CHILDREN OF THE NUCLEAR GODS

Paddy Kelly

CHILDREN OF THE NUCLEAR GODS

DOUBLE DRAGON

FOREWORD

In 1983 a young medical student, short on funds, has enlisted in the U.S. Navy to finish his medical education. Little does he know he is about to end up behind the Berlin Wall in the middle of an international incident, fighting for his life.

While the world is on the brink of nuclear war.

One million years to build civilization.
One minute to obliterate it.

Children of the Nuclear Gods

Dedicated to:

**Commander Dave Harden, U.S. Naval
Intelligence.**

**A man with more heart than any man I have
ever met.**

Bar none.

Children of the Nuclear Gods

INTRODUCTION

All men are defined by the times in which they live. Growing up with daily nuclear attack drills, air raid sirens at every major intersection and going to class past the stacks of olive drab, green emergency rations and cans of water lined up in the hallways of the school was a part of life that is incomprehensible now in the 21st Century. But in the Fifties, Sixties and, in some places, well into the Seventies, students in both the U.S. and the U.S.S.R. spent at least ten to thirty minutes of each school day cowering under their desks, inside makeshift bomb shelters and being falsely led by deluded politicians that if they achieved exactly the right position under their meager, little wooden desks, they could all survive a nuclear attack.

One of my earliest memories as a kid was directly responsible for me spending 16 years of my life in the military. And it was in one of these schools-come-bomb-shelter, at the age of about ten, that it happened.

As John Glen's capsule hurled towards the earth we were all herded into a classroom, the one with the only T.V. in the school, ordered by the Sisters of Perpetual Punishment to sit down, be quiet, and watch the telly. What we eventually saw, after about an hour of torturous commentary, none of which any of us had a hope of understanding, we watched as a small shiny metal capsule under three white and orange parachutes floated from the heavens down into the blue expanse of the Pacific.

"Sister Mary, who are they?" I asked as I watched men in black jump from a helicopter and swim to the capsule.

"Those are men to help save the astronaut. They are called Frogmen."

"Frogmen!" The very name rang with heroism, excitement and endless adventure. There were actually guys who jump out of helicopters into the middle of the ocean and swim like fish!

That's when I knew what I wanted to do with the rest of my life!

The government jingle later mocked as a Pop song in "Duck And Cover!" and the cult film *The Atomic Café* made from actual government propaganda are also vivid memories but seeing the UDT combat swimmers on T.V...

Given this background and given what I did in later life, twelve years in Special Operations, the question occurred to me, as it did to tens of millions of others, how could the leaders of the supposed civilized world reach a point that all civilization as we know it could come within the push of a button of being annihilated?

After several years of research the answer turned out to be quite simple.

They were fucking idiots! Plain and simple.

Although I had to read twenty or so books along with a two meter high stack of articles, treatises and opinions to arrive at this novel it is, as is all my writing, based on actual facts. This book is a work of Roman a Clef not a history book. Although the exact dates of some of the incidents have been altered to fit the story line the incidents themselves are as accurately portrayed as available records allow. Dave Harden and Doc are based on actual characters.

Enjoy the read.

Children of the Nuclear Gods

PROLOGUE

This story is a compilation of true political and military events both historical and personal during my time assigned to U.S. Marine Special Forces and with U.S. Army Intel.

Because they are largely composed of opinion, politics, like religion, is by its very nature controversial. Even the most steadfast researchers and factologists disagree on what certain, 'well documented' events mean. Toss in a healthy measure of skepticism followed by a heaped tablespoon of home grown paranoia flavored with a sprinkle of political bias and the end result is at best arguable.

Following the Carter years, which were unquestioningly marked by weak, even flaccid foreign policy, the overtly aggressive nature which had won Reagan the election, seemed to amplify with each successive speech and each new proposed foreign policy shift, particularly in the military arena, Reagan's distain for the Soviet leadership.

Operation Ryan, the largest counter-Intel operation ever launched in the history of the Soviet Union, was undoubtedly a panic response on the part of the Politburo to Reagan's aggressive approach towards foreign policy. Inclusive in that was his approval of the overt PSYOPS intrusions into Russian territory and the so called 'Star Wars' system which was later exposed as a scam, as the period technology to achieve what was advertised was non-existent.

13

The fact that the most massive and audacious PSYOPS operations were launched in the first quarter of his first presidency is indicative of the mentality Reagan entered into public office with. From all contemporaneous indications Yuri Andropov, the Soviet Premier at the time, had no illusions about which way the foreign policy winds would shift once Reagan got in and so initiated his own covert Intel measures.

Some Americans have argued Andropov was 'backed into' his moves by Reagan's aggression. The historical record doesn't support this.

Andropov's predecessors had long sought conquest by overt force, for example their activities in the Pacific basin, Africa and the invasion of Afghanistan less than two years before Reagan was elected.

It was no coincidence that almost immediately after Ronald Reagan took office the American hostages, after 444 days as political prisoners of the far left Iranians, were released.

By way of example, the year-long pointless negotiations with the Iranian terrorists pretending to be students showed no actual signs of resolution during Carter's tenure but when, the day after Reagan got the keys to 1600 Pennsylvania Avenue, Tehran magically offered a solution.

There is no shortage of proof that Moscow was advising the hostage takers, (atheist communists advising radical Muslims? That would have been interesting to see!), but it was just one more step inching us closer to the inevitable confrontation of September 1983, the story you are about to read.

The war between the U.S. and the U.S.S.R. had been being fought by proxy since 1947. Ergo there was little doubt that shortly after the 1980 American election an army commanded by someone who wrote Cyrillic, liked vodka and was used to cold weather would be advised that they, like the Persians who sought to conquer the world, would no longer be allowed passage through The Hot Gates.

Sparta had a new king.

On the other hand, the shoot down of the passenger liner KAL flight 007 on August 31st, 1983 which may or may not have actually been a passive probe to agitate Soviet defenses over one of their most sensitive installations, Petropavlovsk Naval Air Base near Vladstok, and was certainly one of their most vulnerable, was the bitter icing on the cake for Andropov and the Politburo.

I was stationed at the Special Operations base in Coronado California as a Marine Force Recon instructor the day the news of the KAL 007 shoot down was made public.

It was Thursday or early Friday morning just before the Labor Day weekend and Dave Harden, a Navy Seal candidate at the time had just finished a beach run along the Strand and I was coming down off the obstacle course aside the BUDS quarter deck building.

He'd asked me if I'd heard the news. I hadn't and he filled me in about the shoot down. We both agreed we would be issued orders within the next 24-48 hours.

At that point we improvised a mock scenario

where-by an aide enters the White House and reports to Reagan that we have an incident and that KAL 007 was actually a probe.

We were wrong, it probably wasn't but it wasn't until a decade later that the world learned there had been an American spy plane in the area.

All those years later when I read about the RC-135 surveillance aircraft that had been in the area I suddenly empathized with my father when I told him they found out FDR pretty much knew that Pearl Harbor would be attacked at some point and also that a retired military investigator finally discovered what had happened to Glen Miller's plane back in 1944 when it vanished over the English Channel. Two incidents which had remained mysteries for years and which had profoundly affected my father and his generation.

This is a work of historical fiction, however the names, dates and places are factual. With the exception of the events of the last few chapters which are loosely based on what happened, the events leading up to my involvement are true.

The U.S./U.S.S.R. military and political events which transpired through the month of September of 1983 transpired pretty much as written.

As with all my novels I write books dealing with events which have never been novelized before and I decided to write this book because I've had endless discussions with people who submit to the popular, incorrect belief, that the Cuban Missile Crisis was the closest we'd ever come to a nuclear exchange. This is incorrect, there have been several others.

However, I was not able to find anywhere in the archives when or where the order to launch nukes was actually given by either side save for the one written about here.

I believe the September-November 1983 incident to be the only, and hopefully the last, time that such an insane order will be issued.

***

"Nobody intends to put up a wall!"

-**Walter Ulbricht**, Leader of the GDR, June 15,
1961.
Weeks before the Berlin Wall was erected.

"A wall is a hell of a lot better than a war."

- **John F. Kennedy,** August 1961
Weeks later as the Berlin Wall was being erected.

CHAPTER ONE

Greenleaf Point, Potomac River,
Washington D. C.
July 4th, 1983
14:45 EDT

Dating to the Colonial Era Fort Lesley J. McNair, a joint forces base and home to Naval Sea Systems Command, or FTMCNNAVSYSCMD in Nav speak, sits right on a northern bend of the Potomac River.

Established in 1791 it was the site of the first federal penitentiary, served as the execution grounds of the Lincoln conspirators as well as the base of operations for Walter Reed and his research which led to the cures for yellow fever and malaria.

Ironically its name sake, Lesley J. McNair, was killed in a friendly fire incident when 77 Army Air Corps planes bombed friendly positions during *Operation Cobra* in the battle for Normandy.

Technically a U.S. Army fort, it holds pride-of-place for a naval detachment of the U.S. fleet as well.

This day however, as the thermometer reached 87 degrees and the humidity climbed, was one of the few times on the station that the entire fort's compliment were allowed to wear civilian clothes, lounge around, drink beer and, except for an unlucky few, were not required to report for duty.

It was America's 207th birthday.

Americans are proud of their bar-b-que tradition.

Bigger, better hamburgers, fatter, juicer hot dogs and enough chicken to keep Ethiopia fed for a year. But a Navy bar-b-que is a sight to behold.

A week earlier, by order of the Station Commander, twenty, 55 gallon diesel oil drums had been cleaned out, trucked over to the repair ship *U.S.S. Ajax*, cut in half down their long axes and had iron cross legs welded to their undersides. After the addition of iron grates on top, the resulting 40, man-sized bar-b-ques were then brought back to the parade ground early on the morning of the Fourth, lined up end to end, 20 on the port side of the parade ground, 20 on the starboard and stacked with high grade charcoal.

By ten hundred the home fires were burning and by high noon 10,000 beef burgers, 11,000 hot dogs and 14,500 chicken legs were sizzling away as nearly the entire station's compliment of 11,000 officers, petty officers, NCO's and enlisted men, half with family members in tow, formed four orderly lines which snaked back across both baseball diamonds, out past the Officer's Club and nearly to the front gate.

It was the mother of all bar-b-ques.

On the North side of the base just inside the Bachelor Enlisted Quarters, a young seaman dressed in cut off jean shorts and a dark red Boston Red Socks tee shirt scrambled in through the rear entrance, ran up the passageway and ducked into the office adjacent to the front entrance on the quarter deck.

Under considerable duress he rummaged around for a pink pad of pre-printed dockets, tore the top one off and took a seat at one of the half dozen typewriters, removed the cover and inserted the docket into the carriage.

As was usually the case in the office someone had left the radio on and he tuned out the pleasant voice of the female commentator as he typed.

"... It was announced today that the installation of the Pershing II missile systems along the East-West German border has been completed.

The Pershing II's are nuclear capable and are designed to be launched from road mobile vehicles in order to make them more difficult to find. Estimated flight time to Russia's capital, Moscow, is between six and eight minutes thus giving the Soviets little or no ..."

Just as he finished banging away the Officer Of the Deck came around the corner and through the half-opened door detected the staccato of the keys slapping paper. The tall, lanky O.O.D. eased the office door full open and stuck his head in.

"Kcarney! What the hell you doin' on the Quarterdeck in your civvies?"

"Sorry Lieutenant! I gotta finish these reports mosh skoosh!" The kid didn't look up as he continued to hammer away on another.

"You do know what day it is? I mean they do celebrate the Fourth in New Yawk, don't they?"

"Can't say sir, I'm from Bas-ton sir and shit yah we celebrate it! We're the ones picked the fight, remember?!"

"Then shove the hell off!"

"But sir, I told the Master Chief I'd have these laundry reports done by noon!"

"We'll you missed that ship by a coupl'a hours!"

"Aye, aye sir. I know."

"What was her name?" The lieutenant slyly asked.

"Ohh ... it wasn't like that Lieutenant! I mean ..."

"I'm sure the Master Chief will still retire on time next week without a few laundry reports."

"I know sir, but the Master Chief -"

"He'll understand. And if he doesn't, you tell him the Company C.O. wants to have a chat about that half-empty bottle of 12 year old scotch he has stashed in his lower desk drawer." Kearney smiled up at the Lieutenant.

"Now get the hell outta here, that's an order! Un-ass the A.O. and go get some of that fine chow the U.S. taxpayer bought us for fighting back the Red tide and keepin' the world safe for democracy!"

"Message received loud and clear sir!" The kid pulled the docket from the typewriter, stowed it in a drawer, scrambled past the lieutenant and out the office door, saluting smartly as he passed. "Seaman Kearney request permission to leave the ship, sir!"

"Get the hell outta here, numbnuts!" The officer smiled and was using his pass key to lock the office door when Kearney yelled back into the barracks.

"Janean Sir!" The kid called back as the L.T. walked to the front entrance in time to see Kearney jogging across the parking lot.

"What?"

"Janean, sir. Her name was Janean. Janean from Jersey! And she was a goddess! I think I'm in love!

Happy Fourth L.T.!"

With a smirk still hanging on his face the O.O D. adjusted the bill of his cap and raised a hand to block out the sun as he stared out across the Potomac and watched a white, 38 foot Chris Craft slowly meander upstream.

"Someday." He mumbled to himself as he turned and walked away. "The day after retirement!" He ambled back into the barracks to continue his rounds. "The **very** day after retirement!"

****

Only one of the two used-to-be sailors with a perspiring bottle of Budweiser in his hand and sheltering in the wheel house of that 38 foot Chris Craft Cruiser, gazed out the port side and across at the massive, tax payer financed bar-b-que as he cruised by. The slightly older, bald, bearded one continued to stare straight ahead as he manned the helm.

"Ya miss it, Chief?" His tall, gangly friend asked.

"Miss what?" He adjusted his glasses as he grumbled a reply

"Miss what?! What the hell do you think?! The Navy!"

"Fuck the Navy! Months at sea, shit chow and no matter how high you go in rank there's always some asshole tellin' ya how to do your job a better way. Fuck that shit!" His normally pale complexion reddened slightly.

"So Chief, how do really feel?"

"Fuck you!" He drained his bottle and tossed it overboard onto the river. "You see I'm in civvies, don't ya?"

"Yeah. So what's yer point?"

"Quit callin' me Chief, god damn it!"

"Jesus John, you're bitchier than normal!"

"Pass me another beer."

"Maybe you need something stronger than beer!" He rummaged through the Styrofoam cooler and passed John another cold bottle.

"I always need something stronger than beer."

"How's about I take you out and get you laid tonight?"

Retired Chief Warrant Officer John Walker didn't answer nor did he encourage any more conversation with his friend for the remaining twenty minutes until the pair had reached his rented slip at The Yards Park, on the Southwest Waterfront.

After stowing their fishing gear in the trunks of their cars, and a half-hearted commitment to, 'Do it again soon', the pair parted company in the parking lot.

It was approaching half four when Walker hopped on the 395N heading home to the Oceanview district of suburban D.C. just outside Norfolk, about ten miles north of the marina.

In an effort to quell his anger at his current domestic situation he switched on the radio.

And in other news, the Reagan Administration appears to have taken another body blow as

*Secretary of the Interior James G. Watt has been
found guilty of 25 counts of perjury and obstruction
of justice and sentenced to five years' probation, a
$5,000 fine and 500 hours of community service.*

"Fuckin' bastards!" Walker mumbled to himself.

PROBATION, for 25 counts Jim?! The female
co-anchor declared.

Probation, Lucy!" The male anchor shot back.

*That were you or me Jim, they'd toss us in a hole
and throw away the key!*

*No question Lucy! And the best part is . . . HE
STILL GETS TO KEEP HIS JOB!!*

Is this a great country or what, Jim? She added
with mock pride.

*Land of the Free. Unless you're not a politician,
then you have to pay, don't ya?* The female co-
anchor picked up the commentary.

*This latest White House Headache comes hot on
the heels of the conviction of Assistant Secretary of
Housing and Urban Development Phillip D. Winn's
conviction for multiple counts of bribery just
months ago!*

*You're tuned to DC Radio FM106.4 on your FM
dial. All news, all the -*

"Fuckin' bastards!" Walker declared out loud as
he flicked off the radio and lit a cigarette.

Twenty-five minutes later he was pulling up the
driveway of his four bed, split level, red brick house
and parking next to his white 4X4. A tall, young
man, thirty-ish, stepped through the front door out

25

onto the porch.

"Hey Mike. Glad you made it in. Anyone else here?" Walker called up to the porch as he retrieved his fishing tackle and headed up.

"Laura's in back manning the bar-b-que. Cynthia called, she can't make it but Margret and her guy are due over in bit. How're they biting?"

"Not a fucking nibble." Walker entered the well-furnished house. "Any sign of Wentworth?"

"Jerry rang, he can't make it. Said he'll try and make it over tomorrow."

Out in the kitchen Laura was lifting marinated chicken breasts out of a Tupperware bowl as Walker snuck up from behind and covered his daughter's eyes with his hands.

"Hi dad. Welcome back. I smell your clean hands so I guess there were no fish?" They gave each other a peck on the cheek. "Be right back in. I've gotta get back out there or the coals will die." She said.

"Malarkey! You stay here, sit yourself down, and talk to your old man. PETTY OFFICER WALKER!"

"PETTY OFFICER AYE SIR!" Mike yelled back from out in the living room.

"Give your sister a hand! Get the hell out on the galley deck and man the bar-b-que! ON THE DOUBLE! POGUE!"

Laura giggled to herself.

"Moving on the double sir!" Mike grabbed the bowl of chicken breasts and his beer and headed outside to the back deck. Laura finished washing her hands and was drying them as she pulled up a chair to the oversized kitchen table.

"Sure is hot in here." Walker made an exaggerated gesture of wiping his brow. "Man could work up a helluva thirst in this weather."

Laura rose again and retrieved a bottle of beer from the double door fridge just as the doorbell rang.

"I'll get it." She opened the beer for her father then left the room to answer the front door.

John sat, casually sipping on his beer and mulling over how well his life had turned out. His house, his car, a 4X4 in the driveway and a boat in the marina. His own detective agency and a couple of good kids.

Not bad for a kid from D.C. who was one step ahead of a lengthy jail sentence for petty theft.

He glanced at the kitchen clock over the doorway. 18:45. He checked his Rolex which read 18:47. Rising from his seat he pulled a chair over to the doorway and climbed up to correct the clock. After setting the time pieces within seconds of each other he returned the chair, retrieved his beer and started to wander out to the back porch where he could see Mike was filling a large china plate with half a dozen hot dogs and a few assorted burgers.

By now Laura had opened the front door but apparently had not yet let the caller in and on his way across the kitchen Walker thought he heard whispering coming from the front door. He changed direction to investigate and arrived in the front room in time to see his ex, Barbara, stumble through the front door holding a can of beer. She was halfway to a good drunk and the years of neglect and border line abuse were festering to the surface.

She went straight for Walker.

"I been calling you all day! Where you been?!" She demanded. Laura had sense enough to head back out to the kitchen with the excuse of helping her brother at the grill.

"Out!" John casually snapped back.

"Out where?"

"Barb, look. Look real close!" Walker held up his left hand, displaying the ring finger. Even the tan line was gone. "Notice anything missing?"

"Yeah. As usual your give-a-shit meter is empty!"

"What'a ya want Barb?!"

"I want money!"

"Barb, you're not getting any more money."

"I want money!!"

"For what? All the years of lessons you gave me?" He queried.

"What lessons?!" She challenged.

"Lessons in how to be one miserable son-of-a-bitch."

"You're just one smug bastard, ain't ya?!" She snarled.

"DINNER'S READY!" Laura called from the kitchen.

"That why you used to close your eyes during sex? Couldn't stand to see me enjoying myself?" He took the can of beer from her hand as she fell back onto the couch.

"Fuck you!"

"Snappy come back but, not any more sister! Them days is gone." He drained her beer, set the can on the coffee table and chased it down with a swig of his Budweiser.

"I sath FUCK YOU! BASTHARD!"

"DINNER IS SERVED!" Laura again yelled into the front room.

"I need ten grand!" Barbara demanded.

"For what? Another face lift? Don't you wanna wait and see if the first one takes?" Out in the kitchen Laura had set the table.

"Dinner's ready?" She meekly said still standing in the middle of the kitchen. Mike began fixing himself a plate. "Or not." Laura mumbled, depression quickly setting in as she plopped down at the kitchen table. "Maybe we'd better put these back on the grill." She suggested. Mike shrugged, did a shot of tequila and began reloading the rest of the burgers and dogs back onto the serving plate and headed back out to the deck. He unceremoniously dumped the whole plate back onto the oversized gas grill, closed the lid then stood facing out to the small, manmade lake out behind the house, chicken leg in one hand, bottle of tequila in the other, tuning out the intense negativity emanating from the parlor.

"YOU OWE ME GOD DAMN IT! YOU KNOW GOD DAMNED WELL YOU OWE ME!" Barbra scowled. Walker remained nonchalant in his retort.

"The kids are grown, out of the house and supporting themselves! Read the divorce papers! You signed em' same as me! No more alimony!" With unexpected energy and coordination Barb sprang from the couch and backed John into a corner by the window.

"I know what you're doin'!" She leaned in close and poked his chest with her index finger. "Don't think I don't know what you're doin'!"

"What's that Barb?"

"You know! And don'th think for one New York Thirty seconth that I won't tell them!"

"Ya know Sweetheart, I think the love's gone out of our relationship. Go back to rehab, will ya?" He patted her on the cheek, ducked out from under her arm and headed in the direction of the kitchen.

"MIKE! COME IN HERE AND DRIVE YOUR MOTHER HOME!" John yelled as he finished his beer, set the bottle on the mantle and grabbed his denim jacket from the hall coat rack and made for the front door. Barbara trailed him halfway across the living room then fell back onto the couch as Walker darted out the front door.

Outside the house the muffled sound of the 4X4 being fired up in the driveway was briefly heard then quickly faded into the distance.

Barbra reached across the coffee table to retrieve her empty can of beer and tilted it to her lips.

"SHIT!" She flung it across the room just missing the family portrait on the mantle and slumped further down on the couch.

"Rehab! Rehab is for quitters!" She mumbled to herself.

***

Paddy Kelly

Night Moves Lounge
Polish Hill District
Pittsburgh, Pennsylvania

"Pittsburgh, Pennsylvania!" He spoke with the resignation of a condemned man mounting the gallows. "I left New York City for fucking Pittsburgh, Pennsylvania!"

The thirty year old sailor in dress whites at the end of the bar threw back another drink as the juke box changed records. The bar clock read a quarter to midnight. Early yet.

"You left New York for a girl, dumb shit." Down in the center behind the bar, leaning on one arm as he flipped through the latest issue of *Shaved*, the stocky, black bartender Jake, drawled out the retort, before leisurely perusing the sparsely occupied bar room. He shook his head as he returned to his literary endeavors as the sailor continued his quiet rant.

"What the hell was I thinking?" Sitting alone at the end of the bar, Petty Officer Second Class McKeowcn held up two empty shot glasses to signal the barman for a couple of refills.

The fake grass thatching over the bar was held together by dust and grime, the plywood cutouts of crossed palm trees above the door to the toilets in the back hung peeling and sagging and the furniture throughout had suffered multiple assaults.

There was a reason every night was two-for-one night at the *Night Moves*.

Founded on the misery of thousands of Viet Nam vets, *The Lounge* had been a local watering hole

31

since the early days of the Viet Nam War but thanks to Richard Nixon's economic policies had quickly transitioned into somebody's dream gone bad and was now on the verge of being condemned. Again.

The late 30-something woman with the shoulder bag big enough to smuggle a dead body in continued to lean on the juke box as she pretended to give a shit about which record selection she wanted to hear. It was apparent that her struggle to maintain her once stunning good looks was weakening.

There was a dangerous brush with excitement when she briefly glanced over her bare shoulder at Petty Officer McKeowen, smiled a lop-sided smile and turned back to punch a couple of more buttons before taking her seat next to a guy half her age who obviously had mistaken the place for some kind of gay leather bar.

"Obviously you weren't thinking, dumb shit." Came the follow-up answer to McKeowen's last query by way of the burley bartender.

Sea Of Love wafted out of the Wurlitzer and permeated the room.

"Thanks for the support Jake! And you're supposed to be a friend!" McKeowen snapped back.

"Let's don't be presumptuous!" The bartender said pouring the drinks. He glanced down the bar and heard the sailor mumbling out loud to himself.

"Could'a had that job in the Village if I stayed in New York. Or grad school, FREE! If I signed that teaching contract! But noooo! You dopey bastard!"

The barman came down with the drinks, set them next to McKeowen then leaned in to the not-yet-drunk-but-feeling-no-pain sailor.

"Hey man, do me a favor will ya?! Shut the hell up, or at least find somebody else to talk to. Ya scarin' the clientelé."

McKeowen glanced around to spot a late middle aged couple in a corner playing tonsil hockey, two teens with a half a dozen empty beer bottles in front of them struggling to remain upright and an old codger shuffling to the little boys' room about five minutes too late. Juke Box Lady and her leather buddy were also making nice-nice as they were rounding second base as she fished his hand out of her bra.

"I'll try and keep it down. Wouldn't want to disrupt the romantic ambience of the room." McKeowen quipped.

Just as the bartender took his leave Juke Box Lady waited until her boyfriend went to the little boy's room then rose from the table and with silver, sparkly platform shoes clip clopping across the floor and wandered over towards McKeowen.

His eyes shot immediately to the white hot pants to the place where there was supposed to be a little triangular peep hole at the top of the thighs. There wasn't one.

"Hey!" She greeted, being sure to bend over farther than required as she reached to pull out the bar stool to his right. He tried not to focus on the elongated cleavage as she flopped her big bag onto the bar.

"Hey yerself." He greeted back as he slid one of the loaded shot glasses over to her.

"Mind if I -"

"Not at all. Grab a seat. So, what's a nice girl like you, blah, blah in a place like blah, blah blah?" She smiled and took the whiskey. He glanced down at her almost shapely thighs. "Fishnets. Very stylish." He tried not to smirk.

"Thank you." She threw back the whiskey like a seasoned pro. "So what's your -?"

"Her name was Tanya."

"Tanya huh? That why you hang around classy joints like this talkin' to yerself?"

"I loved her, she loved me. Then we finished college, no work. Her mom, who takes the warm and fuzzy out of the word cunt, came in late in the second act and next thing I know instead of sharing our dream apartment in the city I was sleeping in the back seat of my 1979, steel grey, SAAB 1000."

He swallowed his shot, stared at the empty glass as he twirled it in his hand and then suddenly flung it across the room into the almost-realistic fake fire place. The old man cheered, gave an enthusiastic ovation and tried to stand but couldn't. The bartender wasn't quite as appreciative.

"HEY MAN! Where the fuck you think you is, Russia or some shit?!" McKeowen peeled a tenner from the small stack of bills on the bar in front of him, waved it at the bartender and slid it across the bar. Juke Box Lady signaled for another round. McKeowen fished out another note.

"Lemme guess. You had plans, they went to shit so you moped around for the better part of two weeks ..." She preached as McKeowen held up three fingers. "... called in sick and now you're out tryin' ta get laid to wash her outt'a your hair! That about it?"

"Ya say it like that, sounds like a forgotten chapter in some old book."

"Chapter might be stretchin' it. Maybe a couple'a pages, three at most." She countered.

"Are you tryin' to minimalize my most recent emotional trauma?"

"Not really." She defended as they had another drink.

"I just wanna put people back together." He confessed.

"Whose broke?"

"Trauma. I got a knack for emergency medicine. If they're breathin' when I get there, they'll still be breathin' when the chopper takes 'em out. And that ain't braggin'! Seven years I've never put a dead patient in an ambulance or on a Medi-vac."

"So all you really wanna do is save people's lives?! That's admirable!"

"Save people's lives. And blow shit up."

"What?"

"Special Operations. We all double up on jobs. It's sort of a unique skill set."

The bartender set two more shots on the bar and Juke Box Lady wasted no time peeling another tenner off McKeowen's pile.

"Done like a true pro!" McKeowen jibed as he watched her pass his money to the bartender.

"What's dat supposed ta mean?!"

"Just sayin', done like a real professional."

"Hey chuck you Farley! I ain't no hooker!"

"Hey easy sister. Just alludin' to sex. I mean, that's what it's all about isn't it?"

35

"What are you talkin' about?! Who said anything about having sex?!"

"Just tryin' ta get ta know ya. It's like in Bridge. If you don't have a good partner, you better have a good hand. Know-what-I-mean?" She turned away from him. "Hey, honest mistake, Sweetheart. Let me make it up to ya." She smiled, settled down and swung around on her seat back in to face the bar. "Just let me know exactly how much ya need per hour and ..."

She slapped the bar and turned red.

"You're a real asshole! Ya know that?" She blurted out.

"So I've been told." She pushed back from the bar, hopped off her stool, grabbed her shoulder bag and headed for the door.

"Don't forget to write." He threw back his shot, reached across and took hers and signaled for two more. The bartender signaled back 'no' by way of his middle finger.

"Apparently we've been cut off." McKeowen informed the two empty glasses.

"HEY, ASSHOLE!" McKeowen looked around for the source of the yelling. "YEAH YOU! POPEYE THE FUCKIN' SAILOR MAN!"

It was the leather clad Village People reject who apparently had no sense of humor about his 'date' who had been sitting at the bar with McKeowen.

McKeowen glanced over at the irate idiot in time to notice he was brandishing a stiletto switch blade and heading straight for his end of the bar.

"WHAT THE FUCK ...?!" Jake the bartender yelled as he dropped his girlie magazine and vaulted the bar in one leap to land just behind the leather festooned baboon but had to reach forward to grab him by his left arm and swing him around 180 degrees.

This was perhaps not the wisest maneuver from the big black fella who was accustomed to intimidation by size. It never occurred to people like him that the Principle of Bigness did not apply when dealing with real life crazed, Sicilian, pimp types.

As Guido the Killer Pimp swung around, the bartender didn't feel a thing. At first. However, the bartender's size counted for something and the force of the spin he put on the pimp was enough to make him stumble to the right buying the bartender time to gain the upper hand. As the pimp was slammed back against the bar he was momentarily defenseless and that was all she wrote.

The first punch glanced off Guido's right cheek but the second broke his nose, the third his jaw and the fourth ensured his rhinoplasty bill would run into the tens of thousands, not counting rehab.

An unconscious, profusely bleeding Guido crumpled to the floor like a wet rag doll.

As the big man began to breath heavier from the exertion he winced in pain then immediately found it rough going to try and take in a deep breath. His hand shot to his abdomen, he backed away from the slumped, lump of pimp, fell to his knees and collapsed backwards onto the bar room floor.

The blood trail looked like somebody had emptied a couple of bottles of ketchup on the deck and a third all over the black man's exposed belly.

"SHIT!" McKeowen had already been on his feet since the Killer Pimp initiated his antics and so was at the wounded man's side in seconds assessing his injury. He carefully lifted away the flaps of the sliced open Tee shirt and slid Jake's hand away. The blood was flowing too steady to see anything but the anomaly which caught his attention was a small rise in the otherwise smooth and steady blood flow off to the left side.

Gastric bleeder! McKeowen thought to himself. He immediately guesstimated the location of the bleeder and with his left hand pinched a flap of flesh with his thumb and forefinger. The flow slowed noticeably but didn't abate.

Simultaneously with his right hand he monitored the carotid pulse.

"JAKE! JAKE, CAN YOU HEAR ME MAN?!" The barman was slipping in and out of consciousness but was able to squeeze out a smile, then attempted to speak. McKeowen leaned in closer.

"Guess ... somebody else ... gonna have ta lock up tonight." Jake struggled to whisper.

"You're gonna lock up tonight Bro, same as always, now stay with me man! You're gonna be alright!" He quickly surveyed the bar room. The two teens were now awake and on their feet a couple of yards from their table between McKeowen and his patient. "HEY! YOU TWO, HERE NOW! I NEED YOUR HELP!" They traded dumfounded looks then scurried over. He addressed the girl first. "Go around behind the bar. Call the operator tell her you have a stabbing at the *Night*

Moves Lounge, next door to the *Big O*! Tell her we need an ambulance now!" The girl took off to make the call. "And bring me back one of those bar knives and shit load'a bar towels!"

"What are you, like some kind'a doctor or something man?" The young guy asked.

"Somethin' like that. Find me something to raise his feet up onto then get his shoe laces off and tie 'em around his upper thighs, tight." The half sober teen stared down at the 12 inch wound. "Anytime this week, Champ!" McKeowen snapped.

"Shit! Sorry man!" The kid got right to it and did a good job. The girl returned with a stack of bar towels.

"JAKE? JAKE, YOU WITH ME MAN? TALK TO ME BROTHER." He leaned in to listen for breaths. They were there but becoming weaker and a bit erratic.

"What else man?" The teen asked.

"I need a bottle of vodka and a bottle of whiskey." The kid took off.

"How long for the ambulance?"

"She said ten to fifteen minutes." The girl shot back.

"Shit! Alright, here's what we need to do. I'm holding his artery closed right now but it's still leaking. We have to stop it." The girl was now turning a bit pale. "You up for this? I need you, I can't do this by myself." He explained. She pulled herself together. "You okay?!"

"Yeah. Yeah. I can do it."

"Good girl! Now, I need you to fold one of those over long ways and gently pack it into the wound.

She quickly obeyed but hesitated when it came to packing it in.

"Good job. Now, I need you to fold two more towels, lay one across his chest and, when I tell ya, exchange the one in his wound for a clean one. You got any hairpins in your hair?" She responded instantly and pulled three from her French braid which immediately fell down around her shoulders. McKeowen let go of Jake's neck and took the bobby pins. The boy returned.

"Here's the vodka and here's the Irish. All they had was Jameson's. That okay?"

"It'll have to do." Mac answered. The kid fell to his knees and set to opening the bottles.

"What do I do with the bloody one?" The trembling girl asked.

"What'a ya want with the booze Doc?!" The boy interjected.

"Don't call me Doc, god damn it! Take the vodka in your right hand, pull the pour spout out and put your thumb over the mouth of the bottle halfway. On my signal douse the hell outta the area I'm pinching, you got that?"

"Like a fancy French chef with cookin' wine!"

"Yeah, French chef." In the distance a siren could be heard. "And here comes the cavalry!" McKeowen mumbled as he daubed the area searching for the bleeder.

"What about the whiskey?"

"Remove the pour spout, take the bottle in your left hand and raise the whiskey to my mouth and give me a swig." Smirking, the kid complied. By now the drunk old man had slid his chair over to the scene and was leaning forward arms on knees watching the show.

"What do I do with the bloody towel?!" The girl reiterated.

"Just toss it outta the way. Okay, we all move when I count three, okay? All on the same page?" The teens nodded. "One, two, three!" The girl removed the blood soaked towel which had absorbed a considerable amount of blood to reveal torn mesentery and a glisten of large intestine.

As the wound again began to fill, the kid acted quickly and saturated McKeowen's hand and the area around.

"Hold the next towel in closer! Dab the area between my fingers when I let go. Ready, now!" They alternated pinching and dabbing until, he saw something. "There you are you little bastard!" It was the partially severed small artery.

Just as he was about to apply the pin the two ambulance attendants burst through the front door with the grace of a pair of wounded bulls in a china shop.

"Jesus Christ! You guys know how to make an entrance!" McKeowen cursed.

"Where's the patient?" The dumpy one asked.

"See if you can guess!" The kid shot back.

"Okay, stop!" Mac spread the bobby pin wide and slipped it over the exposed pinch of tissue surrounding the bleeder.

Bright red blood still seeped steadily while he prepped a second pin and quickly applied it. The arterial bleeding stopped.

"YESSS!! WE DID IT!" The kid yelled.

"Easy Chef! We ain't out'a the woods yet!" There were numerous veins and smaller vessels still leaking. He turned to the ambulance attendants. "You guys got any suture kits or forceps out in that rig?"

The pudgy attendant fished a pair of curved Kelly's out of his shirt pocket and tossed them to McKeowen who immediately applied them to the largest of the still leaking vessels.

The girl repacked the wound with a clean towel as McKeowen rechecked Jake's pulse and respirations. Both were slow and thready but palpable.

"Chef, what's your name?"

"Reginald. But my friends call the J Man."

"Makes sense. J Man, you like music?"

"What loser doesn't?!"

"Exactly. I need you to keep time for me. Put your fingers here on his neck. Feel anything?"

"Yeah! I got his pulse, but it feels weak."

"I need you to tap your hand on your thigh in sync with Jake's pulse. Think you can do that?"

"No prob man!"

"Also I need you to watch the bar clock, count the beats for me and tell me his pulse every thirty seconds. Think ya can handle that?"

"You got it Doc!" McKeowen winced.

"Alright, get outta the way. Let's get this guy transported." The tall lanky ambulance driver ordered.

"Negative! He needs to be stabilized. You got I.V.'s on board that rig?"

"Yeah, of course. But ..."

"BUT WHAT?!"

"We ain't allowed to use them without authorization of an M.D. first."

"Get out there, get me two large bore needles, 16 gauge, two Ringer's Lactate and a bag of saline. And a shit load of Gelfoam."

"What's Gelfoam?"

"Fuck! Get me the I.V.'s, needles and a pack of sterile 4X4's!"

"But ..."

"Hey, Bush League! You wanna stand around here playin' pocket pool and watch this guy bleed out, or you wanna do your job and help save a life?" By way of an answer both ambulance attendants scrambled out the door.

"And one of you check that guy out!" Mac nodded over towards the crumpled up pimp. The tall one scurried over to the unconscious lump who had his nose on the left side of his face.

Ten minutes later with an I.V. draining into each arm, Jake the bartender was being loaded into a white, 1980 Cadillac ambulance which had been backed up to the front door as a pair of cops sat in a cruiser behind the ambulance drinking coffee.

"Is he gonna make it man?" The kid asked McKeowen who was sprawled out on the bar room floor, in his blood stained dress whites staring at the stamped metal ceiling. The bottle of Jameson's in his left hand.

"I think so kid."

"MAN! That was some awesome shit! Like you knew exactly what you were doin' the whole time!" Mac slowly sat up. "Where'd you learn all that shit?!"

"I read a book." He lifted himself off the floor, took a long swig from the bottle and handed it to the kid. "Here. You guys know Jake?" McKeowen asked the kids.

"Yeah. He's a cool guy. Let's us drink in here all the time. But only beer."

"He usually keeps the keys in the cash register. Lock up for him and drop the keys off with the cops, would ya?"

"Yeah, YEAH! Totally cool man. Will do. Absolutely!"

"And leave the cash in the register!"

"No prob man! No prob!" The kid turned toward the bar room and shouted loud enough to wake the dead. "ALRIGHT! CLOSING TIME! YOU DON'T HAVE TA STAY HERE BUT YOU CAN'T GO HOME! EVERYBODY OUT!" The old man staggered to the door.

"What'a about the mess?" The girl asked as she perused the blood splattered bar floor.

"Leave it for the cops." McKeowen suggested as he turned to leave. As he pushed through the front door and started to turn left to head back to base he caught sight of Juke Box Lady, knap sack sized bag slung over her shoulder and leaning against a lamp post.

"What took ya so long? I was beginning to think ya didn't love me anymore." She said. He walked up and leaned his forehead into hers. He gave her a slight peck on the lips.

"Your back or mine?" She asked as she took his arm and they meandered down the side street.

"Man, you scared me back there! When I saw that psycho comin' afta' ya' I thought you was dead for sure!"

"Nah, don't worry about me Sweetheart. When I die I'll die peacefully in my sleep, like my grandfather." They turned the corner and headed down the block. "Not screaming and yelling like the people in the back of his car."

****

CHAPTER TWO

Evening nautical twilight had passed into dark shortly after John Walker left his house. He was now a good twenty miles North into Maryland when he turned west and passed through the affluent section of Falls Church and under Memorial Parkway. He drove for another eight miles keeping careful track of his mileage. Leaning over as he drove, he popped open the glove box and fished around for a piece of note paper. He referenced the hand drawn map on it and at a predetermined intersection turned back South onto County Road 703 and drove to an isolated strip of two lane country road.

Slowing the 4X4 he cruised for a few minutes, counting the telephone poles through his open passenger's window as he drove. At telephone pole #27 he pulled onto the soft shoulder, spotted the black, red and white *'No Hunting'* sign and killed the lights and shut down the engine.

Being careful to mask the open flame of his lighter he lit the last of his Marlboros, checked his watch, slid his seat back and relaxed.

A short time later he took his last drag, stubbed out the butt and glanced at his watch.

"Six and a half minutes. Impressive." Reaching under the passenger's seat he produced a half full, brown paper, shopping bag with its top folded over several times. Climbing over the seat he exited the passenger's side, glanced around, and climbed the small earthen berm into the knee high shrubbery

46

directly behind the telephone pole at the foot of the woods.

He crumpled the bag up as much as possible without disturbing its contents and then sat it down, on its side. Glancing around in the dim light he spotted a couple of discarded Coke cups, a McDonald's burger wrapper and some French fry boxes. He collected them up and scattered them around the bag. He checked his watch and a few minutes later was back on County road 703 again heading South.

At the town of Mosby he turned north.

Five miles away, just South of Lake Barcroft, at the same time Walker was coming up to the main intersection an identical brown paper bag was being snugged into a niche at the stump of a large oak tree. The man who planted the bag was now back in his black, Chrysler Cordova heading south to the West end of 703.

Twenty minutes later Walker pulled over on the East bound side of the two lane, macadam road, under a broken street lamp and stopped. He killed the head lights, put it in neutral and jumped out of his vehicle. He glanced up and down the dark road, made his way behind the lamp post and with the aid of a small, red lensed Mag light began to search the immediate area around the stump of the oak for the other brown paper bag.

After ten minutes his efforts yielded nothing. With more vigor he widened his search gradually turning frantic.

Scurrying back to his vehicle he triple checked the note paper against his surroundings then jumped back into the 4X4 to hightail it back South.

County road 703. Telephone pole. *'No Hunting'* sign.

No paper bag.

Over the next forty-five minutes, in-between experiencing a cascade of confused emotions from abject fear to giddiness, Walker made two full runs between the two drop sites.

Reality eventually kicked in and on his third return south he aborted the hunt and headed back towards the interstate.

Approaching the 395 intersect John slowed down and glanced at the big, green overhead directional signs.

'NORTHBOUND TRAFFIC KEEP LEFT'

Head north or go home? He mentally debated.

'SOUTHBOUND TRAFFIC KEEP RIGHT'

"Head north or go home?" He mumbled.

A tractor trailer creeping up on his slow moving vehicle blasted his horn hard several times. John jumped high enough that his head hit the roof of the cabin.

"FUCK IT!" He swung the wheel right and drove with renewed determination.

He fished around in his pockets for a cigarette and came up with the empty Marlboro box. Cursing, he threw it out the window and started rummaging around the glove compartment. His senses on full alert he suddenly picked up the distant wail of a siren.

"Shit!" Quickly scanning the right side of the road for an off ramp he found none. He gazed into his rear view mirror. The siren grew louder as flashing blue and red lights came into view over the rise in the road behind him.

From between the seats he pulled a 9mm Colt, quickly ejected the mag, checked the action on the slide and reinserted the mag seating it several times more than necessary.

He could now make out the State Trooper's silhouette in the driver's seat of the cruiser as it quickly closed the distance between them. He cocked a round into the chamber, clicked off the safety then snugged the weapon between his legs, tight up to his crotch, muzzle down. He flipped on his indicator, slowed down and glided into the far right lane to pull over.

Despite the cool breeze wafting through the open windows, a light sheen of sweat covered his face.

He pulled onto the shoulder and in a flash, the cruiser sped by him.

With both hands at 12 o'clock on the wheel Walker fell forward and squeezed his eyes shut.

It was nearly midnight when he pulled into the all-but-empty parking lot of a roadside Ramada Inn, pulled around to the far corner of the building and shut down the engine.

Bathed in the red neon glow of the sign, he sat staring out the window, back over at the interstate and the sporadic whir of the occasional passing car.

Thirty minutes later he made the decision to check in.

***

"But he's an officer!" The slender brunette reached across and switched on the bedside lamp.

About a week or so after the bar room incident McKeowen had met a dental student at the Naval hospital. They met just after she had broken off her engagement to an officer. Things developed and they started dating.

"How can he be an officer? He's not even in the military!" Doc argued.

"He's in the Air Force!"

"Exactly!" McKeowen replied. She pulled the sheets up over her pert breasts. "If he was serious about your engagement he wouldn't have been gallivanting all over town every god damned night!"

"Sometimes he had business. Air Force business." Realizing the transparency of her argument her emotions turned back to fear.

"He's a medical records officer, he doesn't even have a real function. The guy's a dial tone!" McKeowen continued.

"If he said he was coming over he'll come over!"

"If you're hintin' at a ménage à trois, forget about it! Especially since last time when I sobered up next to my cousin!"

"That's disgusting!"

"It's a joke!"

"Is everything a joke to you?! HE'S NO JOKE! HE KNOWS KARATE!"

"Karate huh?"

"YES! Now be serious god damn it! I'm scared!" Just as McKeowen slipped out of bed and donned his trousers there was a knock at the door followed by yelling.

OPEN THE FUCKING DOOR LINDA! I KNOW THAT LITTLE SCUMBAG IS IN THERE!

McKeowen mouthed the words 'little scumbag', buttoned his trousers at the waist line leaned over to the woman cowering in the bed and kissed her on the forehead.

"I'll just see who that is. Don't go away. Be right back."

"Be careful!" She warned as he mocked a karate kata on the way out of the bedroom.

Dressed only in his trousers, McKeowen opened the front door. Two feet away stood a disheveled, obviously drunk Air Force lieutenant in full dress uniform. McKeowen made eye contact and smiled.

"AHHH! Girl Scout cookies! We'll take two boxes of Chocolate Mint and one Vanilla Cream Sandwich. Say, do you guys still do oatmeal raisin?"

He heard the two shots before the pain registered. He didn't feel the first round as, in slow motion, it tore through his lower belly and lodged in the kitchen wall behind him. It was the second round that knocked him back, stumbling to his ass before he fell backwards to lie face up on the tiled kitchen floor.

Intuitively knowing what happened, the girl screamed, ran out of the bedroom and fell to her knees at his side still screaming.

"NOOO!! NOOO!! YOU SICK FUCKING BASTARD!" She screamed at the lieutenant as he stood in the doorway, smoking .45 in his hand.

McKeowen couldn't see anymore but was somehow aware of her pounding heavily on the floor and shaking him.

"WAKE UP! WAKE THE FUCK UP!"

"MAC! MAC! WAKE THE FUCK UP!" Suddenly she was yelling with a man's voice.

"MAC! Wake the fuck up! There's a call for you!" McKeowen moaned, rolled over and covered his head with the pillow.

Eventually he shook off the grey haze of sleep and climbed out of bed. Still naked, he opened the bedroom door to be confronted by his disheveled friend, Heinzy, also a corpsman in the Naval Reserves. They were stationed together in Pittsburgh.

"Jesus Christ Mac! This place smells like a fucking brewery! How much did you drink tonight?"

"Technically it's a distillery, not a brewery. Only one. Bottle."

"One bottle!"

"I told you, I'm trying to cut down." Mac fell back to sit on the edge of the bed rubbing his head. "Got any morphine?"

"You get caught here in my dorm and I'm on the street! Look, I don't mind ya crashing here while ya get your shit together, if you ever get ya shit together, but ..."

"Fuck you."

"You're welcome here but at least get your sperm dumps to call during the day when I'm in class, will ya?! I got a Genetics exam tomorrow!" Heinzy chastised as he vanished out across the hall and behind his bedroom door. Mac shuffled out and lifted the receiver from the hall table. He recognized his C.O.'s voice straight away.

"Commander Dunn! It's half past one!"

You think I'm callin' to check the time?

"Negative sir. I just want to say in my defense, I didn't do it!"

Do what?!

"Whatever it is you're calling to blame me for."

Relax shithead. I got news. The Commander relayed.

"What kind'a news? We been activated or something?" He stood up straight and listened carefully. "Uh huh. Yeah. Uh huh. Okay. All reserve medical personnel to report for active duty at once! Full alert! Got it sir."

With a shocked look plastered across his face Heinzy burst into the hallway and froze in his bedroom doorway just in time to see Mac flipping him off.

Heinzy shit himself yet, you twisted bastard? Commander Dunn asked.

"Negative sir. He's just making for the head to puke up his supper."

Okay shit bird, here's the scoop. I know how happy you are about hanging out in Steeltown and going to reserve meetings once a month for a whole $76. So, I'm gonna tell you about a priority message I got this evening from SINCPAC Command.

"I'm all ears, said the brave young stud."

Well, that's good but, you listen too, because I pulled some strings and you owe me.

"Yes sir. I'll call my sister. She doesn't normally do officers but in this instance –"

As of about five minutes ago you have a choice of

53

release from reserve duty to be reassigned to NAB Coronado as the only HM ever to be assigned to Force Recon training facility and have a chance to be the first ever HM to earn the 0321 NEC. Or you could hang around here and maybe make HM1 in ten to twelve years. The NAB slot goes fleet wide at 0001 hours tonight. Take your time. No pressure.

"0001 when?"

Tonight.

"Commander, that was a half an hour ago!"

Which is why I already sent your name into The Bureau of Naval Personnel in D.C. by Twixt three hours ago. Your orders are cut and will be at the TWA desk at the airport.

"When?!"

One hour ago. Your wheels up from Pittsburgh at 02:45, touchdown in San Diego is 05:30.

"Just in time for morning P.T.! I don't get a say? I mean what the hell you gonna do around here for a decent corpsman?"

You been hangin' around here for the better part of 11 months fucking off and trying like hell to pickle your liver and get arrested. Time to move on and get on with your life. Get the fuck out'a here and get back on track, will ya?!

"Yeah but ..."

Don't forget to write. The line went dead. Heinzy stood over him peering down.

"What was that all about?"

"I think I just volunteered for Force Recon."

"Coronado?!"

"Maybe Benning first for Jump school." Doc drank in the moment as Heinz fell silent and turned to leave then turned back.

"Hey Doc."

"Yeah?"

"You know I really don't give a shit about you one way or the other but, watch your ass out there. Coronado ain't the Reserves. Out there you ain't **playin'** Navy no more. Those guys are the real deal. They do it as a profession. They're the top 1% of the top 1%, and it ain't only because they're the best. It's because they got a death wish. They're adrenaline junkies. They don't expect to ever see retirement."

"Heinzy! I didn't know any better I'd almost think you cared."

"Be flip if you want to but guys die or get fucked up in training out there all the time! And their reward for graduating? First in behind the lines if the balloon goes up."

"Heinz, if I'm gonna snuff it, it sure as hell ain't gonna be in training!"

"All I'm saying is, watch your ass out there young pup! There's a lot'a shit going down right now around the world, and if your lame ass makes it through that course, you may not be an instructor for long. If the balloon does go up, Force Recon will be one of the first units shipped out." Mac had already started packing his sea bag as they spoke.

"Whew! Thank god for that!" Mac sighed.

"Why 'thank god'?"

"At least it won't be those lame assed, glory hounds!"

"Who's that?"

"The SEALS, those amphib squids get all the P. R.!" He turned back into the spare room he was using. "One more thing Heinz."

"Yeah?"

Doc stopped packing and made eye contact.

"I owe you." Doc added. Heinzy walked away.

"Forget it! You need anything asshole, just call!" Heinz closed the door as he retired to his bedroom, Doc continued packing and ten minutes later, with his single sea bag, he was ready to go.

"HEINZY!" He called across the hall into his shipmate's bedroom.

WHAT? Heinz answered through the bedroom door.

"DID YOU REALLY MEAN WHAT YOU SAID WHEN YOU SAID, 'JUST ASK'?"

I SAID, JUST CALL.

"HEY HEINZY!" Doc called out.

WHAT?!

"I NEED A RIDE TO THE AIRPORT!"

FUCK YOU! CALL A CAB. Ya prick.

"All right, all right. I respect that!"

'Bout time ya respected something!

"Also appreciate ya takin' me in."

No problem.

"Sneakin' me into the university cafeteria for chow and all."

I get it! Good luck out there.

"One more thing, then I'll leave ya alone."

What Doc?

"Loan me a tenner for the cab, will ya?!"

There was rummaging around in the bedroom and a hand popped out of the doorway with a tenner in it.

"Thanks man."

Asshole!

****

It was just after 3 a.m. on the seventh floor of the twelve storied Ramada, pacing back and forth in room 763 in his sleeveless, white Tee shirt and boxer shorts, that /john Walker finally accepted the fact that he had two chances of sleep that night; slim and none. And Slim had just left town.

As he passed the single bed and night stand for the tenth or fifteenth time he stared at the cheap print of the Spanish bullfighter above the 12 inch screen TV. His mind raced through a variety of scenarios.

FBI? CIA? But if it was the Feds, why didn't they bust me at the drop site? He sat down on the edge of the bed.

Maybe it was the Russian's fuck up? They screwed up before, twice in the last six years! Maybe again? Maybe they were spooked by something? Maybe they just got the date wrong?

The phone rang, Walker jumped. Out of pure reflex he killed the bedside lamp and carefully inched along the wall to the window. By the light of the half open bathroom door, while standing to one side, he carefully brushed the curtains aside to peer down into the dark parking lot. It rang again. Nothing but a red VW under a lamp post and a motorcycle two lanes over. Returning to the bedside table, he slowly lifted the receiver.

Mr. Wainwright, room 763? There was hesitation

57

in the caller's voice.

"This is Wainwright, who is this?"

Sorry to wake you sir. You drivin' a cream 4X4, sir?

"No." The line went dead as Walker slammed the phone down. The desk clerk quickly hung up.

"It's a white 4X4 numb nuts! Call him back!" Down in the lobby the night clerk stared at the man in the black suit and blue bullet proof, FBI vest on the other side of the half-moon desk. "Tell him there was a mix up." The long haired teen was a bit more shaky the second time around.

Back up in the room Walker realized the clock was ticking. The only direct evidence he had on him was the small envelope with the dead drop instructions, a few black & white photos of the site and the directions. He momentarily considered burning them but his contingency instructions from the KGB in the event of an abort were to try again in seven days' time. Ergo he would need the info in a week.

More importantly he needed the $200,000 he'd be paid for the drop. John was busy deciding where to stash the hand drawn map and papers. He was in the bathroom when the phone rang again.

FUCK!

"I'm trying to sleep here! What'a ya want?"

Sorry to bother you again uhh ... Mr. Wainwright, but ... there seems to have been a mistake.

"Yeah? What kind'a mistake?"

*The vehicle involved is a **white** 4X4, sir.*

"Involved in what, exactly?"

A drunk backed into the side of your vehicle. He's been arrested but, the Maryland P.D. need you to confirm your vehicle registration. There was a long pause on both ends of the line. *And that you're the owner sir.* The clerk quickly added. Walker thought for a moment.

"Awright. Lemme get some pants on and I'll come down." After hanging up he quickly continued to peruse the room.

Behind the mirror? Too obvious. Ice machine in the hall! Best way, outside the room! Then they can't say they found it on me.

He fumbled into his trousers and shoes, clipped his .38 Special onto his belt and threw on his short sleeve, Baby blue Dacron shirt. He grabbed the envelope and made for the door.

NO! Mustn't be caught with the evidence! He darted back to the bed and stashed it under the mattress.

Carefully undoing the safety chain, he turned the lock as quietly as possible, cracked the door and peered out into and down the hall. Nothing.

Jerking open the door and drawing his weapon in one quick move he took up an offensive stance and scanned from the elevators down and across the hallway to the ice machine. All clear.

As the last free act of John Walker's life, he scurried back to the bed, retrieved the envelope and made it back out into the hall.

"FREEZE WHERE YOU ARE, FBI!" Walker spun to his left. Two FBI agents wearing bullet proof vests had jumped out from a room opposite the elevators and a third from behind the ice machine with 9mm's holding a bead on his head and chest.

"This what you lookin' for Warrant Officer Walker?" The agent nearest the ice machine held up a clear plastic bag of $200,000 in used 50 and $100 bills while keeping his 9mm service revolver aimed at John's torso.

Walker's mind instantly flashed back five years to one of only two face-to-face meets with his KGB handler.

"You are the most experienced we have John! The very best!" The Russian handler commended.
"Goddamn right!" Walker had replied.
That was now ancient history.

"Lose somethin'?" A second agent displayed the crumpled bag containing over 100 stolen classified U.S. Navy documents wrapped in a white plastic trash bag. Walker swung his weapon to the right to get a bead on a second agent.

"DON'T DO IT JOHN! DON'T EVEN THINK ABOUT IT!"

Almost as fast as he aimed his weapon Walker realized the first agent had shifted his aim to Walker's head. The hopelessness of his situation finally registered. Gently laying his gun on the floor he placed his hands behind his head and surrendered.

The agents rushed him, kicked his pistol out of reach and in seconds he was pinned to the corridor wall by two of the agents while the third maintained a zero on the back of his head.

They quickly frisked him, and once satisfied he carried no concealed weapons, yanked off his black running shoes, cuffed the retired spy and forced him into an adjoining room.

Inside the larger double room a small army of agents was waiting and he was unceremoniously stripped naked as they wasted no time in divvying up his clothes for inspection.

Different agents seized each piece of clothing, examining them in microscopic detail. They even took his metal-framed, reading glasses and inspected them for microfilm. He had been forced to his knees in the middle of the room as they tore his clothes apart. Now naked, surrounded by FBI agents and with two separate weapons drawing a bead on him the world seemed different.

"Fuckin' pack of wild animals!" Walker mumbled. A senior agent squatted down at Walker's side.

"What's that John? Didn't quite get that." John didn't answer. "I know what you're thinking John. Lawyers, judges, court room proceedings. Maybe some leniency after you shill some bullshit story about financial hardships. Problems at home. Business gone bad. A wife who doesn't love you anymore."

"Fuck you Dick Tracy! I'm too important a spy to be prosecuted. It's only a matter of time before your bosses realize they can use me as a double agent. I know more about espionage than all you James Bond wanna-be's put together!" He broke into a wide smirk as another plot hatched. "Besides, what real evidence you got on me? The KGB sure as shit ain't gonna testify. And there ain't no prints on that bag."

The agent who had been examining an envelope came up to the one crouched next to him, the one Walker guessed was the head cop, and addressed him, ignoring their prisoner.

"Photos of the drop are from a micro cam but he didn't have one on him. Handwriting is foreign, Eastern European, as is the grammatical syntax. Both probably supplied by his contact. He's got big backing. Russians, maybe the ChiComs."

"Anything in the van?"

"We've got a team down there now. Briggs radioed in. The photo lab confirmed the infra-red night shots at the drop were him."

"HMMM! What'a ya know about that John? Photos of you at the drop site!" Head Cop smiled as he assumed a complete air of nonchalance. "Anything ya wann'a talk about John?"

"Not to you Junior G-man. After they figure out my true value, I'll have a drink and talk to your boss. Maybe he won't reprimand you too much!"

John watched as the tattered remnants of his clothes were thrown into a black garbage bag and his personal possessions were put into a brown envelope and sealed with a red 'EVIDENCE' sticker.

"We're done here." One of the agents announced.

"Okay Spy Boy, let's go." Two of them lifted him to his feet by the arms, he was cuffed and led to the door.

"Hey! What the fuck?! Ain't you gonna give me no clothes?!" The two agents holding him nearly tripped over each other to respond.

"What'a ya think boys? Should we march him through the lobby in his birthday suit?"

"With a fucking body like that, could become a public safety issue."

"Fuck it, cover him in a sheet."

"Alright, knock it off! Give him his trousers and shirt."

Minutes later, handcuffed and sitting in back of the unmarked car flanked by two agents, riding through the night enroute to his isolation cell in the Baltimore City Jail, Walker stared out into the dark, mentally reviewing his every move in the past 24 hours.

Feigning nonchalance, as he gazed out the window, in dire fear of his future, the volume on his internal dialogue hit 10.

*How **the fuck** did they learn about the dead drop? Certainly not smart enough to figure it out for themselves!*

Someone switched on the car radio as they took the next cut off.

"... in other news, Presidential National Security Advisor Robert "Bud" McFarlane boarded a plane this morning to fly to London. When questioned at the airport as to the reason for his apparently sudden trip, Mr. McFarlane explained it was a routine meeting of economic advisors in Britain associated with manufacturing and trade.

We'll have more news at seven. Meanwhile stay

tuned to WNBC World News."

From the front passenger's seat Head Cop, one of four agents in the car, peered into the rear view mirror and read Walker's face.

"Still trying to figure out what went wrong John?" Walker didn't answer he just turned back to stare out the window.

He knew what went wrong, how they had tracked him.

"Arthur warned me about that bitch!" Walker grumbled. "Never trust anything that bleeds for a week and doesn't die!"

"Ya should've paid her more alimony, John."

"I should've put a fuckin' bullet in her head is what I should'a done!"

Head Cop smirked and exchanged glances with the driver before he commented over his shoulder to Walker.

"Wives huh?! What'a ya gonna do?"

CHAPTER THREE

JFK International
Jamaica, Queens, New York City
August 31st, 1983

As Hitler turned his attention to the West of Europe early on in World War II the Parisians were not impressed by England's-all-too-late efforts to counter the former paper hanger's continental rampage. So it was decided, as a preventative measure, the largest stain glass window in the world, the façade rose window at Notre Dame, all 4,000 plus pieces, would be disassembled piece at a time, labeled with a special code devised by the French patriots and hidden throughout the country side.

Now, 40 years later, the Notre Dame South Rose window was the second largest stain glass window on the planet behind the Sower's window at the American Airlines terminal in JFK International, in Jamaica, Queens.

A heavy-set, late middle-aged American and his wife standing in line at the Korean Air Lines check-in counter stared at the giant, rectangular stained glass widow and its abstract, non-descript forms as they waited.

"I don't see how that's art!" The graying man unapologetically declared as they slowly shuffled forward.

"That makes two of us." Concurred the stout woman. "Did you take your pills this morning?"

She asked without looking up from her book.

Attention customers, attention customers. We regret to announce that due to technical difficulties KAL flight 007 flying from New York to Seoul, South Korea via Anchorage, boarding at gate 15 will be delayed by thirty-five minutes. Once again, due to technical difficulties KAL flight 007 which will be boarding at gate 15 will be delayed by thirty-five minutes. We apologize for any problems this may cause.

"SHIT! We're not gonna get outta here til after midnight!" The tall, former construction worker cursed at the announcement.

"Ben! Mind your language!"

"Sorry Doris. Just you'd think with Washington royalty aboard they'd have their act together." He nodded to a gaggle of reporters behind them in line who encircled a U.S. senator absorbing his pontifications about the recent Reagan Administration scandals.

"Yes I took my pills!" Ben grumbled.

Doris patted Ben's arm.

"That's alright dear. It's just I worry about your blood pressure."

"Thank you Doris." He replied with sincerity. Just then a member of the senator's entourage approached the couple.

"Excuse me sir?" The young man, wearing a three piece suit he was yet to grow into, stood directly in front of Ben and lactated a broad smile. Ben quickly perused the kid.

"What?"

"The Senator wonders if you'd mind if he went ahead of you to the ticket counter?" Ben was momentarily confused as to whether he should laugh out loud or tear into the senator's revoltingly YUPPIE assistant. His comeback had been formulated years ago as he gradually became fed up with American politics.

"Why? So he can hurry off to the lounge and squeeze in one more drink on the government's teat before takeoff?" Doris hoped her husband had remembered to pack his extra blood pressure tablets that morning. "Son, bad enough me and my tax money is payin' for your little junket, now you want me to step aside and let the Senator from the great state of ...'"

"Georgia, sir. He's a Democrat from Georgia." The kid proudly announced.

"So?! Who gives a shit?! The answer is no!"

"Next please!" The smartly uniformed girl behind the ticket check-in counter called.

Ben deliberately took his time as he slowly handed in his ticket and documents over the counter.

*****

Save for the Soviet Union, President Reagan saw most of the rest of the world as by-standers in 'The Big Show'. There were no shortage of comparisons between his short lived B-acting career and the way he appeared to approach the world political stage.

However, the one other government that he did feel he needed behind him was The United Kingdom.

Margret Thatcher and her Conservative government were the Ying to Reagan's Yang particularly in attacking labor and the working man's tenuous hold on the little power they had.

Like urine overflowing in a public urinal, Thatcher thought Ronnie's trickle-down theory of economics was a good thing. Therefore it was quite a shock to him when she joined in with all of the rest of Europe and Asia in condemning his Strategic Defense Initiative program, euphemistically dubbed 'Star Wars' by the U.S. press.

Primary opposition, from all sectors, was based on a policy of the anti-weaponization of space by either superpower as it was deemed that if one side armed up, the other would quickly follow.

Earlier that month Robert "Bud" McFarlane, National Security Advisor for Reagan, had been dispatched to London after Ronald Reagan, much to his chagrin, was rebuffed by the so called Iron Lady when he assumed her backing for his Strategic Defense Initiative was a done deal.

Already condemned by most of the civilized world for what they saw as overly aggressive warmongering and a flagrant violation of the Outer Space Treaty of 1967, Reagan was particularly keen to go to extreme lengths to extend the 'special relationship' and gain Thatcher's backing.

McFarlane's mission? Convince Thatcher that *Star Wars* was a good thing.

The day after leaving Washington Thatcher was cornered by McFarlane at a small, closed meeting prior to a dinner. Thatcher continued the same party line rhetoric she tossed at Reagan the week before, reiterating that her moral conscience would not allow her to back the weaponization of space.

Suddenly, at an opportune moment, McFarlane leaned into her and softly mentioned to her that the President believes that there could be upwards of $300 million in sub-contracted work earmarked for British contractors attached to the SDI program if it were to come to fruition with congressional approval.

Thatcher sat back in her chair, smiled an evil little smile and glanced back at McFarlane.

"I think that something might be able to be arranged." She quietly uttered.

Thatcher's backing for SDI, despite her earlier vehement moral convictions and ignoring the increased tensions with Moscow, was essentially bought with a promised bribe of three hundred million dollars. Every man has his price.

Apparently so do women.

So the world was once again burdened with a renewed lethal standoff of Cruise and Perishing missiles deployed in Central Europe against Soviet SS20's deployed along the western front of the Iron Curtain skirting Eastern Europe.

***

About the same time the senator's young apprentice in line at JFK was learning exactly how much the American public revered its politicians, at the back of the terminal a dark blue coverall clad individual flashed his ID badge to the black security guard who checked the photo to the man's face, noted his Black & Decker tool box then escorted him down the terminal hall to a short passageway between the men's & lady's toilets to a steel grey, security door. The stocky guard blocked the keypad with one hand as he punched in the six digit code and then held the door open for the workman and watched as the KAL logo on the back of the man's coveralls disappeared around the corner at the bottom of the metal stairs. He watched the door close and returned to his station as the man made his way down some more stairs to ground level.

It was a chilled but clear New York night as the dark figure exited out onto the tarmac and consulted a folded over piece of paper he pulled from his breast pocket.

Checking in both directions he headed off to the left and with the luminescent skyline of New York City in the distance it was a mere five minute walk across the poorly lit, noisy tarmac until he reached his destination, Hanger #7.

He suddenly crouched and feigned rummaging through his tool box as a tractor towing an empty luggage trolley pulled up not far from the hanger's entrance and halted beside a second baggage handler he hadn't seen when he first entered the tarmac. The overweight driver of the empty tractor yelled over to the younger worker shifting a large mound of baggage off a wagon and onto a conveyor belt.

"Hey Mickey, where the hell's the rocker handle

for the luggage trolley?!"

"How the fuck should I know?" He snapped back as he roughly tossed a dark blue Samsonite suitcase across the conveyor which slid off the other side and onto the ground. "Man! Fuck this luggage! I'm going on break!"

"Thank you Mickey. Welcome aboard, nice to have a new employee to help out." He put the tractor in gear and pulled away. "You know there's no 'I' in asshole!" He yelled over his shoulder as he drove off.

Careful to stay in the shadows, the man quietly watched as the driver pulled the luggage tractor around side of the hanger and wandered off back towards the terminal.

It was five minutes before the 22:00 coffee break and Hanger #7, save for the Boeing 747 sitting half in half out of the giant doorway, was already abandoned. The man checked his watch.

Korean Air Lines flight 007 Heavy had just finished up with her standard pre-board mechanical checks and was due to depart for Seoul via Anchorage, Alaska in less than two hours at 23:50, EDT.

With a sense of calm urgency the man ascended the roller stairs which were snugged up to the port side, forward passenger's hatch and made his way up to the cockpit. Once inside he set to work with the efficiency of an emergency room surgeon.

Removing a pilot's flight control handbook from his tool box he opened to a pre marked page titled; 'Pre-flight Checklist'.

With a small, battery operated screwdriver he

unscrewed and removed the cover plate to a toggle switch on the console to the right of the pilot's seat, and disabled the ship's Inertial Navigation System or INS relay wire. He then proceeded to install a hand held, wrist watch-sized, self-contained INS unit. He then expertly rewired the new INS unit to the aircraft's main computer.

As a redundant measure he reversed the On/Off switch of the Way Point Navigational System so it would appear that 'Off' was 'On' and vice versa.

This meant that it would appear that the flight crew had either forgotten or neglected to activate the WPN which was essential to locate the electronic beacons' impulses which dotted their entire flight path. Should they track off course they would, in theory not realize it.

Six and a half minutes later he was around back of the hanger near the perimeter fence, climbing into the back of a black, Ford Cordoba with his tool box and removing his KAL coveralls to reveal a charcoal grey three piece suit and dark blue striped tie.

Less than an hour later the jumbo jet was rolled up to the gate and boarding commenced as the flight crew climbed into the cockpit and settled into their pre-flight duties.

The black Ford had long since vanished into the night.

****

Like a model out of a TV commercial the

beautiful impeccably uniformed, Korean, thirty-something KAL Head Stewardess weaved her way through the passengers crowding the aisles as they loaded their carry-ons into overhead bins and meandered about looking for seats. Reaching the cockpit, she knocked twice then entered.

"How're we looking back there?" Asked the veteran captain as he continued checking the overhead control panel.

"Hye-su, marry me!" The young navigator sitting at the table off to her right proposed to the stew without looking away from his control panel. The attractive stew didn't miss a beat.

"You know I would Dae-ho, but there's a problem."

"What is it my love?"

"You couldn't possibly expect a girl of my caliber to marry a lowly navigator!" Bae, the co-pilot switched off his head set and spoke into his dead mike.

"May Day, May Day, May Day! This is Navigator KAL flight zero-zero-seven. I've just taken a direct hit and been shot down in flames! May Day, May Day, May Day!"

The young navigator took the ribbing well.

The pilot's on-board intercom crackled to life, he flicked the "open" switch and a female's voice reported.

Top side, passenger report. She relayed.

"Main deck here, go ahead topside." The pilot responded.

"Top side we have twelve passengers First Class, twenty-three Business, everyone else Economy.

73

Also, 130 connects in route."

"Rug rats?"

"Twenty-two all tolled."

"Any medical conditions, pregnancies or allergies?"

"Two food allergies only Captain. Nuts."

"Well, get a couple of straightjackets and keep them quiet! Wouldn't want to disturb the other passengers!" Dae-ho said into his mike.

A sense of humor so subtle one hardly notices it. Where do you come up with them?! The reporting stewardess cracked.

"V. I. P.'s?" Asked the pilot. She read from the manifest.

Congressman Lawrence McDonald and a platoon of aides.

"Thank you. Hye-su, make sure the Senator has all he needs, prep the crew and let us know when everyone is tucked in." The Captain directed the Head Stewardess.

"Will do Captain." On the way out she couldn't resist a pat on the head of the navigator. "Cheer up Dae-ho. There's someone out there for you!" She stepped through the cockpit door back into the cabin. "You just have to find him."

"Captain, switching crew to main channel." The captain announced and all crew members checked they were on the right channel and adjusted their headsets. "Tower, this is KAL zero-zero-seven Heavy requesting commo check." Chung-cha, communications officer for the flight radioed the tower. There was a few seconds delay and his headset came to life.

"Read you loud and clear KAL zero-zero-seven, stand by on this frequency for taxi instructions and be advised you will then proceed on a heading of two-two-zero degrees to Bethel, Alaska. I say again heading of 2-2-0 degrees, how copy, over?"

"Tower, KAL zero-zero-seven, copy two-two-zero degrees enroute to Bethel. Out."

"Good sailing zero-zero-seven. Tower out."

****

Meanwhile, Senators Jesse Helms of North Carolina, Steven Symms of Idaho and Carroll J. Hubbard, Jr. of Kentucky were seated in one of the many lounges in the sprawling East Terminal waiting to board 007's sister aircraft 015 scheduled to depart about fifteen to twenty minutes behind 007.

The four senators were all enroute to Seoul, Korea to attend scheduled ceremonies for the thirty year anniversary of the U. S.-Korea Mutual Defense Treaty.

It was no coincidence that *The Eagle Lounge* was a mere five minute walk from the gate and, at a window table adjacent to the bar, Congressman Lawrence McDonald, who had left instructions with his aides to come and get him when the boarding was nearly complete, sat with them. They had just ordered a third round when an aide approached them from the front entrance.

"Senator McDonald they're ready for you and your party to board now. Senator Helms I'm afraid there's been a change in the flight plan." The aide added.

"What kind'a change?"

"Sir, as Senator McDonald's flight has been delayed by 30 to 35 minutes our flight has been bumped back as well."

"By how much?" Hubbard asked.

"We're not sure yet Senator, but I spoke to the KAL desk and they assured me that as soon as they have confirmation they'll announce it. Probably not more than a half an hour sir."

The drinks arrived and had no chance of survival beyond the three minute mark and as McDonald ordered one last, last round, he threw a fifty on the table.

"What the hell you doin' boy?!" Hubbard protested.

"The people of the great state of Kentucky will be pleased to pay for this!" McDonald said.

"When we get to the hotel in Seoul the great state of Kentucky can buy all the bourbon she wants. For now, the people of the great state of Georgia will pay for proper whiskey!" He tossed two twenties on the bar and slid the fifty back, downed his drink and left.

With most of the passengers tucked in chasing sleep, the cabin crew attending to their hospitality duties and the flight crew confidently finishing up their pre-flight checks, final clearance was given by the ATC's and Korean Air Flight 007 was wheels up at eight minutes to midnight, Eastern Standard Time, headed for Anchorage via the Bethel, Alaska beacon station and on the first leg of their journey half way around the world.

*

Kenai Radar Station
Eastern Shore of Cook Inlet, Alaska
04:37 Local

The only way up the formidable mountain was via the four to five foot wide, dirt road by four wheel drive vehicle. In the daytime. Weather permitting.

At the end of the trail, on the highest peak of the mountain, stood a complex antennae array. The adjoining, small log cabin was deceptive as it was actually a sophisticated commercial radar station serving as a living quarters. From the outside the crude cabin could have been mistaken for someone's low budget, summer get away house in the swamp lands of Northern Michigan.

It was here that alternating two man crews took forty-eight hour shifts of four hours on and four hours off, on a twenty-eight day rotational basis with a two week break off.

Inside the basic but fully functional station a set of bunk beds stood against the opposite wall from the multiple radar screen console and by way of a kitchen there was an upright fridge/freezer, two hotplates, a tea kettle and a two slice toaster. The overall appearance of the room was more like a frat house or a cheap hostel than a commercial radar facility, such was the mess. The only occupants at present were two late twenty-something locals.

"Hey, did anybody check in while I was in the shitter?" The young guy in the Official Alaskan State uniform; blue jeans, red flannel shirt and Detroit Red Wings ball cap, asked as he retook his seat at the monitoring station.

"No, not in the last half hour to forty-five minutes since you been gone. Why?" The kid in the darker red flannel shirt sporting a Montreal Canadians wool cap and laying on the bottom bunk systematically popping Cheez-Its into his mouth quipped.

Detroit, now sitting in front of the three radar screen monitors was flipping through a digital readout on a green screen computer built in to the table surface of the console.

"Hey, I'm reading a KAL flight out'a New York on screen 3, followed by another KAL heavy about 100 miles or so behind it. And I just called up the flight plans they filed before leaving JFK."

"So?" Cheez-Its lethargically queried.

"According to their flight plans they're both heading to Seoul."

"And your point is?"

"Okay Meathead, navigation 101! If two aircraft of the same make and model take off from the same location, and are heading to the same place, they should have filed the same flight plan. No?"

"Yes, but did they?"

"Yes they did, but ..." Cheez-Its guy slid off the bed and wondered over to the radar screens where his colleague was pointing to the first of two blips which was noticeably north of the second.

"That first guy looks kind'a wide of the mark." He commented.

The two continued to watch the screen for a full five minutes. The blip marked 'KAL007' continued to drift slightly more to the west as it descended south.

"By about six or seven miles I make it."

"Maybe they forgot to switch their auto pilot to INS mode after their last way station?" Cheez-It suggested.

"Or they did switch it over but they're still in Heading mode?"

"Where was their last way station?"

"Should have been Cairn Mountain." He pointed a spot on the screen north east of the blip.

"Anybody out there we can contact to confirm they flew by there?"

"No. It's just a beacon."

"Maybe the beacon's out?"

Detroit adjusted screen #1 and a read out which listed the three beacons within a two hundred and fifty mile radius. All were signaling as operational.

"You're taking flying lessons. What'a you think?"

"I'm learning on a Piper Cub! Those guys go to school for years to fly those monsters! Plus you gotta have at least ten years behind the stick to even be considered!" They continued to watch and pushed their brains for a decision. "We did have a class about on board INS systems." Cheez-Its remembered.

"What's that?"

"Inertial Navigation System. It's an on-board

computer system that tells when you're off course, but you have to have your auto pilot programmed to pick it up. Plus it doesn't kick in if you're over seven or eight miles off course, something like that."

"That sucks!"

"Can't we radio them?"

"No, they're way outta range!"

"Can we radio somebody to radio them?!"

"Yeah, how's that gonna look on your next resume?! 'While a junior radar operator in bum-fuck Alaska, applicant caused panic on board a Boeing Heavy by advising the vastly experienced pilot that he was on the wrong course!' Let me know how that works out for ya!"

"Point taken."

"Even if we could radio them we don't know their freq's, or if they're on HF, VHF or what."

"Shit! Hope they're okay." The quintessential awkward moment set in.

"They must know what they're doin!"

"Yeah. Yeah, they must know what they're doin."

Neither spoke with conviction.

****

"KAL zero-one-five this is KAL zero-zero-seven, do you copy? KAL zero-one-five this is KAL zero-zero-seven, I say again do you copy?"

"KAL zero-zero-seven, KAL zero-one-five, we copy. Over."

"Zero-one-five we seem to be experiencing a

little difficulty reaching our next way point by radio and we have a revised ETA to pass on. I say again, we have a revised ETA. Could you relay radio message for us to Flight Service Station, Anchorage. Over?"

"Zero-zero-seven, zero-one-five, say again your ... mess ... arbled. Ov ..."

"Zero-one-five, we are experiencing difficulty reaching our next way point by radio and we have a revised E-T-A. I say again, we have a revised E-T-A. Could you relay radio message for us to Flight Service Station, over?"

"Zero-zero-seven, zero-one-fiv ... have ... tried HF and VHF, ov...?"

"Roger-we-have-tried-both-HF-and-VHF.   Can you relay for us? Over." The captain called over his shoulder to the navigator. "Is there weather between us and them we don't know about?"

"No sir but, given our location and altitude radio interference is not unusual."

"Zero-one-five, zero-zero-seven did you copy message, over?"

"Zero-zero-seven ... ill rela ... over"

"Shit! Damn communications packages! We can put men on the moon and talk to them clear as day but can't talk to an aircraft a hundred miles behind us!"

Little did the captain realize that he had missed his guess regarding the distance between his aircraft and their sister flight KAL 015. By almost 400 miles.

Less than an hour after takeoff from Anchorage the Alaskan station at King Salmon had also been tracking 007 nearly thirteen miles north of where they should have been. However, not knowing their flight plan and having no reason to suspect anything was wrong, no one saw any reason to take action.

KAL 007 was now outside its maximum expected course deviation by six times the norm.

*

CHAPTER FOUR

U.S.M.C. Force Recon Training Facility
Naval Amphib Base
Coronado, California

Dressed in jungle boots, Navy issue swim trunks and a green and gold tee shirt with the Force Recon emblem over the left breast, Capt. Coats, C.O. of the Force Recon training facility, looked like something right out of central casting. The blue-eyed, black haired, well-built Marine officer took a seat at his desk, reached across and switched on the radio as he opened a large brown envelope and removed a sealed personnel record.

Signing on right at the tail end of Viet Nam, Coats had missed the 'Big Show' but was determined to make up for lost time. He was the only dual qualified Marine officer in the Corps which meant that he'd earned both Marine Force Recon and Navy Seal badges, back to back, which meant he could talk all the shit he wanted and there wasn't a god damned thing anybody could do about it. But it wasn't in his nature to talk shit, he was the kind of guy who just got on with it.

To quell any lingering questions regarding his motivation for Special Operations, he was also jump and scuba qualified and wore Navy gold wings, not the Army lead sled.

He returned to his coffee while reading the file on his new incoming corpsman as he followed the morning news.

"... with news on the hour. Good morning San Diego! It's five o'clock in the a.m. Here are the headlines.

In the ongoing Senate investigation of the Department of Housing and Urban Development, the Assistant to the Secretary of HUD, Deborah Gore Dean, was today convicted of three counts of conspiracy to defraud the federal government, one count of having accepted an illegal gratuity, four counts of perjury and four counts of engaging in a scheme to conceal material facts.

President Reagan's Press Secretary made a brief announcement following Dean's sentencing. He called the latest White House scandal, 'An unfortunate, but isolated incident'.

Dean was sentenced to three 21 month sentences to be served consecutively. However, legal experts say she will likely serve about a year, either in a low security prison or under house arrest."

"Bastards!" Coats cursed under his breath, switched off the radio and returned to the morning's paper work.

Meanwhile, a couple of miles away, McKeowen and the Recon School's Executive Officer, Lieutenant Stratford, were enroute from the airport, approaching the expansive Coronado Bridge connecting San Diego to Coronado Island.

Lt. Stratford, four years in age younger than Captain Coats, but only a year and half less in seniority than his boss, was a different package altogether.

Blond haired with hazel eyes he was the kind of guy, like Michael J. Fox or Leonardo DiCaprio, who would still be getting carded at bars and night clubs when he was forty.

Save for the fact that his entire vocabulary wasn't limited to 'like', 'awesome' or 'totally' he could've passed for your run-of-mill, Southern California surfer bum.

In reality Stratford was a laid-back Seattle Grunge type with not even the slightest concept of an agenda towards his career. Whenever the subject of why he enlisted came up he told it like it was.

"We fell in love. She dumped me for a guitarist. I signed up." Far from that simple, Doc would get to fill in the blanks as time went on.

Stratford was along for the ride, however long it lasted.

It was early dawn and from downtown San Diego the sun wasn't yet visible but once they had climbed to the apex of the two mile long Coronado Bridge, the burning red-orange horizon out over the Pacific stretched as far as could be seen in either direction. It was the first time McKeowen had ever seen "The Coast" and compared to the industrial, steel grey, confined spaces of Pittsburgh or New York City, Doc had the sensation he was on the other side of the known universe.

"JESUS! It's like something out of a movie set!" He asked as his ears perked up. "What's that rhythmic pounding? Sounds like a giant's heart beat through a stethoscope!" The L.T. didn't answer, he just pointed out to sea. Doc nearly fell out of the moving jeep.

Coming in sets of eight to twelve, about a mile out to sea, he could see the ten foot beach breakers which marked the inland border of a surf zone that started at least 150 meters on the seaward side of the beach.

Just remember, when you get out there, you ain't in Kansas anymore!

Heinzy's words echoed in his head.

"Don't worry. Corpsmen don't go in the water." The L.T., mistaking Doc's bewilderment for apprehension, informed him.

"Why the fuck not? Sir."

"Medical support stays on the beach."

"And if you and the troops are a mile out and there's a casualty?"

"We'll swim him into you."

"There are sharks in that water?"

"It's the Pacific ain't it?"

"Jellies? Barracuda? Debris?"

"Yeah, what's your point?"

"You know how long it takes for a man to bleed out from a small shark bite let alone something more serious?"

"Can't say as I do Doc."

"Thirty seconds. Maybe. If he's lucky." The L.T. looked over at his new corpsman. "Providing he doesn't attract other elasmobranchs because then you got a whole platoon in the hurt locker!" McKeowen added.

"You tellin' me you wanna get wet?"

"Sir, I didn't leave the magnificent smog ridden, polluted, acid rain drenched, freezing climes of

86

beautiful, downtown Pittsburgh P.A. to come all the way out here to these god-forsaken sun drenched beaches and cursed, drop-dead gorgeous, scantily clad women just to suffer the constant 72 degree temperatures and eat burritos!"

"Okay." The L.T. shrugged. "I guess you can get wet."

"I will cover all evolutions side-by-side with you and your men."

"Recon Marines, Doc. Not men. Marines."

"Apologies, sir."

"Ya see that black-brown rise in the rocks out to your left?" As they crested the apex of the bridge the lieutenant pointed out over the ocean.

"Yeah."

"Dat eez Meh-hee-co. Tijuana." As they began their descent of the bridge Doc glanced to the right.

"Hey! That's the hotel they used in ..."

"Yeah, *Some Like Hot*,1958. Monroe, Curtis, Lemmon. It's the Hotel Del. Hotel Del Coronado."

"Love that film!"

"The two lane road running North-South is Silver Strand Boulevard, The 'O' course and pretty much all physical training takes place on the beach side of The Strand. All the academic stuff is on the other side at the Amphid base." The more the lieutenant spoke the more Mac's enthusiasm was building. "All the military beaches are color coded every few hundred meters. The first jetty south of the hotel is Red Beach One, that's the federal property boundary. We have to keep south of that or the natives get restless."

"South?"

"Our southern border is that sunken area out there, about five miles from Red One. They call it Silver Strand. But we operate as far as the Mexican border sometimes on runs and such." Doc was standing in his seat holding onto the windshield of the battleship grey Willy's jeep looking over the bridge's safety rail.

"Don't jump." The L.T. said.

"What?"

"Don't think about jumpin'."

"This bridge is a hundred and fifty feet off the water! Who the hell'd be that stupid?"

"Over two hundred foot off the water and Navy SEAL students would be that stupid. Well, two would-be-SEALS."

"I don't get it." He fell back into the seat.

"About a year ago two dumb shit candidates saw a movie. In the film two Navy Seals, actor types, drove by here and one of 'em jumped out of the jeep and over the rail. Then quietly swam ashore."

"The real jumper live?!"

"Oh yeah. He lived. He'll never walk again. Or have kids, much less fuck. But he lived."

"Sounds like a real dumb shit move." Imagining what it would be like to smack into the concrete waters of the San Diego bay from that height, McKeowen leaned over and peered down at the channel again. "Where was this genius from that he couldn't tell the difference between real life and the movies?"

"Texas."

Ten minutes later they were pulling in across the road from the SEAL training compound and a gate guard saluted smartly as McKeowen and the X.O. drove through the front gate and pulled into the first structure on the left. Doc threw his seabag over his shoulder and they headed in.

It was the first in a short row of olive drab green, Quonset huts marked only by a small, red, wooden sign staked into the narrow, impeccably groomed lawn. Gold letters declared:

Amphib Warfare School
Coronado, Calif.
U.S.M.C. Force Recon

"Celer. Silens. Mortalis."

"Celer. Silens. Mortalis?" McKeowen queried as they entered the hut.

"Swift. Silent. Deadly."

"Catchy."

Once inside, Doc saw the open space was neatly sectioned off into thirds perpendicular to the long axis of the hut and again divided exactly in half down the long axis. They turned right down the narrow passageway, made their way to the very rear of the hut and stopped just short of the partitioned off area on the right marked, 'B.A.'.

"B.A.?" Doc queried.

"Bad Attitude." Stratford quipped.

"Fuck you. Sir!" A tall, trim but well built, black Gunnery Sergeant on the other side of the hut replied to the L.T. from behind his desk.

"This is our new doc, Doc McKeowen." The L.T. introduced.

"Sir, I don't prefer to be called ..." It was at that point that Mac reluctantly resigned himself to being called Doc for the remainder of his time in the forces. The Gunny came out from behind his desk to shake McKeowen's hand.

"Gunny Genne Senior NCO for Basic Amphid. We teach the grunts how to disembark vessels without breaking a leg, drowning or getting their asses shot off."

"Sounds like a valuable skill Gunny. HM2 McKeowen. Nice to meet ya."

"Don't mind these guys Doc." The L.T. advised nodding to the half dozen desks and personnel on the other side of the chest high partition. "The Corps siphons out the misfits and rejects and sends them here. The only qual to be an instructor at B.A. is to show up with all five appendages. Or in the Gunny's case, four and a half." The Gunny saluted the lieutenant allowing his middle finger to stick out. Doc more than appreciated the banter. Ever since he finished his first tour in the Navy McKeowen found the unassuming nature and lack of hidden agendas of military service types to be relaxing, comfortable even. It's hard to sweat the small shit when you're liable to wake up dead or mutilated one morning.

In the civilian world a guy constantly had to watch his back because in Civ Land you could never tell what the hell anybody meant by what they were saying, much less if what they were saying was what they meant.

The L.T. led Doc through two neat rows of unattended, large grey, steel desks over on the starboard side of the hut just across from the B.A. area to an empty desk in back. Save for a plaque where a name plate should have been, the desk top was bare. Doc picked up the plaque and read aloud.

"'Doc H's two rules for success. Rule #1: Don't sweat the small shit. Rule #2: It's all small shit!' Huh! The last corpsman?"

"Yeah. Doc Hernandez. Great guy. We all miss him."

"Rotated duty stations?" Mac asked. Gunny Genne, who couldn't help but hear the conversation in the small space over the partition, looked up from his work, straight at the L.T. who was staring down at the deck.

"He was lost. On a jump."

"Wife?" Doc asked.

"And two kids."

"Naturally!" McKeowen dropped his sea bag to the deck. "This my desk now?" Stratford nodded. Doc carefully placed the plaque back in the exact spot he had found it. "Let's just keep this here." The L.T. cracked a barely perceptible smile of appreciation. Doc noticed. "What? Sounds better than celer, silens, mortalis."

"Just leave ya gear here, let's report in to the C.O."

Back up the passage way they stopped at the last door on the starboard side of the hut where the L.T. pounded on the bulkhead next to the door three times hard.

"WHO?"

"Lieutenant Stratford with the new Corpsman Sir! Permission to enter!"

"Permission granted!" This wasn't his first time around Marines but Doc had forgotten how different the green side of the Navy was.

They both entered, stood at attention in front of Captain Coat's desk and sharply snapped to attention. Mac raised his hand to salute but was stayed by the L.T. Still perusing McKeowen's orders the C.O. addressed Doc without looking up.

"Marines don't salute indoors unless under arms."

"Roger that sir. Sorry. My mind's still on the blue side sir."

"We'll have to work on that. You always report to a new duty station in civvies Petty Officer ... McKeowen?"

"Sir I ..."

"The Petty Officer's luggage was misrouted at O'Hare, sir." Stratford interjected.

"I was told you were flying out of Pittsburgh, HM2 McKeowen."

"I did sir, via Chicago. I suppose somebody at Personnel figured it'd be cheaper than a nonstop to here. Sir." The lieutenant wasn't the only one who could pull a plausible excuse out of his ass on short notice. Sign of a good troop.

Coats squinted his eyes and scanned both their faces. He wasn't sure if the L.T. had said something to do with McKeowen's excuse and the pair conspired to bullshit him before they showed up or if Doc was that quick on the uptake. Either way he decided to let it go.

"McKeowen. Undergrad in biology, qualified EMT, twice recommended for the lifesaving medal.

Scuba qualified. How did a reservist swing a billet at Scuba School?"

"Kissed the right ass the correct number of times at just the right angle, sir."

"Expert Rifleman Badge, Expert Pistol, .45 or 9mm?"

"Both sir."

"Naturally, why'd I ask? Originally from New York City. Well, we won't hold that against you. You Irish, petty officer?" Coats lay the folder on his desk and made eye contact with McKeowen.

"Negative sir. Second generation Scots-American Sir,"

"Coats is English. What do you make of the British Empire Petty Officer?"

"Nothing sir. She seems to be making a fine mess of things herself."

"You realize the British conquered half the world?"

"A truly amazing feat sir. Especially given they had such a hard time of it at a little wooden bridge up in Sterling against a bunch of rabble in skirts, sir." Stratford fought back a smirk. "Then again, it took God Almighty Himself to keep the Scots from conquering the **entire** world, sir."

"Yeah? How do you figure?" Coats challenged.

"He made whisky sir." Doc answered in a matter-of-fact attitude. The C.O. chuckled.

"I know your orders are to report for duty at zero six hundred this morning but seeing as how you're just off the plane and flew all night I'll give ya the day off to get settled and squared away. Tomorrow there's an instructor's meeting at zero nine hundred here. Sunday we're free. This is the last day of formation week and we've accumulated enough warm bodies to commission a class on Monday. Most of today will be taken up with troop orientation. Lieutenant Stratford will explain your duties and what's expected of you. Questions?"

"A few sir, just to help me get oriented to RECON."

"I'll fill ya in on the way over to personnel." The L.T. offered.

"Anything else?" Coats asked. Stratford took up the question.

"The Doc is gonna need some swim gear Captain." Coats tilted his head to the side and glared at McKeowen.

"That so Doc? You wanna play with the big boys?"

"Sir, amongst all these big boy Marines, the U.S. Navy saw fit to assign a Corps-MAN. Consequently it is my sworn duty to abide by some wisdom my dad passed unto me when I wuz but a young 'un. There are three things on God's Little Green Acre what are completely useless. Balls on a priest, tits on a nun and a corpsman sittin' on the beach while his troops are a half mile out beyond the surf zone."

"I got a feeling you're gonna fit right in here Doc. Welcome aboard." The C.O. stood and extended his hand and Doc smiled as he took it.

"It's great to be aboard sir."

"Here's a copy of the roster and the course syllabus, the L.T. will square you away with the rest."

Once back outside the headquarters hut they

turned left and headed further into the amphib base.

"What time's the morning swim L.T.?"

"Formation is 03:45 over there on the beach, behind the Enlisted Club. We kick off at zero four every morning save Sunday. Morning swims, one mile, are in the bay for the first month until the candidates are acclimated to swimming in the dark in formation and they're ready to tackle the surf zone at night."

They talked as they continued up the one main street which was flanked by low, cinder block, government buildings. Foot traffic was sporadic at that hour on Saturday morning and vehicular traffic was non-existent.

"How often do you run classes?"

"Three to four classes a year if we have enough candidates show up."

"What do they have to do to qualify to get here?"

"How they qual is they bust their asses for a year or more back at Battalion proving they have what it takes to exceed the course standards then, if their C.O. approves their request, they get to take the screen test, which is basically the same as the SEALS screen test except they also have a twenty-five mile forced march with full gear the same day."

They passed the swimming pool which McKeowen noted was surrounded by a ten foot chain link fence which in turn was shrouded in a green canvas curtain obscuring view of the pool from the street. Thus cordoned off, Mac wondered if some top secret training maneuvers took place there but, not wanting to seem too naïve, didn't ask. Stratford continued with the tour.

"Fleet wide as many as five to six thousand a year try out. Out of those about 30 to 40 per class get to come down here. Because we get our money from the Department of the Navy we have to be more selective than the SEALS. While they're waiting for orders they're temporarily assigned to Battalion Recon to teach them the basics, land navigation, tracking potential targets and most importantly advanced swim techniques. By the time they get here they're in good enough shape that 15 mile beach runs and mile long open ocean swims with gear aren't gonna wash them out."

"Sounds like a respectable program."

"It's upgraded and improved about every six months. Ever since Nam we realized of all the branches, Spec Ops evolves the fastest. An added burden is, with the exception of SCUBA training, we have two months to achieve the same run, swim and patrol standards the folks across the road have six months for."

"What about jump school?"

"We use the Army's school out at Benning but they have to prove themselves here before we agree to give them a four week vacation at an Army school."

"Injuries, casualties?"

"We try to make it as realistic as possible to save lives but it's not unheard of that guys die or are crippled in training. Touch wood, other than the usual near drownings, broken bones and soft tissue injuries we've not had any casualties in the year I've been here, but there's injuries every class. Once we're into the swing of things they're only getting four to five hours sleep a night, plus we train on Saturdays, so there's only one day off. Not counting Hell Week."

"Hell Week?" Doc inquired. The L.T. brandished an evil smile.

"You're gonna love it, trust me." He motioned towards a large flat building off to the left. "Chow hall. There's no time for chow before the swim today but I'll see you get some extra time for lunch later."

"'Preciate it. Where do I live?" Stratford pointed across the two lane road to a WWII styled barracks. "Jesus!"

"What?"

"Same architect as my college dorm back in New York."

"Senior Enlisted Quarters. You're cleared with the OOD but if any of the senior NCO's give you shit, let me know and we'll square it away."

"Senior NCO Quarters? That mean I get my rack made for me?"

"Just like the Hilton Doc! Technically, since we've never had a corpsman assigned to us there's no assigned billet for a corpsman so the base C.O. ordered you billeted in there." McKeowen stopped and gazed across the street.

"L.T., how the hell did this slot come open anyway?"

"No fucking idea Doc. There was no billet here before. From what we heard somebody in D.C. made some phone calls down here. Spoke to the base Commander who referred him to Captain Coats, next thing we know we get a twixt sayin'

97

make ready, we're gettin' a full time corpsmen."

Doc smiled and mumbled. "Commander Dunn!" He looked around. "Huh! Barracks right across the road from the chow hall! I'm getting to like this place already! Just outta curiosity, what did'ja do for medical coverage for your hazardous evolutions before if there was no billet for a corpsman?"

"Put in a request for medical support 24 hours prior then waited for the dispensary to send over whatever fat, lazy, give-a-fuck, Black Shoe, corpsman was available so he could sit on the beach in his air conditioned ambulance, read gay porn and fuck off." The L.T. slapped McKeowen on the shoulder. "But now, looks like we got us a for real doc, hey Doc?!"

"What's a Black Shoe sir?"

"A non-Special Operations qualified individual. A regular troop, you know, a puke!" Stratford took notice as Mac glanced away. "Somethin' the matter Doc? Just now you looked away. And I saw ya wince in there when the C.O. shook ya hand."

"I don't like bein' called Doc, that's all."

"What's the issue? You're a corpsman ain't ya?" To firmly but respectfully make his point Mac made eye contact.

"That ain't the point."

"Well?"

"I got an issue with somebody else called Doc."

"Another corpsman?"

"No." Stratford waited for more details. "My father."

"He a corpsman too?"

"No, never served. Punctured ear drum."

"Well, if that's the biggest problem you have to deal with here you're gonna make out like a thief. Doc." The L.T. stepped to the side as McKeowen made his way down the sidewalk towards the Admin building.

"Hey Doc!" Stratford called cross the street after him.

"Yeah?"

"You're from New York, ain't ya?" The L.T. called over.

"What about it?"

"Where did you ever see a shark bite?" Doc smiled.

"*Jaws*." He called back. "See ya on the beach L.T."

****

CHAPTER FIVE

15:47 Local
NORAD
Command & Control Facility
Elmendorf, Alaska

The North American Air Defense Buffer Zone reaches well south into the Bering Sea and extends, by agreement, down into the Northern Pacific. The Soviets, likewise, have similarly restricted airspace from the Bering Straits to the northern islands of Japan.

This effectively leaves, for a relatively short distance by jet airline standards, a narrow strip of air space about fifty miles wide intended to allow commercial aircraft to and from the Far East to access North American airspace.

Not realizing they were so far off course, KAL flight 007, for the last twenty minutes, had been closely monitored by both the National Security Agency, through the North American Aerospace Command aka NORAD, at Elmendorf Air Base as well as by the Soviet Far East District Air Defense Forces on Sakhalin Island.

Given their airspeed and rate of drift, the inevitable happened. At approximately 15:51 hours local KAL 007 entered Soviet air space over the Kamchatka Peninsula.

The sprawling radar & control room at Elmendorf which requires dozens of full time operators and supervisors, is tasked with the

Command and Control of a half dozen squadrons, fighters and bombers and is the largest C&C air control facility in the Western United States and Canada.

From his glass encased office, the duty officer, Lieutenant Kaminski, looked up from his desk and down on to the bank of monitoring stations on the operations deck below him where he noticed one of his troops at console #11 intently referencing his radar screen, busily using his slide rule and making notes. Kaminski decided to go down and investigate.

"What is it Polk?" He peered over the airman's shoulder one hand on the back of the airman's swivel chair the other on his console.

"Sir, I have an unidentified aircraft, which appears to be near the outer, south west boarder of the NOPAC boundary. But a few minutes ago he skirted the no-fly zone."

"Can you fix him down?"

"I did sir and from a reverse azimuth I'm guessing, if he's a legit passenger liner, that he's supposed to be in the Romeo-20 corridor."

"Call up the outer westerly marker for Romeo-20." The airman adjusted the display mode on his screen and the iridescent green image enlarged with a superimposed red line tracing the east-west outer boarders of the flight buffer zone.

"Western marker for Romeo-20 is 18 miles east of Kamchatka, sir." He indicated across the screen with his slide rule.

"Course and speed?" The officer inquired.

"He's steady at four-niner-zero, holding at two-six-five degrees, sir.''

"Well done Polk. Maintain tracking."

"Yes sir." The lieutenant made his way back to his desk and placed a land line call on his secure phone. A pleasant female voice came on the line.

Good afternoon, NSA desk.

"This is Lieutenant Kaminski at the radar facility."

How may I help you Lieutenant?

"We're tracking an unidentified aircraft traveling south by south west along the outer marker for the Romeo-20 flight path."

Stand by sir, I'll notify the Duty Officer.

"Thank you ma'am." A minute later a man came on the line.

Who am I speaking to? The gruff voice demanded.

"Lieutenant Kaminski, NORAD tracking facility. Who is this?"

This is the NSA Duty Officer. Lieutenant, there's no need to track that aircraft. We are aware of its presence.

The L.T. was puzzled but knew better than to give into his suspicions when dealing with the No Such Agency people. He hung up and passed the order for Polk to disregard the blip and then returned to his paper work. He wrestled with the idea of blindly accepting the NSA's terse order, but as a precaution decided to enter the incident in his daily log anyway.

There was a good reason the 'hands off' order was given by the NSA Duty Officer. There was another aircraft in the immediate vicinity. And it wasn't a civilian airliner. It was a USAF RC-135 Reconnaissance aircraft. A state-of-the-art spy plane.

A model the Soviets were well familiar with.

****

In the First Class section of the KAL plane all of the passengers were sleeping but one. Hye-su, the Head Stewardess, noticed one overhead light still on and a man staring out into the pitch black of night. Senator McDonald was wide awake and preoccupied with his thoughts. She quietly approached and leaned into his seat area.

"Senator, can I get you a drink? Tea, coffee?"

"That's very kind of you stewardess, but the last thing I need right now is caffeine!"

"We have caffeine-free beverages. Maybe a white wine to relax?" He was taken in by her engaging smile, dark eyes and soft, beautiful features. He set his pen and paper aside and purposely taking a dramatic pause before he spoke, looked up at her.

"May I speak with you a moment?" McDonald asked.

"Of course."

"Are you from Seoul?"

"Nearly. I was born in a small village just to the south, but raised in the city. School, university, my first job."

"First love?"

"Something like that." She smiled and took a

seat on the outer arm rest of the empty seat next to the senator.

"What'a you make of all this Cold War stuff? I mean, what'a you think the Korean people, the man on the street, what'a you think they think?"

For Hye-su humiliation mixed with suspicion was tempered with a dash of flattery that a ranking politician should be interested in her opinion of world affairs. She drew a breath before answering.

"In Korea we have lived as a divided people for thirty years, more than a generation. Consequently there is an entire generation who have grown up, and are now raising their children, in the shadow of fear. Fear of invasion, war. Nuclear war. Many of us throughout the Orient feel that the Russians and Americans do not fully understand the forces they are dealing with, that they are too insulated from the realities of war to comprehend its consequences. Some see your countries as a pair of small children who have somehow wound up playing with a loaded gun with no safety catch." Hye-su suddenly became aware of her impromptu dissertation. With all pretense of political superficiality quickly evaporating, the senator sat motionless as she continued. "In Korea, hopelessness is tempered by hope. Hope that your leaders will come to their senses before it is too late." McDonald shifted in his seat. She raised from the seat and stood up in the aisle.

"How do we feel about the so called Cold War?" She continued. "We think that so long as President Reagan and Premier Andropov continue to play one-upmanship, it is inevitable that they will needlessly bring the world to the brink of extinction. And so, it is difficult to respect men with their priorities so far off track. Rightly or wrongly, many extrapolate these feelings to those who follow these men as well."

McDonald, mesmerized by her frankness, was unsure how to react.

"Would you like that wine now?" She politely asked.

"Maybe a whiskey."

****

If the Soviets ever had anything that approached the size, complexity and capability of the Elmendorf facility in the U.S. the facility they dropped billions of rubles on located on Sakhalin Island and her adjacent facilities south of Kamchatka on the far east coast of Russia were it.

It is from here the Soviets sought to fend off the imaginary hoard of capitalistic barbarians in protection of the Motherland as much as the Americans were prepared to battle off the millions of heathen, godless commies poised to over run their fair lands, enslave their families and steal their McDonalds.

Fighter squadrons, bomber squadrons and squadrons of squadrons of personnel to support those squadrons were posted all up and down the eastern seaboard of the U.S.S.R. from the Arctic Circle to the northern border of North Korea.

The actual primary radar tracking facility, a

heavily fortified bunker complex, was on the southern tip of Sakhalin Island itself. A small cluster of block houses, barracks, several residences set apart from the radar facility and a lighthouse comprised most of the island's settlement.

"Comrade Major, an unidentified blip has entered into the F.I.R." The Lieutenant operator called cross the dimly lit chamber.

"Show me." The major crossed the room to where the junior officer pointed to one of two dozen blips on his screen.

"Here, approximately two minutes ago."

"Follow and track him. I need times, speed and projected course as soon as you calculate them!"

"Yes sir." The major started back to his desk in the adjacent command bunker of the main radar facility. Just as he reached for the red emergency alert phone, it began to sound its impatient, high pitched double ring. A senior sergeant at a nearby desk picked it up.

"Radar sta ..."

"WHO IS THIS?!" The sergeant didn't recognize the voice but the fact that the ranking officer in his presence was a major meant that whoever had the audacity to open a phone conversation with an angry interrogative could only mean one thing, this was a problem far above his pay grade. He handed the receiver off to his C.O.

"This is Major Solodkov, Duty Officer at Sakhalin tracking station." Solodkov recognized the perpetually angry voice. "Yes Comrade General Kornukov. A short while ago we picked up an unidentified aircraft moving south, south west across Kamchatka."

"Have you intercepted it yet?" The late fifty-something general demanded rather than inquired.

"Two pilots have just been sent up." He quickly gesticulated to the sergeant who understood and, picking up another line, relayed an order to scramble two fast movers immediately with coordinates to follow once the jets were airborne.

"However General, we do not know what is happening just yet." As he spoke, Solodkov referenced a floor mounted, metal framed printer still furiously spitting out paper. "It entered our airspace at 15:51 and has just exited over international waters. It's heading straight for our position on Sakhalin possibly to Terpienie Bay. Somehow, this looks very suspicious to me General, I don't think the enemy is that stupid. Can it be one of ours perhaps?"

"Hold on Solodkov." Through the phone the major heard Kornukov yell to one of his subordinates.

Get me the Commander of Air Defense Forces, now! Seconds later Kornukov heard someone pick the receiver up off the desk at command headquarters.

"Who is this?"

"General Anatoli Kornukov, Commander of Sokol Air base on Sakhalin. Am I talking to the command post of General Valeri Krymnaskya?!"

"This is General Valeri Krymnaskya, Commander Air Defense. What is the problem General?"

"At 15:51 tracking picked up an unidentified

aircraft moving south, south west across Kamchatka. We've scrambled jets to intercept but haven't yet located it. Possibly by now it is over neutral waters. General, what are your orders?"

"ORDERS?! WHAT DO YOU THINK ARE MY ORDERS?! DESTROY IT! DESTROY ON CONTACT!!"

"Simply destroy it? Even if it is over neutral waters? Are the orders to destroy it over neutral waters?"

"Do you not remember in June when the Americans flew six aircraft for twenty miles into our airspace and we responded too slowly? How many senior staff were relieved of duty?"

"I remember General!"

"Then your memory is functioning well! IS THERE PERHAPS A PROBLEM WITH YOUR HEARING COMRADE GENERAL?!" There could be no doubt, Krymnaskya was in panic mode.

"No Comrade General! I understand. Destroy it. Even if it is over neutral waters. I understand." Kornukov was relieved when he heard the phone slam down on the other end of the line. "Destroy it. Even if it is over neutral waters? Oh, well." He mumbled to himself in disbelief then resumed the line with Major Solodkov. "Major?"

"Comrade General?"

"Shto vy otpravili?! What did we scramble?"

"Sir we sent one MiG-23 and one Su-Flagon when the intruder was about 60 miles from the Kamchatka coast over The Sea of Okhotsk. Now it is nearly 80 nautical miles away."

"Pass the order for the Air Traffic Control crew

108

to guide our jets to the intruder's location. I'm coming down to the control deck."

"Yes sir!" The major passed the order to the Vozdushno Transportnii Konttrol, or the ATC's as Kornukov left the Headquarters of Centre Generalnii and hurried over to Solodkov's radar room.

****

Meanwhile on the flight deck of KAL 007 the crew were having a leisurely conversation about conditions in the vicinity of 015 as compared to their flight conditions. They had been having a bad patch of radio com, but for a brief period the clouds cleared and the weather allowed the two aircraft to resume communications.

"We are now having an unexpected strong tailwind. How much are they getting back there?" The co-pilot noted as he addressed the navigator. "How much and which direction?"

"Their wind is coming from two-zero-six degrees." The navigator informed 007's co-pilot.

"Ask him how many knots?" The navigator again did as requested and was surprised at the response from 015.

"They got so much! We still got a headwind. Sir, they are on 215 degrees, at 15 knots of wind."

"Is it so? But according to flight plan, wind direction should be 360 at 15 knots, approximately." The Captain countered.

"Well, it may be like this sometimes." Came the

navigator's response. The co-pilot switched subjects.

"I have heard that there is currency exchange at the airport now?"

"Yeah, right in the airport!"

"What kind of money? Dollars to Korean I mean."

"Not sure, but radio in and ask them to check."

"It's right in the domestic building too." The navigator added.

"Nice!"

****

Kornukov stormed into the radar facility and headed straight for the main radar screen to direct things himself.

"Major, did you pass the order to ground control to direct the interceptors to the intruder?"

"Sir, they have it in sight now."

The General was now at the main radar screen and calling directions over to the head Air Traffic Controller, Lt. Col. Titovnin, sitting at the next desk over.

"Who is flying the Flagon?"

"Major Osipovich, general. Call sign eight-zero-five."

"Bring him up, bring Osipovich up to the prescribed distance." He directed Kozlov, the Combat Controller at Sokol Air Base sat at the desk on the general's other side. The general manned the radio himself. "Eight-zero-five, do not engage the target from the aft hemisphere. You do not engage him right on the tail! Maintain angle of approach!" There was an immediate response.

Roger, executing, sir. His eyes intently glued to the sweep hand of the radar screen, the General handed the mike back to Kozlov.

"Kozlov stay with him!"

"Yes General but it's difficult because we lost several radar dishes last week in the storm. There are blank spots in our radar blanket." The General picked up a random headset and spoke loudly into it as he stared at the screen.

"Faster eight-five-zero, the target is entering the zone above the one hundred kilometer waters!"

"Sir, he can't hear you on that headset." Kozlov moved to where the General stood in front of the main screen and reset his channel. "Try now sir."

"Don't forget eight-zero-five, the target has cannons in the rear!"

Roger, understood. Executing. Came the static laced voice of Osipovich.

Not exactly a patient man to begin with, Kornukov was growing more so. "Eight-five-zero faster, the target is entering the zone above the one hundred kilometer waters!"

Wilco. Seconds later Osipovich, piloting the Su-Flagon reported. *Have intercepted intruder on heading two-four-zero. Am observing, over.*

Kozlov pulled back his headset and called over to the General.

"He has the target in sight!"

"Ask him if he can actually see it, and how many jet trails are coming from it!" Kozlov requested.

"Eight-zero-five, how many jet trails are there? If there are four jet trails, then it's an American RC-135 for certain!"

Titovnin, the Head Air Controller spoke up. "Can you see the target eight-zero-five?"

I see target on screen only. Came the reply.

"Roger eight-five-zero. Report when you achieve lock-on. How copy?"

Good copy control.

"Kozlov! What, don't you understand? I said bring him up to a range of four to five kilometers to identify the target. You understand that weapons are going to have to be used now and you are holding him at a range of ten?! Give the pilot his orders!" Kornukov demanded.

Moving in at combat approach attitude, from below and on the left, Major Osipovich spotted flashing anti-collision strobes in the murky distance.

I see it!

"Yes, sir. He sees it on the radar screen and visually. On screen and visually." Titovnin relayed to the entire room as he switched on the public address speakers. All eyes and ears in the room now focused on Titovnin's station.

I am locked onto target. Osipovich reported.

"He has locked on, he is locked on." Titovnin relayed to headquarters via a third line. A few more moments of tense silence followed.

Target isn't responding to the contact.

"Eight-zero-five, is the target's heading still 2-4-0?"

Affirmative. Target's heading is 2-4-0 degrees. Titovnin looked over at Kornukov who signaled by

112

gesturing as if he were turning on an imaginary switch. Titovnin relayed the order.

"Roger eight-zero-five. You are cleared to arm your weapons then switch to channel seven."

"Will comply." From his cockpit Osipovich peered through the pitch black as best he could as he obeyed the order by arming all weapons while maneuvering closer to his target. A minute later he came up on channel seven.

"Major Osipovich, I am giving you to Gen. Krymnaskya." Titovnin handed his mike and headset over.

This part of the conversation was primarily, as per military directive, to record events for the inevitable post mortem which would occur in the after action reports. Although at odds as exactly how to incinerate the earth and destroy all civilization as we know it, one thing the Russians and Americans did agree on was the inescapable need for paperwork.

"Comrade General Krymnaskya, good evening." As he spoke, Osipovich carefully monitored his speed and distance from his target. "I am reporting the situation. Target designated #60-65 is now over Terpenie Bay just off the East Coast of Sakhalin and tracking at two-four-zero degrees, 30 kilometers past the State border. The MiG fighter from Sokol is 6 kilometers away. I am presently locked on and orders were given to arm weapons. I have executed this order. The target is not responding to calls to identify. He cannot identify me visually because it is still dark, but I still have him locked on."

Osipovich reported the detailed situation for the

benefit of the recorders running in his aircraft and on the ground.

"We must find out, maybe it is some civilian craft or God knows who!?" Kornukov desperately proposed. Krymnaskya immediately protested.

"What civilian? It has flown over Kamchatka! It came from the ocean without identification. If he crosses the State border again I am giving the order to attack!"

It is a given that there are significant differences between a military RC-135 reconnaissance aircraft, particularly in length and wing span, and the passenger aircraft flown by the Korean Airline pilots. However, both are similar generation Boeings and in the dark, at night at 500 miles per hour from a one to three mile distance, viewed from an angle ...

As if the situation weren't complicated enough, there is virtually no difference on a radar screen.

And then there's the fact that Reagan and Andropov were hell bent on erasing the world if it meant altering either's ideology.

*

As Osipovich's Su-15 closed the distance to the passenger aircraft, the flight crew on 007, bored and relaxing while riding on auto pilot, were chatting about currency exchange at Gimpo Airport in Seoul and bantering with each other.

Most of the passengers rested, slept or prepared themselves for their various tasks while awaiting their arrival in Seoul. The cabin crew went about their routine business of fixing drinks and snacks and making everyone as comfortable as possible.

"Korean Air zero-zero-seven, Tokyo. Go ahead."

"Tokyo, Korean Air zero-zero-seven requesting climb to three- five-zero thousand to save fuel."

"Requesting three five zero feet?"

"That is affirmative. Presently maintaining altitude at three-three-zero."

"Korean Air zero-zero-seven, Tokyo radio, roger. Stand by, call you back." The Tokyo ATC operator quickly referenced 007's flight plan and checked the surrounding traffic situation and called back.

"Korean Air zero-zero-seven. Clearance granted. Climb and maintain flight level three-five-zero."

"Ah roger Tokyo. Korean Air 007 leaving three-three-zero at this time. Climbing and will maintain at three five zero."

"This is Tokyo radio, roger zero-zero-seven. Out."

KAL 007 decreased speed as it climbed, causing the pursuing Soviet fighter to instantly draw a beam of but below the jet liner, yet still remain unseen. Osipovich quickly radioed in.

"The target is decreasing speed. I am going around it. I'm already moving in front of the target."

"Increase speed, 805!" Titovnin ordered.

"I have increased speed!"

"Has the target increased speed?"

"No, it is **decreasing** speed."

Osipovich and the radar facility seemed to be having a problem coordinating their efforts.

"I have slowed and am again behind target. I'm now approaching the target. Going in closer, to a distance of about 2 kilometers. Target is currently at about 10,000 metres has slowed and appears to be climbing to take evasive action. What are my instructions?"

"Roger eight-zero-five. If possible, take up a position for attack." Titovnin instructed.

"It should have been earlier! How can I chase it? I'm already coming again a beam of the target! Now I have to fall back again!"

Kornukov had been monitoring the transmissions.

"Cut the horseplay at the command post, what is that noise there? I repeat the combat task order! Fire missiles, fire on target #60-65!" Kornukov barked.

"Wilco."

"Comply and get Tarasov here. Take control of the Mig-23, his call sign is one-six-three. Call sign one-six-three, he is behind the target at the moment. Destroy the target!"

"Task received." Titovnin sought to get Kornukov off his back and so relayed the order. "Destroy target #60-65 with missile fire, accept control of the MiG fighter from Smirnykh."

"Carry out the task, destroy it! Oh, god damn it!" Kornukov stomped his foot. "How long does it take him to get into attack position?! Target is already getting out into neutral waters!! Engage afterburners immediately! Bring in the MiG-23 as well! While you are wasting time it will fly right out!" Kornukov sounded as though he were thirty seconds from a stroke.

"Eight-zero-five, open fire on target! Try to destroy the target with cannon." Titovnin instructed.

*

"Tokyo Radio, Korean Air zero-zero-seven reaching level three five zero. Will hold here until next way point."

"KAL 007, Tokyo roger your altitude at three-five-zero."

*

"I am dropping back. Now I will try a rocket." Osipovich reported.

"Roger eight-zero-five." The MiG-23 pilot then broke into the radio chatter.

"Control, this is One-six-three, I am five kilometers to target. I see both Osipovich and target."

"Eight-zero-five, approach target and destroy!" Titovnin reiterated for Kornukov's benefit.

"Roger, I am in lock-on mode."

"Eight-zero-five, are you closing on the target?"

"I am closing on the target, am in lock-on. Distance to target is now four kilometers."

"Afterburner. AFTERBURNER, 805!" Kornukov shouted into his mike.

"I have already switched it on." Osipovich in his Su-15 replied.

"Launch!" Titovnin shouted into his mike. Osipovich came back straight away to report a Zulu

117

Golf condition. His fuel light was on indicating he was running out of fuel.

"Eight-zero-five reporting Zulu Golf, repeat, Zulu Golf."

*** * ***

In the cockpit of KAL 007 a loud thud followed by a barely perceptible jolt interrupted the casual conversation. Of its own accord, the aircraft began to slowly climb.

"What's happening?" The Captain demanded.

"What?"

"Retard throttles! Systems check!" The Captain barked.

"Engines normal sir."

"What about the landing gear?" As the plane continued to gain altitude all hands frantically engaged in their designated systems checks. The emergency procedures recording began to sound its robotic voice.

Altitude warning. Altitude warning.

"Landing gear?!" The Captain asked. "Landing gear?!" The Captain reiterated.

"Negative, sensors indicate still retracted."

"We're climbing! Why are we climbing?!" The navigator asked.

Altitude warning. Altitude warning.

"Gear attitude normal Captain." The engineer reassured.

"I have executed launch." Osipovich reported to control.

"Well, what do you hear there?" Kornukov requested.

"He has launched." Titovnin relayed.

"I did not understand!" Kornukov glared at the ascending blip on the radar screen.

"**He has launched**." Titovnin repeated.

"He has launched?! Then follow the target! Follow the target! Withdraw Osipovich from the attack and bring the MiG-23 in there! NOW!" Kornukov shouted.

Target destroyed. Osipovich confirmed.

"Eight-zero-five, break off attack to the right, heading three-six-zero." Titovnin ordered Osipovich.

"Control, repeat I am Zulu Gulf. I am breaking off attack." Osipovich was by now flying on fumes.

"Control, this is one-six-three. What are my instructions?" The MiG-23 requested.

"Fuel remainder 1,600." Osipovich reported.

"One-six-three, standby."

"Control, this is one-six-three, request heading."

"Control, Eight-zero-five, I'm coming in empty!"

*

"What? What?" The KAL co-pilot wasn't the only one frantically ripping through the emergency procedures systems checks as the huge aircraft

119

continued to climb on its own.

"I am not able to drop altitude!" The Captain declared.

Attention emergency ascent! Attention emergency ascent!

In the passenger cabins drinks, left over meals and personal paraphernalia slowly spilled off seat serving trays and onto laps. Luggage shifted in the overhead compartments and two of the stews lost their balance and tumbled to the deck.

"We're still gaining altitude!" The captain reiterated as he let both hands off the yoke. "This is not working. This is not working!"

"Try manually." As suddenly as it had started the cockpit warning track reversed itself.

Attention emergency descent! Attention emergency descent!

"Cannot control manually Captain!" The co-pilot exclaimed. The decent was gradual and a collective sigh of relief ran through the aircraft.

Attention emergency descent!

"What was that thud we heard?!" Just then the Head Stew burst into the cockpit.

"Sir, I think there's something hit the back of the plane!" She blurted out.

"Damage report?"

Attention emergency descent!

"I don't know sir. Whatever it is, it's behind the rear fire wall!"

"Anyone hurt?"

"Doesn't look like it, but the passengers are beginning to panic."

Autopilot has now been disengaged. Engage

manual control. Autopilot has now been disengaged. Engage manual control.

"All right, get back there, keep everyone calm, tell them its weather and discreetly see if you can see anything out on the tail section from the rear window or to the rear of the fuselage behind the snack area. Call me on the closed line as soon as you see something."

"Yes sir!"

The robotic voice of the emergency warning system droned on in its emotionless tone.

Autopilot has now been disengaged. Engage manual control. Autopilot has now been disengaged. Engage manual control.

"Engines are normal sir."

Put out your cigarette. This is an emergency descent.

"That can't be right!" The flight engineer was completely stymied. All systems appeared normal but the aircraft wasn't responding to the primary controls.

Put out your cigarette, this is an emergency descent.

"Captain, give it all of both!" The engineer suggested. The captain complied and was shocked at the panel readings. The elevators weren't responding.

"Can that be that right?!"

Put the mask over your nose and mouth and adjust the headband.

With the aid of a second stew to rake away the back part of the aft fire wall panel, Hye-su's face went pale as she peered through the small chink they had made. She had discovered their problem.

Although one of Osipovich's proximity missiles missed the aircraft the other had taken out part of the rudder and stabilizer, one rear elevator and had locked the other in the downward position.

Somehow pressure was being maintained in the small space in front of the damaged area but Hye-su suddenly felt sick to her stomach as the realization hit that it was only a matter of time.

**

At this point the Soviet commanders became aware that they could still see their target on their radar screens, apparently maintaining altitude and, knowing that it had been fired at with two rockets, became confused.

"What is happening, what is the matter? Who guided him in?! He locked on, why he didn't shoot it down?!" A shocked and dismayed General Kornukov demanded. "Eight-zero-five, are you returning to base?!"

"I am executing! What is the distance to the airfield?!"

Back on board 007 the co-pilot took over radio control from the engineer and continued to attempt to establish commo with Tokyo.

"Tokyo radio Korean Air 007! Tokyo radio Korean Air 007!"

Put the mask over your nose and mouth and adjust the headband. Fit your own mask before assisting children.

"Korean Air 007, this s Tokyo control. Go ahead." Accentuated breathing clearly discerned during the transmission indicated to Tokyo control that an oxygen mask was being worn.

"Roger ... Korean Air 007 ... ah, we are ... experiencing ..."

Put the mask over your nose and mouth and adjust the headband.

"Captain ascent phase seems to have ... abated. We are now ... leveled out at pre-incident altitude of ... 35,000 ft., Forward acceleration readouts ... appear to be back to pre-incident rate of ... zero acceleration, and air speed ... has returned to pre-incident velocity." The engineer reported.

Yaw movement causing oscillations, which began at the time of missile detonation, continued to decrease and momentary relief swept through the pilot's cabin. KAL 007 now began the descent phase of its arc. Oxygen masks, which dropped down throughout the passenger compartment of the aircraft, exasperated the already panic, injected atmosphere.

"Captain, losing all compression!" The engineering officer reported. "We're experiencing rapid decompression!"

"Descend to one zero thousand immediately!" The Captain ordered.

Attention emergency descent. Attention emergency descent.

"We have to set this right, NOW!" The engineer instructed. Meanwhile, the flight crew had their hands too full to maintain communications and, on the ground, Tokyo Air Traffic Control began to become concerned.

"Korean Air 007, radio check on channel one zero-zero-four-eight." No response came. "Korean Air 007, radio check on one zero-zero-four-eight."

Attention emergency descent. Attention emergency descent.

"Stand by on speed!" The engineer instructed. "Stand by to reset speed. Stand by, on my command. Stand by. Stand by. Set!"

Put out your cigarette. This is an emergency descent.

Put out your cigarette. This is an emergency descent.

"Korean Air 007, radio check on one zero-zero-four-eight." Overhearing a controller's slightly excited voice, the Tokyo tower ATC supervisor wandered over to the ATC's console as he attempted to establish com. "Korean Air 007, radio check on one zero-zero-four-eight."

Put the mask over your nose and mouth and adjust the headband. Fit your own mask first before assisting children. Put the mask over your nose and mouth and ..."

*

"This is 1-6-3, I'm executing left to a heading of 1-8-0. Altitude 7,500 meters." The MiG pilot reported.

"Roger that 1-6-3, heading is 1-8-0."

"How many missiles were fired and did Osipovich see the missiles explode?" Kornukov frantically inquired.

"I believe he fired two missiles, Comrade General." Titovnin responded.

"Ask him, ask him yourself, get on channel seven and ask Osipovich did he or did he not see the explosions?" Kornukov demanded.

"Right away. 8-0-5, this is control. Did you launch one missile or both?"

I launched both. Osipovich radioed back as he focused on getting his empty aircraft safely back to the airfield.

"Did you **observe** explosions?"

*Yes. Two. I repeat, **target destroyed**!* Osipovich angrily reported.

"Control, this is one-six-three. Roger, confirm two missiles fired. Explosions observed. Also roger heading one-five-zero at 7,500. Now executing heading two-one-zero degrees."

*

"KAL zero-zero-seven this is Tokyo radio. Korean Air zero-zero-seven, this is Tokyo radio. Korean Air zero-zero-seven, Tokyo. Do you copy?" The ATC glanced up at his supervisor standing to his left. The Supervisor nodded to continue his attempts.

*

"Control one-six-three, roger new heading two-one-zero degrees at 7,500 meters. Target has turned to the north."

"The target turned to the north?!" A shocked Kornukov asked. North was further into Russian territory.

"Affirmative General."

"One-six-three move in and destroy it!" Kornukov ordered.

There was another minute of silence as Kornukov ripped off his head set and now paced in ever widening circles as he crept closer to meltdown.

"Well, I understand that I do not understand the result! Missiles were fired! Why is the target still flying God damn it! God damn it to hell!! Well, what is happening? I am asking! Give the order to the Controller, what is wrong with you there? Have you all lost your tongues?"

Non-response of his staff was motivated by the fact that no one knew if Kornukov was addressing them or speaking to himself.

"Comrade General, I gave the order to the Chief of Staff, the Chief of Staff to the Controller, and the Controller is giving the order to..." Titovnin countered.

"How long does it take for this information to get through?! Can you not ask the results of firing two missiles? What were the results?" Kornukov grabbed the headphones from the table and threw them at the offending console.

"One-six-three, do you see the target?" Titovnin requested.

"No, I don't see it. Executing heading 360 for second pass."

*** * ***

By this point there was hardly standing room around the main tracking console in the control tower at the Tokyo airfield.

"Tokyo radio to KAL zero-zero-seven, do you copy? Tokyo radio to KAL zero-zero-seven, do you copy? Switch. Tokyo radio to KAL zero-one-five, do you copy?" The Supervisor turned to a female ATC to his left.

"Hiroko, get on console three and try a VHF frequency to KAL 015."

"High!" The young ATC scurried to her assigned console and manned her head set. "Tokyo radio to KAL zero-one-five,. Tokyo radio to KAL zero-one-five."

Tokyo radio, KAL zero-one-five here, roger your call.

"Zero-one-five Tokyo radio requesting you attempt to contact Korean Air zero-zero-seven ..." She blinked tears from her eyes as she spoke. "Korean Air zero-zero-seven and, er ... and ask him to relay his position please?"

Roger Tokyo, stand by. Switch.

The tower group listened intently as the request was relayed.

KAL zero-zero-seven, this is KAL zero-one-five. KAL zero-zero-seven, this is KAL zero-one-five come in. There was no response. *KAL zero-zero-seven, this is KAL zero-one-five ...*

In the tower there was complete silence as all

127

other traffic had been asked to maintain 5 minutes of radio silence. *KAL zero-zero-seven, this is Korean Air zero one fiver.* Silence ensued. They repeated. *KAL zero-zero-seven, this is Korean Air zero one fiver.*

"Tokyo radio to KAL 015."

"Korean Air zero-one-five, go ahead."

"Tokyo radio to KAL 015. Ah ... would you use ... er ... HF please or VHF over?"

"Tokyo radio, KAL 015. Ah roger, wilco."

Tense seconds seemed like hours as the group of ATC's, now augmented by some of the oncoming staff of the next shift, crowded tighter around the petite Hiroko in contact with 015. There was absolute silence as they listened in on the distant transmission.

KAL 0-1-5 to KAL 0-0-7. Korean Air zero-zero-seven, this is zero-one-five.

In the tower, gut wrenching pauses stabbed at each break between transmissions. *Korean Air zero-zero-seven this is zero-one-five. Do you copy?*

Some of the ATC's looked up to the Supervisor. A few looked down at the floor.

Ahh ...Tokyo radio, Korean Air zero-one-five. Ahh ... unable to contact KAL zero-zero-seven at this time. How copy? Hiroko looked across the room to her supervisor who nodded back.

Tokyo tower, Korean Air zero-one-five. Unable to contact KAL zero-zero-seven at this time. How copy?

The Supervisor nodded again. Hiroko swallowed hard.

"Good copy zero-one-five. Thank you for your

help. Tokyo tower out."

Zero-one-five maintaining course and frequency. Out.

****

"Sir, target is at 5,000 meters and appears to be in initial stages of spiral descent over Moneron Island." Titovnin reported.

"5,000 meters?" General Kornukov was shocked.

"Affirmative. Target is turning left, right, then left again. Apparently it is descending in a controlled spiral."

"Destroy it, use the 23 to destroy it!" Kornukov roared into his mike.

"Roger, destroy it. Understood." Titovnin passed the order on another channel, but Kornukov, now concerned the situation was getting beyond his control, was growing more impatient for confirmed results.

"Well, where is the MiG fighter God-damn it?! How far from the target?!"

"Comrade General, they cannot see the target."

"They cannot see the target?!"

KAL 007 had by now descended below 5,000 meters in its slow spiral over Moneron Island.

"Sir, the target appears to have dipped below our radar! Perhaps they are trying to evade us! One-six-three do you have eyes on target?!"

"Negative, I don't see it. No visual at this time."

"You know the range and you know where the target is! It is over Moneron, God damn it!"

Kornukov continued to attempt a self-induced stroke. "ORDER ONE-SIX-THREE TO SEARCH THE AREA GOD-DAMN IT!"

"One-six-three search the area, by order of comrade General Kornukov!"

I don't see anything in this area. I just looked! The MiG pilot radioed back.

"They lost the target, Comrade General, in the area of Moneron. The pilots do not see it, neither the one nor the third aircraft we dispatched. The radio forces have reported that after the launch of the missiles the target entered a right turn over Moneron." Kornukov plopped down in a chair like a rag doll just gone through the wash and having no idea what exactly just transpired, was coming to grips with the fact that no matter what had just happened, the shit was about to hit the fan at headquarters.

"Comrade General," Titovnin attempted to convey. "The target is descending and presumed lost over Moneron."

"Uh-huh." With glassed over eyes Kornukov displayed the dreaded 1,000 yard stare.

"General, are you okay?"

"Yes, descending. Lost over Moneron"

****

The Tokyo tower supervisor continued to stare intently at the thin green line as it swept around the face of the radar screen, desperately wanting to see a blip.

An eerie, almost ominous white glow partially illuminated the half dozen air traffic controllers' faces as they still huddled around the main radar screen.

At 18:56 hours, thirty minutes after KAL 007's estimated time over the NOKKA beacon check point and after repeated attempts to re-establish communication had failed, two things occurred.

Tokyo Air Control Center notified several Air Traffic Services and military units via direct speech links of its inability to establish radio contact with KAL 007 and requested them to conduct a communication search.

Secondarily, Search and Rescue orders were issued to all appropriate Japanese units.

Approximately twelve minutes after ATC's on the ground in Japan realized KAL 007 was off course, her blip along with 269 men, women and children, officially became a statistic.

*

CHAPTER SIX

Force Recon Training Facility
Naval Amphib Base
Coronado, California

H ell Week, simply put, is a week of unmitigated hell. All the worst physical and mental torture that instructors can muster is heaped on the candidates at one time, with no sleep, no dry clothes and little or no time to eat. Located at about the halfway point in the 8-10 week program, theoretically Hell Week is supposed to weed out the mentally weak and is not necessarily oriented towards washing people out of the program. However, there has never been a candidate yet gone through the program who would agree with that theory.

Like the plaque over the BUDS quarterdeck says: 'The only easy day was yesterday!'

In reality Hell Week is intended to weed out the individuals who would likely bail out on their team members when the shit got thick. This is accomplished by means of all the bad shit you've ever heard about U.S. Navy/Marine Corps Special Operations training. And then some.

If McKeowen was ever going to gain anyone's respect as a potential operator, it was here that it was going to have to happen.

Now in his third week as an instructor/trainee Recon candidate, HM2 William McKeowen had made it past the daily one mile swims and the regardless-of-surf-conditions four mile timed beach runs immediately followed by the one to two hour Physical Training P.T., sessions and the open ocean swims. Being a former gymnast he was able to clock up one of the fastest times on the 'O' course and he considered himself in reasonable shape by the time the class reached the dreaded pool week, also known as 'drown proofing', an evolution which culminated in having your feet and hands tied behind your back and being thrown into the deep end of the pool where you were required to survive for 1 hour. On an instructor's signal you were then required to dive to the bottom of the pool, retrieve a piece of gear in your teeth, usually a fin or mask, surface, brandish the piece of gear to said instructor then, given a nod, swim to the shallow end of the pool. Hands and feet still tied.

McKeowen dropped the mask halfway to the finish and had to repeat that part of the tasking but both Stratford and Coats were pleased to see he reacted instantly to correct his situation still finishing ahead of three quarters of the other candidates. Oh yeah, all this was done a la buff. In the nude. Apparently no room for false modesty in Special Operations.

Back in the instructor's showers Lieutenant Stratford found Doc at his locker drying off.

"What'a think?" Stratford probed.

"Fun. I especially like the naked part. When's it get tough?" Despite being glib McKeowen knew he had been through a tough evolution. He felt it in his lungs as well as every muscle in his body.

"Report to the C.O. soon as you're squared away

and he'll tell you what he's got for you." Doc was surprised and more than a little curious.

"Do I need to dress for the occasion?"

"Negative, P.T. gear is okay." Little could he know but his jungle boots, UDT shorts and recon gold and green tee shirt would be all he would wear for the remainder of his time in Recon.

"Will do L.T." Doc replied.

Less than fifteen minutes later McKeowen was standing in front of Captain Coats' desk with Lieutenant Stratford seated off to the side.

"We have a bit of a dilemma Doc." Coats opened the impromptu meeting.

"Sir?" Coming in through the back door of Recon as he did McKeowen suddenly worried that some pencil neck had caught Commander Dunn's finagling of paper work and now it was time to pay the piper. He instantly decided that if he were to be sent back to the reserve unit in Pittsburgh he would quit the military altogether and seek work there in California.

"You're not officially a candidate but as a concession to us having a dedicated pecker checker assigned here, the base Commander was adamant that you go through each and every evolution that the candidates go through so that you understood exactly what we're trying to do here. If you don't fuck up, this will become a permanent slot meaning all HM's looking to be assigned to Force Recon will have to go through the course before they qualify to be stationed with a Force Recon unit."

This of course was all news to McKeowen.

"You mean they're thinking about creating a new

slot?"

"Not just a new slot Doc. A new Military Occupational Specialty. They're gonna designate the MOS 0000/0321. If **you** make it through."

"No pressure eh sir?" Was all he could think to say. Stratford picked up the conversation.

"Sorry to be the first to tell ya Doc but you're a guinea pig."

"Now I get why this slot was put up!" Doc declared.

"Think of yourself more as a pioneer Doc." Coats encouraged.

"You know what makes a pioneer sir? An explorer with an arrow in his back." Doc quipped.

"Hell Week is coming up and we can't ask you to go through it and act as our corpsman at the same time. It's not practical."

"Then don't." Suddenly he had both officers' attention. "Don't ask me to do both. Just pull a Black Shoe corpsman from the dispensary as you've been doing since before I showed up while I go through the evolutions. He sits in his ambulance on the side lines reading whatever gay porn he's into and if anything serious turns up, I'm right there. I'll make sure the ambulance is properly equipped to deal with anything that might come up so we don't have to waste time transporting the casualty."

"Not too sure how ..."

"Sir, Black Shoes are great to have around for pluggin' holes and evac'ing casualties, but when that's not an option, they're tits on a bull."

"That your professional evaluation Doc?" Coats asked.

135

"After eight years as a black shoe, a hundred and ten percent sir! There isn't a patient I can't stabilize for transport if I get there in time and he's stabilizable."

"Doc, you're not lettin' your ego write checks your ass can't cash, are ya?" The L.T. pushed.

"I sure hope not Lieutenant, but in eight years I've treated at least five or six dozen serious, emergency cases, civilian as well as military. If they were breathin' when I got there, they were breathin' when they were med-evac'ed out which probably means they were breathin' when they reached a competent medical facility!" Everyone traded glances. "Short of a cardiac bypass, there's not much I can't do in the field. As long as my med kit, the one I pack myself, is on station." The two officers exchanged glances. Stratford shrugged.

"Okay Doc, guess that's settled. You'll go through the evolution as a student and change hats if somebody gets their ass in a sling." Captain Coats directed.

"Thank you sir." McKeowen turned to leave.

"And Doc, you'd better bunk with the students Saturday night." McKeowen smiled at the heads up about when Hell Week would start.

"Aye aye sir!" Stratford stepped out after Doc and caught up to him in the passageway.

"Stabilizable?" Stratford queried.

"What can I say? I get emotional about my work."

"Stabilizable?" Doc stopped walking and stared at the L.T.

"I'm not gonna live that one down, am I?" After

a pause he walked away.

"Stabilizable?" Stratford called after him.

"With all due respect, sir." Doc signaled back over his shoulder with his middle finger.

*

J. Edgar Hoover F.B.I. Building
935 Pennsylvania Avenue
Washington, D.C.

A few blocks south of the International Spy Museum in Washington D.C., between 9th & 10th Streets, lies the J. Edgar Hoover F.B.I. Building.

Up on the 7th floor of the FBI HQ, off in the southeast corner lies Briefing Room "A" which sits directly adjacent to the Director's office.

The middle-aged man in the medium priced, three piece suit and striped tie glanced across the hall and up as he entered his office. The twenty-four hour clock above the entrance to the briefing room read 15:33.

He checked for something on his desk, found it and moved back across the hall to the briefing room and took a seat at the head of the massive, 30 seat conference table.

Minutes later a Navy Lieutenant in his dress blues and carrying a brief case shackled to his wrist stepped off the elevator. As he made his way down the hall heads turned. Mostly women's heads. Two secretaries at a water cooler stopped what they were doing and stared.

"Are they shooting a sequel to *Officer And A Gentlemen* we don't know about?" The middle-aged blond asked.

"I don't know, but if they are I'm available for the bedroom scenes!" Her colleague quipped as they both zeroed in on the officer's aft quarter.

Should he ever get tired of the rigors of naval life, Lieutenant David Harden could always find work as a double for Richard Gere.

The fact that Harden was a morphological doppelganger of the famous actor was not lost on his friends and classmates at university leading to no few pranks on unsuspecting co-eds and cops alike.

Harden made his way to the Director's office, when he noticed the Director over in the briefing room who had, in the meantime, been joined by two other agents. He entered the room and greeted the three.

"Director?"

"Yes, come in."

"Lieutenant Harden, Office of Naval Intelligence. Here to give your people the briefing sir."

"Come in Lieutenant. I'm Director William Webster, this is Bill Holby, Director of Intelligence and this is Jim Doherty Assistant Director of Intel."

"Mr. Holby, Mr. Doherty, glad to meet you."

"Wish I could say the same Lieutenant." Replied Holby.

"What have you got for us?" Webster got right to the point.

"Not as much as we'd like, I'm afraid." Harden

set his brief case on the table, produced a key from his trouser pocket and unlocked it from his wrist as he took a seat to Webster's right. The two intel men pulled up chairs to his left. Harden read from a thin file folder.

"John J. Walker, born 28 July 1937, Scranton, Pennsylvania."

"Huh!" The Director grunted.

"What?" Holby queried.

"A homegrown spy."

"Gets better. He joined up in 1956 after being arrested for burglary. Offered the option of jail or the military, he chose the Navy."

"Fucking great! The Press is gonna eat this up with a god damned spoon! Why the hell didn't he sign up in the Army?!" Doherty, who was former Navy, commented.

"What the hell difference does it make?" Snapped Webster.

"With all this Israeli shit last year, those two idiot sailors the Russian embassy gave us last month and this asshole, Nav Intel is getting the shit beat out of it. And all this right after we lambasted the Brit's Intel services for their leaks!" Doherty added.

"How bad did he hurt us?" Webster asked.

"Bad Director, and he's not cooperating. But we think we might have an ace-in-the-hole." Harden continued.

"What's that?"

"Although not to the same extent, his kid is in on it. Apparently they're pretty close to each other. The kid is about to be picked up in the next 48 hours. As he's on deployment at sea, Walker won't know we have his kid. The interrogation people think if they wear Walker down a bit then let him see his kid for the first time at the arraignment he might crack and want to deal."

"Any indication **exactly** how bad he hurt us?" Asked Webster.

"As far as we can piece together he's been operating since the late Seventies, maybe longer. The latest reports indicate that he sold them code cards for both the KL-7 Adonis and the KW-37 Jason cipher systems."

"So what's that mean, exactly?"

"Those are the codes for both the Navy and Army's primary systems."

"This guy wasn't half-assing it was he?" Doherty interjected.

"Our saving grace is that the KL-7 was phased out a few years back." Harden added.

"Well that's something at least!"

"However, since he's not talking we have no way to know what kind of progress the Reds may have made in extrapolating the decoding of our transmissions based on the KL-7 models."

"This just keeps getting better and better. What else?" Webster pushed.

"According to his service record he's done time at the Anti-Sub Warfare base up in New London so we have good reason to believe that our SOSUS technology may have been compromised."

"What in the hell is 'SOSUS'?" Doherty asked. Holby spoke up before the lieutenant could answer.

"A very expensive, underwater surveillance system which monitors sub traffic via a network of submerged hydrophones."

Webster rubbed his forehead, sat back in his seat and sighed. "I need a drink." He declared.

"It's our primary tracking system." Harden continued. "It follows underwater traffic by cavitation of the screws on a sub's back wash. Based on the fact that we've noticed a marked decrease in Soviet sub traffic in the last 19 months, we have no choice but to believe they've developed some kind of new counter system. Or a new screw design to reduce cavitation."

"So, you're just not picking them up?"

The Lieutenant made eye contact with Webster before answering.

"Probably not."

"How in God's name did he manage to access so much secure information?! And at that level of classification?!"

"Let me put it too you this way gentlemen," Lieutenant Harden replied. "The general consensus on The Hill is that as off now any shopping mall in the country has better security than the United States Navy."

"Maybe we should just hire Sears and Roebuck for security!" Webster quipped. "Anything else? He asks with great trepidation."

Lieutenant Harden carried on with his brief as he produced another folder.

"There's an Alfred Wentworth, a radioman and former student of Walker's from when he was out in radio school at San Diego."

"What about him?" Holby asked.

"We need to know the latest from your side on

Wentworth." Harden requested.

"From our surveillance of Walker," Webster explained. "...we know Wentworth to be an associate. I sent a couple of agents out to the trailer park where he lives and with no pressure Mr. Jerry Wentworth agreed to let our agents search his trailer. They found this." The Director produced a floppy disc sealed in a plastic, zip lock bag.

"Anything on it?" Harden asked.

"No direct intel but it's filthy with circumstantial evidence. Meeting times, dates, places along with monetary amounts to be exchanged."

"Can I keep this?" Lieutenant Harden asked.

"No, we need it for evidence but I'll get you a copy before you leave." Webster noticed a small handful of his people milling around outside in the hallway. "Lieutenant the troops appear to be gathering. Anything else I need to know before we let them in?"

"Yes Sir. There's something I won't be covering when I brief your folks this afternoon. I've been instructed to discuss this with you alone." Harden discreetly indicated the Director's two colleagues.

"Jim, Bill, excuse us for a moment?" Webster requested.

The two agents maintained their professional demeanor as they excused themselves. Harden switched seats so that his back was to the door while still facing Webster and waited until he heard the door close before he spoke.

"Does the name Ryan mean anything to you Director?"

"No. Should it?"

"Something called Ryan? Maybe the name of a place, a person? Something out of context?"

"No, sorry Lieutenant. Nothing." Harden sat back in frustration. "Something I need to know about?"

"Our analysts have deciphered it on several occasions but have no idea what it means. It's suspicious because it's almost always out of context to the rest of the message."

"You think there's a connection with the Walker ring?"

Harden hesitated, pursed his lips and looked down before answering.

"I was cautioned to use my discretion on broaching this to you. It's imperative, at least for now, no one on your side of the fence be told about this."

"How in the hell can I tell anyone when I don't have a clue what you're talking about?" Harden accepted the dead end.

"There's no mention of the name itself in connection with anything we have so far from Walker. But a lot of secondary intel, times, meets etc... mentioned in other communiqués are in exact coordination with some of his movements." Harden explained.

"You people think this Ryan fella is pretty high up the ladder?"

"Whoever he is he's way above Walker. The big fear now is he's some international operator running several cells at once, right here on home ground."

"Shit!"

"Our sentiments exactly. However, there's a

bigger concern."

"Which is?"

"Which is that nearly all the communiqués intercepted which mention Ryan can be traced directly to a higher source."

"Higher source? How much higher could they go?"

"The Kremlin." Webster fell back in his chair and stared at Harden. He took a deep breath before he spoke again.

"We'll get you everything we have on Wentworth."

"Thank you Director. Additionally I'm authorized to request, unofficially of course, that if your people discover anybody else you suspect is associated with the Walker ring, let us know before you move on them."

"I don't see a problem there. Anything else Lieutenant?"

"Yes sir, the floppy?"

"Here, take it by my secretary's desk on the way out. She'll burn you a copy. Leave the original with her." He handed the clear plastic bag to the Intel Officer.

"Will you want to sit in on my briefing sir?" Harden queried.

"I'll give you a brief intro but I can't hang around. I've a 16:30 over at NSA. Get them up to speed on what we have so far on this whole mess."

"Yes sir."

From the day John Walker's Ex went to the FBI, realization of the seriousness of the situation had spread through The Bureau like gonorrhea in 1967

Saigon.

In time honored tradition Webster initially ordered no one outside the small team of agents directly associated with the Walker case was to be let in on the dirty little secret. However, almost immediately an obstacle arose. The documents confiscated after Walker's arrest were technically property of the U. S. Navy.

Within 24 hours Webster had made the decision to set up a meet with someone directly from the office of the Chief of Naval Intelligence to have his deputy personally hand over the docs and ask ONI to keep it in their back pocket until The Bureau was happy they had the whole Walker ring in custody.

ONI agreed but back in The Bureau there had been some foot dragging as the necessary personnel to be put on the 'Need-to-Know' list, or BIGOT, were assembled. Those twelve department heads were the people now filing into in the briefing room. When they were all in and seated Director Webster took the podium.

"Good afternoon ladies and gents. Sorry to pull you away from your duties on short notice, but events are moving rapidly in the Walker case. In short, The Cold War just got a little hotter." Webster quickly took a mental head count. "Lieutenant Harden here of ONI has prepared a briefing. Obviously everyone, and I do mean everyone, will be briefed on a need-to-know basis and everything you hear here today is, for now, classified as T.S. No notes, no recordings no hard copies of anything. You will give Lieutenant Harden your full and undivided attention. Thank you."

Several studious agents stowed their note taking material and listened up.

"Thank you Director Webster." As Webster and Harden crossed paths in front of the room they shook hands and the Director leaned in to whisper into the Lieutenant's ear.

"When you get back to the office tell your boss I'd like a meet." Webster requested.

"Will do sir."

"As soon as possible." Webster added. Harden nodded his ascent then moved to the podium. Webster paused at the door as he left. "And people, I don't need to tell you. Quash the rumor mill! The last thing we need is a bunch of scuttlebutt floating around The Capital about Russian spies!"

Harden took the podium.

"Good afternoon ladies and gentlemen. As our primary perpetrator was captured less than forty-eight hours ago this is merely a preliminary report." Harden spoke without referring to his notes. "Chief Warrant Officer John Anthony Walker, U.S.N., Retired, has used the most common of the M.I.C.E. motivations for entering into the spy trade craft. Money. We have reason to believe that the enterprising Mr. Walker has been spying for the KGB as early as 1972 possibly from as far back as the late Sixties."

The Director motioned Holby out into the hallway where he took him by the arm and guided him down the corridor.

"I'm gonna need your eyes and ears all over the place in the coming weeks Bill."

"Jesus! You think we're infiltrated?"

"There's no mention of that but we have to take all precautions. Let's call it an extended need-to-know situation."

"Okay, I guess."

"Keep everything fragmented. The department heads will learn everything they need to know for now in Lieutenant Harden's briefing." Webster informed him as they slow walked down the long hallway, Holby now a step behind.

"Sir have we gotten any of this stuff on Wentworth over to The Agency yet?"

"They're aware of the general situation, but not in on the details yet. A classified memo is being drawn up as we speak. It'll be sent out by secure courier as soon as it's approved by the White House Security Adviser. I spoke to The Chief this morning. He wants a mass meet of all the heads of all the agencies tomorrow." The Director informed. The Chief' translated to President Reagan.

"Is it that serious?"

"He's calling all the agency heads personally. Said it was going to be a working lunch, day after tomorrow."

"That's not so bad."

"A working lunch starting at zero-six thirty!"

"That's not good." Holby conceded.

"The fallout hasn't even started. If it's as bad as ONI says it is, the repercussions will be years in the making."

"And as a strategy for our long range plan?" Holby asked.

"Near as I can tell, temporarily limit

147

transmissions, scrap all our codes, get to work writing new ones and recall all our burst transmission devices."

"That's gonna take some time. And while that's in process?" Webster stopped abruptly and turned to Holby to make eye contact before answering.

"Pray to God we don't go to war!" Holby stopped dead in his tracks and stood alone calling after Webster as the Director continued down the hall to the elevators.

"Director!" Webster rang for the lift and looked back up the hallway.

"Yes?"

"Commies don't believe in God!"

*

Command & Control compartment,
CVN-68 *U.S.S. Nimitz*
22:42 Local, Port of Haifa, Israel

The nerve center of any combat ship is the Command & Control compartment or the C&C, where all orders for internal functions for that vessel originate and where all incoming and outgoing traffic is received and sent from.

The Petty Officer at the telex console looked up from his pulp fiction novel as the twix printer sprang to life. Putting the book aside he tore the newsprint grade paper off the machine, read it and, without a word, pushed his roller chair across the compartment straight for the Executive Officer sitting on the other side of the small space.

"When?" The X.O. inquired after reading the message which had arrived via the Atlantic Fleet Commander.

"Sir, seconds ago." With an urgent but puzzled look the X.O., a Lieutenant Commander, read it again and began to calmly give orders.

"L.T., enter this message in the ship's log as of twenty-two forty-three."

"Aye aye sir." The X.O. passed the message to the Lieutenant.

"Petty Officer, standby for further traffic. Notify me immediately if anything else comes in."

"Aye aye sir!" The X.O. moved to the ship's sound powered telephone as he rendered the orders.

"Quarter Deck, this is the Bridge. Identify."

"Bridge, Officer Of the Deck, Ensign Haskins sir."

"Has the C.O. gone ashore yet?" There was a brief pause.

"Bridge, the log shows negative Sir. Captain's still aboard."

"Any other personnel ashore at present?"

"Save for ship's surgeon and two corpsmen away for supplies, none sir."

"Very good. Bridge out."

"O.O.D. out."

"Petty Officer Nugent!" The Lt. Commander said.

"Sir?"

"Get on the 1MC ... no, as you were. Quietly secure a duty messenger to the Captain's quarters. Word message to read; 'X.O. requests Captain report to the bridge at his earliest convenience.' Get that out on the double!"

"Will do sir." Nugent quickly exited the space through the watertight door into the passageway to secure one of the two couriers, known as 'runners', constantly standing by. The X.O. once again utilized the ship's telephone.

"Quarter Deck, Bridge here."

"Yes sir?"

"I need the Captain of the Guard up here on the double."

"Roger that sir. He's in the Officer's Mess having chow."

"Well now he's finished chow. Have him report to me on the double. This is a priority."

"Will do sir. Anything else?"

"Yeah. Until further notice no one leaves or boards the ship without permission from the Bridge. Understood?"

"Roger that sir. I'll post guards at both gangplanks."

At that unusual order the few sailors in the C&C stopped and stared.

"X.O. out"

"O.O.D. out."

Down on the main deck guards were hastily posted and after issuing them their orders the O.O.D. returned to his post on the quarter deck.

A minute later, back up in the C&C, 'Attention on deck!' was sounded as the ship's C.O., still in his skivvy shirt and trousers, stepped through the watertight door.

"As you were. What's the problem Don?" By

150

way of an answer the X.O. handed the C.O. the telex which concerned one of the ship's Intel personnel. His reaction was immediate.

"Son-of-a-bitch!" The C.O. shook his head. It wasn't possible to know all of the six thousand plus sailors on board the carrier, but the C.O. certainly knew everyone in his Intel Division. "You notify the Marines yet?"

"Their Duty Officer's enroute. I thought it prudent to play this as quietly as possible."

"Good call." Just then a young, extremely strack Marine officer bearing a side arm accompanied by two riflemen came into the space and smartly saluted the C.O.

"Lieutenant Dumbrowsky reporting as ordered sir."

"At ease Marine. We have an incident here and we want it handled as quickly and quietly as possible."

"Understood sir." The C. O. passed the Marine the telex.

Petty Officer Mark Walker suspected Soviet spy. Detain and arrest with all due urgency!

"He's off duty Lieutenant, so he could be anywhere on the ship." The X.O. cautioned.

"We'll locate him, sir." Dumbrowsky shot back.

"Pick a rendezvous point, grab a messenger and send him to get a corpsman to meet you. We need a complete body search and we'll need a complete, independently verified, inventory of everything on his person, in his space and in that compartment to include all his shipmate's possessions." The X.O. directed. "Also get us a list of all the shipmates from his section and have them drop whatever they're doing. In their own handwriting, I want a complete list of everything they brought aboard, including contraband."

"Tell them they won't be charged for anything they declare." The C.O. added. "Also keep him under close guard until he's off the ship. The crew gets word of what he's accused of they may try to take matters into their own hands."

"Understood sir."

To the Marine the seriousness of the situation was sinking in.

"Questions Lieutenant?"

"Negative sir."

"Make it so!"

"Aye sir!" The Marine saluted and was gone, his riflemen in tow.

On his last day of freedom in the Twentieth Century, Petty Officer Mark Walker was quietly at work down in the Enlisted Quarters writing a letter to his father, whose fate was as of yet still unknown to the hapless double agent.

He was just sealing the envelope when the three burly Marine guards burst through the hatch into his space and found fifteen pounds of various classified materials in his foot locker. They proceeded to confiscate everything in the compartment.

Including Petty Officer Michael Walker.

*

CHAPTER SEVEN

NTSB OFFICE
Anchorage, Alaska
07:25 Local, September 2nd

The National Transportation & Safety Board had seen some gruesome and horrendous accidents in its short sixteen years since its creation by the U.S. Congress but this one was far different. Not just in terms of numbers of casualties, but what appeared to be the most blatant, unprovoked act of war on a civilian craft since the Germans sank Lusitania back in 1915.

The Anchorage office, to which territorially the investigation of the loss of KAL 007 fell, is nestled on a low lying area of a mountainous terrain off the northern sound of the Gulf of Alaska.

One of the busiest offices of the NTSB, due largely to the many small aircraft used to negotiate the rugged Northwest terrain. The office was honchoed by a hard core veteran of the most sophisticated transportation accident and safety organization in the world. His name was James Michelangelo and by all accounts he lived up to the magnitude of his name.

As he entered his office he sat his over-sized mug of coffee on his desk and flicked on the radio which sat atop the steel grey filing cabinet, took a seat and perused a partially completed form on his desk as the radio sprang to life.

153

More breaking news in the ongoing Housing and Urban development scandal concerning bribery of Washington officials by selected contractors for low income housing projects.

Thomas Demery, a Republican and Assistant Secretary of HUD, today pled guilty to multiple counts of bribery and obstruction of justice by misleading the investigation.

Joseph A. Strauss, also a Reagan selected Republican and former Special Assistant to the Secretary of HUD, was convicted of accepting payments to favor Puerto Rican land developers so that they could receive HUD funding.

"Bastard politicians!" Michelangelo quietly declared.

He heard the phone ring in the outer office quickly followed by a voice on his intercom.

Washington office on line one, sir.

"Thank you Linda." He switched lines. "Michelangelo here."

Jim, it's Bill.

"Morning Bill. I'm just in. I got your fax about the Tacoma crash. I'll-"

Forget that for now. Quick question. How far along on this KAL thing are you? Michelangelo was alerted by the lack of normal salutation in his boss' voice.

"I started a preliminary AAR-74 about an hour after we got word from the ATC guys which was about four hours after she vanished off the radar screens. I put in the calls and the investigation teams are assembled. Soon as I know where to send

154

'em they're wheels up and enroute. Why?"

The radio continued in the back ground as they spoke.

Samuel Pierce, another Republican and Secretary of Housing and Urban Development, because he made "full and public written acceptance of responsibility", was not charged. However, Silvio D. DeBartolomeis, was also convicted on several counts of perjury as well as bribery.

Jim I ask because this morning I had a visit from two guys from the State Department. Michelangelo's boss explained.

"State Department?! What'd ya do? Get caught asking about Communist party membership?" Jim laughed, Bill didn't.

Bastards tracked me down while I was on my morning jog.

Michelangelo reached up and turned down the radio.

"I'm listening."

You're to stop everything you're doing on it, send everything we have, originals and copies, straight to The State Department. Effective immediately the NTSB no longer has jurisdiction in this case.

"Sounds like somebody's been reading too many Forsythe novels!" Michelangelo cracked.

Maybe so, but whatever they got going on out here, it's above my pay grade. This one sounds worse than the '69 hijacking.

"Okay, if you say so. I'll get the ball rolling."

And Jim!

"Yeah?"

Be careful. Full paper trail on this one. And on second thought, send it straight to my office via secure courier. I'll handle it, get the picture?"

"In Technicolor"

Michelangelo took a moment to gather his thoughts and to digest the implications of what had just transpired as he stared at the full wall maps of the Alaskan territory which papered the wall across from his desk.

In 27 years of government service, he'd never heard of, much less experienced the U.S. Department of State resting an investigation from anyone much less the NTSB. There had always been full cooperation between the two agencies.

After a minute or so he flicked on the intercom and buzzed his secretary.

"Linda?"

Yes Director?

"Orders from the top! Notify the team leader in the KAL case to tell his men to stand down, mission cancelled. Tell them to forward all info gathered so far to my office immediately."

Will I inform them of a change of plans?

He thought for a moment.

"Tell them to get me their info, relax and take the day off. I'll see if there's anything more I can wrangle out of the Washington office. Tell the team leader to stay close to a phone."

Will do sir.

He reached over and turned his radio back up.

The special news broadcast now playing, which was usurping the normal morning programming, was exclusively devoted to the disappearance of KAL Flight 007.

...the flight, which was previously reported to have landed safely in Russia, is now presumed to be lost somewhere over the Northern Pacific.

****

Coronado Amphib Base
Sunday night
00:01 hours

It doesn't get much more upscale than Coronado, California. Casually lounging on the very southern tip of California, the palm festooned marina, with its dozens of expensive, blue canvassed yachts ad sail boats served daily as the picturesque motivation for dozens of would-be Cézannes, Gauguins, photographers as well as inspiration for cheap post cards.

It's the place of honeymoons, anniversaries and has served as locations for dozens of motion pictures. The spectacular ocean sunsets are nature's daily free matinee for thousands.

Down next to the pristine beach the Sunday evening diners at the posh, upscale Hotel Del Coronado lined up to routinely pay $100 plus per plate for a three course meal to enjoy on the lovely beachside veranda. Drinks not included.

However that night, the first explosion suddenly intruding on the beachfront course was followed by half a dozen others. From over on the other side of the 200 meter rock jetty just south of the hotel yelling and screaming was accented by sporadic bursts of rapid machine gun fire, bright white illume flares and strings of grenade simulators. Most of the out of town hotel clientele applauded what they thought was a complimentary fireworks display.

The Marine Force Recon candidates on the other side of the jetty had a different impression.

"GET THE FUCK OUT! OUT, OUT, OUT! FORM UP ON THE BEACH! NOW!" Literally less than three minutes earlier the entire student contingent were tucked snuggly into their racks snoring away.

Then the shit hit the fan.

"EVERY ONE OF YOU PEOPLE KNEW BEFORE YOU SHOWED UP ON MY DOOR STEP THAT THIS ENTIRE COURSE IS BASED ON THE PREMISE OF MIND OVER MATTER." Coats yelled as the troops quickly assembled.

Captain Coats noticed, in between lighting off training ordnance and yelling, while all the other students scrambled out onto the beach, a lone student had chosen to sit on the low wall outside the barracks entrance and take his own sweet time to lace up his jungle boots.

Amidst the noise and confusion of the other instructors harassing the half asleep students Coats casually strolled up to the student, leaned down to him and spoke.

"Little trouble with your laces Marine?"

158

"No sir! I just wanna be sure they don't open while we're out there."

"Good thinking Marine! Attention to detail saves lives!"

"Yes sir! Aye aye sir!"

"You take your time and do what ya gotta do. Don't let us hold you up."

"No sir. Thank you sir. Be right there."

"I'm sure you will." Coats commented as he strolled away.

The student's ass overhung one side of the low wall where he sat and that's exactly where Coats tossed the next grenade simulator as he averted his eyes from the blast. The next time he turned to look for the theoretically 'dead' Recon Marine he was flying across the sandy beach heading for the surf zone, the ass of his camouflage trousers smoldering.

"SO GET IT THROUGH YOUR BRAIN PANS PEOPLE! I DON'T MIND AND YOU DON'T MATTER!"

As McKeowen double timed through the doorway and out onto the chaos of the midnight beach with the students, Stratford's words from the night before rang in Doc's ears.

Remember Doc, there's one critical difference between you and the students: You can't ring out.

Fairly heavy shit, McKeowen thought to himself as he nearly tripped over the door jamb of the barracks.

Cold. Cold and wet were the enemies to be conquered during the next week and every candidate knew it. For anyone who thought he would make it for any length of time still dry, they had another think coming.

The first command came before all the troops had actually formed up in squad and platoon order out on the beach. Staff Sergeant Instructor Ricky Keese, a weapons expert, casually strolled over to the partially assembled formation.

"DROP PEOPLE! 100 flutter kicks followed by 100 good morning darlings then get wet! Let me hear you sound off ladies." In seconds the entire class were on their backs and doing flutter kicks.

"ONE, TWO, THREE ONE SIR! ONE, TWO, THREE, TWO SIR ..."

At the completion of the warm up, lower body workout, all the students by platoon sprang to their feet, came on line parallel to the sea, locked arms and singing *The Marine Corps Hymn*, dutifully marched off into the cold autumn surf zone. It took less than 30 seconds before the entire company resembled a giant load of dirty laundry on its first wash cycle in God's washing machine. Arms and legs flailed and tangled as the three meter beach breakers pounded the shore and anything in between it and the high water mark.

They had barely struggled back to the beach to reform up, most on hands and knees, when orders were once again barked out, this time by Stratford.

"LET'S START THE WEEK RIGHT! SUGAR COOKIES PEOPLE!" Doc looked up the beach through the darkness and saw Coats standing, arms crossed, white smoke drifting around him like Lt. Kilgore on an LZ four years earlier. McKeowen smiled and like the rest of the class dropped his soaking wet body onto the sand and rolled around to make the familiar Special Operations 'sugar cookie'.

Important to have sand up your ass for the next week. Doc mused to himself as he rolled around.

For the members of Class 83-04, Hell Week had begun.

*

West German police today report the arrest of 176 protesters as a peaceful, anti-nuclear rally turned violent at the Rhein-Main U. S. Army airbase outside Frankfurt am Main.

Several dozen were injured as the peace protesters were denied access to the Lindenbaum Strasse outside the main U. S. airbase in the city.

A spokesman for the protesters claim they were assured access to the road to peacefully voice their protests over what they call, "American Imperialist disregard for the safety of European citizens".

This following the wide-spread deployment of the Pershing missile system by the United States in July and August. The highly mobile, nuclear capable missiles were deployed to counter the already present, Soviet SS20, long range ballistic missiles, which are also believed to be nuclear capable.

This is Lynn Shillingworth, BBC One, London. More news at six, thank you for listening. Be safe!

*

By Wednesday night, night umber four, Class 83-04 had lost 12% of the sixty-four candidates from their date of commissioning. Given that the SEAL attrition rate was upwards of fifty percent and the Army Green Beret's Phase One program regularly sustained a 65-75% attrition rate, statistically speaking eight candidates may not sound very devastating.

However, given that these Marines had already spent up to a year in a ready company, whose sole purpose was to prepare them for the rigorous Basic Amphib phase of Force Recon where they were exposed to all manner of techniques they would undergo while at Coronado, to be driven to 'ring out' or be medically dropped was a big deal.

The Marine Corps' approach to special ops training was to retain the candidate for training as long as possible without compromising the standards and thereby add as many recon qualified Marines to the Corps as possible. The additional eight months training in land navigation, long distance forced marches, infiltration, scuba and parachuting to follow Coronado would then be a relatively easy trek for the candidates.

The Marines, as the bastard child of the Navy, are continually in the unfortunate position of having to depend on the U.S.N. for funds. Therefore money was always tight, and at a price tag of upwards of $200,000 per Marine to get through the course, (not counting Jump and Scuba school), the Commandant of The Corps, Gen. Robert H. Barrow, who during the battle for Quang-tri province flew his own recon missions and thus imposed over 1,000 enemy confirmed dead, took a personal interest in Recon Marines.

The student hierarchy at the school was fashioned on the organization of actual operating teams. There was a Class Leader, an Assistant Class Leader, four Platoon Leaders and eight Boat Team Leaders with each boat team consisting of eight Marines. This organization was no less critical to the proper operation of the course overall than was that of the instructors and their commanders in Washington, D.C.

One of the first tasks upon arrival at the school was for the instructors to break the potential Force Recon candidates into boat teams. This was not done by rank as, unlike BUDS/S SEAL selection, there were no officers, all Recon students were enlisted.

Doc was intentionally assigned to a strong boat team so that in the event he were called away from them on a medical emergency, the team wouldn't suffer. This also made him the odd man out on a nine man boat team. This in turn created a unique situation where-by before each task the boat team leader would yell over to McKeowen as they prepared to undergo the next evolution.

"Hey Doc! You a student or instructor on this one?"

"Unless you fuck up and get hurt, I'm a student!"

One element in the student's favor during Hell Week was that in a continuous five and a half day period there were a limited number of different evolutions which could be organized and so the instructors were compelled to repeat several of them. This, by design, allowed the student teams to adapt techniques to enhance the ability of the individual boat crews to operate as a team instead of eight individuals.

Tonight, it was just shy of 21:30 chilly and windy, when the boat teams ran a quarter mile with the 350 pound, black rubber 3IBS's, Inflatable Boat, Small, carried on their heads. They ran from their staging area back near the "O" course up to the jetty on Red Beach One, the Navy's property line and the Northern most marker near the Hotel Del.

Any Red Beach exercise, being the closest beach to the civilian side of the coast, always drew a crowd. Tonight Rock portage was on the menu. Here the candidates were taught and then practiced how to beach their boats onto rocky shores or landing sites.

As the entire beach line from San Diego County to the Mexican border was more or less sandy beach, the few jetties were the only place suitable to hold the hazardous evolution.

The small crowd, drawn by the late night commotion, had formed about a hundred meters off on the North side of the jetty to watch the show.

An extremely well dressed, elderly but stately woman, carrying her shoes and moving slowly and deliberately down through the soft sand, approached the crowd and found herself standing next to an apprehensive young girl in jeans and a sweater, arms hugging herself against the nip in the night air. The woman glanced over as the girl pulled her sweater tighter around herself to combat the chilly wind.

"What's happening? Are those Navy Seals?"

"No ma'am. They're Force Recon Marines." The girl answered as they looked out over the twenty yard wide jetty.

The old woman's equally well dressed husband a few steps behind made his way over to the girl and his wife.

Under the six foot surf pounding the jetty at different angles the first team slammed into the rocks, lost control of their IBS and scrambled to escape the jagged boulders, push back out and reorganize.

"I've always wondered what makes them want to do that sort of work?" The old woman mused as all three stared out at the dripping wet, shivering and fatigued candidates dressed only in tee shirts, swim trunks and neoprene swim booties.

The young girl smirked.

"Motivation. Devotion. The need to affect a maximum impact. But mostly the desire to serve with men of a certain caliber." The young girl responded, her eyes never veering from the action.

The old man drew back slightly and studied her.

"What's your name, dear?" He asked.

"Cheaney, Jennifer Cheaney." She replied continually staring at the candidates as they purposely crashed their IBS's into the ragged jetty, fought to climb out of them onto the large chunks of black rock and then wrestle the hundreds of pounds of wet IBS up out of the water behind them.

Nervousness suddenly crept into the girl's voice.

"My twin brother is in one of those boats."

"Brave men!" The man commented. "You come

from a military family?"

"My father served in Viet Nam, as a Green Beret."

"He must be very proud."

"He was killed during an operation to rescue some South Vietnamese doctors." She responded.

The man appeared slightly embarrassed and quickly tried to compensate.

"I'm sorry for your troubles. Well your mom must be very proud."

"She's not that gone on the idea. I had to sneak out of the house and drive down from Redondo Beach to get here. We planned this behind her back before my brother started training." The man smiled over at her. "He's to throw a chem light up in the air if he's made it to this phase of training."

"SECURE BOAT!" Someone called out from deep in the murky darkness as the IBS's continued to crash into the ragged, plankton coated rocks.

The old man suddenly grasped the girl's hand and pressed a bank note into it then leaned in to whisper in her ear while more yelling could be heard mixed with the pounding of surf as it echoed in the back ground.

"When those boys finish their training, I want you to take your brother over to the hotel ..." He nodded back at the Del Coronado, "... and buy him a steak dinner. Then, get him to ask for the Roosevelt Suite." The girl pulled back and stared at the strange old guy. "You two will be my guests for a weekend." She stared first down at the $100 bill then at the old man. "Bring your mom if you like. Maybe it'll soften her up." He suggested as he walked away.

The elegant, old woman loudly whispered as she trailed behind heading up the beach back towards the hotel.

"He's on the board of directors." She informed.

Flabbergasted, the young girl looked over at the men scrambling through the surf and over the vicious jetty in time to see, seemingly in slow motion, a green chem light float up into the air.

****

It was sunrise Friday – Last Day. Last day of Hell Week. A time which was the entire, immediate focus of every man's life as a member of Class 83-04. Each individual's resolve was such that 'They', the opposition, the bad guys, the instructors, could do anything to the candidates and no one, short of broken bones or worse would quit today. By the student code of rules it simply wasn't allowed.

However, in the ensuing last five days of non-stop torture they had forgotten about the Recon Olympics.

Now able to reduce their continuous shivering to a minimum as the big heat tab in the sky peeked over the horizon, they were ordered to form up by boat teams, ground their IBS's, which had been their constant companions since Wednesday, and stand by for orders.

It was in the warmth of the mid-morning sun that the students found themselves on the obstacle course once again.

They had just completed the all night, "Around the World" paddle, a 45-50 mile excursion around Coronado to the 32nd Street pier section over on the mainland where half of the Pacific Fleet was anchored, and back again.

By this point in training each of the remaining candidates had run this obstacle course a minimum of fifteen times and because of this all had gradually crept below the mandatory passing time with each man having reduced his personal time with each run. All were now well below the required time.

Now they would start the last evolution before securing for the weekend and a two day recovery period to try to catch up on five nights of lost sleep and tend their blister covered bodies.

But first, they were going to run the obstacle course yet again. Only this time they would do it carrying their 350 pound IBS's, the boats they had lived with day and night for the last week.

"Teams, stand at ease!" Lieutenant Stratford called out as he mounted the low instructor's podium at the starting point of the course. "For this evolution the rules are simple! You and your boat team will negotiate each and every obstacle clearing them in the prescribed manner with your IBS's." He carefully scanned the formation for any overt reactions from students which would signal the instructors to keep an eye on as they went through the barrier of what was generally considered to be the make or break week in training.

Most of the students, the ones with the where-with-all to have scooped out the course evolutions beforehand from the previous classes, realized what

168

was coming.

Which did absolutely fuck all to relieve their apprehension.

"Teams will launch at two minute intervals. The team with the best time secures from Hell Week and is exempt from all duty for the weekend. The remainder of the class will do it again."

The teams, some literally holding up other team members who were too weak to stand, still maintained their military bearing.

"The rotations will continue until all boat teams are off the course save the last one. As this is a 'must-past' evolution, the last boat team will be subjected to an Instructor's Performance Review on Monday morning and probably be recommended to be rolled back to the next class. Where they will, of course, be required to repeat Hell Week." This garnered some reactions. "If your team is stuck on an obstacle and another team reaches that obstacle you will finish the obstacle immediately or make way and allow them to pass through the obstacle. Failure to do so will result in your team returning to the start point and beginning again. What is life without rules but chaos, isn't that right gentlemen?!"

"SIR WHOO-YA, SIR!" The class responded as one.

Stratford glanced over at Doc, attached to Team Three as he had been since that Sunday. While Stratford's eyes were on McKeowen, McKeowen's eyes were on the ground, bent over, hands on knees as he tried to focus through the pain of the golf ball sized blisters on both feet and his bone wrenching fatigue.

However, at that particular point most eyes were on Boat Team Five, a strong team with somewhat of a celebrity on board.

Jason Schultz, alias "Forklift", because he could lift almost anything a conventional forklift could, was five times Ohio Weight Lifting Champ, two times Midwestern Conference winner for under twenty-fives and had been favored to take the National Championships which would mean an invite to a seat on the '84 Olympic team, national fame and a guaranteed future, when he decided to enlist in the Navy. This despite the fact that, except in the movies, he had never seen an ocean.

"We will launch in numerical order. BOAT TEAM NUMBER ONE, FRONT AND CENTER!" Team One's Team Leader gave the order for high boat carry and the team double timed over to the start point.

"Good!" Doc declared as he leaned over to his Team Leader who stood next to him.

"Why good Doc?" The Corporal asked.

"We get a free tutorial on how best to do his thing before we launch."

"Or how not to!" The Team Leader acknowledged.

"Tell your team to pay attention."

"Roger that Doc."

On the L.T.'s command Team One took off and easily cleared the first obstacle, a simple log balancing requirement, using a high boat carry. Team Two moved into position and was launched two minutes later.

Team Three worked well together and so had

170

planned their strategy while awaiting their turn. It was simple. No hot dogging, constantly communicate and don't come in last!

They sailed, if that level of struggling can be called sailing, until they reached obstacle #13, 'The Weaver', a six foot high pyramid comprised of 12, 5 inch steel pipes welded to a frame in parallel formation with 18 inches between them. The rules called for the negotiator to 'weave' between each of the pipes to the top and then weave back down the other side.

Team Four were closing in on them from behind when Doc yelled at the team member closest to him.

"Start weaving through and when four of you are through we'll hand the boat off over the fucking thing to you and we'll go through."

"What if Stratford tags us?" The Team Leader asked.

"Him tagging us is a maybe, Team Four up our ass in about ten seconds is a for sure!" There was no more discussion as they put Doc's idea into motion.

Then came the call that corpsmen train for their whole lives but never want to hear.

"CORPSMAN UP!" It was across on the other side of the course.

McKeowen grabbed his waist mounted M-1 medical kit which he had grounded in preparation to negotiate The Weaver and dashed towards the L.T. who stood among Team Five, their boat grounded next to them. It was Forklift laying in the sand propped up on his elbow and holding his left leg about midway down from the knee.

"Hold on mate. You're gonna be alright!" Doc

opened his kit and broke out his stethoscope then applied it to the patient's mid tibia. Crepitus is the sound of broken bone rubbing against bone. There was crepitus.

With intense desperation motivated by the fact that the entire last six weeks of his life boiled down to this moment, Forklift reached up, grabbed McKeowen's arm hard, pulled him in close and made eye-to-eye contact as he whispered.

"Doc! Just let me finish this last evolution and I'll be a med drop!"

Doc looked back into Forklift's eyes as the rest of his team stood by awaiting the verdict. There wasn't a trace of pain to be seen on the big man's face, only the inescapable desire to finish what he started.

"I got this sir." Doc said to Stratford who then wandered off to monitor the remaining teams. Doc dug through his bag and retrieved two rolls of medical tape and a 4 inch wide Ace wrap.

"Team Leader, get your team going. He'll catch up." Doc instructed. Forklift forced a smile to his face. "The Battalion surgeon hears about this and I'm changing bed pans on the geriatric's ward! You owe me a drink cowboy!" He proceeded to tape the leg in a herring bone formation then wrapped it as tight as possible with an Ace wrap followed by another herring bone wrap in the opposite direction. He reached back into his bag and produced a syrette of morphine.

"What's that Doc?"

"Morphine."

"I'd prefer you didn't." Schultz protested.

"You sure? Pain's only gonna get worse."

Forklift struggled to his feet and quickly limped away towards his team. "See ya at the finish Doc." He called back.

By now Team Three was nearing the last obstacle and Doc kept an eye on team Five as he ran through the next few obstacles to avoid disqualification and catch up with them. But the worst wasn't over. Despite having wrapped and taped Forklift's leg in record time, fate intervened.

Boat Team Five's Team Leader, now in front of the team, was nearing the top of 'The Skyscraper', a 20 foot tall, four tiered platform affair, when he slipped and tumbled backwards. Nimbly righting himself on the way down, probably thinking to do a parachute landing fall to break the momentum, he hit hard on both feet and broke his right leg at the ankle.

Before McKeowen could react and without the slightest hint of hesitation, Forklift finished The Skyscraper, limped over to his team mate, threw him over his shoulder and yelled "HOLD ON!" as he proceeded to climb to the top of a ladder to negotiate the next obstacle.

'The Slide For Life', a 100 foot rope slide starting from about fifty feet up. With his team mate clinging to his massive back like a human haversack, Schultz eased them both down the rope and successfully completed the obstacle.

From over on the finish line the hair on McKeowen's arms stood on end as he watched Forklift's team leader quickly take charge, reorganize his team and with two wounded men, one hobbling along carrying the other casualty on his back while the other six team members struggled under the extra weight of the 350 pound IBS, pushed on through the last few obstacles to collapse across the finish line as one.

Even Coats, who wasn't supposed to be, was impressed.

**

CHAPTER EIGHT

Rancho del Cielo
Santa Barbara, Calif.
09:45 WPT, September 2nd

Rancho del Cielo, "Heaven's Ranch", sits just northwest of Santa Barbara, California. It is a sprawling 700 acre property surrounded by a small yet scenic mountain range. Replete with rolling hills, a small forest, rivers and a lake, it is something right out of a movie set, a movie set with a chunk of land set for a movie star-come-president.

Also known as the Western White House it's here that President Reagan hosted heads of state such as Queen Elizabeth II and Prince Philip, Duke of Edinburgh, German Chancellors and Margret Thatcher.

It was in the conservatively decorated dining room amongst the family photos and plaques hanging on the white plastered walls that he approved and signed the historic *Economic Recovery Act of 1981*.

But today Ronnie, dressed in his favorite cowboy boots and jeans, was sloshing around in the shallow, muddy soil, helping a ranch hand repair fencing on a slope on the western end of the property.

In between being preoccupied with the developing Beirut situation, where it seemed the entire population were on the verge of civil war between Muslim and Christian factions, Reagan was

175

on a three week excursion to the western states to press the flesh and raise funds for the party, and spend a few days on the ranch to try and decompress, when his itinerary was fatefully altered.

From down by the ranch house an aide worked his way up the hill, made his way past the Secret Service contingent who all stood off to the sides at respectable distances and handed the President a Telex.

Reagan winced as he read the message handed him.

"Has this been confirmed?"

"Apparently so Mr. President."

"Up to **300 hundred** civilians dead?!"

"Exact numbers are not confirmed yet sir."

"Give me the phone." Reagan took the brick-sized cell phone, extended the aerial and pressed one button. While he waited to be connected he gave the "round-em'-up" signal to his Secret Service duty officer and nodded thank you to the aide who headed back down the hill to the house. A female voice came on the line.

Yes Mr. President?

"Charlene, is Secretary Schultz available?"

Yes sir. Please hold.

Mr. President? Schultz came on the line.

"George, is this Korean Airlines thing confirmed?"

Unfortunately sir it is, from several sources.

"Have they gone completely mad?! Civilians!! What in God's name are they doing shooting down civilians?! More importantly, where there any

176

Americans on board?" There was an uncomfortable pause on the other end.

We think about fifty. And sir...

"Yes, what is it?" Reagan prompted.

Senator Larry McDonald was one of them. On his way over to participate in the 30th anniversary of the American-South Korean Treaty. For one of the few times in his life Reagan felt a burst of profanity well in his throat, but fought it back. *Japan and Korea have both pledged full support.* Schultz added in an attempt at buffering the news.

"Where do we stand legally?" He asked Schultz.

As it was a Korean aircraft they have legal right of salvage and as of an hour ago, they've transferred salvage rights to us and the Japanese.

"What's in motion?"

I've authorized The Seventh Fleet to ready a Search and Rescue mission which they've informed me task Force 71 is mounting as we speak. They've got a submersible aboard the Narragansett and Admiral Cockell is enroute by helo to assume overall command. All pending your okay, of course.

"Bill's a good man. Get me updates." The President confirmed.

By now the six man Secret Service detail were rounded up and standing by. Reagan left his tools where they lay and began to make his way down the shallow hill.

"What happens if we don't find any survivors?" Reagan probed.

Under the circumstances sir, and it doesn't look good, protocol is 72 hours then it turns from a Search and Rescue to an S.A.S., Search And

Salvage operation. But that can be determined at the appropriate time. Schultz informed.

Reagan stopped and focused on the next question.

"Wreckage? The black box?"

We've re-tasked the required NORAD satellites and are awaiting updates on the current imagery. But it looks like the Soviets have dispatched everything they've got to the area.

"We need to find that box before they do!" The President demanded.

I understand Mr. President, but with no way to beat them to their own waters and half the Soviet navy on the move to the area as we speak, we need to take all precautions to avoid an international incident.

"I concur. Is there any good news?!"

The Japanese think they have some radio chatter from the Russian aircraft prior to the incident. We'll know something by tonight, tomorrow morning at the latest.

Reagan was already nearly all the way down the muddy hill, the SS men in tow, as he continued the debriefing.

"I'll be airborne and enroute in about an hour. I'll keep the lines clear on Air Force One, meanwhile you have my authorization to officially order everything you've done so far but give absolute priority to that black box! The Commies are probably preparing a massive propaganda campaign as we speak, no doubt to include blaming us! We **must** know what happened up there to be able to defend ourselves and apportion blame where it belongs!"

*

Two weeks and a day after the victories of Hell Week, Doc McKeowen was two days and a weekend away from being the first U.S.N. HM to graduate and thus qualify as a Force Reconnaissance Marine.

It was a Wednesday afternoon and earlier he had taught a class on poisonous snakes and insects and was coming in off a beach run when he was intercepted by Gunny Genne who had been practicing on the obstacle course.

"Hey Doc, got a minute?" Gunny called over to him. Both men out of breath and covered in sweat ambled over to the instructor's podium near the start point and took a seat.

"For you Gunny, I got two minutes."

"There's been a schedule change over in Basic Amphid and I'm down a man."

"Should I have a bad feeling about this Gunny?"

"Nah! Should be right up your alley. We got an active duty team of operators coming in for refresher training tonight and I need a safety swimmer to cover their water evos."

"I got a navigation class to teach in the morning, Gunny."

"That's okay, I can take that. I ran it by Captain Coats and he okay'd it if you're up for it. Says you can have a two day pass if you help us out."

"Four days off! Not bad for six to eight hours

work babysitting some operators. Shit, what'a I gotta do and where do I sign-up?" They stood and made their way back across The Strand to the Quonset hut offices.

"All you got'a do is pack a lunch, ride in a chopper and wait for someone to get hurt, which ain't very likely because they're all high speed low drag experienced operators."

"Sounds easy enough. What kind'a refresher stuff they gonn'a be doing?" Doc asked.

"Helo casting, beach infil, SPIE rig, hell hole work on a CH-47 the usual fun stuff but we just need you around for the water work stuff."

"If something goes south, then what?"

"Then do some daring hero, medical shit, save **his** ass and maybe get **your** ass put in for a medal."

"Sounds like fun." Mac affirmed as they entered the hut.

"Ya know, I knew there was a reason I didn't listen to all that shit they was talkin' about you when you first came aboard Doc, bein' the only squid and all." Gunny quipped.

"Strange, that's what your wife said when I was kissing her good bye this morning."

"Yeah she likes a little bit a white boy sometimes. Reminds her how good she got it with a black man."

Back in the office area Doc spied a big, off-white, plastic box which occupied most of the Gunny's desk and stepped over to examine it. The contraption had a small, iridescent green TV screen in the front of it and jutting out of the bottom like the jaw of a Neanderthal, was a monster-sized keyboard.

"What the hell is this thing?" Doc asked as he leaned in and stared like a chimp looking at a television for the first time.

"It's a Commodore 64!" Genne proudly smirked.

"What the hell's a Commodore 64?"

"A computer Doc."

"What's this little box next to it?" McKeowen perused the black, shoe-box-sized unit sitting next to the monitor.

"A floppy disc drive."

"What the fuck is a sloppy disc?"

The Navy had just begun a fleet-wide adaptation of the desk top computer and the admin centers at each command were issued a limited number of them. BA had one, Recon had none. Computers don't do so well in the open sea. Even if you put a life vest on them.

"I heard of them. Seen a picture of one on the cover of *Time* magazine." Doc lightly pecked at the keys but the machine wasn't on. "You know how to use one of these things Gunny?"

"Yeah they teach ya about 'em in a one week course over on mainside. They use games as learning aides. Come around when you're free, I'll give you briefing on it."

"Games?"

"Yeah. I'm pretty good at chess, so to get the hang of it I used the chess program."

"Chess program? Pretty heady stuff for a jarhead. Do ya ever win against this thing?"

"Fuck no!" Gunny walked over to the far corner filing cabinet to file some records from his desk.

181

"But I beat the shit out of it at kick boxing!" He smiled.

It was then that Doc noticed the right side of the plastic casing had an appreciable sized crack in it.

**

The Kremlin
Office of the General Secretary
Moscow

For a full five centuries the official residence of Russia's leaders and their families has been The Kremlin.

A foreboding and mysterious place to Westerners, often pictured as a single building housing the ultra-secret KGB, a medieval prison for dissenters of The State and a place where people were randomly executed.

Like most widely disseminated information of the Cold War era, none of this was accurate.

The triangular shaped Moscow Kremlin is a collection of structures surrounded by a 2 kilometer plus wall enclosing an area occupied and fortified since the Second Century B.C.

The Moscow Kremlin's renaissance architecture, originally built from the stones of the Chudov Monastery and its adjoining convent, was burned several times, partially destroyed by Napoleon on his retreat from Russia and remains the Kremlin's Palace of Congress used for all Communist forums and meetings.

The famous Tsar Bell, housed in one of the many cathedrals in the Kremlin, weighs in at 202 tons, is the largest bell in the world and was accidently split during forging. Consequently it has never been rung. Muscovites believe that this bell will one day ring on its ascension to heaven during Armageddon. An Armageddon such as might be triggered by a nuclear war.

In view of the increasing political tensions, Armageddon had recently re-entered the common vernacular in both the West and East and it was this very event that Yuri Andropov, General Secretary of the Communist Party of the Soviet Union's Central Committee, had on his mind as he sat in his office in the Kremlin's main administration wing across from the Palace of Congress.

Currently he had to focus hard to pay attention to the rhetoric he was presently hearing.

In a corner of the wide, plush office a large, console model television was on as was the bulky VCR on top of it. A half dozen Politburo members stood gathered around the TV set, mesmerized by the videotaped broadcast they were watching.

Filling the screen from a stationary camera was a tight shot of U.S. Secretary of State George Shultz who stood at a podium reading from a prepared statement. For dramatic effect he read in an angry, halting fashion.

In conclusion, the United States reacts with revulsion to this attack. Loss of life appears to be heavy. We can see no excuse, what so ever, for this appalling act! There was absolutely no justification, legal or moral, for what the Soviet Union did!

General Secretary Andropov, alias Prime Minister in Western terms, was pensive as he waited for Andrei Gromyko, his longtime friend and Minister for Foreign Affairs and final member of the emergency meeting, to arrive. On a signal from one of the Politburo members a well-dressed aide moved across the room and shut off the television then closed the doors of the polished mahogany cabinet as Schultz was cut off.

By the time Gromyko showed up ten minutes later, the debate was in full swing. Andropov stepped back behind his desk, took his seat and brandished a red folder.

"This is the report I have received this morning, upon my official request, from Colonel Chairman Chebrikov of the KGB and endorsed by the Defense Ministry." He passed the file to the aide who selected a page and began to read.

'We are dealing with a major, dual-purpose political provocation carefully organized by the U.S. special services.

The first purpose was to use the incursion of the intruder aircraft into Soviet airspace to create a favorable situation for the gathering of defense data on our air defense systems in the Far East, involving the most diverse systems including the Ferret satellite.

Second, they envisaged, if this flight were terminated by us, the U.S. would use that fact to mount a global anti-Soviet campaign to discredit the Soviet Union.'

"As they are now clearly attempting to do!" Loudly declared Dmitriy Ustinov, Minister for Defense.

"Exactly Comrade Minister!" We must make some sort of a statement!" Andropov insisted as he stood behind his oversized desk. "To remain silent is neither practical nor politically sound. These are not accusations which may be allowed to go unanswered!" The half dozen ministers, all members of the politburo, were formulating their opinions fueled by their anger at the Americans.

"I agree. Silence is not an option." Sergei Tarasenko of the Soviet Foreign Ministry had given long hours of thought to how to handle the seemingly unmanageable but inevitable task of how to face the world press. "But we are here to reach a consensus as to **what** must be said. Certainly the Americans are going to claim they are expecting an apology and will likely push the Koreans to attempt legal action in the International Courts."

"The International courts, bah! For all the good it would do them!" Andropov scoffed.

"There can be no admission of guilt! Out of the question Mr. General Secretary!" Ustinov was adamant. "Besides, they crashed into the sea! No one will ever know for sure what happened!"

"Eventually Dmitriy, wreckage will be found. We must face that fact." Tarasenko insisted.

"Andrei is right. There is always wreckage. You see it on the television along with little men with long necks wearing glasses poking through the carnage with pencils and note pads." Vitaly Vorotnikov, Chairman of the Council of Ministers argued.

"They crashed into the sea at a thousand kilometres an hour, into waters that we control!" Ustinov vehemently countered.

"We are not sure exactly where they went down!" Tarasenko, becoming increasingly passionate about his calls to come clean to the international community and admit the mistake, aiming his comments directly at Andropov. "Regardless of if it was in our waters," He continued, "... or international waters it was only a few kilometres either way. Additionally, it's been nearly twenty-four hours, there could be wreckage spread from Sakhalin to Seoul and all over the Western coast of Japan!" He was becoming irritated and shifted in his seat. "The best policy is to make an admission of the facts as we know them! The World Press will otherwise enter into conjecture and the whole thing will become an endless quagmire of accusations and counter accusations ending who knows where!"

"And exactly how does Sergei Tarasenko propose we make this admission of guilt to the world, Mr. Secretary?!" Ustinov was on his feet as he spoke.

"It was our fighter jets who are responsible! We can easily claim pilot error, weather, ANY NUMBER OF REASONS, COMRADE MINISTER!" Tarasenko yelled back from his seat avoiding eye contact with Ustinov.

Andropov sat back and held up a hand to regain

control. He spoke quietly and distinctly.

"There are limits to offense of pride to which a nation can be expected to endure!" Andropov spoke firmly enough to quell the flares of temper as well as to get the discussion-turned-debate back on track. "We will make our announcement at a specially arranged press conference, most likely outside of the Soviet Union's territories and we will make it in our own good time, NOT when pressure from the Imperialist press dictate!" Everyone took a breath as Ustinov sat back down.

Andropov deliberately shifted to a softer tone as he continued. "I've spoken with Minister Korienko. He agrees."

Quiet prevailed.

Andropov signaled for the single senior aide standing by to leave the room. The aide nodded in acknowledgement and slipped out through the huge oak doors.

"Comrade General Secretary, have any American vessels arrived yet?" Vladimir Dolgikh, of the Secretariat quietly enquired.

"The first of them was spotted leaving Okinawa last night." Ustinov reported. "Undoubtedly they will be steaming at full speed, which means they are due on station within the next few hours. We have aircraft standing by to report as soon as they arrive. Meanwhile the Japanese have begun their search aided by the Koreans." Ustinov explained.

"The Japanese are minor players in this scenario, but I want ALL vessels to steer well clear of the Koreans! Is that understood?!" Andropov demanded. "Send word to the overall commander that I don't want anyone within ten kilometres of ANY Korean vessels, to include fishing boats. Give them as wide a berth as possible!"

"Yuri, you understand how that could hinder our search efforts for the black box? Ten kilometres means the Koreans could find the wreckage first and-"

"AS WIDE A BERTH AS POSSIBLE!" Yuri slammed his palm on the desk and instantly became embarrassed by his outburst. He then again altered his tone. "The last thing we need is to give the Americans the excuse they are looking for!"

"Comrade General Secretary, do you really think-"

"That Reagan's war mongers engineered this entire thing? Absolutely and without question! Do you think it was coincidence that there was a U.S. spy plane in that exact area at that exact same time? Can you, Nikolai Tikonov, an educated man, look yourself in the mirror and convince yourself that, of what you can be very sure were two very experienced Korean pilots 'just happened' to stray hundreds of miles off course, to **coincidentally** fly over one of our most secret installations?" He pressed.

"In point of fact, I never really ..."

"Of course it was not a coincidence!" Andropov sprang to his feet and leaned both hands on his desk. "It was completely planned! It's time you accept the fact that these men know no limits! They tried to eliminate Castro with a poison cigar! When that failed they tried a god-damned exploding shoe! Like in a comedy movie!"

Most in the room remembered the headlines of the incident back in the Sixties and despite the severity of the terse atmosphere, were forced to stifle a laugh.

Intentionally or not the General Secretary relieved at least some of the tension in the room. Even Andropov allowed himself a smirk before continuing.

"Comrades, we must never lose sight of the fact that these men form their moral basis from their cinema films! They are living in a movie and the world is their cinema!"

Ustinov took over.

"The Comrade General Secretary is right. We didn't make the mistake of firing on their aircraft with their ridiculous, childish incursions in the Spring so now they want to 'up the ante' as Reagan puts it in those ludicrous cowboy stories of his."

Sensing things were once again veering off track, Tarasenko, who had been scribbling some notes, interrupted.

"Mr. General Secretary, if I may?" Andropov nodded.

"Before we met this morning I took the liberty of sketching out a possible response to the American's accusations. We could use TASS to broadcast it, thus avoiding the need for anyone to appear in front of the cameras."

"Read it please."

"An aircraft, flying without lights, has been intercepted by Soviet fighters after it violated Soviet airspace over Sakhalin Island. The aircraft failed to respond to warnings as it continued on its flight towards the Sea of Japan."

"And what has become of this mysterious ghost flight, they will ask?" Ustinov challenged.

"This can be dealt with when we locate the wreckage and have more definitive information. This will buy us some time as well as force the Americans into their next move."

"I'll tell you straight away what their next move will be Comrade Minister Tarasenko," Ustinov pushed. "I don't think –"

"Add the adjective 'unidentified' before 'aircraft' and we will use it." Andropov directed. He winced in pain as he shifted in his seat. It was clear the situation as a whole was beginning to weigh on the General Secretary. "What do you think Andrei?" Andropov asked.

Gromyko, sitting to his immediate right, considered his words before answering. As he did there was a knock on the door.

"Yes?" An aide entered, apologized for the interruption and made straight for Andropov, handing him a folded note, which he read.

'Dr. Chazov has arrived with the nurse.
It is time for your dialysis treatment.'

"Ten minutes." He answered as he folded the note and placed it in his jacket pocket. The aide nodded and left.

"What I think Mr. General Secretary, is that we should, carefully, very carefully, observe the Americans very closely these next few weeks."

"I agree." Ustinov echoed. "President Reagan

has gone on record as opposing every significant arms limitation agreement since 1963, whether negotiated by Republican or Democratic administrations! He pretends in the press to be an advocate of the SALT arms limitation talks, even tries to take credit for their initiation! But the fact remains we have not come to one actual agreement on any of the major points we have agreed to discuss. It's as if the people of the Soviet Union are sponsoring a never ending lunch date between the so called negotiators! Reagan's record speaks for itself!" Ustinov spat.

"With the Americans giving little ground at the SALT talks ..." Vitaly Vorotnikov interjected.

"'Little ground'?! They are moving like a bunch of snails!" Yuri added. "This Pershing missile business, continuous incursions testing our defenses and now these public political attacks it's difficult to tell what they are planning, let alone thinking."

"We will issue Sergei's statement. Comrade Ustinov, direct Marshall Ogarkov to prepare a presentation for the press."

"Yes Comrade General Secretary."

"I will review it when finished. Distinguished gentlemen, if you'll please excuse me. I have another appointment to keep." Andropov requested.

The politicians excused themselves and went off to their respective appointments.

"Andrei, a word." Andropov asked of Gromyko before he reached the door.

When the room had cleared a puzzled Gromyko approached the still sitting Andropov.

"In a few days' time, I'm awaiting some

information, I will call a meeting with some of the security people. I would like you to speak to Dobrynin and have him delay his return to America until after this meeting. Also, I would like you to attend."

"Of course Yuri, but Anatoly must be at the U. N. for the opening of the General Assembly on-"

"He will be there, he will be there. Can I count on you?" Yuri reached across the desk and offered his hand. Andropov smiled but did not stand as they shook.

"Of course Yuri." Gromyko, the only member of the inner circle with knowledge of exactly how severe Andropov's medical condition was, had kept the oath of secrecy he had taken to his friend when Yuri was first diagnosed.

What Gromyko couldn't know was that his advice of keeping a close eye on the Americans had already been acted upon.

Andropov had, more than six weeks ago, ordered 50 more secret agents, augmenting the 150 already spread across Europe, be sent to the West to observe and report.

As much heat as Andropov and the Politburo believed the Reagan administration had so far heaped on them, the Russians had no idea how far from rock bottom things really were.

However, the Politburo were not the only ones who were about to be forcibly taught an abject lesson in international politics run amok.

*** * ***

Doc took note of the dark, slightly windy conditions and the fact that the sea was getting a bit choppy as he waited at the helo pad which jutted out into the channel on the far end of the Amphib Base. He checked his watch again and mumbled to himself.

"If this were a date she'd have to be twenty-one years old, blond hair, blue eyes, rich and own a liquor store for me to still be hanging around here!" Dressed in his Recon green and gold tee shirt and swim trunks and coral booties he noted also that it was cooling off and with any prolonged exposure in the water hypothermia of the troops would be a risk.

Twenty minutes later, as dark was setting in, a CH-46 Chinook came in over the horizon and across the Strand from the seaward side.

"Helluv'a way to run a circus!" McKeowen cursed.

Doc secured his watch cap to his head with a hand to keep it from blowing off in the rotor wash and backed away as the banana shaped helo lightly touched down.

Two soldiers, whose ranks were indiscernible, disembarked and Doc met them halfway to the ramp as it was still being lowered. He could see there were several other personnel inside the bird. The tall one came up and offered his hand.

"Sergeant First Class Quinn, Army Spec Ops, this is Captain Fisk, zero-nine-six Team Leader."

"HM2 McKeowen, Force Recon."

"Didn't know they had Navy Corpsmen that were Force Recon qualified." Fisk replied.

"They don't, yet sir. You got another medic with you?"

"No. He took one in the calf in Beirut. He'll be alright in few weeks but that's why we requested you."

"We appreciate your support." Quinn added.

"Anything for our boys in uniform. Sergeant Quinn, am I early, I was told 21:30?"

"No you're dead on time Doc, we ran into a snag. Our assigned pilot and flight crew were called away on a rescue. Some civilian yacht jockeys got their shit in the wind and needed help getting home. They gave us a last minute replacement crew."

"Fuckin' reservists!" The captain standing next to Quinn spat as he chewed on his unlit cigar stub.

"I don't know sir. Some of my best friends are reservists." Mac tried to lighten the mood. It didn't work.

"Well, let's get this fuckin' show on the road!" Fisk ordered. Doc picked up his med bag and swim fins and followed them up the ramp onto the chopper.

Quinn briefed Doc as they mounted the ramp which was raised halfway after they were inside.

"Plan's simple." Quinn briefed Doc. "Our last three ops have been in desert areas of operations. The C.O.'s decided we need to brush up on water borne ops a little so we're out here as your guests for three days of refresher training." Doc gave the thumbs up as Quinn continued to shout over the rotor wash and they lifted off.

"The op order calls for two or three passes over the water, out of sight of shore, about a mile out in this darkness I figure, then the bird comes back around, recovers the team via the Jacob's Ladder, then we do it again. On the last past, we form up in the water and head for shore." He indicated a wrist compass to indicate how they would navigate in.

"Need me to swim in with you?" Doc asked. Quinn looked surprised.

"We were told you were gonna stay in the bird, but if you're up for it, glad to have you along."

"Didn't bring my brand new Armani swim wear just to look good!" Doc nodded down to the deck to his Navy issue Rocket fins.

Quinn smiled and offered a high five then switched on his water proof lapel radio to brief the captain who was across the aisle on the other side of the bird. Quinn's brief on the new arrangement was not received well. Fisk didn't use his radio to respond.

"Fuck no! This ain't no joy ride god damn it!" Fisk yelled. "We're here to train! The medic stays on board!" Doc couldn't help but hear and made direct eye contact with the cantankerous officer.

"All due respect sir, I'm not a medic. I'm a Navy corpsman!"

"Whatever ya wanna call yerself is okay by me son, but your ass is stayin' up here in the bird. Last thing I need to worry about is givin' Captain Coats back a broke medic!" It was all Mac could do to bite his tongue. Fisk leaned across and shouted orders to the Team Sergeant. "Quinn! Jump stick order. You lead, lieutenant last, the team in between." Obviously Fisk would stay with the helo.

"Got it sir!" Quinn tapped Doc on the knee.

"Sorry."

"Fuck him!" Doc mouthed to Quinn who smiled.

The bird turned seaward and revved to full speed. Out over the partially open ramp everyone watched the shore lights fade and finally vanish altogether. The team moved into position sitting on the deck facing each other on either side of the Hell Hole, a 30 inch square hatch in the very center of the helo's deck. Doc sat off to the side next to Quinn who undid the four safety latches as he and another member of the team lifted away the hatch and passed it to the ship's crew chief who stowed it under the rear seating area. Quinn leaned over to McKeowen.

"We'll come in at around 20 feet to launch. The idea is to get out as quick as possible to maintain a tight formation in the water and clear the bird in case it's hit." Quinn explained. "After the last man's out hold on. The bird's gonna do a combat flair to simulate avoiding small arms fire." Quinn spoke as the team donned their fins then, just as in a parachute jump, all eyes were glued to the ready lights on the starboard side of the ship, up near the ramp.

The red light came on and the Crew Chief gave Quinn the thumbs up. The Team Sergeant slid his ass up to allow his legs to dangle down through the hole. Doc leaned forward and peered down through the hole. Nothing but blackness.

Maintaining constant commo with the pilot, the crew chief squatted with one hand on Quinn's shoulder, the other holding on to a seat stanchion next to him.

The green light snapped on.

"GO!" He yelled at Quinn as he slapped him on the back and the next man opposite slid to the hatch. As the team members alternated sides and disappeared through the hole into the pitch black darkness Doc and the Major watched intently until the last man, the team's L.T. slid into position.

Suddenly, just as he lifted his ass off the deck to launch down through the hole, the helo flared and shot up at a 45 degree angle throwing the L.T. across and partially through the hatch slamming his chest against the opposite edge of the hole knocking the wind out of him. As his stunned body slithered down through the opening he hit the back of his head on the back edge of the hatch and went limp.

"SHIT!" Fisk cursed. Doc quickly hit the deck leaned over and peered down through the hole. He watched in horror as the young lieutenant was visible much longer than Doc thought he should have been for a twenty foot fall into the black of the Pacific.

"Get back to the infil point and drop altitude ASAP!" Fisk ordered the crew chief.

"Sir how we going to find them in this ..."

"Look for their strobe lights, dumbshit! Fuckin' do it!" The crew chief yelled instructions into his headset as he dashed to the back of the bird, hooked in his monkey harness to the bulkhead and fell to the deck on his belly to peer over the edge of the still partially raised ramp. Doc followed suit and was shocked to see that they were already at least 500 hundred feet in the air, maybe more. He quickly realized there was no second monkey harness.

He immediately spotted first one then two, three and four strobes flick on and he could see the tiny glimmers slowly moving towards one another to form a small cluster. Doc rolled over several times and banged into the crew chief as the Chinook banked hard to port and circled back to the infil point.

At the same time, down at sea level, Quinn quickly took charge and issued orders.

"Activate your strobes and form up! Sound off for head count!" All were present and fortunately, two of the team members had located their unconscious lieutenant fairly quickly, activated his shoulder mounted strobe light and partially inflated his UDT vest as they swam him over to the small cluster of bodies slowly bobbing in the eight to ten foot swells.

"How's he look?" Quinn inquired. While holding on to the shoulder straps of the L.T.'s swim vest both men answered with one word.

"Fucked!" Quinn noticed blood trickling from the L.T.'s nose.

Back up in the bird Doc's wheels were spinning at full speed. If the course had impressed one thing on him, aside from the inherent dangers of realistic training, it was that the sea was an unforgiving bitch.

As the helo dropped in altitude Doc changed into his fins and donned his mask.

"You got a Jacob's ladder on board right?" He shouted at the Crew Chief.

"Yeah!" He pointed up at the tightly rolled up and stowed, 65 foot long, cable and aluminium

198

Jacob's ladder. "Why?" The crew chief yelled back.

"How long to get it rigged up?"

"About fifteen minutes give or take. But it takes two men." Meanwhile Fisk had made his way down to the rear of the chopper.

"Where the hell you goin' Petty Officer?!"

"For a swim, sir."

"The fuck you are son-" Doc raised a hand and cut him off.

"Sorry sir. With you in a minute." The short tempered Army captain began to seethe but remembering he was in Navy country and picturing typewritten reports of how one of his junior officers getting seriously injured on a routine training op might look, he wasn't sure how far to push it.

With the swim team's strobes on, their faint outlines were now in sight, about 100 yards out. "Tell the pilot to hold here!" McKeowen instructed the crew chief. The bird slowed to a hover and, looking over the ramp, now about fifty meters out, they could see Quinn's team floating and slowly bobbing in a lopsided circle. The crew chief relayed the order and the helo stopped moving about a hundred feet off the deck.

"You said two men to rig the Jacob's?" Doc asked.

"Yeah." Chief shouted back. Doc leaned in so as to be out of ear shot of the captain.

"Think you can manage with one man and an officer?" Doc nodded at Fisk.

"If that's all we got, guess we got no choice." The crew chief smirked and shrugged.

"Good now lower the ramp to just below level,

get your pilot to hold as close to the deck as possible and keep the rotor wash away from the team. If that L.T. is unconscious and on his own you'll drown him, got it?"

"Roger that."

"Are you on the same freq as the team radios?"

"Yeah!"

"Good! Give me a thumbs up when we're at a hover. As soon as I'm away, rig the ladder and stand by. We'll relay instructions as soon as I assess the L.T.'s condition. Green?" The crew chief gave the thumbs up. Doc turned to the captain and slung his med bag over his shoulder.

"Sorry captain, you can court martial me later sir."

"Asshole!" The officer mumbled to himself.

Doc sat on the edge of the ramp, struggled to see the undulating ocean through the dark and held his breath.

$269 a month! I must really like this shit.

He grabbed his balls and pushed out and away from the ramp.

Due to the sea's constant movement most aircraft altimeters are only accurate to 10 feet or more when over the ocean. Compounded by the pitch black of the night and darkness of the sea it's impossible to get an accurate determination of your altitude.

The fall felt inordinately long however he didn't hit quite as hard as he thought he would but he did lose his mask on impact and cursed himself for not having held it in his hand as he had seen the SEAL trainees do on cast and recovery exercises.

It was only minutes later until Doc was able to swim up to the assembled team.

"The fucking bird flared too early! The L.T. wasn't clear of the hole!" Doc reported to Quinn.

"I saw. He must've been nearly three times normal height when he launched! Fuckin' reserve pukes!" Quinn cursed.

"You got com with the bird?" Doc asked.

"With the captain, yeah!"

Doc, partially inflating his vest to avoid having to tread water as they bobbed up and down with the waves, was already examining the L.T. He was out cold, appeared to have a concussion and was bleeding from the ears and nose. Some mild respiratory difficulty indicated possible broken ribs but probably no or little internal damage, most likely just bruising. But, seeing the red pool in the water surrounding the L.T.'s legs, he quickly cut away the trousers and found the real problem.

On impact the officer had sustained a double compound fracture of both legs. The right tibia and fibula protruded through the skin just above the ankle, while the left tib-fib had torn through the skin in front of and just below the knee.

This poor bastard's time in Spec Ops is finished. McKeowen mused to himself as he worked. *On the up side, he's probably got a disability check coming for the rest of his life!*

Doc continued to speak to Quinn as he worked. "They're gonna rig and lower the J-Ladder."

"We'll never get back up the ladder with the L.T. out!"

"Don't need to. You guys can make it into shore no problem. If the bird can drag us up to the surf zone you and I can get him through the zone and onto the beach. Radio the bird to have an ambulance standing by south of the jetty on Yellow Beach Two. The bird can hover us in and relay our position if we drift so the beach unit can adjust."

"Sounds good." Quinn responded.

"This cold water will help slow the hemorrhaging but he's defiantly on the clock! First we gotta do something with that bleeding, otherwise we're fucking shark bait. Anybody got any shark repellent on their vests?" Two of the men did. "Soon as we get his bleeding under control pop your canisters, one on each side."

Doc unstrapped his own UDT vest, removed it and, after tying the patient's legs together, strapped the vest around the calves and inflated it a little more.

While treading water he dug through his med bag and retrieved several four inch gauze bandages and two bulky compresses and some Gelfoam.

Enlisting help, as Quinn and another soldier held the unconscious L.T. stable, he handed the bandage rolls off to one team member, the compresses to another but packed the Gelfoam, which absorbed some sea water but still helped, into the wounds himself.

Relieved that the bleeding appeared to be halted, he then paddled back around to the head and began to monitor the vitals while instructing the team members, who were all trained in basic first aid, in how to wrap the legs and splint them to one another using bandaging as ties.

Meanwhile Quinn had established commo with the helo, explained the situation and was directing the Crew Chief in manoeuvring the lowered ladder slowly over to their position.

Once over the team's location, Quinn directed the other team members to take the flanks to swim in while he and Doc each hooked an arm through the bottom rung of the J-Ladder, grabbed a shoulder strap each on the L.T.'s swim vest and let the chopper gently tow them in. As they skimmed half under half over the water McKeowen instructed the Team Sergeant.

"Sergeant Quinn, tell the helo to let the dispensary know to have an O.R. ready. Tell them to relay 'double compound fractures both legs, EBL one pint plus-"

"His blood type's O Pos." Quinn called over to Doc who was visibly impressed that Quinn was right there with the info. "A good Team Sergeant knows all his team member's blood types. Fucking corpsman taught me that." Quinn called over.

"Fuckin' corpsman!" Doc smiled as they gently cut through the night sea.

It was a good twenty to twenty five minutes until they reached the outer border of the surf zone and were able to see the flashing red lights of the ambulance on the beach where it was a simple matter to let go of the ladder and float in on the surf where they rendezvoused with the awaiting ambulance.

Ten minutes later the unfortunate young lieutenant was across the strand, had been gassed and was under the knife in his first steps to a very long recovery.

***

Doc's two day pass turned out to be a sleep in on Thursday and a priority meeting in Captain Coats' office on Friday morning. Lieutenant Stratford sat on the side lines as McKeowen stood in front of the C.O.'s desk once again.

"The surgeon who let you scrub in said you had your shit together." Coats stated and asked at the same time.

"Thank you sir. I was a bit lucky, but I damn sure have an increased respect for the dangers of training."

"The surgeon's a light colonel. He thinks you deserve an att'a boy." The captain added. Doc shrugged. "False modesty Doc?"

"No sir, just ..."

"Just ...?"

"Nothing sir. I appreciate you passing that on. Is that why I'm here Sir?" An uncomfortable feeling ran through McKeowen as Coats did something he rarely did. He smiled.

"Stand at ease Doc, have a seat."

Shit, 'have a seat', this must really be bad. Mac thought to himself.

"Thank you sir." McKeowen took a seat opposite Stratford at an angle to Coats' desk.

"Let me ask you a question ..."

"Nine inches fully hard, sir."

"Bad jokes aside, how do you feel about heights?"

"Me?! Why?"

"Because in the entire Corps you're the closest thing we have to a Force Recon qualified Hospital Corpsman."

"Jesus!" Doc fell back in his seat.

"You didn't know that Doc?" Stratford asked.

"No, no. I was just thinkin' sir. If I'm the best you've got, the Corps must be in some deep shit!"

"No doubt we are." Stratford interrupted, "Particularly now with the Reds shooting down civilian airliners and the bru-ha-ha over missiles in Germany, but our immediate concern is getting you up to qual so the Navy can see squids are able to come through here and come out the other end in one piece." Coats looked over at Stratford and shook his head.

"What the lieutenant is trying to express in his own down home, rustic style is ..."

"I get the idea Captain. It's not his fault. Personally, I blame the parents. Lack of a father figure and all."

"Be that as it may, a billet has opened up at Camp LeJeune at Second Force Recon and they hold a permanent slot at Fort Benning for each jump class going through. How would you like to go jump out of airplanes?"

"I think I would like that very much sir, so long as the birds aren't being flown by reservists."

"That's fair enough." Coats and Stratford smiled

as they exchanged glances. Doc picked up on it.

"Sirs, with all due respect, you two look like the cats that ate the canary. And how come I feel like I'm covered in yellow feathers all of sudden?" The two officers smiled out right.

"You drink Doc?"

"Sometimes, but not usually at 09:30." Doc became more suspicious as Coats reached into his desk drawer and removed an official looking piece of paper and handed it to McKeowen.

"Bad news Doc. Looks like you're not gonna be around for graduation." Coats informed him. McKeowen was flabbergasted and sat bolt upright.

"Sir! I swear to god I didn't give that fucking captain any shit! He was primed and cocked before he even ..."

"Relax Doc. Read the paper." The L.T. suggested.

The 'paper' contained official orders. Orders to the teams in Force Recon, 2nd Recon Battalion, 2nd Marine Division, Camp LeJeune, N.C. with orders to Jump School at Fort Benning in route. Doc went from flabbergasted to excited, confused then back to even more excited.

"L.T., what's this mean? Exactly."

"It means, you've already got your scuba bubble, as of today you are Force Recon qualified so, as long as you don't fuck up at Benning, you'll have all the boxes checked to be a real live operator. I talked to the C.O. and he's gonna have orders cut and sent to D.C. to get your 0321 MOS designator into your record."

"By the time it gets all the signatures and rubber

stamps on it you'll be outt'a jump school and over at LeJeune." Stratford added.

"This means a lot L.T. Seriously."

"The door." Captain Coats nodded to the Lieutenant who pushed the door closed as Coats produced three paper cups and a bottle of Glen Levitt from his desk. "Sorry you won't be around for the graduation next week Doc."

"Not me sir. Now I can get drunk tonight."

"By the way, I also got this yesterday morning by Twix from Fort Bragg." Coats passed Doc a copy of a Twix message. It was a recommendation that McKeowen be put in for a medal of commendation.

Signed by Captain Fisk, U.S. Army Special Forces.

"Shit! I guess not all officers are dicks!" Doc's eyes shot up from the Twix to Coats then Stratford.

"I mean Army officers! I meant to say 'Army' officers. Sirs."

"Don't break anything at jump school Doc!" Coats said as he lifted his cup by way of a toast.

"Or do." The Lieutenant raised his cup.

**

207

CHAPTER NINE

09:22, EST, September 4th
Joint Chiefs of Staff
Conference Room
The Pentagon

If you passed him on the street, dressed in civilian clothes you'd mistake him for the friendly guy down the road who you see every Sunday on his way to buy the newspaper, or think maybe he was the local school teacher. The reality was very different.

At sixty-one years of age, a ramrod posture and sporting a greying head of close-cropped hair, General John William Vessey, Jr., was not only the last WWII combat veteran still serving on active duty as well as the longest serving member of the U.S. Army, he was also the tenth Chairman of the Joint Chiefs Staff.

Vessey began his long and distinguished career as an enlisted man working his way from private all the way up through the enlisted ranks and receiving a battlefield commission during the slaughter of the landings at Anzio, Italy in 1943.

Later, during the Korean War, he served in various infantry divisions while gaining his bachelor's and master's degrees in Political Science.

While serving in Viet Nam, at a firebase behind enemy lines, he and his small force were decorated for having fought off thousands of Viet Cong in a frontal assault, killing over four hundred of them and wounding hundreds of others.

Prior to the Marines deployment to Beirut, as part of an international peacekeeping force, Vessey had warned the administration not to send Marines to Lebanon as part of the police keeping force. The Marines were sent and just weeks later, 241 Marines were killed when a truck bomb was driven into the headquarters building.

The president recalled the Marines.

More recently, the magnitude of the Grenada situation was brought home when Reagan not only received near world-wide condemnation for the incursion, seen largely as an action to offset the damage America suffered by the bombing of the Marine barracks in Beirut, but Ted Weiss, a Democrat, introduced a bill to impeach the President for the controversial invasion.

Throughout the shit storm that ensued, General Vessey maintained a firm and decisive hold on the reins of military leadership.

In short, John Vessey was by no means a short sighted, desk jockey of a 'paper general'.

Now that things were heating up again Ronnie, as well as most of the big dogs on The Hill, were more than happy to have someone of Vessey's proven caliber at the helm of the military.

Reagan felt compelled to cut his three week working trip out at Rancho del Cielo short and had radioed ahead from Air Force One on his way back to Washington that the JCS were to be convened to address what was being played up as the Soviet's latest incursion in a string of international human rights violations.

The long rectangular table sat perpendicular to the long axis of the windowless room and all the seats save one, the one at the head of the table, were occupied. A moment later General Vessey's command presence emanated through the room as he entered.

"Lights please. Map." Not bothering to take his seat, he moved straight to the wall-sized screen which had already been lowered. He activated his laser pointer as the armed Military Police sentries backed out into the corridor and pulled the doors closed behind him and assumed guard.

The collection of the highest ranking men in the Free World were extra attentive.

"Good morning gentlemen. At the President's request and in accordance with formulating a suitable response to the Korean Airlines incident, I've been authorized to bring you up to speed on some developments we think relevant.

As you will learn, you were not briefed earlier on the details I'm about to divulge as it was deemed more politically prudent not do so." Every man in the room interpreted the phrase, 'you were not briefed earlier' in the same exact manner. It meant 'kept in the dark.'

"What you're about to be briefed on has been 'Eyes Only' for O-10 levels and above since its inception six months ago. Other details are known only to a very small handful of people, only one of which is a civilian." A wall sized map came into focus and illuminated nearly the entire wall behind General Vessey.

"To further emphasize the nature of what I'm

about to present to you, there is no paper trail. Anywhere. It's been referred to, and will continue to be referred to simply as, 'The Game'."

"Is there an outline, guidelines, anything General Vessey?"

"Nothing. NO paperwork. And there is to be none until further notice. Which will not be forthcoming." The slide changed to a view of the Atlantic with the Eastern Seaboard of the U.S. on the left of the screen and the European mainland on the right. Greenland and Iceland were top center.

"What you're looking at is obviously something we've been concerned with since the end of WWII. A topical of the Greenland/Iceland-United Kingdom corridor, alias the GIUK Gap." As you know since the mid 60's the Soviets have been running this gap utilizing Bear bombers with fighter escorts. We would divert or launch interceptors, the Soviets would keep to their outer markers until they knew we were there and then slip back up deeper into their own territory. None of this is news to you."

"What's our best guess as to why they would risk retaliation for something like that? I mean why do it?" It was Gen. Paul X. Kelley who was about to take over as Commandant of the Marine Corps.

"Because they can." Vessey answered. "The fact that they make these flights in predictable patterns flying at 20,000 to 27,000 feet at slow cruising speeds indicates to us that they want us to know they're there. They're testing us."

Again the slide changed as Vessey moved to the other side of the screen.

"Then we started The Game. In the beginning all

we'd do was send bombers over the North Pole to get their radar installs to kick on. Next time we'd send fighter-bombers to probe their Asian or European peripheries. At peak times, the operation would include several maneuvers a week. We'd send them at irregular intervals to make the effect all the more unsettling. Then, as quickly as the flights began, they'd stop, only to begin again a few weeks later."

"Kind'a like poking a stick at a dog through a fence!" Someone commented.

"Except with a dog reactions are predictable." Vessey responded. "The aim of The Game was twofold. To probe for weaknesses in their defenses and to test their reaction times and methodologies."

"To what end General? We have most of that data and over the last six to eight years nothing seems to have changed much. I mean, who made the decision to play this provocative and dangerous game?!"

Vessey could sense slight resentment in the Army general's tone, probably from being 'kept in the dark'. The Chairman rightly guessed it could be infectious.

"The man who sold our most valuable codes to the enemy. John J. Walker made that decision for us." There was considerable shifting of positions as the name rang home once again, this time with a more profound significance. "Now that they have our codes things have been happening. In short, we feel the balance of power may be shifting."

Slightly rebuffed by the idea the Soviets could be ahead of the good guys, it was General H. Robert

Barrow, current Commandant of the Marine Corps who posed a question.

"Do our intel services have any hard evidence of that Chief? I mean that the Reds are ahead?"

"As a matter of fact—"

"General, if I may?" Vessey was cut off in his response by Admiral James D. Watkins, current Chief of Naval Operations who stood as he interrupted the Chief of Staff. Vessey extended his arm in gesture for the Admiral to field the question.

"General Barrow, among other things, the noticeable decrease in Soviet submarine detection is taken as a clear indication that when the Soviets turned our man and were sold the intelligence they were, they were able to apply it to improve their stealth capabilities. It wasn't due to decreased activity that we weren't able to detect them, as we believed. We couldn't find them because they found a way to defeat the cavitation principles our SOSUS systems were based on."

SOSUS or Sound Surveillance Systems were a multi-billion dollar, under sea hydrophone system to track surface and sub-surface sea traffic around the globe. The SOSUS system was one of the secrets sold to the Soviets by the Walker spy ring.

"We know the subs were there thanks to cross references in our HUMINT networks," Admiral Watkins continued.

General Barrow nodded in understanding. "That being the case, we have to assume there are other intel advances we don't yet know about." The Admiral nodded back at Vessey and retook his seat.

"Thank you Admiral." Vessey resumed his

briefing. He nodded and the slide changed again, this time to a view of the Pacific detailing the western U.S. and the Kamchatka Peninsula off the Russian East coast.

"This is a one to one hundred thousand satellite photo of area where the Korean airliner incident occurred. After about a five hour, cross country flight east to west, KAL 007 refuelled and took off from Anchorage to continue south by south east. Slide please."

The same view of the pacific coasts of Russia and the U.S. came up again but with two red route lines from Alaska to points south. "The dotted red line indicates the planned route of the KAL aircraft, that is the flight plan they filed with the NYC ATC, while the solid red line traces the known route from Anchorage to an estimated crash point just below Sakhalin Island."

"The relationship is that this area between the Soviet Union's perceived airspace and our outer Pacific marker is essentially their GIUK corridor and we don't think the fact that they casually took out a civilian aircraft with almost 300 civilian men, women and children onboard, in this area, was a coincidence, much less an accident. Lights please." Vessey switched off his laser pointer and slipped it into his pocket as the projector went off and the lights came up.

"Now we have orders in the next evolution of our ongoing strategy-"

"Which is?"

"Which is to step things up. The CIA and the NSA think that Ivan is up to something and the

President wants to know what it is. Admiral?"
Again Watkins stood and took the floor.

"Our guys at ONI need more info on how the
Reds have adjusted their protocol and procedures
since the FBI nailed Walker and we had to rejig our
codes. We think there have been some significant
alterations in Soviet Intel protocol."

"Significant Admiral?"

"Game changing, General."

"So we're gonna see if we can nudge them a little
harder and see if they kick?" General Barrow
queried.

"Exactly. The boys over at Air Force Surface
Intel think if we can get them to turn all the toys on
at the same time, or at least most of them, ONI can
discern patterns and techniques which will help
them update their intel in the way the Reds have
reconfigured. This may in turn yield some clues as
to how much of our mail they were given."

"Jesus Jim! Are we still in the dark about how
much he sold them?"

"The short answer is yes, we don't know. He's
not talking." More than one member shifted in his
chair. "He thinks we're gonna offer him deal to play
both sides of the fence."

"Fucking guy's delusional!" Barrow's
commented. The Admiral continued.

"On the up side, FBI Director Webster thinks
they have an angle. His kid. Walker doesn't know
the FBI have him. They're gonna leverage him and
see what they can get out of him."

"Do we think the Reds are gearing up to launch
an operation?"

"That's exactly what we need to determine. Back in August a joint Allied exercise comprised of over 80 U.S., Canadian and Norwegian ships, headed up by the U.S.S. Eisenhower, managed not only to breach that gap undetected by Soviet radar and air surveillance, but were able to encroach to well within missile and aircraft striking distance."

"Sir, are we to understand that these extremely dangerous and provocative missions are still to continue just to see if 'Ivan will kick' so to speak?!"

"It is more imperative now, more than ever, that these psychological exercises, although in different format from the original PSYOPS exercises, continue." Vessey interjected.

"Especially in light of the shooting down of the Korean airliner!" The Admiral added.

"General Vessey, sir, if I may raise a question?"

"Yes General Gabriel?"

"Is it true we actually had a surveillance aircraft in the area at the time of the shoot down?"

"Yes. And if our intel is correct the two aircraft may have actually crossed flight paths just before the Soviets launched their fighters."

There was not a man in the room who at some point in his career hadn't been closely affiliated with or worked directly for ONI, CIA or the No Such Agency, ergo the reality of the possibility of a bait and switch scenario by one of these agencies was lost on no one.

"How soon before?" General Gabriel probed.

"It's difficult to say exactly how long before but as near as we can figure it ... about seven minutes before." Vessey replied as he carefully monitored their reactions. "Gentlemen, there was a U.S. Air Force RC-135 surveillance plane in the vicinity, but we have no indication at this time that there is any possibility the Soviets picked up on the 135 then mistook the Korean passenger plane for the spy plane. The decision we are faced with now is how to brief this and our intended plan to the President and the Secretaries of the Cabinet –"

"Or whether or not to brief them on it at all!" General Gabriel added.

"We can't just NOT tell them!" Barrow protested.

"No but we can be selective about the information we DO tell them."

"What the hell's that supposed to mean?"

"It means there's no reason they have to know there was actually a 135 in the area at the same time." Gabriel insisted.

"Plausible deniability is supposed to relate to the president." Vessey reminded them.

"I don't believe I've ever seen that written down anywhere gentlemen." Watkins said. "It's an air route we've used before and have slated to be used again in the future. Isn't that right General Allen?" Allen, the Air Force Chief of Staff drummed the fingers of his left hand on the table top and looked down before he answered.

"It is now. I guess." No one spoke for the better part of a full minute. The decision had been made. Vessey, cleared his throat before he spoke for the last time that morning.

"Gentlemen, more has been fucked up on the battlefield and misunderstood in the Pentagon

217

because of a lack of understanding of the English language than due to any other factor! So I'll be perfectly clear regarding where I stand on this situation. My strategy has always been one of preventing war by making it self-evident to our enemies that they're going to get their clocks cleaned if they start one!" He perused the group again gauging their reactions. "To that end, as of zero nine hundred tomorrow morning, for the first time since The Korean Conflict, I'm advising the President that we should move to DEFCON 3!"

Save for General Vessey, what the JCS didn't know was that Reagan not only knew about the KC-135, but was being updated on the Top Secret incursions in a private brief aboard Air Force One even as the JCS were meeting.

In fact, save for General Vessey himself, Reagan had been ahead of the JCS from the day after he took office when the scheme of limited incursions was first hatched.

That there was always the outside chance that a civilian airliner would stray across the path of a military intel aircraft, especially in light of the fact that the intel plane's flight plan would be highly classified, was also a subject of great debate when Schultz first approached Reagan with details of the plan eleven months ago.

The final decision by Reagan, Schultz, Vessey and their advisors was that the odds were near impossible that such a thing would ever happen. And if it did, no reasonable nation would destroy a passenger airliner loaded with vacationing civilians.

At least that's how it looked on paper.

*

'Legs' are the U.S. Army's version of what the U.S. Navy Spec Ops guys call 'Black Shoes', non-Special Operations qualified personnel. For legs, more precisely non-Airborne qualified people, Jump School can hold a special intimidation.

Long days, early morning runs in combat boots, regardless of weather, seemingly non-stop calisthenics, which are also administered at the least little provocation, endless inspections and a special feature seemingly unique to the U.S. Army, an endless supply of meager portions of really bad chow.

For a Special operations sailor, Marine or soldier, who was at the end of his Special Operations training, Jump School was a four week holiday with refreshing morning runs limited to five miles, very few calisthenics by comparison, pointless inspections, and chow was never an issue. The food at Fort Benning was so bad that most Spec Ops guys refuse to eat it and opted to wait until the day was over and eat off post.

At the moment Petty Officer 2nd Class 'Doc' McKeowen, now nearing the end of his three week stay at Fort Benning, Georgia, was standing his last company inspection following the five mile morning run.

While most of the airborne candidates spent three to four hours an evening spit shinning boots and starching their inspection uniforms,

McKeowen, like all the Navy and other Marine Spec Ops candidates before him, simply purchased an extra set of camouflage blouse and trousers and a second pair of boots, then spent the 10 extra bucks a week to have the family of locals just outside the post gate spit shine and starch their uniforms each day. Thus their evenings could be more productively spent drinking and cruising the bars for local talent. Talent of the female that is.

Charlie Company's Head Instructor, Sergeant First Class Dillon, a career soldier and former Ranger who stood five foot seven and nearly as wide at the shoulder was a man Doc had come to respect as much for his professionalism as his unexplained tolerance of McKeowen's unprecedented pranks. Although Doc's pranks sometimes earned Charlie Company group punishment, much to the aggravation of the officers in the company, McKeowen reasoned the instructors had 12 hours a day to fuck with the students, which the instructors took full advantage of. Consequently showing a little spirit, by pushing back a bit, was more than warranted.

As for the complaints of the student officers training with Charlie company, his reasoning was simple: "Fuck 'em!" Of the ten officers in the company only two would ever see a jump slot, the rest wanted a pair of jump wings to decorate their pretty uniforms and milk the prestige jump wings garnered to get points to make rank. Essentially, after jump school, they would never jump again, worse yet they were robbing slots from real soldiers, troops who wanted to jump out of airplanes and serve in airborne units.

His opinion was more than reinforced when at the graduation ceremony all but one of the officers refused 'Blood Wings', the practice of awarding the student his wings by removing the stay buttons on the back of the wings before pinning them to his chest, directly into the pec muscle. Sometimes with a follow on punch just to make sure the wings were firmly embedded and wouldn't fall out.

The military constantly taught that attention to detail saved lives so one of Dillon's favorite fuck-fuck techniques was to spot a group of students crossing an open area and feign yelling the last of the five point procedures required when exiting the aircraft, "Check canopy!"

This was accomplished by keeping your legs together, running your hands up the riser straps of your chute harness and visually inspecting that all of the panels on your canopy were intact, as on older chutes a panel would occasionally blow out on deployment which in turn affected steering of the chute.

Dillon had fun with this by sometimes yelling, "Check Annie's knees!" or "Check can of peas!" or other assorted variations of the order. Anyone who moved to check canopy obviously hadn't paid attention to what he said and was thus subject to punishment.

That morning as SFC Dillon meticulously worked his way down the rank of immaculately groomed and polished soldiers, standing the big company inspection prior to their last jump and graduation on the drop zone in front of friends and relatives, he was being particularly fastidious.

In fine Spec Ops tradition Doc had prepared his latest caper.

Probably, as a little entertainment for the crowd which had gathered off to the side of the landing zone to watch the jump Dillon, as he reached the end of the front rank, yelled what Doc had been waiting for every single day for the last week and a half.

"CHECK CAN OF PEAS!" There was tension due to the inspection, last jump graduation etc ... so most of the company were faked out and mimicked going through a canopy check.

Additionally, espirit de corps dictated that when your fellow company members were undergoing punishment you joined them. So, as the entire company, save a few of the officers, dropped to do the mandatory 20 push-ups to pay for their mistake, Doc remained at attention, reached into his left cargo pocket and produced a can of peas. As everyone else was on the ground counting out push-ups, he held the can high, then promptly and loudly sounded off.

"SERGEANT! PEAS, GREEN GIANT, BABY, LE SEUR, TYPE ONE EACH! ALL INTACT, SERGEANT!"

The crowd were confused, Charlie Company alternately moaned and giggled and Dillon, possibly for the first time in his life as an instructor was flabbergasted. But McKeowen also noted the fact that Dillon had to fight back a smirk.

Doc did push-ups that day on the air field until the aircraft was ready to load, Dillon instructed the

Jump Master to make him do push-ups on the deck of C-130 until they reached altitude, hooked up and jumped, and Dillon sought him out on the DZ to make sure right after Doc had gathered and secured his jump gear, he resumed doing push-ups at the turn-in point.

A short time later, while back in the ranks they both smiled as SFC Dillon pushed another instructor aside to enjoy the privilege of issuing Doc his blood wings.

There was an extra punch in the chest to be sure the pins embedded properly.

**

There were no shortage of local parties in and around Benning the night of Jump School graduation and although the U.S. military didn't want to waste any money on keeping people around any longer than necessary, they did have the good taste to allow for the swollen heads the following day and so the new grads at least had a bed for one more night.

The following morning was Saturday and as he was only travelling a short distance north up the coast, Doc McKeowen was given until Monday to report aboard up at Camp LeJeune.

It was just after 10:00 when he reported to the Benning school admin to check out of the post and receive his orders to his next duty station.

In the admin office he approached the cutest of several young female secretaries sitting at one of the

223

four long lines of desks. As she typed away on her big bulky, government issue typewriter he approached, gave his best smile and looked down at the phone on her desk.

"Excuse me, is there a landline I can use?"

"You can use this one. Is it off post?"

"Yeah, Coronado."

"Is that in North Carolina?"

"No miss. California."

"Oh! I'm sorry, students aren't allowed personal calls from Army lines."

"This isn't personal. I'm in the Navy. I'm calling the Marine Headquarters at the Naval amphib base at Coronado, California. It's the Special Operations base."

"OH! Ya'll's a SEAL?"

"No ma'am. Recon. Marine Force Recon."

"Wait! You're in the Navy ..."

Doc quietly began to count to himself. Slowly. *One. Two. Three ...*

"But you're blah... blah... blah! But you wear ..." *Nine... Ten... Eleven...*

With her chin in one hand, elbow on her desk she stared up at him, glassed over eyes and gaping mouth poised to catch any errant flies that might mistakenly flutter by.

"Yes. That's exactly right, miss. I'm in the Navy but serving with the Marines."

"Just dial '9' to get out."

"Thank ya'll kindly, ma'am."

The phone rang straight through to the amphib base and the operator connected him to the Recon school. Lieutenant Stratford picked up.

224

"L.T. Doc McKeowen here!"

Doc! Got your lead sled do ya?! Stratford asked using the derogatory Navy term for Army jump wings as opposed to the gold wings issued by the Navy.

"Yeah, yeah I do sir. It was a fucking blast here. I mean it ain't Coronado, but ... Just need you guys to know ... aw you know."

Yeah, I know, Recon's the greatest thing that ever happened to you, it's changed your life etc ... etc ... etc. Ya ball-less bastard! Can't even say thank you!

"You want a thank you L.T.? Get my ass back there as soon as my tour in the teams is up. Meanwhile you'll just have to deal with black shoe corpsmen!"

EEERRR! Wrong answer Doc. The umbilical cord has officially been cut. While you were on vacation at Benning the D.O.D. authorized us one new slot for each class from now on. For a squid! Looks like we're gonna have us a permanent corpsman slot.

"Shit L.T.! That's good news, I guess."

Also found out the teams, as always, are short. Three new operating teams have been authorised to come on line by the end of the year.

"Well, at least we got work for the next few years! Guess I'm off to catch up with 2nd Force."

Word has it they're cookin' something up for the Spooks in D.C. to track down the scumbags that blew up the barracks in Beirut. With any luck you'll get in on the action.

"Fingers crossed. Give my best to the Captain,

sir. Any luck we'll cross paths again. See ya when I see ya L.T.

Not if I see you first Doc. Keep your powder dry Doc! Out.

****

CHAPTER TEN

10:12, EDT, September 5th
The Oval Office
White House

The television was on in the Oval Office and there was standing room only. It was as if Leonardo Da Vinci came back from the dead and reposed *The Last Supper* using U.S. heads of state for the apostles.

The president sat at his oversized desk while in front and to Ronald Reagan's right was Secretary of State George Schultz, alias "The Sphinx" due to his balding head and constant lack of expression. He sat next to William Casey, Director of the Central Intelligence Agency who sat on the couch across from Lt. General L. D. Faurer USAF, Director of the NSA. As was to be expected, the Inner Sanctum was also decked out with the usual collection of high ranking entourage.

Virtually every U.S. television station, as well as most of those in the civilized world, was tuned to a press conference which had been set up by the Soviet embassy and was being broadcast live from the United Nations General Assembly Hall.

Dressed in full military regalia Marshal Nikolai Ogarkov of the Soviet Air Ministry had been talking, largely through a translator, for the better part of an hour and a half. His charts, graphs and photos mounted on multiple artists' easels behind him occupied the entire presentation area.

Finishing, he laid his pointer on the table before him and faced the full to capacity amphitheater, cleared his throat and spoke in a controlled voice in heavily accented yet discernible English into the microphone which had been provided for him.

"Additionally, the regional air defense unit had identified the aircraft as a U.S. intelligence platform, most likely an RC-135 of the type that is known to routinely perform intelligence operations along a similar fight path." The rumblings began.

"In any event, regardless of whether it was an RC-135 or a Boeing 747, the plane was unquestionably on a U.S. or joint U.S.-Japanese intelligence mission, and the local air defense Lieutenant made the correct decision. Two hundred and sixty-nine lives of innocent victims notwithstanding, I submit that the Soviet Union acted rationally."

Needless to say, to the majority of observers gathered at the conference, some of whom actually came believing they were going to hear an apology, this went over like a lead balloon. "The real blame for this tragedy lay with the United States, not the USSR!" Ogarkov firmly asserted.

Questions from the floor, as had been agreed upon, were next and started at first in a controlled manner but quickly deteriorated to the point of barley controlled chaos until Ogarkov was compelled to terminate the conference by leaving the floor.

The television picture then switched live to Seoul Airport where dozens of hysterically grieving relatives were strewn about the floor of the waiting room wailing uncontrollably. One old woman pounded her temples in disbelief. A reporter with a big mike came into view. Reagan reached across his desk for the bulky remote and shut down the TV.

"Well, in view of that little show and tell, I firmly believe that we need to institute an active if not aggressive, campaign in the United Nations to spur worldwide efforts to punish the Soviets through any means possible!" Reagan blurted out. "Comments?" The President threw out.

Faurer of the NSA took up the baton.

"Ogarkov's so called press conference is a cover up from beginning to end! By no stretch of the imagination was that a spy plane! I would advocate commercial boycotts, lawsuits, and if possible, denial of landing rights in our territories for Aeroflot!"

"There can be no doubt that all efforts must be focused on indicting the top leadership as being ultimately responsible for this, however they spin it!" Spat Faurer.

"If he doesn't condemn this action Andropov has lost what little marbles he has!" Bud McFarlane, special advisor to the president, commented.

"Bill?" Reagan asked. In lieu of an answer Casey stepped over to Reagan's desk leaned in and whispered into his ear. Reagan reached for his intercom and called out to his secretary.

"Geraldene, where's Marine One?"

The duty officer has it on standby sir.

"Tell him we need it around front in ten minutes, we're going over to Virginia. And have the kitchen rustle up some coffee and sandwiches for the ride over."

"Yes Mr. President."

"And pass the word to the gates, no press! Tell them they'll be something shortly."

Yes sir. The connection clicked off but almost immediately clicked back on again. *Mr. President?*

"Yes?"

I'm sorry sir, but the press seems to have gotten word and are gathered out on the South lawn. The Marine Guards are herding them back to clear landing space for Marine One. Do you want me to send word to have them escorted out?

Reagan quickly glanced at Schultz who shook his head to indicate 'no'.

"No Geraldene. We're in a hurry so I guess we'll run the gauntlet and take our chances."

Yes sir. Good luck sir.

"Thank you Geraldene." Reagan sat back in his high back black leather chair, his wavy pompadour covering the presidential seal on the head rest. He addressed the group. "Bill Casey has arranged for us to be briefed by some of the folks over at Langley so I want everybody to meet over there for a strategy meeting in one hour. I want all the department heads who were involved in the tracking, monitoring and any intel on this incident on standby for information." As he spoke Bill Casey and General Faurer lifted and reset the couch which had been turned to face the television.

"I'm going to arrange an emergency press conference for immediately after the meeting at Langley. George, I'd like you to take that conference."

"Yes Mr. President."

"Grab a couple of staff writers if need and start crafting something while I'm over at Langley. Aggressive, condemnation but no details about where we are or what we have on this. I don't want to give any indications about what we're going to do, at least not yet. They'll defiantly hear from me later." Reagan directed.

"I understand." Schultz answered as he scribbled some notes.

"Bill, General Faurer, will you ride over with me in Marine One please? No aides."

Once outside they made it across the South lawn and past the barrage of reporters being held back by the White House Marine contingent, into the VH-3 Sea King and in minuets were on their way.

As the rotors loudly whined to full and they gently lifted off Reagan began to rehearse words in his head, words he would use for the inevitable speech he would make at the U.N., on the very spot where the Soviet Air Ministry General stood less than an hour ago.

"... an act of barbarism, ... born of a society which disregards individual rights ... the value of human life and seeks constantly ... to dominate other nations!"

Reagan stared out the window of the impeccably polished helicopter as it slowly rose above White House level and rotated back to the south. With the South Portico now growing smaller in the distance he heard a voice, deep in his head.

Is this where it starts?

****

McKeowen felt the invigorating, crisp mountain air as he rode shotgun in the jeep which wound its way through the heavily forested terrain. He took in the deep green forests and rolling hills of Camp LeJeune, North Carolina which struck him as the polar opposite of the sea air, wide open spaces and deep blue turquoise of the California Pacific.

The old growth pine forest was not the ocean environment he had come to love and felt completely at home in, but was no less a universe away from the slums, sewers and constant racial violence of the city.

As on all U.S. posts and bases, as in most foreign militaries as well, the Special Operations team houses and administration areas are located away from the rest of the base and such was the case for the 2nd Force Recon Marines at LeJeune. Isolation from legs and black shoes was not only desirable due to avoiding contact with the less disciplined, slovenly units, but as of late had come into good use to avoid the new breed of Politically Correct officers who sought to make advancement by reporting 'violations' such as not having sleeves rolled up correctly, posting Playboy centerfolds in your private locker or most black shoe officer's favorite feature to attack, the use of profanity during a run while calling cadence.

These of course were the same officers whose misplaced attention to detail would get their people lost, injured or worse in the real world. Avoidance of this mentality, universally labeled as "Mickey Mouse bullshit", was a primary motivation for signing up in Special Operations and willingly suffering the endless physical and mental stress required to get through qualification.

Doc was driven from the main gate to a small group of buildings situated well back in the wooded area of the camp and dropped off at the headquarters building, a WWII .wooden structure not much more sophisticated than the Recon school Quonset hut in Coronado.

"Well McKeowen, what have you been doing for the last few months?" The Major behind the desk in the team room asked as Doc dropped his gear and handed in his orders.

"Pretty much non-stop reporting aboard duty stations since leaving Pittsburgh Major."

"Well Doc we're real happy to have you report aboard here. We don't have any dedicated corpsmen, and you're the first one I've ever met with an 0321 designator."

"If I'm not mistaken sir, I'm the first. But I spoke with my X. O. a few days ago and apparently there's a permanent billet now at the school."

"Well that's good news. On the operational side you're just in time for *Operation Northern Wedding*."

"Which is sir?"

"A NATO training op they run every four years. Pretty big deal. This year it's being run to coincide with a new operation, *Operation Able Archer*, a paper exercise with a bunch of brass locked in a

233

bunker for two weeks playing a really expensive, giant board game. Kind'a a cross between *Risk* and *Monopoly* only with nukes. First time the top level brass has gotten off their brass and have come out into the field."

"Sounds like fun. We gonna get wet sir?"

"Wetter than a $10 hooker on a drizzly, Seattle payday."

"Looks like I came to the right place."

"I'm gonna assign you to Sergeant Hill, he's the honcho of Team 7. You'll like him. HQ's got something special lined up for him and the team."

"Aye aye sir."

"Meanwhile, go find Gunny Mac and introduce yourself and give the guys a hand packing out. If they don't need ya we'll see you Monday morning 05:30."

"Med gear sir?"

"They'll be an all hands, pre-deployment brief Tuesday after P.T. You'll have a few days next week to organize your med gear and stock up or replace anything you need."

"May I interpret that to mean I have the rest of the weekend off sir?"

"Yes you may petty officer. You are dismissed."

"Good to be aboard sir!"

With a sharp salute McKeowen grabbed his gear and was out the door.

**

13:17 EST
Conference Room X-Ray
CIA HQ, Langley, Virginia

Perhaps as a leftover habit of spying on his fellow actors for J. Edgar Hoover while he was President of the Screen Actors Guild in Hollywood, or perhaps because he, like his arch nemesis Andropov, was genuinely paranoid of the 'Other Guys', Ronald Reagan never really lost his penchant for the cloak and dagger stuff, real or imagined. Ergo when William Casey quietly approached Reagan about a highly classified briefing back in the Oval office, a briefing which he thought himself and the President should attend, Ronnie was more than willing, particularly when he was told it concerned the shooting down of the Korean airliner.

Escorted by four burly M.P.'s and accompanied by the three most important intel men in the 'Free World', George Schultz, General Faurer and William Casey, The President was led down a long narrow corridor at the end of which was an elevator.

Rear Admiral John L. Butts, Director of ONI was originally scheduled to be in attendance however, as the members of the Russian salvage fleet in the Sea of Japan were becoming increasingly belligerent towards the Allied fleet, George Schultz advised The President, who was in agreement with him, that the Admiral should remain behind at naval ops and monitor the situation in the event there was an unforeseen escalation.

Waiting for the elevator in the brightly lit, grey hall no one spoke and when the lift arrived it was all they could do to squeeze eight men into the car. Casey had to request the M.P. closest to the buttons press one.

"B-2." Was all Casey said and in seconds the contingent disembarked into the lower basement of the Langley Building and with a definite, shared sense of purpose turned left, followed the hall to a cross corridor and turned left again. At a pair of sliding glass doors the lead M.P. swiped a card which hung around his neck and they entered an all metallic vestibule, moved to the next door and stopped.

"Thank you sergeant!" Director Casey said and the Sergeant along with his small squad broke off from the politicians and exited out the same sliding doors they had just come in.

Bill Casey stepped forward to the right of the polished steel door and placing his right palm on a clear glass, wall pad while simultaneously setting his eye against a protruding lens. He spoke into a voice recognition microphone.

"Casey, William J. Thirteen-three-thirteen." Hidden servos were activated, a light beam scanned the hand and the door was heard to unlock.

"Thank you Mr. Casey." A recoding said as the double thick door slid into the wall.

"This way gentlemen." Casey directed as they turned right down yet another short corridor with only one door and followed The Director as he entered that room. The door to this room was simply labeled:

"X-RAY"

The room was smaller than you would expect a high level conference room to be but there was the usual rectangular table albeit with only six chairs. A white board hung on the wall parallel with the long axis of the room and in one corner what appeared to be a mini fridge, like the sort you'd find in a cheap hotel room, was mounted on a table. Save for the white board, the walls were bare.

"Gentlemen take a chair please." Casey directed as he moved to a door on the other side of the room and stepped through it. On the other side of this door there was a small square table and one chair, as if it were a corner nook in a café somewhere.

At the table, his left hand resting on a two inch thick folder, sat an ONI intelligence analyst in full Naval dress blues, Lieutenant David Harden.

Behind him the wall was dominated by a large plate glass window on the other side of which was a very large room jammed with main frame computers, their fifteen inch reel-to-reels intermittently whizzing away in their signature stop and go fashion. No sound penetrated the glass.

Most who knew him noticed that it was only at certain times that Bill Casey's New York, Queens dialect showed itself, usually at times of considerable tension.

"They're here." Casey said quietly, his pronunciation of 'here' revealing that this was one of those times.

The Lieutenant's uneasiness was palatable and Casey, the veteran of hundreds of such briefings himself, easily sensed that.

"Harden!"

"Yes Director?"

"You're a make-or-break kind'a guy. Think of it this way, you're either about to be on your way to making full Captain or you're about to dig your own grave." Casey counseled.

"Maybe both." Harden replied as he stood. Harden adjusted himself, tucked the folder under his arm, donned his white combination cap and moved to the door.

As they crossed paths Casey slapped him on the shoulder and made eye contact. "Relax son, you've done this dozens of times. It's just another briefing. He's just another official!"

So says the Director of the Central Intelligence Agency to the low ranking analyst regarding the President of the United States in a time of unprecedented national crisis! Harden thought to himself. *Other than that, just another official.*

Casey ushered the Lieutenant out ahead of himself. As they entered Faurer frowned and glanced over at Schultz. Reagan just stared.

"Sir I've brought the top man we have on Soviet COMINT, ELINT and naval encryption techniques. Lieutenant Harden of the ONI." Casey took a seat next to Reagan.

"Mr. President, General Faurer." Harden greeted.

"Lieutenant Harden, my pleasure. Director Casey seems to think very highly of you." Reagan commented.

"That's very flattering sir, thank you." Reagan indicated a seat for the Lieutenant who politely declined and, as was his forte, got straight to it.

238

"Good morning gentlemen. Mr. President, Director Casey-"

"It's two o'clock in the afternoon!" Faurer barked.

"Sorry General Faurer. I've been working on ... in-"

"Aww leave the man alone Lincoln! He's trying to give a briefing here!" Casey admonished.

Harden moved to the fridge, grabbed a bottle of spring water and gulped a few swigs before replacing the cap and resuming his place in front of the white board.

Reagan and Shultz were struck with the same thought. Whatever this guy is here to tell us it must be pretty damn significant.

"Sir from ours and the Japanese communications intercepts, we learned about the shoot down almost as it was happening. As soon as we were able to analyze the data available we were able to disseminate the information." As all men who truly know their subject matter do, he spoke without notes.

"What was the time gap?" Faurer asked.

"Everything we had was out within three hours, General."000000000000000

"What they did was nothing short of deliberate mass murder!" Reagan made no attempt to mask his contempt.

"We all agree sir, but there's a lot more to it." Harden added as he opened the folder on the table. "Sir, following your authorization of our new PSYOPS initiative back in March, it was deemed that the main idea would be to operate an exercise

239

near maritime approaches to the U.S.S.R., in places where U.S. warships had never gone before."

He now referred to a naval chart he unfolded onto the table, which was prominently stamped with big red letters, 'T.S.' in all four corners. Additionally, various sea routes in different colors were drawn onto the map.

"As you know from previous briefings, we refer to this area as the GIUK ..." He indicated the area on the map he had spread out on the table in front of the group.

"The Greenland/Iceland/UK Corridor." Reagan clarified.

"Yes sir. Following organization of the August-September 1982 exercise, where our ships-"

"How many?" Reagan interrupted. Casey answered the President.

"Eighty-three in total sir. U.S., British, Canadian, and Norwegian ships led by the carrier Eisenhower." Harden continued. "The entire carrier group managed to transit the GIUK Gap, using a variety of carefully crafted and previously rehearsed concealment and deception measures.

Utilizing a combination of passive measures, such as maintaining radio silence and operating under emissions control conditions, mixed with active measures such as radar-jamming and transmission of false radar signals, we were able to go in and then turn about undetected."

"In essence, we created a stealth fleet?"

"Exactly sir. We even managed to elude a Soviet low-orbit, radar satellite launched specifically to locate such activity."

"Uh huh." Commented Reagan. Harden's confidence was boosted as he realized he had the President's interest.

"As the ships came within operating areas of Soviet long-range reconnaissance planes, the Soviets were initially able to identify but not track us. We know this due to the improved altitudes of our P-3 AWAC aircraft which means we were able to monitor their traffic as it originated in the operational areas.

Meanwhile, flying at low levels to avoid detection by Soviet shore-based radar sites, Navy fighters conducted an unprecedented, simulated attack on the Soviet planes as they refueled in-flight. This exercise also included operations that simulated surprise naval air attacks on other Soviet targets. All simultaneously."

"Busy boys!" The general blurted out.

Harden took it as a good sign that Faurer was impressed as he continued to use the map to re-enforce his briefing.

"In a third phase of this exercise, a cruiser and three other ships left the carrier battle group and sailed north through the Norwegian Sea and then east around Norway's Cape, further North and into the Barents Sea. They then sailed near the militarily important Kola Peninsula and remained there for nine days before re-joining the main group."

"So far I'm impressed." Reagan said to no one in particular. "But what I wanna know is, where exactly does this S.O.B. Walker fit in to the fact that the Russians are trying to start World War Three?!"

"Sir, with his compromise of the KL-7 and the

KW-37 encrypt systems the Soviets have virtually all they need to read nearly every Top Secret encrypt we send."

"Well if that's the case then they should have been able to track us anywhere, anytime?!"

"They probably were tracking us, as best they could, we're not sure. But we have to assume they did. And if they did track us, they're not stupid enough to let us know that they knew we were there. As you no doubt know sir, the first rule of spy craft is never let the other side know what you know."

"So what you're telling me is ... we don't know what they know?!"

"Worse yet they could be using their pipelines into our intel channels to feed us false information. That's what we'd do." Harden paused for responses. There were none. "The fleet exercises conducted near the far northern and eastern regions of the Soviet Union, clearly demonstrated our ability to deploy entire aircraft carrier battle groups close to sensitive military and industrial sites, apparently without being detected or challenged, at least early on."

"Uh huh." Reagan mumbled. "Well, when first proposed to me I intended there be some kind of demonstrations of power to deter the Soviets from provocative actions and at the same time display our determination to respond in kind to Soviet regional and global exercises which are becoming larger and more sophisticated, and more menacing than ever before." Reagan stood from his chair and studied the map routes more closely. "Are we satisfied that this projection of naval air and sea power has actually exposed these gaping holes in the Soviet ocean surveillance and early warning systems you describe?" Reagan queried as he perused the others.

"We think so, yes." Casey answered.

"Okay. Once again you Intel boys did good. What are you asking for? More appropriations? You got it."

"Sir ... this is one time it's not all about the money." Harden interjected.

"Explain." The President ordered.

"Although we weren't detected at the time, we have strong reason to believe that, partially due to Walker's treachery, the Soviet leadership, a short time later, discovered our incursions and among other things, cleaned house so to speak."

"You mean they replaced some staff?" The President sought clarification.

"Not 'some staff' sir. If I may be frank, a shit load of staff! High ranking staff."

"So?" Reagan didn't connect the dots.

"Put it this way Mr. President, what the Politburo did was tantamount to you firing the entire Joint Chiefs of Staff."

"We must have really shook them up!" Reagan smiled and nodded in approval.

"Sir, there's more. The repercussions didn't stop there." Harden added.

"Go on."

"Because of this house clearing, combined with the fact that we kept them on alert for nearly three months solid, the Reds are now more paranoid than ever. Most of the present Politburo was around in the late Sixties and memories of the U-2 flights and the Gary Powers incident aren't exactly a distant memory."

"I still don't get your point Lieutenant."

Harden glanced over at Bill Casey who nodded once.

"Sir, in the case of KAL 007, there's at least a chance ... Mr. President that ..." The color slowly drained from Reagan's face as he sat back in his chair.

"Are you saying that there's a possibility ...?"

"Yes sir. It may have been our own RC-135 the Soviets were tracking and when their response aircraft arrived on scene ..."

There was dead silence in the room, to the point that Harden imagined he could hear the main frame computers in the room next door running.

"Lieutenant I know the Soviets committed cold blooded murder! They've done it before, they'll do it again. I know, although I now know in more detail, that we've been taunting them over the fence. And now, thanks to your excellent briefing, where the Walker spy ring fits in. But what I don't know is, why are you proposing that we are somehow responsible ..."

"Indirectly sir."

"Directly, indirectly whatever, for that massacre? Is this leading somewhere? What it is that you're still not telling me."

"Sir?"

"Damn it Lieutenant, there's something else in this intel picture you're not painting for me! Now what is it?!"

Harden had wanted to include that "something else" in the briefing, something he felt would present a possible break in the intel stalemate the U.S. intel people were currently suffering. But, due to lack of all the details was advised against releasing it by both Admiral Butts and Director Casey. He decided to throw the dice anyway.

"A theory, Mr. President."

"A theory?!" Reagan echoed. Casey shifted in his seat.

"An educated guess, more of a hunch really sir." Harden clarified.

"A cockamamie idea more like!" Faurer added. Harden again looked over at Casey who, aggravated by the NSA Director's badgering, shrugged a 'Why not' kind of a shrug. Harden dug through the folder and produced a handful of intercepts.

"On and off there's a name that has been in their traffic for the last 18 months."

"There's a name that appears every now and again in routine traffic you mean." General Faurer sought to diminish the impact of Harden's argument.

"... and it has been showing up more frequently since the GIUK exercise." The Lieutenant countered.

"Appears every now and again in routine traffic but not enough to get our panties in bunch about!" Faurer had no intention of letting an officer so junior to himself get the better of him. Especially a naval officer.

"Codes are about patterns sir." Harden pushed on. "Breaking codes is about finding those patterns. Countering the code breakers is based on hiding those patterns."

"Sounds like a fucking Abbott and Costello routine!" Faurer was not going to let it go.

"That's what stands out about this Mr. President." Harden continued in spite of the interruptions.

"You're gonna havet'a be a little more specific than 'this' Lieutenant." Reagan blurted.

"I think it's a cryptonym, sir." Harden produced three of the intercepts and laid them side-by-side in front of Reagan who leaned over and perused the decoded documents. On each page the word 'Ryan' was highlighted. "Ryan, sir."

"Who or what is a Ryan Lieutenant Harden?"

"No one has any idea sir." Harden said. Reagan grunted. Harden sensed he was losing the only member of his audience that mattered and so began to deliver his pitch a little more quickly. "The thing that stands out is there's no apparent pattern to how they use it. That and it always appears to be out of context to the rest of the message."

"It could just be a false flag maneuver, like the one we used on the Japs at Midway." Reagan suggested.

"I've considered that sir, but the difference here, as opposed to Midway's fresh water condenser fake message, is that Ryan has been appearing for almost eighteen months and with increased frequency." Reagan looked again at the intercepts. "I think there's something there sir."

George Schultz leaned over to The President and, not bothering to whisper, proffered a suggestion.

"Sir, you, I, the General and Director Casey

should speak."

"Okay."

"Lieutenant will you excuse us?" Schultz directed.

"Of course sir." Harden took his water and disappeared back into the closet room.

"General Faurer, what does the Air Force think?" The President asked.

"Air Force Intelligence has so far dissented from the rush to judgment and we'll probably never reach a consensus on this but frankly sir, there are those who fly airplanes for a living who think that the Soviets probably did not know they were attacking a civilian airliner."

"Malarchy!" Reagan spat.

"Sir, between you and I, the people at the Defense Department think that Ryan is a deception and a waste of time. A false flag operation of the highest order." Schultz added.

"Bill, what'a your people think?"

"We've been kicking this particular football around for the better part of a year, Mr. President. We see nothing that indicates we should devote major resources to it, but I don't think we should abandon it all together either."

Reagan slid forward in his seat and perused the group.

"Sir, with all due respect, all the people in the intel community-" Faurer offered.

"SOME people in the community, sir." Casey quickly corrected.

"Most of the people in the community are calling the Lieutenant's theory Harden's Hail Mary Hunch."

"The Office of Naval Intelligence has had some brilliant coups in its time ..." Casey defended.

"Unfortunately not since WWII." Faurer quickly added.

"Gentlemen!" With his open palm The President slammed the table which got everyone's attention, including Harden's in the adjoining room. "Look me in the eye and tell me this is not another case of inter-agency rivalry?" He demanded. No one wanted to be the first to speak. "Need I remind anyone here about Carter's Iran rescue disaster?" The school boys had been scolded by the Head Master. "Exactly how worried are we about this Ryan fella?" Reagan demanded to know.

"Very, sir." After having waited the appropriate amount of time for Harden to squirm and prove himself, which he apparently did, Casey finally weighted in. "Sir if you're considering green lighting Lieutenant Harden, it'll have to be soon. Once you attack the Russians at the U.N. press conference, the whole dynamic is going to change."

"Director Casey's right Mr. President. The Reds did exactly what we expected they would do, denied blame. Now it's our turn and whatever approach we take, from that moment on the rules of the game are set." Schultz added.

"Is there any chance they can turn this thing around on us? Show to within a reasonable doubt, U.S. culpability?" The President wanted to know.

Silence again dominated the room.

"Short of fabricating something, I don't see how." Schultz opined.

"Additionally, we have the radio transmissions

248

the Japanese intercepted." Faurer spoke up.

"Anybody heard those tapes yet?" Reagan inquired.

"No sir, Not yet."

"I want them! Anything else? Anybody?" There were no takers. The President turned and made eye contact with Harden. "Lieutenant!" Reagan yelled.

"He can't hear you sir." Casey rose from his seat and went to the door to the room where Harden waited and opened it part way.

"They want you back inside." He relayed to Harden who was miffed that he couldn't read Casey's demeanor.

Harden entered.

"Lieutenant, you think you can crack this thing before the Second Coming?" The President threw at him.

Harden's entire college, naval and family career flashed through his mind.

"I believe so sir. Yes." He affirmed through a thin shell of confidence.

"Secretary Schultz I want you to give the lieutenant some resources and let him go. Either he'll find something or look like a fool trying to do it." Reagan predicted.

"Yes sir. I'll set it up."

"At any rate, we need all the help we can get right now and I think this young man has something on the ball. Make it happen George. Keep me informed." Reagan ordered as he stood to leave but made no move for the door.

"Yes sir."

"And let's get a copy of a translation of those

tapes ASAP! We need to know what to draft for the U.N. press conference by tonight." Reagan further ordered.

"Will do sir." Schultz nodded to Casey.

"You think you're on to something Ensign?" Schultz inquired as Harden stood by.

"It's Lieutenant, Mr. Secretary."

"Not if you screw this up." Schultz said. Reagan smirked. Harden felt compelled to counter.

"My argument gentlemen is at the very least, we should pursue this until it peters out!" Harden defended.

"What are you looking for in the way of resources?" Bill Casey purposely asked in front of the whole group, already knowing the answer having discussed it with Harden before setting up the meeting.

"I've thought about that, sir. It will require some field work but, between the four main agencies we've plenty of agents. But first I'd like to set up a small task force. We can work out of one of the old offices in the east wing extension of The Pentagon. Based on what we find we can formulate a plan of action, form a team, if required, and assign the field work."

"That is after you've run it by me you mean!" Bill Casey quickly added.

"Who will pass any action under consideration on to me!" Tagged Schultz. All eyes turned to The President expecting him to jump on the band wagon. He didn't.

"Keep me informed." Was all he said.

"Lieutenant Harden," Reagan turned and

shuffled through Harden's intercepts and the map as he spoke. Harden now bent over the table, was looking at them as well. "I left Hollywood when you were a pup. Now it appears we're back in a 'B' movie and the good guys have to find out what the bad guys are up to with their secret plans! Do you truly believe you can do that?"

"Unfortunately sir there's only one man on the planet aside from Yuri Andropov who knows the answer to that question." They exchanged glances over the table. "Viktor Mikhailovich Chebrikov."

"Head of the KGB." Reagan muttered.

*

Unbeknownst to Reagan, Casey, Faurer or anyone on General Vessey's JCS team, even to the man who had devoted the last year of his life to unearthing this super-secret agent Mr. Ryan, Lieutenant David Harden himself, Colonel Viktor Mikhailovich Chebrikov and Yuri Andropov were not the only ones who knew the details concerning Ryan.

In fact knowledge of Ryan was not even restricted to the Russians.

The second incorrect assumption was something that Lieutenant Harden would accidently discover as he was sucked deeper into the quagmire that The Cold War had become.

*

CHAPTER ELEVEN

Karl Marx Allee, East Berlin
16:27 CET, 6th September

A light rain fell over the city streets just long enough to cool the temperature to a mild chill. The overcast sky remained and as the last of the rain drifted away, a middle-aged man in Eastern European styled over coat and fur cap appeared from a doorway on the west end of the Karl Marx Allee just east of where the Warschauer Strasse crosses over the ornate show case boulevard.

A few minutes later, across the street on the south side, a second man, sporting a similar hat but dark brown rain coat, casually strolled to a bus stop bench, sat and lighted a cigarette.

To even the casual observer, who may not have connected the two, it appeared they were killing time, or at least waiting for someone or something to happen.

A quarter of an hour later a very English looking gentlemen in a three piece, pinstriped Seville Row tailored suit came across the lobby of a nearby office building and out through the main exit onto the north side of the busy thoroughfare.

The two men in hats glanced at each other one nodded and, waiting until their intended mark reached the corner, both took off at a slow but staggered pace in his direction.

They followed the man at a discreet distance

leapfrogging each other until he turned and entered the Honeker Insurance building about four blocks west of where they had picked him up.

Although labeled an 'Allee' the Karl Marx, which runs east to west across East Berlin, was actually as wide as Broadway, the Champs-Élysées or the via del Corso in Rome and at this time of day nearly as busy.

Casually milling around across the street Tail #1 watched through the glass double doors of the lobby as the man in the Armani suit rang for and boarded the lift.

He then nodded to his colleague, Tail #2, who was waiting off to the side just outside the ornate twenty storied building. On a second nod Tail #2 ducked into the lobby, stood in front of one of the lift banks and noted the floor it stopped on. Tail #1 signaled for #2 to stand fast in the lobby as he darted across the six lanes of traffic to the adjoining office building, moved through its lobby and emerged one street north of the K.M.A. Minutes later the Mark emerged from the lift and headed out the rear door of the insurance building, turned left and continued west.

Tail #1 now had the lead and picked up on the mark as Tail #2 fell in 100 metres or so behind the two. The surveillance mission continued west.

Once past the central fountain and traffic ring the Mark slowed his pace and began window browsing along the massive landmark book shop the Karl Marx Buchhandlung. When he strolled in through the front door Tail #1 followed as close behind as he dared but once inside was horrified to realize that

253

he had lost his man.

Tail #2, still across the wide boulevard leaning on a tram stop shelter, didn't realize what was happening so minutes later when #1 emerged from the bookshop in a subdued panic and shrugged across the street to his colleague, he got the evil eye.

#2 signaled his mate over and flagged down a cab which they directed to cruise west several blocks then find a place turn around and go east.

It still being mid-morning the parking lot of the Kino International was only sparsely filled with the boxy, little Wartburgs and plastic, four seater Trabi's so the Tails decided to have the taxi pull in and U-turn there. As they slowly circled the lot the mark in the suit was spotted crossing the K.M.A. on the other side.

The game reinitiated until their man ducked into the Friedrichsberg Strasse U-Bahn train station. After waiting until he paid his fare then walked out to the platform the two tails flashed their I.D. to the ticket taker in the glass booth and entered through different turnstiles. As they spotted him at the far end of the West bound platform the two agents split up to cover both ends.

The station's digital clock read 15:43 when the call board flashed the next arrival due at 15:45.

Exactly on time the train pulled in.

The man in the Armani boarded through the second door of the first carriage and his two tails displayed their professionalism as one boarded two cars back while the other waited one step from a door three cars back and out of sight. From the rear of his car the agent closest to the Armani peered around several passengers and satisfied himself when he spotted his mark still there in the first car casually reading a newspaper. The agent leaned back into the crowd and out of sight.

Just then, on the adjoining track, the 15:47 East bound pulled in and by way of announcing its departure, the conductor blew the whistle on the west bound train. The doors slid shut and as the train slowly pulled out Tail #1 was flabbergasted to look out the window and see the Mark waving 'bye-bye' from inside the east bound train as its doors closed over and it started to roll out of the station in the opposite direction.

In the vain hope of re-establishing contact with their mark at the next stop, the two not so professional tails waited around for the next three trains. It was nearly an hour later when they realized they were finished for the day and headed off.

"Did you recognize him? Who was he?"

"Didn't get a clear look at his face but that chap was definitely a bloody Birdwatcher! If not KGB definitely HVA!"

"Do us a favor old boy, next time you have a 'foolproof' plan, try and be less obvious." He chastised. "We're supposed to find out who they are not let them know who we are."

"Thank you ever so much. I'll try and keep that in mind."

The disgruntled British agents stormed off to the exit to find a place to dilute their sorrows before reporting in to their chief the next morning.

The man in the three piece Armani, meanwhile, rode the train to the next station and, with no sense of urgency, took the stairs to the street exit and followed along until he passed the Kaiser Wilhelm Memorial where he turned left to go deeper into the city. About a block and a half on he spotted a well-dressed, man with a receding hairline standing on the corner near a chemist's reading a newspaper. He crossed the street and approached.

"Excuse me, do you speak English?"

"A little, but it would be better if you could speak German." The man spoke over the top of his paper.

"Are you from Berlin?" He asked in German.

"Actually no, but I know the city quite well. Can I help you?" The well-dressed young man replied.

"Yes. I'm looking for an authentic German bier stube."

"Oh, if you cross Friederich Strasse and continue south until you reach the old U-Bahn station, you'll see a place on the corner, Der Struwwelpeter. It's quite nice."

"Thank you for your help."

"I am told the Goedecker Weiss bier is particularly satisfying." He added.

"I'll definitely look into that. Please thank your boss."

The younger man folded his newspaper, turned and disappeared down the street. The man in the Armani followed the other's directions and arrived at the pub.

As he came through the side door he quickly surveyed the premises. Sitting in a back booth facing the entrance sat a man, late fiftyish dressed in an East German officer's uniform with the rank of

Major General. He was also reading a newspaper. Above his head, on the side wall was a large, silk screened poster declaring;

'Goedecker Weiss Bier! Da gibt nur eine!'

"You're late Josef. NATO meeting again?" The officer greeted him in German, however the man in the Armani answered in Russian.

"Apologies Horst, two Englishmen. Apparently they think I'm worth doubling their efforts now." Josef reached into his jacket side pocket and produced a flat package wrapped in brown paper as he slid into the bench across from the officer.

"I brought you a present from our Capitalist friends in the West." He pushed the package across the table. "Who was the new Cutout you used?" Josef asked, referring to the man who had given him directions.

The officer peeled off the paper to reveal a VCR cassette tape. It was a copy of the latest Bond film.

"*Octopussy?*! Josef, you shouldn't have!" He perused the cover jacket. "How do they pick these names?" Horst was unable to stifle his laugh.

Josef switched to German.

"I don't write the films Horst, I just bring you copies for analysis."

"Who is Bond this time?" Horst read the cover credits on the VHS. "Moore! Why do they keep using him? Why don't they use a more masculine actor? Moore just doesn't do it for me! He's just too ... too gay! Why don't they bring back Connery! He's the only real Bond!"

257

"Have you seen this as well?" Josef also produced a copy of *Time Magazine* and passed it to Horst. The cover featured a shield and sword with the flag of the GDR, the logo of the Stasi, and the motto; 'Shield und Schwert der Partei', 'The Shield and Sword of the Party'. The featured article was subtitled, 'The most efficient information collection agency in the world'. Horst smiled as he read over the magazine cover.

"Flattering!" Horst signaled to the barman for two beers and pointed up to the wall poster. He spoke to Josef as he flipped through the magazine. "The new Cutout is a guy named Putin, Vladimir Putin, new recruit. Just using him as a Floater here for a couple of months to get his feet wet. He's shipping out to Dresden next week. Grandfather used to cook for Stalin."

"Huh! Peasant stock. Probably won't go very far. The article?" Josef nodded at the magazine.

"An interview given by a disgruntled employee of the CIA, NSA perhaps?"

"I am informed that the Agency takes great care to avoid disgruntling their employees." Josef countered.

"Yes, we already came across this article last month. Apparently this fellow, an anonymous, low ranking, technical operator, wrote several memos trying to convince the powers-that-be that our technical capabilities on this side of the fence are far more advanced than is generally believed to be the case by the Western leaders. No one would listen, so he went to the ever-ready-to-listen-to-anything against their own government Western Press. And they printed his article."

"And now?" Josef asked.

"Now he is no longer with the CIA. Now he collects his unemployment cheques on the first of the month at the local postal station." Horst informed.

"Perhaps we should send him a thank you bonus?" Josef sarcastically suggested.

The man he was speaking with, Major General Horst Vogel the First Deputy Chief the HVA or the Hauptverwaltung Aufklärung the foreign intelligence service of the Stasi, the Ministry of State Security.

Horst reported directly to Werner Grossman, Deputy Minister and Chief of the HVA.

The HVA service acted as the primary origin of up to 90% of all information obtained by the KGB on NATO nations. The HVA were considered the top information gathering spy agency in the world. Even by CIA standards.

Due to their ability to continually produce valuable material as well as contribute new and improved methods of information collection, the HVA enjoyed a special niche in the Communist's master plan to rule the world.

The glasses of beer arrived and they waited until the barman left to resume their conversation.

"So Josef, what have you brought for me? Something Mischa will like I hope."

"You mean something Markus can continue to placate the KGB Rezident with?" Josef prodded.

"Now don't be like that! Our Russian brothers have been very good to us." Horst countered.

"And the fact that the HVA supplies our Soviet brothers with more than 85% of all the intelligence coming out of the Federal Republic, the most important NATO country, this is of little consequence, yes?" Horst didn't respond, he merely shrugged and sipped his beer. "Horst, we have to push harder for your own SIGINT division. The money is there! You know it, I know it! Everyone knows it! You'll never completely control things until we are independent of Big Soviet Brother!"

"So you are looking to set policy now Josef?"

Suddenly conscious of his rising passions, Josef curtailed his preaching and sat back, beer in hand.

"Horst, you know what I mean. I am straddling the fence here between you for the KGB and Marcus for the HVA. You know I want a permanent posting here and the only way is if you expand your HUMINT force or get a SIGINT operation set up. You've got nearly 4,000 agents, lack of manpower's not a consideration."

"4,500 Josef and they intend to expand that now that both sides are on the verge of severing relations altogether!" Josef set his beer down and leaned into the table but showed no reaction to what his boss had just let slip.

"Horst, someday this will all go away and the only place for you and I will be on the winning side and that will be the side with the technological edge. And as things stand now, HVA are light years ahead of the West and the KGB, without the HVA in the Stone Age as far as information technology is concerned."

"One would never know you are Russian Josef.

One would think you are German." He sipped more beer. "Enough chit chat. What have you brought me?"

"Well to start I can definitely confirm that the new Pershing launch locations are to be rotated every 14 days, three to four days at DEFCON 3 and above."

"Interesting. I would have thought more often. Good, and?"

"Three members of my cell, at three different locations, have been observing the Americans practice their drills. Apparently there is a problem with the uploading mechanisms on the transport vehicles."

"So as of now, they are not able to respond as quickly as they would like?" Horst confirmed.

"That or they will have to keep the rockets in the same locations longer than they wish."

"This is interesting, but eventually they will defeat the problem, no?"

"Naturally but, until then we have time as well an insight into at least one major weakness in their latest missile system. Endless possibilities for sabotage should it come to blows." Horst sighed, leaned forward and became very serious.

"Josef, I need you to talk to me about code sequences for the H&D scramblers. Please my friend, it's been almost two weeks. My men are losing faith in me."

"Horst Vogel, you are Napoleon reincarnate! No matter how dark the night your troops know you will come through for them!" Josef finished off his glass of beer. "Those two clumsy Englishmen cost me some time, I have to run. Must catch a flight out to London."

"Hot date with an English rose?"

"Presentation dinner with Sir Colin Figures. He's giving some nominal award to the Anglo-Russian Freedom of the Press Association. Must keep up appearances."

"British Chief of Intelligence Sir Colin Figures?! You're moving up in the world Josef, congratulations."

"He'll likely not show, but his number two man will be there to shake hands and read his speech." Josef rose to leave. "I'll be in London by six tonight. The awards dinner is at eight. I'll know by tomorrow around noon if I can get the codes you're looking for, so set another communications for day after tomorrow. Use the Classifieds in the early edition of *The Daily Telegraph* this time. I'll verify by Dead Phone between 18:00 and 18:20 that night."

"I'll have an operator on standby."

"And tell your young Cutout this Goedecker beer is a bit like Jane Fonda: too bitter, no body and a bit flat."

"Russians! No taste for the finer things in life."

"Enjoy the film!" Josef replied.

Horst glanced at the back of the video cassette to read the credits as Josef left.

"Huh! Maud Adams. Nice!"

****

Paddy Kelly

U.S. Department of State
C Street, NW
Washington, D.C.

"Charlene?" George Schultz called out to his secretary through the intercom on his desk.

Yes Mr. Secretary?

"There's a bright young spark over at ONI named Harden, Lieutenant Harden. Find him and get him an appointment with me in the next day or so would you please?"

The State House or in the Pentagon Mr. Secretary?

"Here at the State Department but not my office. Have him come to that small meeting room, number ... two?"

Number three sir. She laughed.

"Yeah, three. Getting old, Charlene, getting old."

Will do Mr. Secretary. Any special instructions sir?

"Yes. Tell him to bring his 'A' game. This is his shot at the big show."

Will do sir.

"Thank you Charlene."

Rear Admiral John J. Butts, Director of the Office of Naval Intelligence had never heard of a Lieutenant David Harden, however for the third time in as many days the name once again crossed the Admiral's desk. He made a mental note to track this guy down and have a chat with this Harden as he laid Schultz's message on his desk.

From Butt's office word was sent to Harden's immediate supervisor to have him report to the State

Department office that afternoon at 15:30 and later to report to the Admiral's office to report why he was being ordered to report to the Secretary of State's office.

Sitting on the dark oak federalist chair outside the office of one of the most powerful men in the country, about to pitch an idea that had already been scoffed at by several of Schultz's colleagues and was, as of yet, still unknown to his boss, Harden found it hard to focus. Leaning forward with a deep sigh, he attempted to assuage his nerves by letting his mind wander.

He'd always heard and read that in the heat of battle, when a troop had been hit and was relatively certain he was about to die, his mind flashed back to times and events that comforted him. Home, family, people he loved and who loved him. It was a logical defense mechanism.

He sat his brief case on his lap, his white combination cap on top and let his head again ease back onto the wall and closed his eyes while blanking his mind.

It began to work however, the thoughts weren't as warm and soothing as he'd imagined as images flashed through his mind at an uncontrollable speed.

The rolling hills and endless, golden corn fields of Iowa came to mind. The small town restaurants, pharmacies and grocers which lined the narrow main streets. Accompanying his mom to Midnight mass at St. Agath's on Christmas ...

"Lieutenant Harden?"

Going into town to sign up to be a Navy Seal ...

"LIEUTENANT HARDEN?!"

"YES! Sorry. Yes here." Dave snapped out of his stupor and clambered to his feet.

"Secretary Schultz will see you now." The shiny female face looked down at him.

"Thank you." He followed the pretty secretary into and through the short outer office and in through the door labeled:

George P. Schultz
Secretary of State

The Secretary indicated the chair directly in front of his desk and Harden sat.

Schultz took his time as he read through a brief Harden knew nothing about.

Throughout the short but intense meeting Schultz was curt but professional.

"As I have no direct connection or vested interest in your project or your agency or any other for that matter, I have no stake in whether your hunch is right or wrong Lieutenant, you do understand that?"

"Yes Mr. Secretary."

"But you should know two things from the start. The president has confided in me that he has faith in you, and-"

"With all due respect sir, am I to take it that you don't sir?"

"I was going to say, you're gambling with your career. But I'm given to understand you're a man who's not afraid to take chances."

"Calculated risks, sir."

"Is that why you still persist in seeking orders to Coronado to attend BUDS training at this late date in your career?" Harden was surprised and more than a little shocked that someone that high up the ladder would know that intimate a detail concerning his career ambitions but was too much of a professional to let it throw him.

"I'm still within the age limit sir and, again with all due respect, there have been older men have gone through SEAL training Mr. Secretary."

"But few with your rank." Schultz stared at him intently for a few long seconds then resumed his cross examination. "I'll expect a detailed report each Monday morning, CC'd to Director Casey of what you've been up to for as many weeks as this thing lasts. Understood?"

"Yes sir. Am I to CC Admiral Butts on that Mr. Secretary?"

"Negative. I'll see to it that the Admiral's kept apprised of all your activities and your progress. If there is any."

"Yes sir."

"Meanwhile you're being T.A.D.'d to the State Department."

"I got a memo to that effect sir this morning. Is there any indication how long my Temporary Assigned Duty status will last Mr. Secretary?"

"For as long as it takes. Get your resource requirements to my secretary by the end of the day and I'll see to it-" Harden reached into his inside breast pocket and produced a typewritten list.

"I just happen to have such a list with me sir." Schultz glared at him.

"How convenient."

"I anticipated my relocation Mr. Secretary, so

266

I've also taken the liberty to contact the communications people to re-install the five line phone bank and computer feed lines in one of the old offices over in the south wing sir." Schultz perused the list. "The actual requisition pending your approval of course."

"Of course." Harden realized he was on the high wire. "It appears you know what you're doing."

"Thank you sir, but time is not on our side." Not knowing what else to do Harden stood and waited there, in front of the Secretary's desk until he looked up.

"That'll be all Lieutenant."

"Thank you Mr. Secretary." He turned to leave but halfway through the door Schultz called him back.

"Harden, we've had all three Intel agencies looking at this thing for months without a clue. You really believe you have the ability to tell us what RYAN is?"

"I'll stay at it for as long as it takes, sir."

His mind was a whirlwind of ideas and plans as he went back out through the office door to leave but as he passed Charlene's desk she called over to him.

"Lieutenant Harden, this just came for you from Langley." She handed him a sealed envelope and he stepped to the side to open it.

'Harden, pull this off and I'll personally guarantee you the duty station of your choice.'
- Director Wm Casey

"Does that apply to a school of my choice as well?" He mumbled to himself.

"What's that Lieutenant?" The pretty thirty-something asked as she overheard him.

"AHH ... nothing. Sorry. Talking to myself."

"I do that all the time Lieutenant. As long as you don't answer yourself, it's okay." She made no attempt to avert her sparkling eyes and broad smile as she stared, mesmerized by his face. "Lieutenant, did anyone ever tell you that you look...?"

"That it's okay to talk to yourself as long as you don't answer? Yes, they have." He smiled back. "All the time. Charlene."

She smiled wider, as she stared at his ass until he was out of sight.

****

With the exception of a small circle of White House and Pentagon officials the Soviet's activities in response to the Presidentially authorized military incursions into Russian air and sea space over the last year were virtually unknown. However, thanks to the efforts of the traitor John Walker, the U.S. details of the incursions were known to the Kremlin.

The U.S. command's assumption that their ships and aircraft were undetected last Spring once they were securely inside Soviet territory, were based on the fact that they saw no overt reaction by the Soviets.

This however, by no means, implies the Soviets did nothing. Only that the Soviets weren't stupid

Paddy Kelly

enough to give themselves away.

****

269

CHAPTER TWELVE

Chairman Chebrikov's Office,
Lubyanka Building
KGB Headquarters, Moscow
10:10 Local, September 7th

The day Yuri Andropov moved office into the Kremlin's Presidium ten months ago, Viktor Mikhailovich Chebrikov, now Chairman Chebrikov, moved into Yuri's old desk in the Lubyanka building as Head of the KGB.

Presently he adjusted his glasses as he read to himself, cigarette in hand, from a copy of a recently intercepted Top Secret CIA report which only two days ago was sent to the U.S. Senate Oversight Committee via, what the Americans believed was a secure line.

We believe strongly that Soviet actions are not inspired by, and Soviet leaders do not perceive, a genuine danger of imminent conflict or confrontation with the United States.

Ten years younger than William Casey, the sixty year old Chebrikov didn't share Casey's background in intel work. While Casey had been working with the office of Strategic Services the forerunner of the CIA, during WWII Viktor Chebrikov was working as a battalion commander in the Red Army fighting Germans. To this day the five foot nine Viktor wore the corrective lenses that compensated for his

270

deficient eyesight, the physical anomaly which terminated his military service after the war.

A loyal party member since the days in his homeland of the Ukraine, after the war Chebrikov slid easily into administration and was quickly posted to Moscow first as a manager for the Central Committee and then as Deputy Director of the KGB under Yuri Andropov then Director.

Sharing Andropov's hatred of internal corruption he joined, along with others, to vigorously seek out and prosecute the wide spread political corruption of the Brezhnev hold-over's with such vehemence that several of them blew their own brains out or gassed themselves before they were discovered or betrayed.

The two gelled well and now along with Dmitriy Ustinov, Minister for Defense, the three formed the backbone of the Politburo.

Viktor looked up and addressed the younger man sitting before him.

"Genius!" He quietly declared. "You have perpetrated the ultimate Intelligence coupe! To have the enemy believe exactly what you want them to believe when it is not true!" He then read from an official personnel file, the file of the same man.

"Head of Anti-American operations at 41 years of age, Deputy Director of the First Directorate at 44, Chief of Station in Washington D.C. and, as if that weren't enough, the Colonel who played the key role in the recruiting and handling of John Walker Junior, the Naval officer who handed us the most damaging spy ring ever to operate against the United States!" He closed the file over and gently laid it on his desk. He stood and leaned over his desk to present his hand. "Boris Aleksandrovich Solomatin! Welcome home."

The man in the over-stuffed arm chair in front of Chebrikov's desk stood and shook hands.

"Thank you Comrade Chairman. I regret my return is under such shameful circumstances."

"Shameful? Shameful?!" He stubbed out his cigarette and reached for another, "Because you managed to elude the entire FBI, CIA, NSA and escape America?! After being betrayed by a fellow Russian? SHAMEFUL?! HA! You are legend! Our own James Bond! Soon they will make movies with beautiful, vivacious women about you! Hopefully not with the usual array of ridiculous titles, but still!" Viktor came around from behind his desk and hugged then kissed Solomatin several times more than custom dictated.

"Your accolades are unwarranted, comrade."

"You are too modest Aleksandrovich!" Chebrikov made his way back to his desk where he produced another piece of paper and waved it in the air.

"An article from a *New York Times* interview of a senior FBI agent. Just two days ago! I've been dying to read it to you!" Chebrikov read aloud.

'Solomatin caused us considerable trouble wherever he was posted. He is considered as perhaps the best operative the KGB ever produced. The amount of damage that he has done to the United States is difficult to calculate.'

He lay the article on his desk and shook his head.

"Once again Boris, welcome home!" Chebrikov came back around from behind his desk, crossed his arms and sat on the edge. "Welcome back to help us with this latest fiasco brought on by the politicos who can't see beyond their own ambitions!"

Boris remained noticeably reserved in his acceptance of Viktor's overwhelming praise. But the gnawing curiosity which had been eating at him for the last week prompted him to finally broach his opinion.

"I'm not sure what I can do to help with this ... this political situation you describe Comrade Chebrikov."

"Viktor! It's Viktor, Boris! And what are you trying to say comrade?"

"Just this ...Viktor. While comrade Marshal Ogarkov's performance at the press conference in the United Nations was admirable, it will be blatantly obvious to the Western Press that it was a cover up from start to finish."

"Comrade Solomatin, are you questioning the Party line?" Chebrikov asked, making no attempt to hide his sarcasm.

"The 'Party line'?! If I followed the 'Party line' we never would have had Walker, Souther or any of the others!"

"Souther, the idealist! Pity about that young man." Chebrikov opined

"Do you and the Politburo have any idea how far ahead of the West we are ... were?! And then we shoot down a civilian aircraft full of innocent people. And now I understand the Politburo want to hide it?!"

"They are politicians, first last and always. The truth is their natural enemy." Chebrikov moved in closer to Boris Aleksandrovich and took him by the arm then guided him over to a pair of high backed chairs facing the large window looking down on Lubyanka Square. "We should talk Boris." He threw back the heavy, red and gold, velvet curtains and a diming September light seeped into the room.

"Alarm bells are ringing Viktor. You invite me for a private chat, clear your calendar to see me ..."

"To see a genuine hero fresh from the fight!"

"I have been back nearly two weeks." Viktor moved to the high narrow table against the wall to the right of the window serving as a make shift bar and poured two large Johnny Walker Blue Labels into a pair of rocks glasses.

"I need you. We need you Boris. Your country needs you!" He handed a drink off to Boris and took the seat opposite.

"Don't wave the flag in front of me comrade. Those days are gone. If I walk away right now and disappear to some desert island in the South Pacific I will have served my country as much as any good communist has, now or before."

Chebrikov lit another cigarette, sipped his drink and looked down to choose his words. He was fully aware that Solomatin, after thirty years of service to his country and narrowly escaping the West with his life, returned in the full expectation of a comfortable retirement and a soft gradual decline into old age.

"We are at a critical time in the republic comrade. Reagan is not like Carter, afraid of war.

He will escalate as far as he believes is required so long as he appears the hero to his people. That is why we need men like you. Men the people can believe in. Men who have been there and faced the enemy, in their own den." Solomatin smirked at the obvious cajolery as he sipped his scotch.

"Why do I feel like you are giving me a slow hand job Viktor?"

"Bastard! You want me to speed it up?" He laughed as he slapped Solomatin on the back.

Solomatin paused and thought before he spoke again. He altered tone and now chose his words more carefully but with commitment.

"You know, I had the privilege to meet Yuri Gagarin once at a reception. I asked him, Comrade Gagarin honestly, did you feel fear sitting there strapped into hundreds of thousands of kilos of explosive about to be shot into outer space? Did you experience fear when the rocket began to shake so violently and you realized there were only two ways out, success or death?" Aleksandrovich stopped speaking as he stared out the window at some minor traffic altercation in the square below.

"Don't leave me hanging! What was his answer?" Viktor demanded.

"He said, not as afraid as I was when I returned to earth and realized what they would do with me next."

"Which was?"

"Ask me to be a politician." He went back to gazing out across the square and sipped his deink. "Mother Russia is a conundrum. We've built a communist church in a Christian country."

"Please! Going to church doesn't make you a Christian any more than standing in a garage makes you a car."

"Very clever." Solomatin mumbled. "Point is, I'm not a politician. I'm a spy." Boris affirmed.

Viktor sighed and sat back in his seat. He decided on another angle of attack.

"The Americans and the British have lost several key operatives to us in the last several years. Souther, the Walker family, Aldrich Ames which they don't even yet suspect. We have in turn, lost no one of any significance to the West. We are clearly winning!" Chebrikov took a seat.

"Boris, there are several things in the works, and just now I'm not in a position to allow you to be privy to everything, but I want you to head anti-American espionage efforts.

"I can't go back out. I'm a marked man!"

"I'm not asking you to go back out." Chebrikov leaned forward in his chair and intensified his tone.

"I want you to head anti-American espionage efforts from here, in Moscow." Chebrikov sensed triumph as Solomatin turned his head and made eye contact. "In two days' time there will be a meeting. If it goes the way I think it will, I will have a very important bit of information for you."

"How important?" Solomatin pushed.

"At the chance of sounding melodramatic, it will alter the course of world history."

"That sounds comparatively important." Boris smiled, stood and set his half-finished drink on the table. "you have my word I will sleep on it comrade." He patted Chebrikov on the shoulder and left.

*

U.N. Security Council
General Assembly,
United Nations

At the same time as Viktor was buttering up Boris Aleksandrovich hoping they would join forces, a half a world away U.S. Secretary of State George P. Schultz was advancing one of the key precepts of the Reagan administration's agenda, to discredit the Soviet Union at, what seemed to many to be, an all costs operation.

Schultz sat in the Green Room of the General Assembly at the U.N. applying last minute tweaks to his address which he was about to deliver to an Emergency Session of the General Assembly in coordination with an international press conference. All, ostensibly, to respond to the downing of the Korean airliner, but it was little secret that what he was sent to do was to repudiate Marshal Ogarkov's version of events.

In the last few days the White House had adopted a strategy of releasing a substantial amount of hitherto highly classified intelligence in order to exploit this as a major propaganda coup over the U.S.S.R.

As in all aspects of the American legal system, presumption of intentional wrongdoing was instantaneous, complete and unwavering in the shoot down incident.

That morning prior to the U.N. meeting, to maximize impact of the session, Japan and the United States jointly released a transcript to all the major news networks of the intercepted Soviet communications recorded by the listening post at Japan's northern most point the island of Wakkanai a point actually close enough to the Russian island of Sakhalin to see it.

Through Schultz, Reagan had also issued an official National Security Directive stating that the Soviets were not to be "let off the hook". Schultz, as well as Reagan's entire cabinet and every last member of the U.S. Diplomatic Corps, had orders to initiate a major diplomatic effort to focus attention on the Soviet Union.

To be sure the Soviets got the massage, Reagan further ordered a political overkill maneuver. Schultz's presentation would have back-up, essentially a second act.

Following Schultz, the U.S. Ambassador to the United Nations, Jeane Kirkpatrick would take the floor with a commercially commissioned audio-visual presentation to the Security Council 'proving' the Russians intentionally massacred the innocent passengers of KAL 007.

This presentation would include the use of audio tapes of the Soviet pilots' radio conversations, with translations this time as opposed to Reagan's hurried TV announcement on Prime Time Television the evening of the shoot down when the president's advisors were only concerned with having "realistic" radio chatter as back-up for the president and no translation was provided.

Interestingly the map plan of Flight 007's path in depicting its shooting down, in the Kirkpatrick presentation was essentially the same map used by Air Marshal Ogarkov less than a week prior.

It appeared that, as far as the big picture was concerned, the Americans had forced the Soviet's hand, because shortly following Kirkpatrick's presentation, TASS, the Soviet's official news organ, finally publicly acknowledged that the aircraft had indeed been shot down by a Soviet fighter jet.

But only after repeated warnings were ignored.

*** * ***

For the last five hours the Oval Office had been a hive of activity as Reagan and his advisors struggled to chisel out the exact wording he would use for his televised speech to the world that evening. Following consultation with the three major networks, 8 p.m. was settled on as the ideal broadcast slot. This to reach both coasts at a reasonable time as well as the entire Western Hemisphere, because in reality this broadcast was not intended as a rebuttal of any kind, this was to serve the purpose to initiate an all-out attack on what, in Reagan's eyes, was the enemy of the world; Soviet Russia and her leadership.

He was determined that when the next war started, the history books would record that it was the Russians who will be seen to have started it by firing on and destroying an unarmed civilian aircraft.

The ten arm chairs as well as the couch normally present in the room had been removed and a large round table had been brought in accompanied by a half dozen straight back chairs. In his entire time as President Reagan's Oval Office had never so closely resembled a war room as it did now.

Casper Weinberger, George Schultz, Vice President George Bush as well as various aides, writers, experts and consultants were all present.

Due to his anxious rush to schedule and broadcast his statements about the incident, the actual wording of the statement itself was still in the process of being drafted only hours prior to broadcast time.

The President's secretary buzzed him by intercom however, due to the commotion in the room he hadn't heard it. A minute later she appeared in the office and made her way over to him at the table. He was leaned over chatting with Weinberger when she discreetly bent down and softly spoke into his right ear.

"Mr. President, you requested we keep you updated hourly. You're due on air in two hours, sir. One and a half hours to your make-up call."

"Thank you."

As the politicians conferred lighting technicians, sound people and a trio of set decorators worked around the Presidential desk. At a hectic but controlled pace a tall, pair of full length gold curtains were being hung in front of a fake window with phony trees in the background. The

Presidential and American flags astride a collection of framed Reagan family photos completed the Hollywood-like set. The Presidential Seal was being hung on the front of his desk and gaffers ran electrical cables and erected tall tripod light stands as he rehearsed.

"Sir, 'massacre' works well but don't use it too many times. I think two should do it." Vice President Bush advised.

"How can you use massacre too many times?! That's what it was damn it!" Weinberger countered.

"'... the RC-135 had been on the ground back in Alaska for over an hour when the murderous attack took place.' Do we wanna' use that? Simple math with the round trip flying time will bring that into disrepute." Casey queried. "And the claim that the RC-135 was never anywhere near Soviet territory?"

"Do they have reconnaissance photos of the 135 actually in the area?!" Reagan asked to no one in particular.

"No sir, we think not, or they would have shown them at the ..." Casey answered.

"Hell no they don't have photos of anything! If they did they damn sure would have paraded them out at that dog and pony show they put in at the U.N.!" Weinberger added.

"Do you want to try a run through Mr. President?" Asked an assistant director as he approached the President. Reagan nodded.

Schultz flagged down one of the senior guys from the broadcast crew, a director, spoke to him briefly and then nodded at Reagan. The director climbed up and stood on a chair.

"CAN I HAVE YOUR ATTENTION PLEASE!? QUITE, QUITE, QUITE! ATTENTION PLEASE!" The activity stopped dead in its tracks and everyone looked to the director.

"Thank you. The president needs quite for ten ..." He looked over at Schultz who nodded. "Ten minutes to try a read through, so please get comfortable where you are and be quite. Thank you." Reagan, now behind his desk, ignored everyone in the room and read from the typewritten page.

"My fellow Americans, I'm coming to you tonight about the Korean Airlines massacre, the attack by the Soviet Union on 269 innocent men, women and children aboard an unarmed ..."

As Reagan read Schultz whispered to a nearby senior aide.

"Where's the damn translation of the radio traffic? How the hell am I gonna tell America what these butchers are saying if I don't have the translations!"

"... a crime against humanity that must never be forgotten. An act of barbarism, inhuman and brutal."

"Director Casey the Langley people have hit a bit of a snag with the translations." The aide informed him.

"Talk to me!" Casey demanded.

"The copies the Japanese security forces sent us are second and third generation beta. On top of the fact that a lot of the Russian transmission is blocked or very staticy, they're having a hard time deciphering exactly what's on the tapes."

"Shit! And we're just finding out about this now?! Do what you can but put a foot under it. He's not using a teleprompter for this!" Casey directed.

Reagan continued to read the text from a paper on his desk which called for a full apology, financial reparations and punishment for the Soviets. The text went on to rake up crushing the Czechs, Afghanistan gas attacks and torture. Some of his advisers in the room displayed a visible, negative reaction when he unexpectedly threw those factors in.

"Is he actually trying to get us into a war?!" An aide leaned over to another and whispered.

An hour and a half later, everyone was gathered in the shadows, watching the actual live broadcast from a row of TV monitors as Reagan pushed on.

"The Russians of course refuse to equip their planes with such a device because it would make it much easier for Soviet pilots to defect to the free world. We know that the Soviets have shot down civilian planes before and they will do it again!

I have ordered that the USSR be notified that we **will not** *renew our bilateral agreement on transport. Additionally I have ordered the F.A.A. to revoke, as of the day after tomorrow, the license of the Soviet airline Aeroflot to land on United States soil or her territories. I urge other nations to follow suit as Canada has done by suspending Aeroflot landing privileges for 60 days starting the day after tomorrow."*

In the speech he took great pains to paint the

U.S.S.R. as enemy of the whole world then strategically spent the last two minutes of the speech arguing for his defense budget increases.

"... like the Americans who brought forth this best and last hope of mankind."

Reagan's televised rebuttal on the attack on KAL 007 usurped all other U.S. commercial broadcasting on all three of the majors, ABC, NBC and CBS and started promptly at 20:00 on the evening of 7, Sept.

Late that evening, following the presentation, Reagan was informed that TASS finally acknowledged that the aircraft had indeed been shot down.

The Russians challenged many of the facts presented by Kirkpatrick and most importantly, reiterated the presence of the U.S.A.F. RC-135's path and that it had actually crossed the flight path of KAL 007.

Fully expecting a counter punch from the Reagan camp, the Soviets were not at all taken off guard by the televised presentation. What did draw universal shock however was the vehemence of Reagan's counter attack.

The double teaming of Schultz and Kirkpatrick and the unrestrained lack of diplomacy on any level was seen by the Andropov camp as irrefutable confirmation of the West's collective evil intentions to instigate a war.

Spearheaded by the U.S. juggernaut.

Led by Ronald Reagan.

Tagansky Park
Tagansky, Moscow

As he finished fixing his favourite Turkish tea, Boris Aleksandrovich Solomatin moved to the couch in his study adjacent to the kitchen in his four room Moscow apartment.

Boris was gradually becoming mesmerized by what he was hearing and seeing on his television set. As a high ranking KGB agent he was privileged to have access to one of the limited numbers of satellite dishes allowed by the authorities and so could access most American and European TV stations as well as al Jazeera in the mid-East.

Boris was listening to a TASS taped broadcast of the U.N. presentation of the U.S. Ambassador Kirkpatrick.

He had learned, during the American war with Viet Nam, how the tones of the American news broadcasts were nearly as important as their content in terms of revealing the political attitudes of the governments involved.

Regardless of what he personally believed about the KAL incident, the viciousness of the U.S. political attack was, as far as he was concerned, bristling with challenges both on the political and personal levels. Solomatin saw it as a deliberate attack engineered to challenge the Russian people.

He was not normally given to decisions based on emotion, but in Boris's opinion, the well-rehearsed, well timed expensive dog and pony show staged by Fitzpatrick and Schultz, touched a nerve. By the end of the presentation Comrade Solomatin had made a decision.

Having been in the profession and on the world stage for twenty years, Solomatin fully realized that Reagan's so called address to the nation was also orchestrated to produce more than support for himself and his party. It was composed and had been delivered by a veteran movie actor to agitate protest and antagonism against the Russians on an international scale. In essence to turn the world against the Soviet Union and by default, against the Russian people.

This was a lot for a dedicated Russian patriot to swallow. His opinion was further swayed as he switched TV stations to see anti-Russian protests being staged across the globe.

He left his tea to cool and moved to the phone.

"Viktor, Solomatin here."

Boris! How nice to hear from you. It was Chebrikov on the line.

"Arrange a briefing for me please. If I'm going back into the game through a different door, I need at least to know the rules."

On the other end of the line in his office at Lubyanka, Chebrikov gently smiled.

Day after tomorrow, the Annex. 10:00 o'clock. Acceptable?

"Yes, I can be there."

Great!

"Viktor, just remember one thing, I am not a politician. Politicians and diapers have one thing in

286

common. They should both be changed regularly. And for the same reason."

You have made yourself clear my friend. And Boris, I have a film you absolutely must watch with me! Do you like Maud Adams?

"Who?"

We talk tomorrow.

****

Russian Embassy
Notting Hill
Kensington, London

The old KGB Rezident in London, Anatoly Vladimirovich, had been replaced. He was seen by Lubyanka to be content growing fat and complacent in the decadent West without really earning his Rubles.

Three days after its outbreak the now former KGB Rezident, had still failed to recognize that the very country where he was the Station Chief, England, was at war with Argentina! Unfortunately for his career, despite the mighty British fleet steaming headlong to South America to do battle, Vladimirovich's communiqués to Moscow regarding the start of the Anglo-Argentine war were labeled as nothing more than a 'minor squabble'.

A week later he was back in Moscow with a small desk in the basement of the Lubyanka Building.

The forty-five year old Josef Kuksova's new

promotion to London Station Chief commonly known as Rezident, to replace Anatoly Vladimirovich was the logical progression of his rank, time in grade as well as the status he had attained in his nearly twenty-five years as a KGB operative.

Back in East Berlin Horst Vogel, First Deputy Chief of the East German Intelligence service, the Hauptverwaltung Aufklärung or HVA, had never questioned Josef's passionate ambitions concerning the HVA developing their own Signals Intel division or his questioning of the HVA's Human Intel resource numbers. None of Kuksova's casual questions regarding any of their topics of conversation whenever they met, seemed out of context much less out of the ordinary, especially for an agent who had just been sent to England to head the London office of the KGB.

In contrast to the old Rezident, Josef Kuksova was an agent who's intel had relentlessly proven timely as well as accurate and who himself was the son of a long time KGB man. In all his years with the KGB he had been diligent, resourceful and innovative. No mean feat in a system as closed and repressive as the Soviets'.

"Thank you Iirna. Just off to lunch. Back in about an hour." Josef informed the statuesque, blond receptionist as he signed out at the front desk of the Russian Embassy in the west of London and made for the exit out onto the busy boulevard. He made it a habit to let which ever girl was at the desk know where he was going and how long before he was expected back.

Josef Kuksova had taken up his post as the new Rezident of the London office just over a week ago. Stationed inside the Russian Embassy at the posh Kensington Palace Gardens sector of the city, he now headed north and walked to Notting Hill Gate then turned east and walked to Palace Court where in another ten minutes he was at Queensway.

As he walked he mused at the vibrancy of the colors. The lushness of the plants and shrubbery of the surrounding residences. Thinking back to West Berlin he mused of the many times he had traveled to East Berlin and how, crossing The Wall was like going from a color film to black and white, with varying shades of gray at best.

He spotted a dash of white graffiti, someone's name, splashed across a side wall along an alley off Notting Hill and chuckled at the memory of the graffiti saturated wall on the West side of Berlin. He pictured the East German guards in their fortified towers raking anyone with machine gun fire who was even able to get close enough to the East face of the wall with a spray can, much less being stupid enough to try and paint a disparaging, political remark on it.

London. Berlin. Different planets.

Finally he came upon a small café on a corner, 'Samovar' owned by a Russian immigrant from the Caucasus Mountains. In exchange for generous tips every time an embassy employee visited, the owner, a fifty something named Katrina, proved to be very cooperative whenever she was asked for the occasional favor.

Katrina never knew and never wanted to know if

Josef was KGB or not. If he wasn't then chances were pretty good he was on good terms with the British and it was senseless to wave a red flag at Immigration. And as she still had relatives back in Mother Russia, if he was KGB, it was all the more reason to take the extra beer and cigarette money he offered, be a good girl and look the other way.

The place was less than half full when Josef entered and he greeted the owner with a twenty pound note during their handshake and then discreetly gestured towards the back door. She nodded her consent.

He made his way through the small kitchen and once outside again he casually strolled down the side street where a black Vauxhall Royale with tinted windows and a dark-haired, thirty something man at the wheel sat waiting.

For the past few years the man known as Josef Kuksova to his HVA connections, but as Oleg Gordievsky, his actual birth name, to the KGB and the British Secret Service, had been meeting his MI6 case worker, John Scarlett in and around the same neighborhood.

Disillusioned with the Soviet's brutal tactics in Czechoslovakia, Hungry and as of late Poland, Gordievsky, while stationed in Finland sent out feelers to the West, and was introduced to Scarlett, who immediately struck the Russian as quick, extremely intelligent and, most importantly as showing more initiative than most others. Gordievsky, despite Scarlett's youth and lower rank, liked the fact that Scarlett was able to make promises immediately without asking people for permission which meant he could get things done. A huge asset for someone of Oleg's mentality.

Scarlett was assigned by MI6 as Gordievsky's case officer by request and in their time together the two men had struck up a personal as well as a professional relationship.

After cursory greetings the Vauxhall headed west towards the safe house where they regularly held their meets in a nondescript block of flats in Bayswater bordering Hyde Park.

Fifteen minutes after starting out they turned onto a tree lined, two lane street with attractive well-kept walks, lined with Victorian, stucco terraces. They drove a couple of more blocks until they finally came upon a tastefully decorated two story home carefully dressed to appear to have full time residents. In fact, there was even an elderly man who was paid by the government to live there and keep up appearances. An old age pensioner, should there be any inquiries.

By arrangement the decoy wasn't home so Scarlett pulled up the narrow drive and let them both in through the back door where they made for the kitchen which was also in the back out of sight from the front of the house.

Once there John pulled the shades and set to work making the tea while Oleg cleared the table and produced a large manila envelope from under his overcoat.

"Any incidentals to pass along?" John asked.

"Yes actually. I have new estimates on the numbers of boots on the ground Vogel has in his HUMINT force. Upwards of 5,000."

291

"That's a considerable increase!"

"He says they're planning to increase that as well."

"How'd you come upon that?"

"Given to me by Vogel himself while we shared a pint in Berlin."

"Shared a pint?" Scarlett didn't know whether or not to take Oleg seriously.

"Yeah. Also, no plans to set up his own SIGINT operation just yet."

"Why on earth not?"

"Happy enough using the Russian's." The case Worker poured the tea and set out a plate of biscuits then took a seat at the table as Oleg spread the papers out.

"Did you pass on the false Pershing rotation schedules as well?"

"Yes, ate them up like a hungry puppy. These are some communications documents from the HVA to Dresden for the KGB contingent there." Scarlett produced a pocket sized camera and began to photograph the papers one at a time. "They appear to be semi to low value, dealing with small but across the board increases in surveillance, personnel and something having to do with an operator code named R-Y-N."

"R-Y-N?" Scarlett questioned.

"That's how it was deciphered. Obviously a code name."

"Or an anagram, acronym or something. Ever seen it before?" Scarlett suggested.

"Sorry, no. Unfortunately I don't have access to the original sheets, they're routinely destroyed after being encoded. These came from the electronic transcriptions of the intercept pages."

"I wonder if the increase in numbers have any significance?" Scarlett asked perusing the papers in between taking snaps.

When he'd finished taking two photos of each of the roughly two dozen documents Scarlett went to the fridge and produced some prepackaged hamburgers, unwrapped them and popped them into the microwave. Oleg looked closer at the communiqués.

"I didn't have time at the embassy to read these through, too busy and too many people floating around, but they appear to be fairly routine requests. Of course with all that's going on between the two sides, they could mean something bigger."

"We'll know better who's asking for what exactly when we've deciphered them." John took the last of the photos. "What's the overall atmosphere on the other side of the fence just now?"

"Well, HVA are quite pleased with their technological advances. They're working on a reduced burst system. They think they can get it down to a second or less given enough time."

"That'll be a neat trick!"

"As far as things in Yuri's house, there's no lack of paranoia particularly amongst the Politburo, led by Andropov himself. Hates Reagan thinks he's a delusional lunatic still living in his Hollywood films."

"Yes, well ... I probably shouldn't say anything but there are those of us here who wonder about that as well sometimes."

"He's completely convinced that Reagan is looking to draw him into some kind of protracted nuclear conflict."

"Seriously?!"

"Very much so. There's loose talk as well of sending agents to Granada to monitor the Marines and more agents to Argentina to help the Communist movement there."

"The Yanks'll love to hear that! Any details? I've to send them a blurt tonight."

"None. They don't discuss numbers or anything like that in these papers, there's only indirect references." The burgers were ready and John served them on white bread with some more tea.

"Sorry there's no chips, I know you like them. Did Vogel buy the *Time Magazine* story?"

"Yes, actually, I think he did. Clever by the way."

"Thank you."

"Any mention to further infiltrate Western Europe?"

"Not so far that I've seen. Not from the KGB side of the house anyway."

Scarlett selected one of the documents from the table.

"You're sure of this last bit? About increased infiltrations in Western Europe by the HVA?" John asked.

"I've been ordered to prepare to receive information on as many as a dozen agents myself in the next six months to be stationed in London. It's possible Moscow will order them re-dispersed, but there's no way to know that now."

As they ate Scarlett re-examined the papers.

"Be awful handy if we could give the Chief a bit of insight into this R-Y-N business." Scarlett half mumbled as he continued to peruse the papers.

"Well there's one small bit you can report that might be handy to Lord Sir Colin Figures, KCMG, OBE." Oleg exaggerated.

"What's that?"

"That the People's Soviet Socialist Republic is definitely light years ahead of you in the science of ..." Oleg spat his half chewed burger onto his plate. "... frozen hamburgers!"

**

It's no earth shattering observation in psychology that fear breeds hatred and Andropov's seeds of contempt for the West and consequent growth into full blown hatred, now being fuelled by the ripe fruits of that fear, began almost immediately after WWII.

By the 1950's his hatred was well entrenched and in 1958 he penned a letter to the Central Committee in Moscow, essentially the Politburo, while he was serving in the post of the CPSU's Director of Relations with Workers for the entire Eastern Bloc.

In the letter, which was really a report, he alarmingly wrote about the massive increase in the "Flight of the Intelligentsia" to the West. The well-educated, predominantly young population of the Communist East had seen the writing on the wall before there was a wall and were getting out of the

East before stricter measures were taken to stop travel altogether. The East had suffered a brain drain which eventually reached 20% of the entire East German population.

This report led to Stalin's suggestions which led to the building of The Wall. The wording and tone of Yuri's letter clearly shows early signs of fear of the developing, world-wide political situation. His aggressive ascent of the Commie political ladder into leader of the KGB then to Top Dog of the Politburo sealed the deal concerning his beliefs.

Now thirty years on, Andropov was regularly suffering from ulcers, hypertension and sleepless nights. He wrestled with the fact that not only could the system he had devoted his entire life to be crumbling, but the only apparent alternative to save it, or so it seemed to him, was all out war. A war which was looking more and more to be heading towards a nuclear confrontation.

Reagan on the other hand, clearly believed he had not only a mandate from the American people to save the world from the Godless Commie Hoards, as the Soviets were commonly known, but was in possession of a reinforced mandate from a much higher authority: God Himself.

From his early days as a self-appointed Commie hunter in Hollywood, reporting directly to J. Edgar Hoover ratting out trusted colleagues, Reagan showed he held a clear distinction between those with money and those who had to work at manual labor to live.

It was during the 1946 strike involving the Conference of Studio Unions that he came to convince himself that the strike itself was part of a world-wide Communist plot to take over America. It was at this time that his fear of an alternative system, particularly communism as an alternative system, began to fester into hatred.

This hatred grew and was later manifested by his "Trickle Down" theory of economics, an unmitigated failure, when he reached the Top Dog spot of America's version of the Politburo, The Executive Branch.

In essence both men were driven by a deep seeded and misguided belief of the other and neither had the ability to step back from and look at the bigger picture in order to seek a long term solution.

Worse yet, both men believed they were the bigger picture.

**

It was 22:40 when an aide finally tracked the President down as he was sitting at his desk on the second floor of the White House in the residential area. As he usually did, Reagan was making a diary entry before retiring for the night.

We have many contingency plans for responding to a nuclear attack. But everything would happen so fast that I wonder how much planning or reason could be applied in such a crisis.

Six minutes to decide how to respond to a blip on a radar scope and decide whether to unleash Armageddon! How could anyone apply reason at a time like that?

Also on his mind, along with events of the first week of the publicly broadcast political war of words, was the ongoing, frantic search for the wreckage of KAL 007.

It was not going well, for either side. The Soviets, in support of their fleet and the dozens of civilian fishing boats they had commissioned or commandeered, had also spent 100's of thousands of Rubles while the American bill had exceeded the $1 million mark in the first four or five days.

Standing against the American's efforts was not only the hostile environment of sailing conditions in the Sea of Japan in the Autumn weather but also the fact that the Soviet vessels involved in the search far outnumbered the American's small fleet and, due to proximity to their homeland, proffered ease of resupply and therefore were not necessarily limited by time on station. Additionally they had the benefit of access to the attack pilot and his aircraft's coordinates to guide their search.

Hanging over everyone's head was the possibility of a mishap which would almost certainly escalate into a shootout, something neither side wanted but both were well prepared for.

"Sir?" Reagan was engrossed in his thoughts. "Sir?!" Standing in the doorway of the study the aide called again.

"Yes? Sorry Malcolm. What is it?"

"We've gotten through to the fleet sir, in the Sea of Japan. We have Admiral Cockell on the line via satellite uplink from the *U.S.S. Narragansett*."

Reagan rose to go down stairs to the Oval Office but the aide held up a hand.

"Oh, you can take it from your desk phone sir. They patched it in to your land line."

"Huh!" Reagan stared over at his desk. "A phone attached to the radio!" Reagan grunted in surprise as he looked at the desk phone then retook his seat. "What's next I wonder? Pocket telephones?"

"I don't know Mr. President, but they say a French fella over in France discovered the virus that causes AIDES." Reagan looked up at Malcolm.

"Well I guess that's something, isn't it?"

"Mr. President. Will there be anything else tonight?"

"No Malcolm, thank you, thank you very much." Out of habit Reagan spoke louder than required when he picked up the phone. "Admiral Cockell? This is the President. How are we lookin' out there? Do you have everything you need?"

Yes sir, logistics are superb.

"I need some good news Admiral. Are we any closer to locating the wreckage?"

Speaking from the bridge of his flagship, Admiral Cockell watched a pair of McDonnell Douglas F-4B Phantoms on a low fly-by on their way to escort duty. He raised his binos and scanned the port side. The fighter jets had caught up and over took a low flying P-3 Orion just as it finished dispensing its cargo of sonobouys into the ocean.

"Sir, I promise you that not since the all-out search for that nuke we lost off the coast of Palomares, Spain has the U.S. Navy undertaken a search of this magnitude to locate and recover an object or vessel lost at sea."

Cockell watched as the P-3 climbed in altitude and pulled away just as a second one took its place.

"Admiral you understand the criticality of your mission?"

"Clearly sir, I do."

"We must find that black box!"

"I understand sir. We're running 24 hour patrols. As we speak I'm watching P-3 Orions sweeping for Delta and Typhoon class subs." Cockell could hear the faint chatter of the pilots' radio traffic back inside the wheel house as he stood outside the bridge, his back to the rail.

"Can those black boxes be tampered with?" The President asked.

"In truth sir, it's not my area of expertise, but I suppose anything's possible."

"Well if they get a hold of it you can be damn sure that whatever information they get from it is gonna be tampered with and used as propaganda!"

"Yes sir." The Admiral stepped in closer to the bulkhead of the superstructure and held the transceiver close in to his mouth as he spoke. "Mr. President, are we certain the reports of the KAL aircraft being forced down and the passengers being held on Sakhalin are false?"

"That story was a false flag to buy us time. That and the guys at the Agency couldn't bring themselves to accept the facts when they first intercepted the initial reports that 300 innocent men, women and children had been blown out of the sky by the Russians."

"Yes sir."

"You've probably already been told but I'll repeat it so there's no misunderstandings. Except in the event of overt aggression, I want extraordinary precautionary measures taken to avoid any 'accidental' contact with Soviet vessels. Is that understood Admiral?"

"Yes Mr. President, understood."

"I want ALL vessels to steer well clear of the Russians! Is that understood?! Send word to all ships that I don't want anyone within five miles of ANY Russian vessel, to include their fishing boats. Give them as wide a birth as practical!"

"Orders have been issued to that effect throughout the fleet Mr. President."

"Obviously we don't need any accidents with the Japanese either. We're allies now. The Japanese are not minor players in this game. They have as much at stake as we do."

"I understand Mr. president. They're acting in a very professional manner, and proving to be a valuable asset sir. It's the Russkies we're keeping an eye on."

"Totally understandable. Very well. Best of luck in your efforts and keep me informed Admiral."

"Yes sir, I will." They hung up and Reagan further pondered his diary. He was staring intently at the open leather bound book when he heard a call.

"Dutch honey, you coming to bed dear?" Nancy called from the bedroom suite of the Executive Residence.

"In a minute Nance." He resumed his thoughts, picked up his pen and began again to write.

I feel the Soviets are so defense minded, so paranoid about being attacked that without being in any way soft on them we ought to tell them that no one here has any intention of doing anything like invading them. What the hell have they got that anyone would want?!

When he finished he lay down his pen and shuffled to the bathroom to brush his teeth.

Overall, Reagan did not share other's belief that cooler heads would eventually prevail.

Nancy, concerned that he was taking longer than usual to make one of his normally short entries quietly made her way into the study and over to his desk. She uncharacteristically opened the diary and read the new entries.

She stared blankly at the scribbled writing until she heard him finishing up in the bathroom.

*

CHAPTER THIRTEEN

CIA HQ
Langley, Virginia
19:45, September 8th

Lieutenant Harden had been making little headway on clues as to the significance of the Russian code word 'Ryan', but now nearly a week into his inquiries he believed he might have found a line of inquiry that would open a door which would, with one or two more bits of information, put him where he needed to be.

It was less than a week since getting the okay from the powers-that-be to launch his own investigation regarding the mysterious references in the intercepted Soviet traffic, specifically the code word RYAN.

Now Harden had what he believed to be enough evidence to request the operation be taken to the next level, the formation of an operational team to be deployed for the expressed purpose of uncovering physical evidence to support the now universally accepted theory that the Soviets were up to something big, most likely in Western Europe.

To that end he had obtained permission to liaise with some contacts at the CIA and had been using their facilities all day to track down details connected with the Walker spy ring.

Deciding to call it quits for the night, Harden signed out of the file room at the Langley records wing where he had been working for the last several hours and headed for his car.

"Excuse me sir, you Lieutenant Harden?" Keys in hand, about to unlock his car Dave turned and looked up at what appeared to be two steroid infused military police, their silver helmets gleaming in the yellowish lamp lights of the half dark parking lot. Both men stood a full foot above him.

"Yes. Why?"

"I'm sorry sir, but you'll have to come with us." The corporal said.

"Why?"

"Because you're under arrest." The sergeant answered and as trained, the M. P.'s moved to either side of him.

"FOR WHAT?!"

"Tampering with federal evidence." They moved as a team and one produced a set of handcuffs while the other took his brief case and drew his arms behind his back. It was well past the end of the work day so there were only a few rubbernecks as the military cops led him away handcuffed and set him in the back seat of their olive drab Chrysler.

M.P.'s, being M.P.'s, they refused to talk to him or answer any of his questions enroute to the cop shop and once there they acted little more than automatons as they led him to the desk, unceremoniously dumped his personal belongings on a table along with his brief case and signed in with the Desk Sergeant before leading him back to a row of cells.

Once inside a cell they uncuffed him, the door slammed shut and, despite his demands to know what was going on, he was left alone, uncuffed, uninformed and understanding that this was a pretty serious turn of events in what was, up until a half hour ago, an aspiring naval career.

****

It was sometime early next morning when two different steroid sergeants barged into his cell, re-cuffed his hands in front of him and silently escorted him to what he well knew to be an interrogation room and left him there. Brightly lit, white painted block walls, two metal chairs, one each side of a small table all centered in the ten foot by ten foot room. From his chair facing the door he looked up at the CCTV cam in the corner. The red light was on. He smiled and with cuffed hands waved and mouthed "Hi mom!"

He was left there for some time and had drifted off to sleep, and was leaned over on the table when the door lock rattled, woke him and he looked up into the brightly silhouetted form of a man standing over him.

"Ya know, for a 'bright young spark' you're not off to very illustrious start young man!" Harden cleared his mind and from his seat across the table nearly fell off his chair.

The Director of the CIA, stood in the doorway. "Thank you. You can leave us." Bill Casey directed the guard. "I don't think he's too dangerous. But keep your tasers ready." He instructed the sentry who disappeared locking the door behind him.

Casey sat Harden's briefcase on the floor and reached into his breast pocket as he pulled up the chair opposite producing a floppy disc from his pocket and slid it across the table directly in front of the distraught lieutenant.

"Look familiar?" Casey asked. Harden looked down and grimaced.

"I think I might have seen it before. Somewhere. Sir."

"Who the hell do you think you are son, James fucking Bond?! There's enough political bullshit in this town without having to go around stealing from our sister agencies!"

"I intended to return it. I just –"

"Webster said he gave you permission to copy it! What the hell were you thinking?"

"The information Walker sold to the Russians is property of the U.S. Navy and I am a designated agent of the U.S. Nav-"

"Don't give me that shithouse lawyer crap! Where do you think that shit came from?! Guys like Bill Donovan and I invented that crap to keep the Senate suits off our backs in the old days! You're lucky Webster doesn't want any more scandal or he'd damn sure press charges and –"

"I needed the original!"

"Why?! Why the original?! What's wrong with a copy? We use copies all the time!"

"Yes sir we do and I would have to have gone through half a dozen people in the FBI to get a copy, and then wait while it went through two or three more people on my side of the house. Besides the waiting time, floppies get scratched, creased, misplaced, stolen, lost. Too much heat they warp, too cold they become brittle. I had it right there, right there in my hands. A direct connect with the KGB! Agents don't get too many of those chances in a lifetime sir. You know that. On top of all that when this thing leaks out, which it inevitably will, the FBI will try to claim sole credit!"

"And if it turns into the just as likely blame game? What then?"

"Then they'll blame our side of the house, you know that! Sir."

Casey sat back in his chair and gave a deep sigh of exasperation. "Yeah, I know that." Neither man spoke.

"Well? Did you just give me another ulcer, take a year off my life and disrupt my breakfast for nothing or did you find anything?"

Harden leaned across the table and into Casey, smiled an evil grin and slowly nodded.

"Yes sir. I did."

"Well?!"

Harden held up his still cuffed wrists, the disc clutched between thumb and forefinger. He gave a silly grin, and lifted his eyebrows. Casey remained stone faced.

"GUARD!" Casey called out and when the guard entered he issued instructions. "Sergeant, we need an office, a secure computer and to be left alone."

Most M. P.'s believe themselves to be above the law and regulations and consequently don't take orders very well, especially when those orders come from a recently detained prisoner. Harden knew this and took no small amount of pleasure as he spoke while being uncuffed.

"And two cups of coffee, please. Black." The sergeant sneered at Harden who looked over at Casey who nodded his assent at the Army cop.

Once inside a small side office Harden fed the floppy into the reader slot, closed it over and, after seeing the green cursor begin to flash in the upper left hand corner of the screen manned the keyboard and called up the FBI reports it contained.

"Sir, this file not only contains all the direct connects of Walker, the Russians and their activities, but also all the info the FBI have accumulated pursuant to his and Wentworth's activities since around late '71, early '72."

"Gee Lieutenant, I wonder why Director Webster was so upset?"

"I assume, from a political, P.R. standpoint sir, the FBI will get credit in the Press for what we get from this disc?"

"Yeah, but what's that got to do with us?"

"Trust me sir! Director Webster will feel a whole lot better when he finds out the real value of the information on the disc in relation to our overall Intel situation." Harden punched some more keys and the report's iridescent green letters appeared on the screen. "This document contains a surveillance report on Walker, dated October 17, 1979. This is the last report we have on him before we discovered that Boris Solomatin was his handler."

"Okay."

"I've gone through all the reports on Walker from the earliest date we have, 1972 –"

"Jesus Lieutenant! How the hell long did that

take you?"

"About two hours."

"TWO HOURS?! That all?!"

"Yes sir. Unlike the old Tandy's the new IBM 3600's have a search mode. Type in the word or phrase and it will search not only documents but entire files." Harden explained.

"Impressive!" Casey sat back and stared at the computer. "Why the hell don't I have one of those?"

"It can be arranged sir." Harden informed as he typed.

"I wonder where this technology thing will take us?" Harden, more than 40 years Casey's junior, struggled to suppress his amusement.

"Not sure sir, but probably not where we think." He continued typing. "The word 'Ryan' appeared for the first time in July of '81." Harden continued. Casey leaned in and examined the screen.

"On the Fourth of July?!"

"Yes sir and I think that's significant, I'll explain in a minute. The next time we see it is a few times at the end of the year and then with markedly increasing frequency throughout the 2nd and 3rd quarters of 1982." He pointed to the screen to indicate a string of dates. "Coming into 1983 frequency is maintained and then ..." Casey reached over to the key board and clicked the scroll key.

"Loads of activity in April of that year? How do you account for that?" Casey asked.

"The President started the Strategic Defence Initiative in late March."

"But there's no mention of Ryan on anything we actually got from Walker?"

"No sir and there wouldn't be."

"Why not?"

"Because I think Ryan is very highly classified and very high up. Higher than Walker or possibly even higher than Boris Solomatin."

"Huh."

"Now, you're correct there's nothing direct about Ryan on anything we have from Walker but, the Wentworth discs are loaded with dates, and all of the same dates of KGB and HVA communiqués that mention Ryan can be found on one or more of the Wentworth discs."

"Okay, we got a connect. But where's the Fourth of July fit in?"

"Minimum foreign and domestic military activity during the holiday. Good time to observe troop strengths, stand down and reactivation procedures, assembly times etc..." Harden was pleased to see Casey appeared to be convinced by his line of reasoning. "This is just a stupid wild ass guess, but given that Ryan is still being mentioned in messages and has been for so long and given that it is mentioned to coincide with significant dates of significant activities, like the Fourth, I don't think Ryan is a who."

"Then what?"

"I think it's a 'what'."

"An operation?"

"An operation, a location, a string of locations, not sure yet. Possibly an on-going operation of some description, yes sir."

"That's a pretty impressive SWAG Lieutenant."

"Thank you sir but, my overall concern now is,

do you believe that there is enough here to warrant fielding a team dedicated to investigate Ryan?"

Casey stared at Harden, back to the screen then sighed. He reached into his breast pocket.

"We were not supposed to have this conversation until after you've spoken with Admiral Butts, however ..." He handed a two page, classified report to the lieutenant.

Harden's eyes lit up as he quickly perused through the inter-agency report. On several spots through-out the report, the word 'RyAN' appeared.

"This is dated two days ago!" Harden observed.

"It was intercepted by MI6 three days ago." Casey informed.

"The spelling! They spell it differently. Is that a British thing?"

"You tell me! All I know is that one of their Russians translated it."

"Then that must be how the Russians spell it!" Harden confirmed.

Casey sat back, glanced at the computer screen then back at Lieutenant Harden again and drew in a deep breath.

"We have field operatives already out there, experienced, proven operatives who know the territory. Why should we assemble a new team and not just task a team already in the field?"

"Because, if I'm right, which I believe I am, I just became the U.S. Intel services expert on an unknown, highly classified, Soviet operation that could have serious ramifications of, not only how we use those teams already in the field, but how we conduct the spy business altogether." Casey

311

continued to peruse the screen. "Sir, also consider how long it will take to bring those teams in, debrief them and then re-brief them and bring them up to date on everything we have on Ryan before redeploying them. Not to mention the risks of recalling then redeploying assets after they've been briefed!"

Harden considered it a good sign that he still had Casey's attention so he thought he'd go for broke and play the logistics angle. "We're only talking about a four or five man team at the outside. I'll screen records, pick a few names and submit them to Admiral Butts for approval. Two days maximum. They could be briefed and working on it by Saturday sir."

Again The Director gave no response, he simply rose without comment and gathered his coat and brief case, ejected the disc, removed it from the tray and turned to leave.

"Alright let's go. You've work to do and I'm due over at the Pentagon." Harden had a plethora of questions but reminded himself not to look the gift horse in the mouth. "I want a full typewritten report on my desk by 17:00. Also, be prepared for a Q&A by the Intel heads at 18:00!"

Harden stared blankly. "Questions, comments snide remarks Lieutenant?"

"Only one sir. Do you mind if I dart over to the Officer's Mess real quick? I haven't eaten anything since lunch time yesterday."

"What, they didn't feed you in the brig?"

"I don't suppose they get too many officers in here. I guess they were just tryin' to make the most of it."

As they darted out of the office and headed for the station's exit, they passed through the door, right by the highly irritated Desk Sergeant standing there holding two cups of steaming coffee and a plate of jelly donuts. As they passed Harden stuffed a donut in his mouth and grabbed one of the coffees.

"Thank you Sargent!" He smiled as he passed by.

*

17:55 Saturday 10th
Vestibule of the Oval Office

"I want to be absolutely clear on this!" Reagan spoke in a low voice and made direct eye contact with Howard Baker, the Senior Democratic Party Leader, whom he had cornered in the hall only seconds before. "I don't want any bi-partisan crap on this! You get together with Bob Byrd have dinner, get drunk, get him laid! I don't care, do whatever it takes! I want the SDI appropriations through both chambers by the end of November!"

"Mr. President, the reality of the situation is ..."

"It's time Mr. President." Someone called out to him from the doorway.

"Okay." Reagan answered then strode back into the Oval Office, which once again was decked out with the full array of T.V. broadcast equipment, sound, lights and cameras.

"TWO MINUTES EVERYBODY! TWO

MINUTES!" Somebody in the overcrowded room shouted. There was a last minute flurry of activity, Reagan took his seat behind his desk next to a tele-screen which sported video images of multiple missile trajectories and which was on pause.

A director stood in front of the center camera and began the countdown on his fingers as he spoke.

"Five, four, three, two ..."

"My fellow Americans, thank you for sharing your time with me tonight. The subject I want to discuss with you, peace and national security, is both timely and important. Timely, because I've reached a decision which offers a new hope for our children in the 21st century, a decision I'll tell you about in a few minutes. And important because there's a very big decision that you must make for yourselves."

A pair of senior aides standing in the wings looked at each other in surprise. The speech had not been written by the usual writers and most of the staff knew nothing about its contents or intended purpose.

"Deterrence means simply this: making sure any adversary who thinks about attacking the United States, or our allies, or our vital interests, concludes that the risks to him outweigh any potential gains. Once he understands that, he won't attack. We maintain the peace through our strength. Weakness only invites aggression."

Meanwhile, over at CIA Headquarters in Langley the CIA Deputy Director, John N. McMahon, had been having a coffee in the canteen but was now racing to the nearest house phone. He found one hanging on the wall in the corridor and hurriedly rang a four digit number.

"George, are you near a television?!"

"I'm watching. What the hell is he doing?!" Schultz answered.

"It would appear he's going public with the anti-missile laser beam nonsense!"

"Did he say anything to you about a press announcement?" Schultz queried.

"Jesus no! The last thing we discussed was extending funding for feasibility studies! Our grandkids won't have that level of technology fer cryin' out loud much less our current science people! Did he suggest anything to you?"

"Not a hint! We need a fallout meeting on this tomorrow." Schultz insisted.

"I'll set something up for ten." McMahon assured him. They hung up and the Deputy Director went back to the canteen's television to follow the rest of the broadcast.

This strategy of deterrence has not changed. It still works. But what it takes to maintain deterrence has changed. It took one kind of military force to deter an attack when we had far more nuclear weapons than any other power; it takes another kind now that the Soviets, for example, have enough accurate and powerful nuclear weapons to destroy virtually all of our missiles on the ground.

For 20 years the Soviet Union has been accumulating enormous military might. They didn't stop when their forces exceeded all requirements of a legitimate defensive capability. And they haven't stopped now. During the past decade and a half, the Soviets have built up a massive arsenal of new strategic nuclear weapons – weapons that can strike directly at the United States!"

The United States introduced its last new intercontinental ballistic missile, the Minute Man III, in 1969, and we're now dismantling our even older Titan missiles. But what has the Soviet Union done in these intervening years?

Two senators sat at a local Washington bar, staring at the corner television in astonishment at Reagan's comments regarding no new missiles in the U.S. inventory since 1969 and his further demonizing of the Soviets.

Well, since 1969 the Soviet Union has built five new classes of ICBM's, and upgraded these eight times."

"What can he be thinking?! Is he trying to bluff the Russians or spook them?"

"He didn't get the carte blanch approval he wanted on The Hill for his Star Wars nonsense so now he's trying to bypass us and take it to the people!"

"The Senate are the people who have to decide the funding for such an undertaking and that in turn means you, the people who vote for them must decide."

"Christ! This just two weeks after he calls them

'The Evil Empire'!"

"Three weeks. It was three weeks ago." He dismissed.

"Oh! That makes all the difference! Another round, make it a double!" One of the senators called over to the bartender.

... But with these considerations firmly in mind, I call upon the scientific community in our country, those who gave us nuclear weapons, to turn their great talents now to the cause of mankind and world peace, to give us the means of rendering these nuclear weapons impotent and obsolete.

Tonight, consistent with our obligations of the ABM treaty and recognizing the need for closer consultation with our allies, I'm taking an important first step. I am directing a comprehensive and intensive effort to define a long-term research and development program to begin to achieve our ultimate goal of eliminating the threat posed by strategic nuclear missiles.

My fellow Americans, tonight we're launching an effort which holds the promise of changing the course of human history. There will be risks and results take time. But I believe we can do it. As we cross this threshold, I ask for your prayers and your support for this great land which is the last hope of mankind. Thank you and God bless you.

Back in the White House, still standing off to the side was the V.P. and a senior aide who leaned over and whispered to Bush.

"Mr. Vice-President, if the Press finds out we

don't have anywhere near the technology for that program they'll crucify us!"

"You mean **when** they find out!" An astonished George Bush mumbled.

*

The Lubyanka Building, now the KGB Headquarters, in central Moscow was said to be the tallest building in Russia. Because you could see Siberia from the basement.

The mixed Neo-Baroque and Neo-Renaissance architecture was out of place in the open Lubyanka Square and perhaps that was intentional because the structure certainly jumped out at the public.

The young, army motorcycle courier looked up at the twenty foot tall statue of Felix Dzerzhinsky, founder of the Cheka, the secret police and forefathers, of the KGB, as he rounded the statue which stood sentinel outside.

Compelled to circle twice he was hard pressed to find a suitable spot to park as the place was strewn with construction equipment and materials. A new wing was under construction.

Settling for a spot up against the building, he parked then shut down the little 125cc bike, took the steps to the entrance two at a time and bounded up to the reception desk.

"Chairman Chebrikov's office please. Message from the Presidium."

"Sign here. Second floor, last door on left! The burly NCO grunted. "Be sure to write time, here."

318

He pointed to the last line on the right of the page.

"Thank you comrade! Long live The People's Republic."

"Yeah, yeah." Came the laconic response from the desk sergeant.

With the wasted enthusiasm of youth the messenger didn't wait for the lift but took the stairs, again two at a time.

Heading through the door he was confronted with a long counter shielding a rank of four desks only one of which was occupied.

A pudgy major pushed out from behind the second desk and came to the counter as the boy withdrew a small envelope from his messenger's pouch.

"For the Chairman. From the General Secretary."

"Sign here." He mimicked the ritual from downstairs.

"I will take for him." The Major reached forward but the boy refused to hand it over.

"It is a message for the Chairman."

"Really?!" The major's high speech tainted with a heavy Ukrainian dialect stood out as he leaned forward on the counter and stared at the boy. "I once had a message for the Chairman, Chairman Andropov, I ask him, 'When do I get promotion?!' Do you know his answer?" The boy shook his head. "I give you hint. I used to be general! HAHAHAA!" The messenger failed to see the joke. "Hey boy! You gonna stay in this army you better get a sense of humor! The Chairman is down in The Cellar give me message."

"Sorry major, I have strict instructions. My hand

to Colonel Chebrikov's only!"

"Suit yourself. Have seat." He gestured to the long wooden bench against the bulletin board festooned wall.

✲

The Cellar, Lubyankian for the dungeons, was actually located in the basement and that was where Chairman Chebrikov and his #2 man, Kryuchkov, were at the moment.

They had just taken delivery of a blanket chest sized crate delivered by special unmarked vehicle. Chebrikov signed for the item and the two heavily armed guards who had placed the crate on an iron table against the wall were now closing up the small delivery van and preparing to leave.

Neither KGB man spoke until the van drove back up the ramp and disappeared around the curve to exit the rear of the building.

"Help me get it on the floor." Chebrikov instructed. They pried the lid open and peered down through the dim light into the open crate.

"I've never actually seen one of these things." Kryuchkov commented. I always pictured them as being much bigger."

"Huh. I always imagined they were smaller. And black, not orange." Chebrikov countered.

"Let's get it to a safe place. Give me a hand." They closed it over and carried it down the damp, stone passageway to a narrower hallway off on the right lined with what looked like medieval prison cells and entered the last cell on the left. Inside there was a floor to ceiling steel vault with several shelves.

They wrestled the closed crate onto the bottom shelf, closed over the door, being careful to hear the combination lock engage and Chebrikov spun the dial several times in both directions.

The antique phone hanging on the wall in the corridor buzzed twice in succession. Kryuchkov went out to answer it.

"There's a messenger for you upstairs. He's from the Kremlin."

"You go. I'll be right up. I have to log this in."

Kryuchkov left as Chebrikov pulled the cord dangling from the single light bulb, closed the cell door over and locked it.

****

That evening Harden, encouraged by his recently found mentor, CIA Director William Casey, had given a text book Q&A session to Casey, the #2 man at the ONI, the DDNSA, Faurer's assistant and the man he was warned would be his most ardent antagonist and personally charged by the president to keep tabs on the situation, Secretary of State George Schultz.

All on the day he was released from the brig.

As was becoming Lieutenant Harden's signature trait, he had been one step ahead as he finished drawing up his five man dream team wish list back in his office later that night. That was a Monday.

At his presentation he told them he'd rather hand pick a team versus having one assigned to him and the impromptu intel committee had given him until Friday to not only draw up the list but track the men down and secure written permission from their respective C.O.'s to okay the men's release. No mean feat given he was a mere Navy Lieutenant.

But even if he accomplished all this, which Casey and Schultz had a secret side bet on, he would face the most difficult obstacle.

The ONI, being his parent agency, would have to be persuaded to foot the bill for the operation's fund. And that meant getting it by the Capo di Capi himself, Admiral Butts, a man Harden had unintentionally been avoiding and would happily retire never having met. For this task he knew he would be flying solo.

It was Thursday mid-afternoon and he had sent his ATF, Access to Funds request in on the day after the meeting. Also he was yet to hear back from the SEAL Team Three Commander regarding his request for TAD orders for his weapons and tactics man Ricky Matson.

"Finally I get to meet this character!" Admiral Butts said half out loud, half to himself as a secretary showed him to Lieutenant Dave Harden's one room office in room #327.

Butts, having no sense of humor about having to track Harden down, unceremoniously barged in holding a folder in his hand and a startled Harden snapped to attention from behind his desk.

"This your desk Lieutenant?"

"Yes Admiral." Butts pushed past him and pulled

up the still warm chair and sat behind the desk.

"Not today. I got fifteen minutes for you then I'm due back at Operations." Without otherwise acknowledging Harden the Admiral began reading the file out loud.

"U.S.M.C. Staff Sergeant Ray MacDonald, demolitions NATO and Soviet, standard & improvised. Petty Officer Ricky 'Boom Boom' Matson, Seal Team 3, weapons and tactics. Hospitalman Second Class 'Doc' McKeowen, medical, demolitions and linguistics. Sergeant Danial 'Danno' Byrd, communications and electronic surveillance." He closed the folder over and looked up at Harden, who still stood at attention. "Where do they get these names? Marvel comics? Sounds like a low budget remake of the freakin' *A Team*."

"Sir they ..."

"I don't give a shit Lieutenant! But what I do give a shit about is the fact that all these men are all from different service branches. 1979 Iranian Embassy hostages, *Operation Eagle Claw*, **former** President Jimmy Carter who **didn't** get re-elected? Any of that ring a bell Lieutenant?"

The general consensus regarding the failure of *Eagle Claw* was the multi-branch operation lacked adequate inter-service commo causing it to end in unmitigated disaster.

"Yes sir ... I ..."

"Why would you not want an intact team to deploy? SF, SEALS, Force Recon, men who have trained, worked and deployed together before?" Asked the Admiral with no attempt to hide his disapproval.

"All those men in my request are not only jump and scuba qualified but crossed trained in a second, and some in a third MOS or NSC discipline. Each has at least 3.0 in one European language and all, with the exception of Petty Officer McKeowen, who has served in several global disaster areas, have served on real world deployments. Sir, I firmly believe each man is the best in his own area and therefore the best man for the job. They're all Special Operations qualified with a minimum of eight years each in service. All of which means they are three and four time volunteers. Team work will come naturally to them."

"And another thing, Neu Ulm? Why in hell do you want me to go through channels to get you a billet to operate out of an Army post? The *U.S.S. Lexington* will be on station in the Med in two days!"

"Middle of the Med is a long way off from our intended A.O. sir. Transport, time, logistics these are all factors. More importantly Neu Ulm Army Post will be in the middle of the action during *Operation Able Archer*, the area will likely attract an increased number of Red operatives, if there are any around, we'll spread out to intersect them and be able to cover more ground, it'll be easier to return to a central location and compare notes, prep and call in reports etc ..."

"I suppose you already contacted General Williams at Army V Corps and cleared this with him, clearly explaining there's going to be a bunch of bastard child misfits stomping around their playground during the largest NATO exercise ever staged?"

"Their G-2 has graciously offered us a luxury accommodation on the top floor of a 200 year old, ex-Nazi barracks. That, and the Department of 'Logistics office is only one flight up from your office sir."

"What the hell's **that** got to do with anything?!"

"I didn't have that far to carry the case of Irish whiskey. Sir."

"Uh huh, very strategic. I noticed you don't have a team leader listed Lieutenant."

"Who else would I want to lead these men Admiral?" Butts slid the report folder forward on the desk, sat back and stared at Harden like a dog just been shown a card trick.

"Lieutenant Harden, you've been an intel officer for how long now, four, five years?"

"Five and a half sir."

"Five and a half. And how much of that time have you spent in the field?"

"No time in the field Admiral."

"You're not a field operator son. You're a brains guy. You find the places where we send guys like this in order to get into the shit." Butts used the old political ploy of pausing to give Harden enough rope to hang himself. When coming to Harden's office a few minutes ago he was certain he was going to scuttle the mission before it launched. Now he thought he saw a spark.

"You think you can track down this Ryan guy and find out what the sneaky little bastard is up to when all three major agencies have been working on it for the last six months and come up with nothing?"

"Sir I was the one who first picked up on the code name Ryan and have been on it for nearly a year. I'm convinced it's significant if for no other reason than everyone else is hell bent on ignoring it." Dave finally let himself stand at ease. "It's fairly straight forward Admiral. If I do find Ryan and we can counter him, it whatever, we both wear an extra feather in our caps. If I make a dog's dinner out of the whole thing I look stupid and you still win because you'll know for sure Ryan isn't important."

"You realize you've still got more than half your career in the Navy to serve?"

"Yes sir. Why wouldn't I?"

"Congratulations Lieutenant. Looks like you got yourself an operation. Now all it needs is a name." He pushed away from the desk and stood up.

"Romeo Five sir. Task Force Romeo Five." Butts looked up at him.

"A five man task force?" The admiral scoffed.

"Yes sir. Deception of size is one of the first priorities of Intel sir."

"I'm the Director of one of the top intel agencies in the world! You giving me a basic course in Intel son?"

"Negative Admiral. Five men is all we'll need sir. Once we've discovered the location of Ryan, secondary decisions can be made."

"Why Romeo?"

"It was the designated air corridor the Korean civilians were shot down in."

"Well I guess at least you got something right."

"Admiral, I want to thank you for the opportunity. I won't let you down."

"Don't thank me son. Thank Bill Casey he's the one said if I didn't give you the funding he would." Harden was unable to mask his shock as Butts took the folder and made for the door. Fighting to contain the elation of his victory Harden eked out one last question.

"Sir why did you remind me of my time left in service?" Butts was through the door and on his way down the hall.

"Thirteen and a half years is a long time to be stuck as a Lieutenant."

****

By now Andropov and the majority of Russians clearly imagined a developing world wide plot against them led by the U.S.

No one will ever know exactly what Andropov really believed about responsibility for the KAL shoot down, but whatever it was Reagan's snub of diplomacy and pursuit of extremely aggressive political tactics clearly had their intended effect. They backed the Russians into a corner leaving them no choice but to defend themselves.

President Reagan's decision to use the KAL 007 shoot down to persuade Congress to support his requests for increased defense spending, the MX missile project and his later proposal of the Star Wars system no doubt added fuel to the fire.

A campaign of this magnitude and scope, which

just happened to coincide with the ongoing PSYOPS incursion operations, where there just happened to be a RC-135 in the vicinity of the KAL aircraft was too much to accept as a mere coincidence.

Taken together with the fact that the men of the Politburo were exclusively made up of WWII era politicians who clearly remembered the 25 million Russians lost in the war, in no small part due to Hitler's treachery, one wonders how a war scenario hadn't developed sooner.

The Russians, no less than the Americans, were prone to developing complexes of paranoia and, like the joined continents of Pangaea, their world-wide, future image fit their respective imagined scenarios. This series of events could only have the same effect it has always had and will always have.

The development and propagation of unfounded aggression.

CHAPTER FOURTEEN

The I-95 South
Somewhere between Washington D. C.
& Jacksonville, N. C.
Monday, September 12th

Lieutenant Harden welcomed the five and a half hour long drive south not only to get out of the office where things seemed to be closing in on him but to clear his head and refocus his perspective.

As soon as he had a preliminary plan and had his team list drawn up he decided to pack it in at the office as soon as possible and drive down the coast personally doing the old meet-and-greet to what he hoped would be his new team members.

By coincidence they were all currently stationed on the East Coast and easily within driving distance from D.C. All save Ray MacDonald of SEAL Team Three who was in the Philippine Islands on a hostage rescue mission, but Dave had cleverly waited to contact MacDonald until just after the rescue when he knew MacDonald would be on a natural high. After being informed by phone it wouldn't affect his team status in any way and that he would be free to return to The Teams whenever he wished, he immediately agreed.

Romeo Five had their demolitions man. The only glitch was hooking up with the team in time for a pre-deployment brief due in three days.

Petty Officer MacDonald assured the Lieutenant

he'd sort it out somehow and would be in touch.

And so it was that Harden decided to spend the weekend in his black Suburban in civvies driving down the coast to collect his potential new team members already treating his time away from the office as a kind of a mini-holiday.

At around 15:30 that Friday afternoon, just off Route 17 on the outskirts of Jacksonville, North Carolina Dave spotted an unlit neon sign which, like the last 100 miles of back road had seen better days.

The Bunker
Luxury Accommodation

"Why not?" He shrugged and pulled into the small, gravel covered, motel parking lot.

Opting to keep his clothes bag in the car he registered, paid in cash and left after a friendly but curt discourse.

Camp LeJuene was about a half an hour south and he made it to the front gate at just after 16:00. The Marine guard waved him forward, checked his I.D. and smartly saluted the blue officer's sticker on his bumper as he waved the vehicle through. Harden reached over and flicked on the radio as he passed through.

A million random thoughts ran through his mind as he leisurely took the curves on the long winding, blacktop through the camp. He gradually paid attention to the news broadcast as the pleasant female drawl-tainted voice filled the Suburban.

... the summit meeting, scheduled in Madrid next

week, the first meeting between the two superpowers in nearly a year, both leaders held separate press conferences in their respective capitals. Reagan sent George Schultz and there to speak for the Russians was Andrei Gromyko.

A recording with considerable back ground chatter of a crowd rolled featuring the voice of the Secretary of State George Schultz.

Foreign Minister Gromyko's response to me today was even more unsatisfactory than the response he gave in public yesterday. I find it totally unacceptable!

The voice of the commentator resumed.

When reached for comment the Soviet Union's Minister Gromyko was quoted as stating that the meeting quickly deteriorated into a heated exchange and was quote, '...the sharpest exchange I ever had with an American Secretary of State. And I have had talks with fourteen of them!'

Following the heated exchange, in an unprecedented diplomatic action, the Reagan administration today issued an order forbidding the admission of Foreign Minister Gromyko to land in New York City where he was scheduled to attend the opening session of the United Nations General Assembly in two days' time.

This action is all the more significant given the fact that Russia, now the Soviet Union, is one of the four permanent members of the United Nations. The

*United Nations Charter provides that the host nation is required **by law** to provide access to the U. N.*

Dave reached over and turned up the volume.

Less than a week ago in an emergency session of the General Assembly the Soviet Union was able to use its veto, available to the four permanent members, to block a U.N. resolution condemning it for downing the Korean Airlines flight 007.

Cold War hawk Ambassador Kirkpatrick, stated that the Russian ambassador, still shackled by the Politburo, could not confirm anything regarding flight KAL 007.

Taking things a step further, a White House spokesman today also announced that the U.S. will not renew its bilateral agreement with the Soviets on international transportation which means all Aeroflot Airline flights, as of the 15th of September, will only be available to and from Canada and Mexico.

The moves by the administration prompted an immediate response from the Gromyko camp via the Soviet news agency TASS which suggested that perhaps the U.N. should consider moving its headquarters from the United States to a more rational country.

No location was suggested however, Charles Lichtenstein, acting U. S. Permanent representative to the U. N., under Ambassador Jeane Kirkpatrick responded.

The news commentator's voice was again replaced this time with a recording of Lichtenstein's voice.

'We will put no impediment in their way. The members of the U.S. mission to the United Nations will be down at the dockside waving the Russians a fond farewell as they sail off into the sunset!'

The female commentator finished off the broadcast.

Administration officials were quick to announce that Lichtenstein was speaking only for himself.
Next up, Johnny 'Bubba J.' Kendall with the local livestock reports to include latest in hog futures. This is Mary Jean Copel, WXCN 88.2 FM, Raleigh, North Carolina, thank ya'll for-.

"Jesus, things are heating up with the Big Boys!" Dave mumbled as he switched off the radio and took his bearings. "Hog futures?!' Ha! Hogs have no future!" Harden laughed.

Ten minutes later he was pulling up outside the small, WWII era Force Recon Headquarters building where there was no reception just a Major sitting alone in the back office. He approached and knocked on the door jamb.

"Lieutenant Dave Harden, from Washington. I called ahead sir."

"Yeah I was told." The Major rose to greet him. "Doc McKeowen's giving a class right now, done in about forty minutes." The Major came out to shake his hand. "You're welcome to wait in my office if you like, have a cup of coffee." Harden had purposely seen to it that no hint of why he was there could have been leaked to anyone, including the Major. Therefore, knowing that he was down from D.C., he saw the potential for the awkward situation where the Major would be all warm and friendly and casually stroke him for details. Details he wasn't at liberty to leak.

"Thank you sir, but I think I'll just wonder around a bit, see the base."

"Camp, Lieutenant. It's a temporary installation, therefore it's a camp."

"Of course. A camp." Harden left and drove around the installation and, having been exposed only to the SEAL's side of Special operations was impressed with what he saw.

The obstacle course was twice as long as the one on the beach in Coronado, there were teams running, apparently some distances, with full packs and, thanks to the multitude of lakes and swamp land surrounding all of LeJeune and the Atlantic only a stone's throw away, there was no shortage of water work going on. And, he mused, these are all men who have already gone through training and qualified.

It was just before quitting time when Harden caught up with Doc just outside his team house and explained why he was there.

"So you're putting together this high speed, low drag team and you need a Doc?" McKeowen looked Harden up and down and decided he needed to get stuck into the teams first, before he committed himself to any more blind adventures. "There's 10,000 other pecker checkers in the Navy. Why me?"

"Out of those 10,000 HM's there's only one dual qualified 0321."

"Now you're just flattering me sir. What's next? Dinner and drinks?" Doc continued to unpack his wet gear and lay it out on the drying rack just outside the Quonset hut. "Why me?"

Harden was prepared for the hostility characteristic of men who had gone through a Spec Ops program and came out the other end. They may have been in one piece, but they were never the same as when they went in.

"I read what you did in that bar in Pittsburgh."

"I'm a Corpsman L.T. It wasn't heroics, it was reflex."

"Whatever it was that bartender pulled through, is back at work and there is now a dedicated, labeled seat at the end of the bar, 'The McKeowen Stool'. Apparently no one's allowed to sit there. Even when the place is full."

"Shit! That can't be too often!" Doc said as he made a face, looked down and shook his head. "Ya know L.T. five months ago I was basically on the street. A fuckin' bum regardless of all my training, skills and ed-u-ma-kation ..."

Harden wasn't just there to secure the best corpsman he could, he was on a mission to build a team the likes of which the Pentagon had never seen.

"Then what'a ya say we get the hell out'a *Memory Lane* and look to the future Doc?! There's a whole lot'a shit going down in the world right now Petty Officer McKeowen and there are two kinds of people. Those that are gonna live it and be part of it and them what's gonna read about it in the newspapers and history books. And twenty years from now one of those people is going to tell their grandkids, 'I remember when all those things happened!' and the other is gonna say to their grandkids, 'I was there!'"

"You talkin' about immortality sir?"

"In *Cannery Row* Steinbeck had a character, Doc ... Doc Rivetts –"

"Ricketts sir, Doc Ricketts." Doc corrected.

"Yeah, Ricketts. He said, 'Man's gotta make his mark –"

"'... even if it's only a scribble.'" McKeowen finished. "You come up with that character out of thin air, did you Lieutenant?"

"You wanna make your scribble or what Doc?"

A temporarily speechless McKeowen looked away and pondered the arguments.

"I did think that Korean Airlines thing was pretty fucked up." Doc finally mumbled.

"Fucked up like a soup sandwich in the rain! So here's our shot at doing something about it."

"Yeah? What doing, exactly?" Doc pushed.

"Takin' the fight to them. We operate on the front line in their territory and whenever possible face to face." Doc's face lit up.

"You sayin' we go behind The Wall? Into Poland, Hungry ... East Germany?"

"Not exactly. We have no authorization to do cross border ops. In fact, hoppin' the fence? That's a clear no-no."

"Oh." Doc was visibly disappointed.

"But we do get access to lots of money, all the best gadgets, first tier intel, and immediate travel to where ever we need to be to do the job. Plus you retain all Hazardous Duty pay."

"What about Jump and Scuba pay?"

"Absolutely."

"Uh huh." Doc grunted.

"Do you know who I briefed just over a week ago?"

"November Foxtrot Charlie L.T." Meaning no fucking clue.

"Allow me to enlighten you young petty officer. The head of the CIA, the NSA, the FBI and the Secretary of State."

"The Sphinx himself?!"

"In the flesh. And oh yeah, Ronnie." Harden added. Doc was genuinely impressed.

"President Reagan?!"

"Ronald Wilson Reagan. We're on a first name basis ever since I ... well, never mind. Point is those are the people we'll be working for if I can pull this thing together."

"That's a pretty heavy offer L.T., but to be honest, things have been moving kind'a fast for me lately. Like I said, five, six months ago ... I need time to think about it."

Without the authority to order anybody on the mission Harden was visibly disappointed, angry and frustrated all at once.

"Okay, I thought about it. I'll do it." Doc shrugged.

"Great! You're an asshole but great!" Harden had to stifle his elation lest he compromise what little professionalism he was straining to maintain. If he couldn't win Doc over he stood little chance with the hardcore Spec Ops vets. "Well I'm in town for the night and no other plans till morning. So what'a say we two celebrate our new joyous union Petty Officer?" The Lieutenant proposed.

An hour later the two were in a local bar out on the strip, hard at work attacking their livers.

＊

Lieutenant Harden, never really a drinker in college or throughout his first six years in the Navy, had only recently discovered the therapeutic effects of the occasional rip-snorting drunk. The kind where you wake up next morning not sure if you're actually awake or not and praying to God you're not going to find a sixteen year old girl, a ten year old goat or an empty box of six month old Boone's Farm Apple wine on the floor next to your bed.

But this was not meant to be one of those nights as they faced a long drive first thing next morning, there was work to be done. Plus the team could hardly afford a Team Leader with a head the size of a basketball.

Ostensibly to celebrate his successful okay from The Director on getting the green light for the task force, but more to pick McKeowen's brain and feel him out as far the team's potential attitude, it was Harden who suggested they grab a beer together. So they had driven into Jacksonville to one of the many road side shanty's which passed for bars on and around Route 17.

They picked a spiffy little shit kicker's watering hole called *Sal N' Ella's* not far from Harden's motel.

The logical location to set up the evening's area of operations was the end of the bar, as opposed to a floor table, as it afforded a complete panorama of the rectangular room, to include the entrance/exit and both sets of toilets.

On beer lead to two which begged the first shot and ... It wasn't that long until the booze started to kick in and Harden began to loosen up.

"Nice place." He commented, gazing up at the peeling ceiling tiles and sporadically exposed water pipes.

"Yeah, typical southern shit hole. Just like back in Pittsburgh." Doc retorted as he leaned back and looked over at his new C.O.'s all cap. "Herty the Hawk? Seriously, that was your mascot?" Doc chided.

"University of Iowa. Herty the Hawk mascot for the Hawkeyes!"

"Why Hawkyes?"

"From *The Last of the Mohicans*. After the book came out the people of Iowa became known as Hawkeyes for their hunting and shooting skills. Kill anything at a hundred yards."

"Kind'a like where I grew up."

"Jersey City, New Jersey but you started school in New York on some kind of athletic scholarship before enlisting no?"

"Gymnastics. Eight member team seven of whom got drafted in the "72 draft in the first draw. No more team, no more scholarship. So I signed up. And I damn sure wasn't gonna be a dog face!"

"City University New York at Queensbourgh wasn't it? Pre-med."

"Yeah. How the hell did you know ...?""

"I pulled your record."

"What the fuck is the universal interest in my service record in the last five months?" Doc questioned. Harden stared at him and smiled.

"Gotta say, anybody who reads it is going to be impressed with the first and only Corpsman to have been awarded an oh-three-twenty-one MOS." Not one to take recognition well, McKeowen shrugged off the comments. Harden set his drink down and stared over at Doc. "You don't get it, do you? How the hell you think you got that Top Secret clearance?"

"What'a mean, I don't get it?!" Doc protested.

"You're in 'The Club' Doc. Not very high up, not yet. But you're in the club." Doc got quiet and twirled his drink. "So what was Queensbourgh's mascot?"

"Not important. Tell me more about this club I'm supposedly in."

"The top one tenth of the top 1%. You're in. Special Ops. You're a three time volunteer, you signed the papers, took all the shit they could throw at you dealt with it and now you're on the teams."

"Interesting perspective."

"I should know. I'm one of the guys that find out where the bad guys are and now you're one of the guys that go out there and get 'em. You're an operator." Harden raised his glass and they toasted. "You know, like the Pretorian Guard, Caesar's top guys in his day. The top Germans in the Abwehr back in their time. Roosevelt and Wild Bill Donovan in the Forties. Fairly close to the top."

"Huh! Not sure how I feel about that. I'm just lookin' for money to go to med school."

"Well whatever you're feelin' about it, it's a long fuckin' way from the slums of Jersey City."

"Who said I was from the slums?"

"Seriously Doc, Jersey City?"

"We prefer to call then the Ghetto."

They finished their drinks.

"You need another one." Doc said as he signaled for another round.

"Why? Remember, we're not supposed to be getting' drunk."

"You know what it says in the Bible sir. Buy a man a drink, he drinks for one night. Teach a man to drink and he drinks for a life time!"

Not sure what else to say they didn't say much for a while, the drinks came and suddenly Doc got quiet and stared off into the mirror of the back bar. Harden, an intuitive leader, easily picked up that Doc was lost in himself and refrained for a bit from continuing the conversation.

After ten or fifteen minutes of perusing the farmer-cowboy-Marine festooned bar room and spotting no reasonable prospects in the female of the species department, and polishing off the fourth round, Harden decided it was time to pick it back up. He remained facing out, back to the bar, elbows planted on the edge. Doc came out of his shallow stupor and looked over at his new team leader and decided to jump start the conversation.

"What's your stake in this? Why do you want this so bad? You're a smart guy. Educated, fairly good looking, if you like the young, dashing Naval Intel, *Officer and a Gentleman*, Richard Gere type. You could have anything. Why put up with all the bureaucratic, political bullshit, not to mention the Mickey Mouse, admin shit officers are subjected to and so richly deserve?"

Harden looked down at his drink and spoke quietly but firmly into the glass.

"Because it's a chance at the teams."

"Why the hell you want on the teams so bad?! It's no cake walk! The physical shit in training? That's just the beginning. And all that prestige B.S., it ain't like that. As soon as you're out on the beach one night and some punk, surfer, ass hole who can't make his girlfriend cum hears you're on The Teams he wants a crack at you. And despite the fact you could kill the sperm dribble in the first minute of any hand-to-hand situation, you don't. Not because you don't want to! Hell, the pressure release alone would probably be worth the jail time. In most every state it's an automatic felony charge for a Special Ops guy who kicks the shit out of some limp dick pretty boy, and even being suspected of a felony is grounds for dismissal from The Teams. You don't do it because scum bags like that aren't worth fucking up your career and all you put in to it. So, you suck up the humiliation, frustration and anger and go have a drink."

Harden looked straight at Doc and narrowed his eyes.

"All I'm askin' for is a chance, that's all. I'll deal with all that other shit after the fact." Doc read his intensity and nodded in appreciation. "As far as the Richard Gere crap, yeah it's cool, to an extent. But it gets annoying sometimes too. Bubble headed chicks coming up askin' for autographs, some with their pissed off jealous boyfriends hangin' on their arms. They're hittin' on ya all the time! A few months back I even had a MILF at a restaurant, middle of the day, eatin' lunch with her husband! Her fucking husband!"

"How do ya know she was married to him?"

"I'm an Intel analyst for the Office of Naval Intelligence for Christ's sake! Besides the wedding ring and two kids gave it away." Harden elaborated. Doc smirked. "She comes over to my table, out'a sight of him of course, and propositions me! Already has her fucking phone number scribbled on a fucking napkin!"

"Did ja –"

"Don't even ask!"

"Christ!" Doc took a drink as he imagined Harden's scenario. "If I were you, I'd get myself in a car accident or something! Get that face fucked up ASAP! Shit! I don't know how you live with chicks hittin' on ya all the time! Definitely my worst nightmare!" Harden gave him a 'fuck you' look. "Seriously! Maybe use a blow torch ya know. Singe off the eyebrows and all! I mean I couldn't take them throwing all that pussy at me all the time!"

"You're a fucking asshole, ya know that?"

Harden nodded.

"So I been told ... mostly by women. Friends. Colleagues. My mother." Doc replied as he watched a pair of girls cross the floor and belly up to the bar.

"Little young don't you think?" Harden quietly commented.

"What'a ya wanna do, cut 'em in half and count the rings? The law says eighteen. That's the same number in any language. Besides, they're at least eighteen or they wouldn't be here!" McKeowen took a second look. "Okay, maybe early twenties but who's arguing?"

They continued perusing the premises when Dave got a little introspective and posed a question.

"You have any idea how many fine young men and women are currently serving this fine country in the just United States Navy alone?"

"November Foxtrot Charlie Lieutenant." Doc replied.

"Five hundred, sixty-three thousand, six hundred and twenty! Give or take."

"You should go on Jeopardy. Win us some more drinkin' money!"

"Back in October of 1979, Admiral Stansfield Turner, then Director of Office of Naval Intelligence, in his infinite wisdom bowing to political pressure, eliminated over 800 operational positions. Half the agency! We call it 'The Halloween Massacre.'"

"Rather short sighted of the old man."

"Now we're behind the eight ball big time and the Russkies are way ahead. Hell, you know we arrested a Polish toy store owner in Boston two months ago?"

"For what? Sellin' G.I. Joe's and Barbies in the same boxes?"

"They were buyin' electronic toys by the gross from the Hasbro Corporation, Mattel, Ajax anybody."

"So, good for Hasbro! Stocks go up."

"Not after we got definitive HUMINT that he was KGB! They buy all the electronic stuff they can here, ship it via several intermediate points back to Russia and then pull the stuff apart to discover how it was built."

"Reverse engineering." Doc commented.

"The most expensive phase in any product development is Research & Development. Up to 70% of the overall initial cost. They're saving millions of dollars on R&D and are able to go straight to manufacturing."

"Yeah, probably saving zillions of rubles. What's that, about, eleven dollars and ninety-five cents in real money? Those wily little red devils!"

"KGB & the HVA. Time Magazine claims they're the most efficient information gathering agency in the world!"

"You're getting' a bit worked up L.T., have another drink." Doc signaled for refills while Dave continued his venting rant.

"The intel community is on the verge of a renaissance Doc. A revolution of unparalleled proportions!" Harden declared. "A combined Spec Ops Group where everybody gets invited to the party. Army, Navy, Marines, hell even the Zoomies!"

Harden fumbled a little but finally managed to pull a piece of paper out of his back pocket. It was a sketch of a shoulder patch. He passed it to McKeowen.

"You do this?" Doc asked as he looked it over.

"Yeah."

"Nice work!"

The well-drawn sketch was of a circular patch with a globe and four crossed swords over a globe surrounded by the words, 'Joint Special Operations Command'.

"Huh, JSOC. Sounds like a cheap men's hosiery line. It'll never catch on, they'll never buy it." Doc pushed the sketch back

"Ever since the Carter days and the Iran Embassy hostage rescue fiasco ..."

"Hey, L.T. you think we ought'a be talkin' about this shit here, out in the open I mean?" Dave reluctantly folded the sketch back up and pocketed it.

"Shit, we're only talkin' about the possibility of a combined command. Nothin' classified." Harden defended.

"Well, I think you're crazy. The services'll never work together. Everybody guards his little piece of the pie like it was the last morsel on earth!"

"I may be crazy Petty Officer, but I respectfully disagree! I'm tellin' ya it'll happen! One way or the other it'll happen! The Italians learned that the hard way during WWII!"

"I may be drunk, but in the morning I'll be sober, you sir, however, will still be an officer!" Doc laughed at his own joke.

"Fuck you very much. Seriously Doc, think about it! All the Spec Ops departments under one roof, working towards the same objectives!"

"Yeah, I can see that. About the same time there's a McDonald's in Red Square!" Doc quipped.

"Hey! Boogies six o'clock!" Harden nudged Doc. "Round table in the corner, near the phony book shelves." Doc looked over at the table indicated. Two girls, one brown haired one blond, were busily chatting away.

"Talley ho!" Doc acknowledged.

"What'a think?" Dave asked.

"You're the intel analyst. I'm the guy that gives ya the penicillin shot the morning after." Harden finished off his scotch, set the glass on the bar then turned on his stool to study the evidence.

"Two females, drinking ..." He observed.

"Impressive, Kennedy could'a used you during the Cuban Missile Crisis."

"Fuck you. Two females, early twenties, single, or wanting to appear single. Judging by the glasses, drinking cocktails of some description. If only I could figure out ..." An Hispanic waiter had just bused their table and as he came by Doc flagged him down with a fiver.

"Jes sir, may I help jew?" The waiter asked.

"What are those two ladies in the corner drinking?" The waiter smiled as he answered.

"Pina coladas sir." Doc dropped the fiver on the waiter's serving tray. "Thang jew sir."

"No, thank jew seniõr." Doc leaned into Dave who remained perfectly upright on his barstool and whispered, "Pina coladas."

"Two twenty-something females drinking Pina colada cocktails. Locals, out on the prowl for the night because they're rich –"

"On Daddy's money."

"On Daddy's money, judging by the clothes and handbags, and probably bored."

"How do you know they're on the prowl?" Doc asked.

"Not sure but it adds to the scenario."

Doc looked back over at the table and noted that he and Dave had been noticed. And judging by the way the two girls were now staring with that wide-eyed, gaga, oh-my-god-is-that-who-I-think-it-is look, Dave had definitely been noticed. Doc finished his whiskey.

"You up for it?" Doc challenged more than proposed.

"Is the Pope ... what the hell is the Pope now days?"

"Redundant. Barman, any chance of getting' the loan of a brown magic marker?" The border line cowboy-bartender made his way to the cash register and came straight back.

"Here ya go. Don't forget where ya'll got it from."

"Appreciate it." Doc looked at Dave. "Let's go."

"Ready, willing and able!" Harden slid off the stool and they both headed across the room.

"Smile as we go by." Doc directed.

"Go by... but I thought?" The girls watched then stared in disbelief as the two approached them but at the last minute Doc took Dave by the arm and veered him off and into the men's room, Dave smiled back at them over his shoulder. Once inside, Harden looked at McKeowen and questioned his plan.

"Whiskey Tango Foxtrot, wingman?!" Meaning what the fuck?

"Take your shirt off."

"Okay Doc, but I much prefer the women." He moved to comply.

"First if anybody's the wingman, you're the wingman. Secondly, I'm an old friend from college. We played a little ..."

"Football. We played college football." Dave proposed.

"Too cliché, besides we can read. We swam. We were on the swim team." Doc moved around back of Harden and began to draw a small, irregularly shaped mark with the marker on the back of his left shoulder. "You the 100 meter freestyle, me 50 meter breaststroke."

"You get the breast stroke. Figures." Dave commented, his level of inebriation beginning to surface.

"Okay, you want the breast stroke? I'll take freestyle!"

"Naahh! You suck at freestyle."

"How the fuck you know I'm weak in the freestyle?"

"Read your fitness reports. You take the breast stroke. I'll take freestyle." Harden glanced over his shoulder into the mirror. "What's with the mark?"

"Birth mark. Everyone knows Richard Gere has a birth mark on his left shoulder."

"Nice. I didn't know that!"

"Neither did I, but either way they'll buy it. It's a bit of insurance. Cover story is you're shootin' a film up in D.C., a sequel to *Officer and a Gentleman*!"

"*Officer and a Bastard*?"

"No, *Officer And a He Man*, it's a comedy! Forget the title. You're out in a place where you don't normally hang out, because for just one night you want to be a normal guy and hang with normal people and get way from all those superficial Hollywood types." Doc instructed.

"And my favorite cocktail is ..." They simultaneously answered each other. 'Pena coladas'.

Thus armed they headed back out to score one for the home team in the endless battle of the sexes.

For the rest of her life with her best friend as a witness, Christina Mary Pembrooke of Baltimore, Maryland would always win at least one round of drinks whenever she played *Truth or Dare*. Her standard question?

"Have I ever slept with Richard Gere?"

****

Century House,
Westminster Bridge Road,
Lambeth, Central London

The glass and concrete, twenty-one storied structure overlooking Christ Church looked like a large white cereal box with the labelling removed. Century House, Central London was the location of MI6 headquarters.

Bent over his desk in his 19th floor office was the last place that John Scarlet wanted to be that Sunday morning.

The handler and case worker for NATO's biggest double agent since the onset of the Cold War had planned on sleeping in, having a nice brunch with his fiancée then utilizing the two box seat tickets he had cajoled from a friend who worked with the Chelsea football team to attend the match that afternoon.

Things hadn't gone to plan.

The Director left word that he needed Scarlett's latest update report on the double agent Gordievsky first thing Monday morning as he was to brief the P.M. Of course word didn't reach Scarlett until Saturday evening as he dressed to go out for dinner. With his fiancée.

However, it was just approaching 10:45 so with a little luck catching the match was still a possibility. He glanced up at the green screen on the IBM monitor which occupied most of his desk and stopped typing. He picked up the desk phone and dialled.

"Morning love. Are we awake yet?"

Yes, been up for ages. How's all in the old salt mines? He could hear the clonking of kitchen utensils in the back ground and pictured her fixing tea.

"Up for ages but just making the tea?" He jokingly challenged.

The average house fly lives for twenty-four hours which means if I were a fly I'd have been up and moving for nearly one forty eighth of my life. He

351

heard her sipping her tea. *Everything going to plan down there?*

"Fine, fine. Should be through by half eleven. Depending on traffic we should easily make the match."

If you like I'll wait to eat and we can grab some pub food near the stadium? A smile involuntarily crept across his face at her generous consideration.

"That's part of the reason I love –" The secure line on his red phone buzzed. "Just a sec dear. There's someone on the other line." He put her on hold picked up the other line.

Sir this is Sarah Williams in security. We have an intercept alert.

"Why did you ring me?"

Because Mr. Scarlett, the duty officer doesn't pick up and you're the only one in the building!

"Of course I am. An intercept signal coming from where?"

Sir it appears it could be in the Channel, directly south of here. Perhaps a submarine?

"Get me Charles." Multiple scenarios quickly ran through his head.

Charles Saxon? The operator asked.

"No Dear, Charles The Prince of Wales! YES CHARLES SAXON! WHO DO YOU BLOODY THINK?!"

But ... I don't have his number Mr. Scarlett.

"Why the hell not?!"

Sir we're not authorized to ring Mr. Saxon during off duty hours. He's a G-5. We're not given his number.

Christ! No wonder the likes of Blake and Philby had such an easy time of it! John complained to himself.

"I'll ring him!" A minute later John was on the phone to one of his junior agents. "There's a high frequency radio signal coming from somewhere in the Channel."

And?

"And I want you to get off your bloody arse and find out what the hell is going on before the whole of Britain is put on full alert and people start lobbing nuclear missiles at each other! Do you think you might manage that?"

Ring you straight back sir! The junior agent responded.

Scarlett picked up the other phone but his fiancée had hung up. He redialled and she answered straight away.

John, everything alright?

"Yes, yes!"

Are we going to war yet?

"That's not funny and no we're not. Not yet anyway."

John, what if I just ... The red phone buzzed again.

"Sorry love, just a sec. It's the other line again." He laid the receiver on the desk and picked up the red line.

"Yes?!" Saxon was on the other end.

It appears there's a high frequency radio signal emanating about 100 kilometres south of the capital. The junior agent informed Scarlett.

"Well that's some brilliant detective work Mr.

353

Saxon! I'll bet you're a real thrill to watch *Murder She Wrote* with, eh?"

It's coming in on an unknown high frequency in short bursts. The agent elaborated.

Scarlett sat bolt upright.

"Are you positive?!"

Just rang the commo centre. Yes, I am.

"Get me a helo, and get your arse over here now!"

Scarlett dialled down to security and the same woman guard picked up.

"Put me through to the Army signals division, straight away!"

Yes sir! She switched to a special alert phone reserved for emergency outside calls.

"Signals?" Scarlett asked.

Lieutenant Jenkins Signal Corps speaking. Who is this please?

"Agent John Scarlett, MI6. Jenkins I need you to redirect and scan the South East coast for an unidentified radio signal."

How will we know the one you're looking for sir?

"It will likely be an HF, possibly a VHF, probably not transmitting at UHF and it will be coming in short bursts. Something well above 500 decibels."

Understood sir. Instructions?

"Lock onto it and don't let go! We're flying a team to the area and will be in touch via military radio, frequency to follow. Understood?"

Yes Mr. Scarlett, will do.

"Thank you."

Good luck sir.

354

John darted out of the office and headed downstairs. As he came off the lift the security guard ran up to him.

"Mr. Scarlett sir. I've a message from Mr. Saxon. You're to meet him down the road at the Regency Hilton as soon as possible."

"What in the hell for?"

"He says they can't land the helicopter on the roof here as there's construction in progress and apparently it's littered with scaffolding. Sir."

"So they're going to ..."

"Yes sir. Fly you out from the hotel."

"Why not?" John shrugged.

Fifteen minutes later the last of the bewildered guests who had been gathered around the roof top pool on the Hilton were being pried away from their £25 brunches and herded off the roof. They stared in disbelief as John and his assistant, agent Saxon dashed off the mirrored lift and ran across the marbled hall past the terrified guests and out onto the roof to duck under the whirling rotors and climb into a Royal Marine Bell UH-1.

As they lifted off and rotated south Saxon looked back at the mess the roof top eatery had become as the dumbfounded guests straggled back out through the piles of aluminium chairs, tables and poached eggs.

Once enroute south Scarlett set to work clarifying the situation.

"Who are the local police?" Charles couldn't hear him for the noise and the Crew Chief handed them a helmet and head set each which they donned.

"Who are the local police?" John repeated as he

355

adjusted his mouth piece. Saxon consulted a pocket note book.

"Apparently the Devonshire Police cover most of that area sir."

"Have they been alerted?"

"No sir, I saw no reason."

"Good. When we are ten minutes out alert them to have a single unit standing by when we land, we'll let them know where to meet us once we've found a site."

"Will do."

"NO LIGHTS NO SIRENS! This is a silent operation! Understood?"

"Yes sir." Saxon confirmed.

"Any luck they'll have no clue we're coming." Scarlett climbed forward between the seats and caught the pilot's attention.

"Do you know where we've to go? Do you need my people to radio you instructions?"

"No sir we know it's directly south, on the coast. Besides, we fly by IFR."

"Ah! Infra-Red Radar. Very good!"

"No sir. I Follow Roads. We'll take the A23 down to the M25 cross over then pick up the A22 which will take us straight to the coast."

"I see." Scarlett commented then turned and mumbled to himself. "What a wondrous technological age we live in! The taxpayers would be thrilled."

"We should be able to pick up the signal from about forty miles out and pinpoint it at around twenty. You can direct us from there." The Crew Chief informed them.

Although still under control, John's anger was building.

About twenty-five minutes later the coast was in sight and the radio burst transmissions had been pinpointed to the small fishing village of Eastbourne.

Approximately 90 kilometres due south of London, the village lies just west along the coast from Hastings. A sleepy little village, Eastbourne was primarily the location for second homes of city dwellers and Summer time holiday makers, but there was also an appreciable permanent population which called the medieval-aged village home.

The pilot radioed to Scarlett and pointed down and to the left. "This area here."

"Can you land on the beach?" Scarlett asked. The pilot took them through a quick fly over of the narrow beach.

"Doesn't look too promising sir. Rather small and hilly. Too much of an embankment to safely touch down." John looked out of the other side of the aircraft.

"What about that lawn tennis club? Think you can fit her down on the centre court?"

"That we can do Mr. Scarlett." Saxon tapped John on the shoulder and pointed off to the right. A police car was barrelling down a side road, its blue light flashing away.

"Nice silent operation!" John cursed.

Over on the centre court a young couple decked out in pristine, white tennis garb were batting a ball back and forth while a second police car stood by outside the small club.

A chubby middle-aged officer stepped out of the car and politely waited until the girl had struck the ball out of bounds and then casually strolled across the court one hand behind his back while waiving the other.

"Sorry folks, afraid we're going to have to ask you to delay your game a bit."

"What in hell for?!" Her affronted male partner protested. The officer pointed up to the sky and to the UH-1 coming in at an angle straight for the Devonshire Lawn Tennis Club's centre green.

The club had been alerted and, to the amazement of the half dozen players huddled to the side of the courts, two attendants dashed out and collapsed the net taking it with them as they dashed back to the club house.

"The location appears to be in the village." The pilot reported after landing and shutting down the engine.

"A residence? Do we have an address?" John removed a hand held Radio Directional Finder device from a black case on the deck and switched it on.

"Ask the copper." The pilot suggested and John waved him over.

"Officer, do you know this location?" John pointed to the green lines on the small, circular RDF screen of the helo's dash board.

"Yes sir, it's on Devonshire Park Road. Five minutes from here sir. Hop in the car!"

At the same time, at Devonshire Park Road, #112 sixty-two year old amateur fisherman and auto parts delivery man James Burrows sat in the kitchen in his underwear reading the Sunday morning paper while Gertrude, his wife of 40 years, fried a half dozen eggs and a pound of bacon.

There was a knock at the front door.

"Get that will ya?" He directed.

"Right!" She lifted the pan off the stove and set it on the table in front of him. "Fry ya own bloody eggs!" He raised a hand to stop her, stood grumbling and with newspaper in hand, shuffled to the door himself.

When he opened it two policemen with pistols drawn stood astride Scarlett who presented his bifold I.D.

All three were backed up by several other police cars, blue lights flashing also containing several policemen each. Indiscernible radio chatter from the squad cars filled the back ground.

"Mr. James Burrows? John Scarlett, MI6. May we come in?" Standing slack jawed in his Argyle boxers and white socks, Borrows slowly nodded his consent.

"Will you close the bloody ..." His wife came stomping down the hallway behind him, stopped dead and surveyed the scene then slapped her husband hard on the shoulder. "I told you to pay that bloody parkin' ticket last month!"

"SHUT IT WOMAN! This ain't about no bloody traffic summons!"

Saxon, aiming the hand held RDF in the direction the signal seemed to be coming from led the way in and made his way up stairs to the master bedroom. The large entourage squeezed up the stairs after him.

In the bedroom Saxon made straight for the closet, opened it and rummaged through the shelf above the hanging clothes. Suddenly a faint, rhythmic beeping could be heard as he held up a fisherman's survival vest which he handed over to Scarlett.

Holding up the survival vest Scarlett reached over, switched off the built in transponder which immediately silenced the beeping on the RDF unit.

Scarlett made no attempt to hide how he felt as he threw it at Burrows.

"Are you so dense that light bends around you?! I've got more on my plate than an American politician at an all you can eat buffet sponsored by lobbyists and I've got to come all the way down here for this?! Bloody arsehole!" He yelled to no one in particular as he stormed out of the room with Saxon and the police entourage trailing behind.

Mrs. Burrows arms folded, her husband standing next to her, watched the authorities pile down the stairs and out of the house.

"Fuckin' eejit!" She said as she headed back down to the kitchen.

The ride back to the chopper in the police car was not one Saxon cared to remember but would not likely soon forget.

"How in bloody hell did we pick up a signal from a fisherman's fucking survival vest?!"

"Actually I don't think we did sir." Saxon replied.

"I've got a fucking to-do list longer than a fucking acceptance speech at the fucking Oscars and ... What the hell do you mean, 'we didn't'? Why

360

the fuck am I out in the arse end of nowhere in this god awful weather on a bloody Sunday morning?!"

"I mean sir, we didn't pick it up ourselves, somebody else likely did."

"Like who, for instance?"

"The Japanese Defence Agency actually. Their security service at any rate, picked it up and sent us a priority notice by secure wire. Army intel forwarded it to MI6. That'd be you. Sir."

"Jesus! How in God's name are the Japanese monitoring Great Britain?! We have no intel to indicate they have that technology!"

"They're not sir and they don't."

"You are exactly two steps away from being a fucking filing clerk! If that bloody signal didn't come from a flippin' fisherman's survival vest where in bloody hell did it come from?!"

Saxon manned his headset and spoke to the co-pilot on the internal line.

"Lieutenant, radio in and confirm where that signal we picked up originated."

"Yes sir." The co-pilot radioed back to com central in London." A minute later the co-pilot broke in.

"Mr. Saxon?"

"Go ahead."

"Apparently the signal the Japanese alerted you about originated from a Russian satellite, sir." He reported.

Scarlett froze when Saxon relayed the information. Scarlett stared in disbelief.

The chopper had just reached altitude and was heading back north.

MI6 had no intel to indicate the Japanese had such capability but even more importantly, they had no intel the Reds had a spy satellite monitoring them.

Meanwhile, back in Century House the phone receiver lying on John Scarlett's desk still beeped a busy signal.

*

Sunday morning, well late morning anyway, almost noon as a matter of fact, Harden and McKeowen made good their escape from the motel room where they had spent their second night and after collecting Doc's gear from camp Harden and Doc were on the I-95 heading north back to Washington.

Doc's C.O. at Recon, the Major, had little sense of humor about losing a qualified corpsmen days after he reported aboard but Dave had arranged for orders direct from ONI HQ to be delivered to the Recon HQ Friday afternoon pending Doc's acceptance to join the team. To his credit the Major did wish Doc good luck with the new team.

It was an hour later as Harden's black Suburban sped north in the outside lane, that Doc finally struck up a conversation.

"So who else we got on this dodgy band of thieves L.T.?"

"Funny you should ask Doc." Harden checked his watch, it was 14:45 and they were an hour over the Virginia border when Harden pulled off onto the shoulder of the highway, alongside an open field, put on his emergency blinkers and shut the engine down. Doc noted the last mile marker they passed was MM #62. "C'mon." He nodded to Doc to follow as he grabbed a smoke grenade from the glove box.

They climbed over the crash barrier, made their way down the small embankment then over a waist high barbed wire fence and walked part way out into the adjoining field.

"Keep an eye out to the south I'll scan the western sector."

"Eye out for what? The Russians?"

"Small passenger plane, a shuttle of some sort."

"You want I should break out my med kit?"

"What for?"

"Landing a plane in this field is gonna be a bit dodgy. Looks like it's been plowed up."

Just then the buzz of an aircraft engine came into ear shot.

"Won't be necessary. I got him!" Harden announced as he pointed.

Dave pulled the pin on the smoke canister and tossed it a few feet away. A bright yellow plume erupted and drifted off to the south away from them. McKeowen looked over to the west and saw an aircraft breaking the horizon ten to fifteen miles out. As it approached they could see the plane was a DC-3 with some kind of commercial markings.

At about five miles out Doc could see the port side hatch open and what appeared to be a fully loaded jumper standing in the door.

"You gotta be shittin' me!"

"I wouldn't shit you Doc! You're my favorite turd!" Harden laughed at his own joke just as the jumper dove from the plane at about three thousand feet.

"Who the hell is that show boatin' fucker?"

The passenger aircraft, they could see passengers through the windows, climbed as the door closed over and the aircraft streaked overhead and faded out of sight.

"Petty Officer First Class Ray "Shakes" MacDonald, on loan from Seal Team Three. Our new demolitions man." Harden proudly announced.

"He's in with a bang alright. Crazy fuck!" Doc commented.

They watched as Ray's chute deployed and he steered it due east, over the eight lane highway and to their side of the motorway. With impressive accuracy he closed in on the smoke plume.

At about 1,000 feet he pulled his cargo strap, his pack fell from his body jolting to a stop and then dangled about twenty-five feet below him on its cargo line. Fifteen seconds later he drifted to the ground just forty or fifty feet from Doc and Harden.

"Two down, two to go!" Harden quietly commented as they walked out to greet MacDonald and help him in with his gear.

"Why they call him Shakes?" Doc's question was answered when MacDonald extended his hand in greeting. The result of three helo crashes in one year left him with a permanent Parkinson's-like twitch of the hands.

Fifteen minutes later, with everyone's gear in the back of the Suburban, 60% of Task Force Romeo were back on the I-95 North heading for D.C.

"Staff Sergeant Ricky Matson is out of Marine Force Recon. He's weapons and tactics. He'll meet us in the safe house I have set aside out near the Southwest Waterfront district in D.C." Harden explained as he drove.

"Who's our other guy?" MacDonald asked from his reclined in the back seat.

"Sergeant Danial 'Danno' Byrd. he's coming in from the Green Beret side of the house. Communications and electronic surveillance. He'll round out the Dirty Almost Half Dozen. We're gonna pick him up just outside Alexandria, a small place called Dale City."

"What's the plan L.T.?" Doc asked.

"Get settled in tonight, clean up grab some chow and a beer somewhere and get to work first thing tomorrow. I'll lay out the details in the morning at a formal briefing."

"At the safe house?"

"Negative, I have a room at the Pentagon set aside for us until we get going."

"SHIT!" MacDonald declared.

"What's wrong Ray?"

"I got nuthin' cleaned and ironed sir. I been in route three days solid from the P.I.!"

"Well today's your lucky day Sergeant MacDonald."

"How's that sir?"

"As of zero nine hundred tomorrow morning we are authorized civvies and relaxed grooming standards." Ray kicked up his feet, locked his hands behind his head and smiled.

"I'm liking this job already."

**

CHAPTER FIFTEEN

Kutuzovsky Prospekt
Dorogomilovo District,
Central Moscow
08:25 Wednesday the 14th

The black four door, Chaika limo along with its 10 vehicle, military police motorcade escort pulled into the curb at #26 Kutuzovsky Prospekt precisely at 8 a.m. There was one passenger seated in the back.

The nine story Stalinist style apartment block had once previously housed Leonid Brezhnev and Mikhail Suslov and now, in the same apartment, lived Yuri Andropov.

Inside the top floor apartment on the west wing Andropov kissed his wife Tatyana good-bye and walked to the lift where he was met by his two man 24 hour body guard.

There was no shortage of times these days when Andropov was forced to sleep over at the Presidium in the Kremlin, but last night was a promise he made weeks ago that he and Tatyana would have a quite dinner and an evening together listening to some of his favourite music, Glen Miller, Tommy Dorsey and Harry James.

Downstairs Yuri greeted Andrei Gromyko as he entered the rear of the limo and took the seat next to him. Through the Zil lanes which ran up the middle of all the major motorways and were reserved specifically for senior Soviet officials to preclude interrupting civilian traffic with long government motorcades, Gromyko read from his notes as he ran through their to-do-list for the day on their way over to the Kremlin.

"U.S. Ambassador Hartman has sent word that, 'in light of current events, the present arms control talks in Madrid must regrettably be delayed'."

"Bullshit! Reagan's an actor, he won't let himself be upstaged. What else?"

"Samantha Smith-" Yuri smiled at her memory.

"The little girl from Maine, yes." Andropov affirmed.

"... has written you a thank you note for your hospitality and again wishes you well in your new job."

"She's home safe?"

"Yes."

"Good to know. What else?"

"*Pravda* have requested a comment about Reagan's speech to the people the other day concerning his request to support the Star Wars program and the fact that he also spoke about '... verifiable arms reduction'." Gromyko smirked as he finished the sentence. "'The kind we Americans are working for right now in Geneva.'"

Andropov huffed, shifted in his seat and looked away. Gromyko immediately realized and regretted that he had touched a nerve.

"Can you fathom the audacity of the man?! They've done **nothing** but reject every single proposal put in front of them, have proposed nothing themselves and he tries to play as if we are refusing his proposals!"

"Shall I draft something for the editor?"

"No! No need. I'll have something for them by the end of the day or in the morning. When I get it to you, run it in *Izvestiya* also. What else?"

"The coal miners' strike in Poland. The Polish Politburo requests you-"

"His entire political platform stands on being the tough guy!" Andropov interrupted Gromyko as if he weren't even speaking. "In his world compromise means weakness!"

"This is no doubt why he feels safe flying in the face of International Law and forbids me landing in New York." Gromyko counselled.

Gromyko quickly accepted the fact that it would be a pointless effort to be too tenacious about the to-do list at the moment when Andropov was so preoccupied with Reagan's antics.

They drove another few minutes waiting for Andropov to speak again as he stared out the window. It was only about a five kilometre trip to the Kremlin and, as they were able to by-pass traffic using the Zil lanes, the trip was less than ten minutes long.

The giant gold star of the Spaaskya Tower came into sight as they crossed the Moskva River.

"Which gate Comrade Chairman?" The driver called over his shoulder. Seeing Andropov still distracted, Gromyko answered for him.

"Presidium, North gate."

"I find it interesting he is taking the moral high ground but thinks the way for us to make it up to the dead Koreans is to give their families money!" Andropov scoffed.

"It's the American way Chairman. All things have a monetary price. Human life is no exception." His Secretary for Foreign Affairs explained. Andropov was becoming increasingly agitated. Not a particularly good start to the day, but the rant wasn't over.

"Carter, was a flaccid leader and a weak statesman, but at least you could talk to him, deal with him. Then they elect the anti-Christ! What kind of system is that? Every four years you throw the dice to see who will drive the car, where the camping trip will be and who will lead the songs around the campfire?!"

A few minutes later the two were stepping off the elevator and entering Andropov's office in the Presidium. Gromyko continued to play councilor.

"Americans can never admit defeat. Korea, Viet Nam, Iran. When they botched the Iran hostage rescue, it became apparent that Reagan would succeed against Carter."

"That is exactly why months before he was elected I designed and initiated an operation, a re-enforced surveillance operation!" Yuri lectured in return.

Gromyko seemed only mildly surprised at the revelation.

Inside the office Anatoly Dobrynin, Ambassador to the U.S. was waiting with some papers to be signed. He stood and greeted them. The conversation continued unabated as the guards opened the massive doors and Yuri moved to his desk.

"Comrade Chairman," Gromyko continued, "I

have dealt with a dozen American Secretaries of State and ambassadors. American politics doesn't follow the rule of civilized behavior, primarily because the only rule they feel compelled to follow is that there are no rules. You mustn't take it personally. It's the price of doing business with them."

Andropov sat, took the papers from Dobrynin and began to peruse them. Yuri realized he needed to settle down and so took his time reading over the documents.

"Anatoly, what is this Release of Resources document?"

"Your authorization to release the small fishing boats and personal vessels from the North Pacific search for the black box from the Korean plane."

"Mr. Gromyko, what is your advice?" Andropov asked.

"The Winter is coming. They must be allowed to return to their work to feed their families."

Andropov signed it along with the other few papers and passed them back to Dobrynin who thanked him and left. Andropov turned his attention back to Gromyko.

"I don't dispute any of your points Andrei. My problem now in this forced game of global chess, is his proposal of this Star Wars Defense Initiative which, if it ever comes to fruition, will not only render our entire missile arsenal ineffective, but will almost certainly encourage a first strike by the Western powers!" Gromyko remained silent.

Andropov retrieved a bottle of pills from his desk drawer and poured a half glass of water from a pitcher on his desk.

"The original intention of my surveillance operation was to collect information on the American administration's intentions regarding their actions towards our foreign policy. Now, with the Pershing missile deployment to Western Europe and the increased incursions by the U.S. into our territory."

"What do you call this new, super surveillance mission Comrade Chairman?" Gromyko ventured, not seriously interested in trivial details but seeking to ease the tension in the room by changing the subject.

"Operation RYAN." Yuri casually answered as he took two pills then sipped his water.

"Why RYAN, what does it stand for?"

"Raketno Yadernoe Napadenie."

"Nuclear Missile Attack?!" Gromyko was visibly alarmed as he snapped back to the real world seriousness of the situation.

"Don't wet your pants Andrei! It's only for surveillance purposes." He didn't know why but he felt Yuri was …not lying exactly but not telling the whole truth either.

Andropov already feeling the strain of the early morning made his way over to an easy chair in the middle of the room.

"You appear tired Yuri. Shall I leave?"

"Yes, please. I'm expecting Chebrikov with a report on the American's efforts in the Pacific soon."

"Do you want us to prepare something about the search effort?"

"Say nothing, make no statements for the rest of the day concerning the current situation with the Yanks. We'll talk again this evening." Andropov nodded and waved his hand and Gromyko headed for the door as Dobrynin reappeared but hesitated as the guards opened the door and looked back across the massive, high ceilinged office. Across the room Anatoly made eye contact with Andropov.

"Yuri, you realize there is always the chance the Americans will find the black box recorder before we do?" Andropov slid down in the chair, put his head back, closed his eyes and smiled at the Ambassador's challenge. "Did I say something amusing Comrade Chairman?"

"Rest assured Anatoly, there is **no chance** the Americans will find the box before we do!" Andropov confidently answered as he relaxed in the big overstuffed chair. Dobrynin felt compelled to make further inquiry.

"And, with all due respect comrade, from where does your considerable confidence in this matter emanate?"

"From the fact that I have had the box in my possession for nearly two weeks now." Anatoly smiled. "Safely tucked away in the basement of Lubyanka." Yuri added.

Gromyko stepped back into the room and joined the discussion.

"But the fleet! They are still ..." The penny dropped. "Hat's off to you comrade Chairman! Your time with the KGB was not squandered."

Andropov spoke without moving or opening his eyes.

"I trust the Minister for Foreign Affairs will continue to encourage the world press to believe that we too are looking for the all-important little 'black box'?" Andropov smirked slightly as he asked.

"It is my duty, Comrade Chairman. What else would I do?" Gromyko smirked and shrugged.

"When do you intend to call off the search for the box?" Dobrynin asked.

"When the Americans get tired of playing and go home."

"Will there be an analysis and report of the data on the tape?"

"No. I have ordered Chebrikov to keep it sealed. For now."

There was a knock. The two huge, ornately carved doors opened and a guard announced that Viktor Chebrikov had arrived. Andropov wished Anatoly and Andrei good-bye as they left.

Yuri nodded to the guard to show Chebrikov in.

As the KGB chief, dressed in a dark, civilian three piece, Italian suit and wine colored tie, entered Andropov remained slumped down in the large, overstuffed seat in the center of his massive office, hands gripping the arms of the leather, upholstered chair and staring straight ahead. He did not stir when Viktor Chebrikov was escorted into the room.

Chebrikov motioned the guard away and slowly approached Andropov noticing his eyes were now closed.

"Yuri?" Being one of the two who knew about Andropov's pending and inevitable kidney failure, he became concerned "Yuri? Are you alright?!"

374

Andropov maintained his slumped down position, slowly opened his eyes and spoke in a near whisper.

"The Chinese use two brush strokes to write the word 'crisis.' One brush stroke stands for danger. The other for opportunity." He opened his eyes, paused and slid upright but struggled to stand. Chebrikov scurried over to help but Yuri raised a hand to stop him. "Moral of the story? In a crisis, be aware of the danger." Andropov shuffled across the office to the liquor table. "But recognize the opportunity!" Chebrikov crossed the room and came closer as Yuri fumbled with the glassware. "Care for a drink Comrade Chebrikov?"

"I've not had breakfast yet." Viktor watched Yuri pour a measure of whiskey. "I thought you were supposed to cut back on your alcohol intake, Comrade General Secretary?"

Andropov went to Viktor with a generous measure of Johnny Walker Black label in each hand.

"You will betray me to my medical staff perhaps?" Chebrikov set his drink on a table. "I am on the downhill slide comrade. Point of no return long past. Sit, sit!" Andropov invited with a stern order as he switched on the television, pushed the half loaded ¾ inch tape into the VCR machine on top and turned up the volume on the oversized console TV.

Reagan's image filled the screen. Yuri moved back from the television and mused at the tape recording of the American president preaching to the United Nations. Viktor moved closer to examine the machine as Reagan spoke.

... utmost contempt that I condemn the Korean airline massacre as a crime against humanity that must never be forgotten! It is nothing less than an act of barbarism and inhuman brutality!

"Sony Betamax! Very nice Yuri!"

"SL-8200. Gift from the Japanese Ambassador. I liked my old Rostov, but ... you know."

"I know."

"Listen to his Ranting! Reagan's SDI technology is for one purpose only. To render America invulnerable to Soviet attack, thereby allowing the Americans to launch missiles against us with no fear of retaliation. His ultimate aim? First strike capability!" He sipped his drink. "Fucking movie star cowboy!" Andropov threw back his drink then held the glass in his hand pointing his index finger at the telly but made no comment.

... born of a society which wantonly disregards individual rights and the value of human life and seeks constantly to expand and dominate other nations! Therefore I once again call on the United States Senate to quickly approve the required funding for my proposed SDI program ...

"What do you make of this Korean airlines fiasco Viktor?" Viktor shrugged and responded with a matter-of-fact attitude.

"The same as anyone with a modicum of common sense. The local Soviet air defense commander appears to have made a serious but honest mistake. The situation in that region hasn't been normal for quite some time. His forces had been on high alert and in a state of elevated anxiety following multiple incursions by American aircraft during the entire Spring and most of the Summer. In view of these Pacific Fleet incursions and given that we hate them and they hate us ... the KAL incident was inevitable."

"You really believe that?"

"With all due respect Yuri ..." Viktor picked a grape from the bowl of fruit on the glass top coffee table in front of the couch. "... the truly amazing thing is that something like this hasn't happened before this point, and on a much larger scale." He took a seat on the couch. "If this event causes the course of our histories to deviate in one direction or the other, and I firmly believe it will, 300 civilian lives will have been a small price to pay."

"Is it a verifiable fact that the American planes flew more than thirty kilometres into our airspace and remained there for the better part of half an hour during several, what they probably believe to be secret over flights?" Not waiting for a response Yuri continued to speak as he refilled his glass. "I think the poor unfortunates on that Korean plane were being used as a passive probe to light up our radar so it could be pinpointed and analyzed for blind spots." He signaled with the bottle asking if Viktor needed a refill. Not having touched his drink Viktor declined.

"But they didn't consider it would get shot down." Chebrikov finished.

"EXACTLY! The stupid bastards! They never

factored in conditions at altitude!" Yuri took his drink. "And as a result of this ... circus of incursions, many of our senior officers were transferred, reprimanded or dismissed. They know what they are doing, the Americans! They are trying to temp us into firing the first shot because ..."

"Because they believe they have the upper hand." Viktor added. Yuri harrumphed, turned off the TV and crossed the room. He took a seat next to his KGB Chief.

"Viktor Mikhailovich Chebrikov, why are you still in this fucking game?" Viktor laughed and looked at the floor. "With your lack of connections in the Politburo you have no chance to reach General Secretary. You are only one step to the highest rank you can achieve, save for my job. So why stay until you are too old, or too dead to enjoy old age?"

"Yuri ..." Viktor put a hand on the old man's knee in an act of assurance. "... you know the answer to that as well as I do comrade!" Not intending to drink that morning, Viktor raised his glass before he spoke.

"Vikhod stoit rubl." He said.

"Vikhod dva!" Yuri answered, raised his glass and smiled.

"Entrance costs one ruble. To exit, two." Andropov smirked as he spoke the unofficial motto of the KGB.

Andropov again struggled to his feet, set his empty glass on the table and shuffled across the large office.

"I called you here for a purpose." He motioned

for Viktor to come over. "We covertly began collecting data over a year ago while I was still with KGB."

"Operation Ryan. I thought it was winding down?"

"That was a cover story for the Politburo. There are still questions to be answered, blanks to be filled in, but I will tell you this. From the data I've already seen, I am convinced the Americans are preparing for a first strike attack. Limited perhaps, but they will attack!"

"That's interesting news!"

"Look, come look." Yuri waved him across the room as he went to the corner and retrieved some kind of a long display board on wheels covered in a black sheet. It looked like a 1920's styled university black board on a wheeled frame but was long and narrow.

"Have you determined a time frame for the attack?" Viktor asked.

"I had this brought over from Lubyanka the day after Reagan dictated that Gromyko was to be kept out of the U.S." He pulled the black sheet off the board but it remained partially hung up on one corner.

"Very organized. What is it Secretary General?"

The display was longer than it was high and was essentially a large pane of plexiglass sectioned off by thin, black tape into rectangles. Each rectangle, twelve across and ten down, had a small white label top center, labeled with categories of a sort.

The "board" was actually a mock-up of a glass plotting board like the kind found on board aircraft

379

carriers and other flag ships in the Command & Control rooms. The required information could be plotted on the board from both sides and thus be readily available to Commanders at a glance.

Chebrikov stepped closer to read the headings.

"That was the point at which I realized he truly had no limits!" Andropov declared.

By way of explanation Yuri stepped over to the board, stood with his hands behind his back and perused the various rectangles. He seemed to be contemplating carefully before he spoke again and when he did resume he seemed to be speaking to the plex plotting board rather than to Viktor.

"When I spoke with the Politburo last year they thought me a little mad. I tried to be objective, I tried to present the facts, but they didn't see it. Berlin, 1959 when I argued about losing the intelligentsia to the West. They ignored my reports."

"But they eventually ordered your wall built anyway!"

"After we lost more than 20% of our youth!"

Viktor, more curious about the information on the board, accepted the futility of argument. Yuri pushed on.

"So to make things more graphic I had this constructed." He stepped over to the end and pulled the remainder of the cloth free, letting it fall to the floor. "For the better part of six months I collected and collated information." He suddenly transformed himself into a professor as he picked up a pointer hanging from a hook on the end and indicated the separate squares. "Each square represents a definitive step towards a complete war footing. Strategy based on past history, observable build-up, civilian preparation, current alert status."

"You've made your own cross word puzzle, Yuri."

"Yes. A crossword puzzle that when filled, will tell us the exact time, within a day or two, when the Americans will attack!"

The board's layout was sub-divided into four quadrants: Monitoring of people responsible for ordering the firing of missiles; technicians responsible for maintaining the missiles, facilities from which the attack would originate and miscellany.

"The squares that are crossed out in the white grease pencil represent actions the Americans have already completed in their preparation for war." He indicated the appropriate boxes with the pointer as he spoke. "Exceeding a reasonable excess in intelligence collection. Aggressively expanding their missile program. Scheduling a major military exercise in Europe. Shuffling the cabinet to weigh it down with military minded hawks."

Chebrikov stepped closer and examined the squares. He began see the logic as Andropov continued.

"When all the squares are marked out, the Americans will be ready to strike." He finished his drink. "Most likely on a holiday, deep during maneuvers, when they have a substantial force in place and between midnight and dawn." He stared intently at the board. "Think of it Viktor, it stands to reason. No competition for industry, security for their largest exposed boarder, isolation and defeat for their only real military enemy, reduction of oil, steel and raw materials to rock bottom market prices, world record prices for their oil! its common sense to any strategically minded individual."

"A Dooms Day Board!" Viktor mumbled as he stared and lowered his drink.

Yuri replaced the pointer then moved back to his desk, retrieved an envelope and a document. He signed and stamped the paper, folded it and put it in the envelope which he handed over to Chebrikov.

"This escalation dictates we do something. It is to this end Comrade Director that I have decided on the solution to our planning problems."

As Andropov collected the two rocks glasses and headed back over to the bar, Chebrikov removed the document the envelope and read it.

From: *Premier Secretary General Yuri Andropov:*

To: *Colonel Viktor Chebrikov, Director KGB:*

By this order you have the permission of The Politburo to institute an increase concerning all aspects of *Operation Ryan*. All increases which you deem necessary will be endorsed. This order supersedes all previous orders.

"Do you intend to activate Phase Three of Ryan?" Viktor enquired. No answer came.

As a direct broadcast from the United Nations Building in Manhattan played at a low volume on the desk radio, Yuri poured himself and Viktor another drink and moved to the spacious central window overlooking the vastness of Red Square.

Viktor carefully re-folded the memo and replaced it into the envelope. Andropov folded his hands in front of his face and stared out across the beautiful expanse of the square.

"I fear a kind of military psychosis has taken over U.S. foreign policy Viktor."

The two comrades continued to quietly gaze through the glass at the hundreds of people milling about the square as the first flakes of a light snow flurry drifted down.

Is this where it begins? Yuri Andropov mused to himself.

*

Andropov, the Politburo as well as the entire East German Intel and political structure felt increasingly backed against a wall. Reagan's aggressive approach and penchant for arms escalation over diplomatic talks, especially when contrasted with Jimmy Carter's exceptionally soft approach, caused the Russians to be unable to comprehend much less know how to deal with what they saw as the inconsistencies of American politics.

Prior to the upcoming REFORGER military exercise, warships began operating in the Baltic and Black Seas and routinely sailed past Cape North and into the Barents Sea. Intelligence ships were positioned off the Crimean coast and aircraft carriers with submarine escorts were anchored in Norwegian fjords while U.S. attack submarines practiced with simulated assaults on Soviet SSBN's stationed beneath the polar ice cap.

In the words of one of the JCS, "Out there on the Kamchatka Peninsula they are as naked as a jaybird and they know it! And now we know that holds equally true for the far northern maritime area and the entire Kola Peninsula!"

In short, the U.S. Navy believed it had demonstrated that it could elude the USSR's largest and most complex ocean surveillance systems, defeat Soviet tactical warning systems as well as penetrate their air defences.

The Soviets were less confident they knew every move the Americans were making but, thanks to the traitor John Walker and the KGB's *Operation Ryan*, firmly believed they had the upper hand.

CHAPTER SIXTEEN

Andrews Air Force Base
Washington, D. C.
September 16th

The mass deployment of troops for participation in The Return of Forces to Germany, or REFORGER, training exercise had begun earlier in the month with the ship borne, primarily Marine and Navy troops leaving Norfolk, Virginia and Jacksonville, Florida Navel Stations' in the first week of the month.

Troop movement was purposely coordinated with the mandatory, two week active duty period of Army and Navy reservists and executed in conjunction with the other smaller, training exercises of the participating nations. With full participation of the Allied navies, this was to be the largest training exercise ever conducted by the NATO military with over 100,000 troops in total.

By no means a new exercise, this would be the 15th REFORGER since its conception in 1967 during the Johnson Administration while the war in Viet Nam, which was started as an effort to halt the spread of Communism, raged on. This however would be the largest, longest and most in-depth, sophisticated exercise ever attempted since WWII involving most of the western forces to some extent.

The Boots-on-the-ground portion would go until November 2 when *Operation Able Archer*, essentially a very large sand table exercise involving all the senior military leaders of the NATO forces, would commence with a build-up to and a full simulation of an actual nuclear exchange.

Aside from the tens of thousands of soldiers, sailors and Marines, the support logistics alone required nearly six months prior planning.

But the show case of the whole operation was to be the new code system for the practical inter-unit and inter-service communications, a never before applied system of encoding and decoding using improved burst technology and a whole new code base throughout the NATO forces.

The massive revamp of the Allied code system was due in large part to the Walker family spy fiasco after it was eventually determined that they had passed over a million classified documents to the Communists.

Realizing that troop numbers, hardware and technology were only part of the game, the Reaganites sought to, and were by and large successful at, recruiting the leadership of most of the NATO nation's upper echelon.

P.M.'s, presidents and leaders of all descriptions agreed to participate in the last two weeks of the nearly two month long exercise which would conclude with the simulated nuclear exchange between the NATO forces and the Warsaw Pact powers.

Margret Thatcher the British P.M., the German P.M. Helmut Kohl, Pierre Trudeau of Canada and Arne Treholt of Denmark would "play" along. All of course with Reagan in the driver's seat.

In essence, everyone knew about the upcoming

practice run. Everyone knew that there was a new top secret code system and that the world leaders were going to play along and that it was all make believe.

Everyone knew ... that is except the Soviets.

****

Rhein-Main Air Force Base
Frankfurt am Main
West Germany

To mask their movements as far as was practical, Task Force Romeo Five were listed as civilian contractors from ALCO Engineering in Port St. Lucy, Florida, a fictitious company set up by the NSA through the CIA. They were assigned to fly out of Andrews AFB in Washington, D.C. that morning.

With wheels up at 07:30 they would fly via U.S.A.F. C-141, in civilian clothing and their operational gear was packed in civilian air crates labeled as various 'Instruments'. They lifted off, along with a platoon of the 197th Mechanized Brigade, who were out of Fort Benning, Georgia.

Their weapons locker was purposely mislabeled as radio equipment and was under the close guard of Ricky Matson, a 9mm Colt quietly tucked into a shoulder holster under his jacket, the only individual un-officially authorized to carry a locked and loaded weapon on board the aircraft, but not the only one armed.

387

On paper Task Force Romeo were on a ride-along with the U.S. Army for the duration of REFORGER and *Operation Able Archer* and were there to compose an after action report encompassing ways to improve military mobility in times of conflict.

In reality, they were desperate to find out as much as possible about *Operation Ryan*.

In-flight time was just short of ten hours and so with the six hour time difference they touched down at Rhein-Main Airbase around 23:37 that night.

Located about 130 miles south as the crow flies from Frankfurt am Main it took the men of Task Force Romeo about another three hours in a two and a half ton troop truck, known as a deuce and a half, to reach the main gate of Neu Ulm late that night with all their field gear.

A garrison town since 1841, the strategically located town of Neu Ulm in the BRD affords practical access to the entire Rhineland/Alps area via wide, well serviced roads and its three rivers, the Donau, the Iller and the Danube.

Completely obliterated in WWII by Allied bombing the industriousness of the German people shone through when forty years later not only had the people rebuilt all their bridges and roadways, 100% of which had been destroyed in the three month, non-stop, Allied bombing campaign, but the city itself had been completely rebuilt to a bigger and better standard and extended further into the suburbs.

Now home to the 56th Artillery Command and its supporting units with some 1,500 personnel, the base housed 56 nuclear capable, Pershing missiles.

As they were in civilian clothes TFR-5 were required to keep the O.D. green, canvas rain flap in the back of the deuce and half troop truck pulled down most of the way to blend in with the rest of the convoy, but once they felt the truck slow down and pass over the speed bumps, which indicated they were through the gate, Doc pulled the flap back to afford a view of the post.

What they saw, despite the dark of the evening, shocked them.

Surrounded by young elm and maple trees, the well-lit walks, roads and streets were all impeccably groomed. Perfect row after perfect row of Bavarian styled buildings served as barracks, admin and recreational buildings to present the appearance of a clean, well maintained German village.

The more than adequate street lighting revealed that there was the occasional small monument outside some of the barracks, apparently memorials as there were hand laid, brick foot paths bedecked with fresh flowers set into the trimmed grass which lead to cach.

More like upscale apartments then military barracks, the accommodation at Neu Ulm Army base also took everyone off guard. The rows of three story high barrack buildings themselves were enough to impress any military man.

Each building was immaculately painted, most an off-white or light mustard yellow, and every detail had been seen to right down to each and every window being slightly open at the bottom to the exact same distance.

The deuce and a half, now separated from the rest of the convoy, pulled up outside one of the buildings and Dave Harden hopped out and went inside. He returned a couple of minutes later, stepped up on the foot rail on the back gate of the truck and poked his head into the cargo bay.

"This is us. Number one one eight seven Hunterwasser, remember it. We've got the top floor and the attic spaces. Apparently until yesterday it was a senior enlisted barracks but they were booted out of their rooms and relocated for the duration."

"How to win friends and influence people!" Doc commented.

"Danno, soon as we get everything upstairs, pick yourself one of the attic spaces, throw your commo gear into it and belay settin' up till the morning." Byrd gave the L.T. a thumbs up and started gathering his radio and satcom equipment.

"You okay Danno? Got everything you need?" Ray MacDonald asked as Byrd went to work. Byrd didn't speak he just gave another thumbs up, turned and went into the building, radio gear slung over his shoulder.

"You know for a commo guy he's awfully fuckin' quiet all the time." Ricky Matson observed. "He hasn't uttered a word since we left the States."

"Yeah, make somebody a perfect wife." MacDonald quipped as they shifted gear to the tailgate and began unloading.

Harden continued with his instructions.

"Doc, same routine. Tomorrow, makeshift clinic/sickbay where you see fit and let me know if we need anything else. As per brief we'll have two commo windows per day, staggered as per protocol, zero six thirty and again at eighteen hundred. Ricky come on, I'll give you a hand with the weapons chest."

"L.T., any chance for some chow, its half past two and we've had nothing since breakfast?!" Matson enquired.

"Already sorted Ricky. They knew we were coming."

"Damn, these Germans have definitely got their shit in one sock!" Matson declared.

"There's vending machines in the Rec/TV room on the ground floor." Harden reported.

"Ya know sir, on the trip over Doc talked you up pretty good. Now I'm pissed off on two counts. No food and we got a bull shitter for a Doc."

"Sergeant Matson, in time our love will grow." Harden responded. "First commo is zero six-thirty, so wake up is zero five thirty followed by chow and first mission brief. Byrdo give us a yell when you're up in the a.m." Sergeant Byrd acknowledged with a nod and a smile. "Questions, comments snide remarks?" Harden asked.

"Only one sir. Will you read us a story? That airplane ride was scary." MacDonald asked as Harden helped Doc haul the first of the two general purpose medical chests into the barracks.

A minute later Matson was heard to be loudly cursing down in the rec room.

"SON-OF-A-BITCH!"

"Sounds like Ricky just found out the vending machines only take Deutch Marks."

"Hey Doc, is everyone on the teams a smartass?"

Harden asked on the way up the stairs.

"Well sir, on the O.A. Scale, most operators score an 8.0 or above."

"What the fuck is the O.A. Scale?" Harden asked.

"The scale by which all assholedness is measured. The Officer's Asshole Scale."

The Lieutenant flipped him off as they headed into the room.

***

It was just after 05:45 when Sgt Danno Byrd woke the L.T. who gave Danno the code cards he wore around his neck 24/7 and got ready for the day as Danno made his way up to the attic where he set up his Sat Com dish and small, flat transceiver then prepared to receive the ready signal from HQ back in D. C.

He carefully encoded a successful infill report into the burst transmitter but didn't send it as he waited. First contact was usually made by the teams following infiltration but TFR had arranged for the NSA operators to initiate commo as a test for their new code system using a three second burst method.

A minute later the team's first message came through as hardly more than a beep from a microwave oven. Danno set to work decoding it as he simultaneously prepped to send his encoded reply.

Meanwhile down on the third floor Lieutenant Harden wandered over to Doc and Mac who had their heads stuck out the window gazing down onto the parade ground in front of the barracks.

He wedged in-between the two and looked down on the ersatz parking lot where the company of senior infantry soldiers who used to be billeted in the barracks were standing at ease in formation while a soldier, who apparently was their 1st Sergeant, addressed them.

"They gonna muster here every morning L.T.?" MacDonald casually enquired.

"No, this'll be the last one here, starting tomorrow they're gonna hold muster across the compound near their new billets."

"I'll bet they're thrilled at having been evicted." Doc speculated.

"Fuck 'em. They're legs." MacDonald commented.

"So, Mr. Warmth, how do you really feel?" Harden joked.

Down in the parking lot the 1st Sergeant was making the last of his morning announcements to the assembled troops.

"As you have been previously reformed, we alls havin' some vis-eetors up on da top floor o' dis chere barrackses!"

"Huh! Sounds like officer material to me." MacDonald again jibed.

"Well, he is Army." The Lieutenant shot back.

"You peoples will not be attemptin' to talk to, meet with, or establish any communications with these chere vis-eetors under no circumstances. Am I clear like a crystal ball on that particular point?"

"YES FIRST SERGEANT!" The formation

loudly responded.

"Why are they always from the South?" Doc speculated.

"They yell nicer." Ray remarked as the three withdrew from the window.

"Let's move out." Harden directed and with Matson as a stay behind to guard the gear, they locked the other rooms and headed out.

Once through the chow hall entrance, with Byrd first in line so he could eat and return to relieve Matson, Mac, Doc and Harden followed, presented their fake civilian I.D. cards then took their place in the by now, dwindling chow line for breakfast. Once through the line they took their trays to an empty table on the other side of the huge hall and ate in silence.

Having finished their meal the members of TFR picked up their coffee cups and retired to a table in the far corner of the now all but deserted chow hall, out of earshot. Just as they did Ricky Matson approached with his breakfast tray piled with two of everything and handed the message given him by Byrd to the L.T.

"No fucking Deutch Marks required here!" He boasted.

Harden broke open the deciphered message as Matson attacked his breakfast.

"Okay ladies and gent ... " Harden began, then quickly perused the group. "... ladies. Looks like we have our first assignment. We are to liaise with a rep from MI6 at fourteen thirty today at a café in the ville."

"The ville! Shit L.T.," Matson assumed a John

Wayne voice. "... you sound just like John Wayne in *The Green Berets*, Pilgrim!"

"Mac you have my heartfelt thanks for volunteering to stay back and sort through and repack all the gear to its required field ready status." Harden instructed.

"FUCK!" MacDonald responded as Doc patted him on the back.

"Way to take one for the team, Mac!"

"Merriam Morrison! John Wayne! The Duke! Only guy in the military can jump out of Chinook and not hook up." Ricky commented.

"Apparently our contact will ask for directions to the Danube Boat tour." Harden pressed on.

"What's the authentication phrase sir?" Doc asked.

"We give him directions to Piccadilly Circus." The L.T. informed. "Ricky, Mac, as soon as you two get the gear squared away and secured I want you two to meander up to V Corps HQ in the city. Find a Major Hopkins, he's our liaison. Tell him we need deployment plans for the 1st Cav, 3rd Armor, 8th Infantry and the 11th Armored Cav Areas of Operations. We need to know where the good guys are if we're gonna find the bad guys."

"Roger that sir."

"Meet back at the barracks at 13:00 and give Byrd a hand. Doc and I will be back as soon we finish with the MI6 agent. Additionally, quietly remind the major to disseminate to the troops to report any suspicious characters or behaviors in their sectors. Infiltrators are expected!"

"What about transport L.T.?" Mac asked. Harden

produced three pink laminated cards from his pocket and gave them out.

"We're authorized 3 vehicles, basically whatever they have for us. Give them one of these cards and they'll assign you a vehicle for as long as we need them. Make sure the gas tanks are full and that you get the card back when you turn the vehicle back in."

"Nice! Sir can I get an M-1 Abrams?" MacDonald asked.

"Sure Mac, at three gallons to the mile, you can get a tank, as long as you pay for the gas. Are there any competent questions?" No one spoke up. "No? Good. Doc, you'll obviously tag along with me, just in case they get our beer order wrong. I want to use as little English as possible until we get the lay of the land."

"Jawol mein commandant!" Doc clicked his heels.

"Be ready in ten, Schultz."

"With bells on, sir!"

"Okay, Task Force Romeo Five, we're on the job! Stay awake, keep your heads on a swivel and get the fuck outta here!" Harden ordered. Ten minutes later, in civilian clothes, they met downstairs on the quarterdeck of the barracks.

"Sir."

"Yeah Doc?"

"Might be a good idea to lose the Hawkeyes ball cap."

"Shit!" Harden removed the cap and stuffed it in his jacket pocket.

Twenty minutes later Doc and Harden were

396

being escorted by four M.P.'s through a crowd of about 200, chanting anti-nuke protesters seated on the road outside the main gate as the two made their way on foot to the local U-Bahn train station, Germany's answer to the American subway system, minus the defacing graffiti, panhandlers, crime and late trains.

"Hey Doc." Harden asked once they were on their own and the turbulent din of the ranting protesters faded to the background.

"Yeah L.T.?"

"How'm I doin'?"

"You mean as the H.N.I.C. or as ..."

"All kiddin' aside Doc. It's important. I mean, I live shackled behind a desk, a desk I desperately need to escape. This is my one shot at escaping life as a bureaucrat. I screw this up and I live at the God damned Pentagon the rest of my career."

"What's wrong with the Pentagon?"

"May as well work in a fucking office building!"

They reached the U-Bahn station and descended the stairs, bought their tickets into Neu Ulm and went out to the platform.

"L.T., this is actually my first real world mission too. Combat mission at least, I seen plenty of action but not with assholes shootin' at me. But if the whole thing goes south and, make no mistake if it does go south, there's no doubt you will be to blame and deserve what you get, but if you wind up chained back behind that desk, at least it won't be in just any old fucking office building. You'll be chained behind a desk in the most important office building in the Free World."

The train pulled in right on time and they boarded.

"Thanks Doc. I think." Harden related as they took their seats out of ear shot of the few passengers already aboard.

"Just do what you're best at, the intel stuff and leave the rest to the team. This isn't exactly rocket science. We're here for three, maybe four weeks, we observe and report. Either we find something or we don't. What could go wrong?"

"I really wish you hadn't said that Doc." Dave shook his head.

Twenty minutes later, about a kilometer outside the train station, the two entered the Café Edelweiss off the Carl-Eber Strasse in central Neu Ulm.

They took a seat in the back facing the door and with Doc doing the talking, the waitress took their order.

A short time later they were approached by an impeccably dressed man carrying a tourist brochure.

He was of medium height and as he removed his hat they could see that although he sported very close cropped hair along the sides of his head, he was balding on top.

"Excuse me do you speak English?" The gentleman asked in a strong English accent.

"Yes, a bit." Doc answered with an affected German accent.

"Can you direct me to the Danube Boat tour?"

"Yes of course! But you have to go by way of Piccadilly Circus." The gentleman smiled and took a seat.

"Scarlett, John Scarlett, MI6." He nodded as he

spoke in a low tone.

At that exact instant, given the British accent, Doc thought to himself, *If this guy says, 'On Her Majesty's Secret Service', I'm gonna shit all over myself!*

He likewise introduced himself to Harden.

"Lieutenant Dave Harden, Operational Commander Task Force Romeo. This is Petty Officer Doc McKeowen."

"Sir." Doc shook hands with Scarlett.

"Petty Officer? Enlisted chap in the field? Rather unconventional, isn't it?" Scarlett challenged.

"Sorry Mr. Scarlett. I couldn't qualify for a commission." McKeowen informed.

"Oh?! No university is it?"

"No, I've actually a Master's in Biology. Problem is, my parents are married." Scarlett didn't react but Doc was happy enough to have slapped back.

"Not sure how up to speed you are on current events but I've a good bit of news for you chaps, starting with this." He presented a translated page from a magazine stapled to the original Russian article. "In response to President Reagan's military escalations this article, concerning the Korean airlines shoot down, appeared in *Pravda* day before yesterday."

Asserting that an outrageous military psychosis has overtaken the U.S. the Reagan administration, in its imperial ambitions, goes so far that one begins to doubt whether Washington has any brakes at all preventing it from crossing the point at which any sober-minded person must stop.

The sophisticated provocation, organized by the U.S. special services and using a South Korean airplane, is an example of extreme adventurism in policy. We have given the factual aspect of this action a detailed and authentic elucidation. The guilt of its organizers, no matter how they twist and turn or how many false stories they put out, has been proved.

The Soviet leadership has expressed regret in connection with the loss of human lives that was the result of this unprecedented act of criminal sabotage. It is on the conscience of those who would like to arrogate to themselves the right to disregard the sovereignty of states and the inviolability of their borders, who conceived of and carried out this provocation, who literally the next day hurried to push through Congress colossal military appropriations and now are rubbing their hands in satisfaction.

"Additionally the Moscow based broadsheet *Izvestiya* ran it yesterday." Scarlett added.

"Why do I get the feeling that a few more rain clouds just gathered on the horizon?" Harden queried.

"You're not alone Lieutenant." He began to fix his tea as he continued. "We're working with several assets at the moment but we highly suspect that the Reds are up to something and they're using the Geri's as a screen."

"Except for using the Germans as a front, my people have come to a similar conclusion." Harden spoke casually as Doc kept his eyes casually scanning the empty room and the area he could see outside the café.

"You were likely briefed, as was I, that you lads are to go through your chiefs back at the NSA to contact me, but ..." After scribbling a number on the back Scarlett gave Harden a card. "...you know, just in case the line's engaged."

"Strange looking phone number." Dave commented as he flipped the card over.

"That's because it's not a phone number. It's an access code. Dial the number on the front of the card, all but the last two numbers, wait for the beep then enter the access code. You'll be put through to my secure number."

"Handy!"

"There's something else you need to know."

"We're all ears Agent Scarlett."

"We've not filed an all agency report yet, but last week, on the south coast of England, there was an incident in the course of which we discovered the Russians likely have much more enhanced satellite tracking capability then we've previously believed."

"How so?"

"It would appear they have tracked a signal from the south of England. We thought their most advanced satellite should not have been operable beyond the horizon. Which means they've either re-tasked one of their satellites or launched a new one when we weren't looking."

"Interesting. Presumably you're tracking it?"

"Actually, I'd hoped your people were. Not in our budget at the moment I'm afraid. I've passed on a report detailing the incident to Secretary Schultz's office, no response back as of yet."

"They'll pass it to the guys in the NSA for tracking." Harden relayed. "But I'll mention it next time we get commo."

"Now to the main course." Scarlett said. The waitress returned and Scarlett ordered another tea and waited until she left to resume. "To that end we've an exceptionally valuable asset I'm currently working with. A Josef Kuksova ..."

"Yes, Oleg Gordievsky." Harden said. Scarlett was shocked, angry and put off guard all at the same time.

"I wasn't aware you chaps knew about him!"

"Sorry Scarlett, I guess now you do. I've followed your reports on him since the late seventies."

"At any rate, it would appear you're interested in something called Ryan, sometimes annotated as R-Y-N?"

"We are very much interested in Ryan however it's annotated!" Harden confirmed as Doc glanced over at him.

"We haven't really got much on it, aside from some mentions in communiqués, but Kuksova is due to return to the East on a routine visit next month and we've asked him to do some snooping."

"That's helpful but, it would be much more helpful, if the possibility presented, itself that we might have a brief chat with Mr. Kuksova. Give him what we know, maybe get his perspective."

Approaching another agency about sharing an asset, especially a foreign agency, was a bit like asking your new girlfriend if she would talk to her good looking sister about having a Ménage á trois. If she agreed quality of life would improve dramatically. If not, it was back to Mary Palm and her five sisters while you slept on the couch for an indefinite period of time.

Scarlett sat back and resigned himself to the fact that the Americans were one step ahead, at least on the Gordievsky front.

"Well, in view of the current climate and the fact that you already know about him, I suppose something can possibly be arranged."

Vive la Ménage á trois!

"After all he is back and forth all the time. A **very** brief, brief chance meeting shouldn't arouse any suspicion on either side, I suspect." Harden smiled and nodded at Scarlett's words. "Right then, Lieutenant, Petty Officer, lovely to have made your acquaintance. I will be in touch." Scarlett took his leave from the café.

Harden perused the business card.

"What'a ya think Doc? Think he's got his shit together?" Doc assumed an affected southern accent as he answered.

"Frankly my dear Scarlett, I don't give a damn!" *Pompous Limey fuck!* Doc thought to himself.

****

CHAPTER SEVENTEEN

V Corps Headquarters
Allied Powers Europe
Frankfurt am Main, BRD
11:30, Saturday, 17th September

Since the late Sixties when the French became miffed by the Anglo-American domination of NATO and pulled out of the alliance, SHAPE, Supreme Headquarters Allied Command Europe, has made their home in Mons, Belgium, about seventy kilometers south of the capital.

Regardless of the fact that the complex of contemporary concrete and glass buildings fills a two and a half square kilometer grounds and there is even a directory for the various directories to help visitors find the right office, it wasn't strategically practical to locate all the headquarters buildings in the same place.

After all, the Russians had satellites and missiles too.

To that end the various Corps headquarters are actually located in strategically 'safe' areas of their assigned quadrants of Europe. V Corps was no different.

REFORGER being the first full integrated ground, air and sea offensive exercise attempted, the main objective was to assess how efficiently all three of these nuclear weapons delivery systems could be coordinated i.e. mechanized vehicle, airplane and submarine delivery.

If the prevalent theory of drawing in then trapping the Soviet ground forces before attacking their homeland was to succeed, a timely, coordinated response to any aggression was key. Unfortunately for the Allies, timely and coordinated responses had not been their strong points since the onset of the Cold War in the late Nineteen Forties.

Deep in the heart of Frankfurt, buried somewhere in its own vast complex of military bureaucracy and administrative mayhem was a main office for each of the Allied units now heavily engaged in Operation REFORGER '83.

In the early Fifties V Corps had been assigned as the vanguard of the northern flank of the American sector in Germany and in particular to guard and maintain supremacy of the strategically critical Fulda Gap, running through Germany. The prevailing allied strategy was, and pretty much would remain, that if, (**when** some in many circles believed), the Soviets attacked they would be forced to concentrate into and through the gap where they could be held off long enough for the Allies to rain nukes all over Russia. Theoretically this would destroy the Soviet infrastructure and render further resistance futile. To hell with salting the land, it took too long.

Out in the sprawling parking lot of the V Corps Headquarters, dressed in civilian clothes, Ray MacDonald and Danial 'Danno' Byrd pulled up into a space and made their way through the light snow flurry which now sprinkled the chilled autumn air.

As they entered the gargantuan, 19th Century,

granite laden headquarters they checked in at the massive green, Carrera marble desk centered in the lobby, showed their I.D.'s and were issued visitor I.D. badges which they were required to clip to their left shirt pockets. Following a brief phone call they were told that a Major Hopkins would meet them there on the ground floor, just inside the hallway.

They were then directed up a short but wide flight of marble stairs, through the wall-to-wall bank of eight brass doors and into the bowels of the edifice.

Once through the doors they came out into a wide main thoroughfare of what seemed to be an endless hallway bustling with foot traffic in both directions. Suddenly there was a beeping sound behind them and they were forced to dodge a civilian security guard driving a golf cart, loaded with three four star generals, its large yellow light on top flashing away in time with the high pitched beeping.

"Jesus!" Mac declared. "That's more brass than a store full of women fighting at a shoe sale!"

As they stared, the golf cart slinked its way through the flowing crowd, down the corridor and disappeared. By slapping Ray on the arm Danno signaled that he spotted yet another curiosity which caught his attention. Ray turned to look.

"What the fuck?!" Mac scratched his head as both he and Danno stared at what appeared to be an 18 inch wide vertical conveyor belt with small, narrow steel steps attached every two feet coming up out of the middle of the floor. The contraption rattled up from the basement, through all three lower stories and on up through the ceiling to the three floors above. They stepped closer to look up through the opening when a voice yelled.

"HEY! MAKE WAY!" They looked down and an Army officer was hanging on to one of the steps, standing on another below as he ascended nearly colliding with Mac and Danno. They quickly ducked out of the way then stared as the officer disappeared up into the ceiling.

"It's called a paternoster. Means stairway to heaven, like at the Vatican." They both swung around to face the man they had come to see, Major Hopkins of V Corps. "Nazi's had them installed to increase efficiency. Saves the effort of climbing stairs and there's no waiting for elevators."

"How about those Nazis, huh?" Mac quipped. "A contraption named for a Led Zeppelin song!" Judging by his lack of amusement the major wasn't a big Rock n' Roll fan.

"Major, didn't I see this building in a WWII movie one time?" Mac asked.

"Probably more than one time Sergeant!"

"Petty Officer MacDonald sir, this is Sergeant Danno Byrd." Byrd nodded as he shook Hopkins' hand.

"Major Hopkins, V Corps G-2." G-2 was the Corps level intel section. "This is the old Nazi Armored Division Headquarters. First Armor Division captured it in forty-four during our push to Berlin. What can I do for you two?"

"We're from Washington, special task force, here from the duration of the exercise."

"Oh yeah! My secret engineers. So secret I don't

even know what the hell they're up to!"

"Most of the time we don't either." Hopkins maintained his façade of non-amusement. "Sir." Mac quickly added. It didn't help.

"I'm a little busy here. What can I do for you two?"

"Sir we need deployment plans for the 1st Cav, 3rd Armor, 8th Infantry and the 11th Armored Cav, primarily areas of operations. We need to know where the good guys are if we're gonna avoid them and find the bad guys."

The Major crossed his arms over his chest and sized the two operatives up.

"Why the hell you two in civvies?"

"Temporary Assigned Duty to one of the security agencies, sir."

"Fucking TAD'd to NSA! No wonder it's on the QT!" Hopkins cursed.

"Must be to avoid SNAFU's!" Mac added with a smile but quickly concluded that Major Hopkins and humor were oil and water.

"Sorry we're not at liberty to get into details sir, but ..."

"But my ass! I don't give a good God Damned! We're jumping through our asses here! Half these high ranking desk jockeys think this thing is for real fer fuck's sake! Nobody wants to screw up and look like an idiot so they're all wound up tighter than a big base drum!"

As they were talking a First Lieutenant approached and pulled the Major aside. After a brief word the Major set off back down the massive hallway calling back over his shoulder. "Wait out by reception. I'll get the plans pulled and have an orderly run copies down to you. You can sign for them out there."

The Lieutenant approached Mac and Danno.

"Sorry guys. Something going on as the G-2 and G-1's bang heads. Everybody wants to do things their own way. Sometimes ya wonder if we're all even on the same team workin' towards the same goal?"

"Lieutenant?"

"Yes sergeant?"

"It's Petty Officer Lieutenant. Is this whole circus just for REFORGER?" Mac asked.

"Yeah, pretty much."

"Why the fuck is everybody so uptight all the time? It's like they're all constantly wired to 220 cables!"

"Hey, why change anything?" The L.T. shrugged "You fellas need a ride back?"

"No thanks Lieutenant, we have a motor pool issue. Okay if we swing by at this afternoon and collet those plans?"

"Sure, why not?"

"I think we're gonna leave the car here and catch a cab into town. Get some lunch and peruse a bit. Come back by later. Is there a problem with language with the taxi drivers?"

"Yeah, usually."

"Shit!" Danno muttered.

"What'a we do if we don't speak German?" Mac asked.

"If you don't speak German, don't worry about it. Neither do any of the taxi drivers. They're all Turks.

Just like the hookers, all foreigners, little or no German or English. You just grunt and point."

"Except with hookers there's no meters attached, hey Lieutenant?" Ray joked.

"Don't laugh! Wait 'til you see the Red Light District in downtown Frankfurt!" The L.T. hopped on the paternoster and disappeared down through the floor.

"Amazing!" Mac said.

"What's that?" Danno enquired.

"Thirty-eight years after WWII and the same mentality predominates. The same mentality that helped us get our asses kicked in Nam."

As they headed back out to the lobby Danno looked over at Mac. "Ja suppose he was serious about hookers and meters or was he joking around?"

"Sounds like a challenge to me Danny Boy! Let's find us a Turk taxi and head into town!"

****

"Take the next left then follow the road." The Captain directed his jeep driver as he wrestled with the canvas side flap to secure it against the light rain. The driver turned on the wipers.

"Yes sir. What exactly we looking for this time Captain?" It was a cold wet morning with virtually no traffic as they made their way down the rural, two lane blacktop.

"Not exactly sure but the liaison's office said they had multiple complaints that the power suddenly going out between Bad Hersfeld and Friedewald about an hour ago."

Getting soldiers, sailors and marines all pumped up and then giving them weapons of war, ammo and vehicles to conduct a military exercise longer than a day is inevitably going to result in some damage to civilian property. During an exercise scheduled to last nearly two months involving up to 100,000 troops was a recipe for disaster.

The Allied governments were fully cognizant of these facts and so for this exercise appointed twice the normal amount of D.C.O's or Damage Control Officers, to investigate and report on civilian damage.

The Captain and his Corporal driver/translator had been very busy and now just over a week into REFORGER '83 they had been going non-stop for the last three days sleeping in barns and sheds but mostly living out of their 1963 Willey's jeep in-between driving the length and breadth of the V Corps sector investigating, cataloging and reporting accidents and damage to civilian property and vehicles.

Two hours earlier they had just finished investigating a nineteen year old truck driver, private type, who ploughed through a restaurant in a small village, out the other side and into, what was until that morning, the village's only bakery located in what was a 350 year old, Tudor styled building.

With the exception of several broken bones, a concussion and a pregnant woman's water which broke, there were no other injuries, strewn amongst the layers of smashed cakes and breads. That is until the Polizei arrived and had to pull several of the iron pipe wielding, village youths off the deuce and half truck while the driver cowered in the rubble-covered cab of the vehicle.

The day prior, in another local community, the two investigators spent most of the afternoon counting recently planted oak saplings which had been purchased, after 14 years of fund raising, in what was the village's latest attempt to reclaim land damaged in WWII. The total count was just short of two hundred trees, now reduced to fire wood by the two M1 Abrams tank crews who decided to see who could take out more trees with their vehicles in a straight run to the other side of the wood.

Presently the two man D.C. control team were on their way to seek out the location of yet more stupidity.

"Disney Castle, this is Mickey Mouse Zero-Six, Radio check, over." The Captain spoke as he manned the jeep's radio.

Mickey Mouse Zero-Six, good copy. Report when you arrive at site of incident, out.

"Roger Castle. Mickey out."

"Why are all the teams on this mission named for cartoon characters?" The driver asked.

"Because this whole fuckin' thing is a cartoon! Even the upper command structure realizes that! Reagan and Andropov! Two paranoid delusional bastards both old enough to remember when Jesus was a corporal, each with one foot in the grave, who are willing to incinerate the world over whether or not we buy our hamburgers with rubbles or dollars!"

"So how do you really feel sir?"

"You don't want to know!"

The D.C.O. and his driver had been driving along the two lane blacktop for about twenty-five minutes when the corporal pointed across the road to the right.

"Think I found the problem sir."

"SHIT!" The Captain reaffirmed as he too spotted the problem.

The line of telephone/electrical poles which ran parallel and about fifty meters in from the road weren't there, at least they weren't standing erect.

The first three or four they came across looked as if they had been pulled over to the left side inwards and towards each other. The next four or five were flat on the ground and the last one they spotted, over 100 meters down the road, was crossed over the top of another, as both lay like two over-sized sticks of cinnamon, on top of an AVLB.

An Armored Vehicle Launched Bridge, is a two part folding, 8 to 10 meter bridge mounted on a tank chasse and used for assisting armored vehicles in crossing rivers and ravines. The bridge structure itself being capable of supporting up to sixty tons and spanning 10 meters when mounted on the tank chasse, stands a good 5 meters tall folded up. This rises to a height of over 20 meters high during deployment.

Sparks still spat from the electrical lines draped across the ground on either side of the armored vehicle.

In an effort to quell the wide-spread racial unrest plaguing the Army in the Post Viet Nam era voluntary segregation units were experimented with. These were informally called cohorts.

Apparently this cohort of all black soldiers, a five man crew and one officer had suffered a major, collective brain cramp and decided they didn't need a road guide to dismount and direct them safely under the telephone and electrical lines running parallel to the local road despite the fact this was a required by regulation and was standard military procedure when passing under low obstacles in these types of vehicles.

The officer apparently allowed them to just go for it bringing the communication and electrical lines with them when they attempted to drive over the rail crossing snagging the utility lines on the upper section of the vehicle.

As the D.C.O.'s jeep pulled up to the mess he ordered the driver to pull over and park well clear of the lightly sputtering wires and he got out approaching the scene on foot.

One of the crew stood on top of the AVLB's main hatch scratching his head, while two, who had been zapped by the initial contact with the electrical wires were recovering, sitting up against the damaged poles and being comforted by the other two. Part of the deploy mechanism on the AVLB had been welded to the bridge joint on contact with the 440V power lines.

Following a quick survey the Captain returned to man the jeep's radio.

"D.C.O. Mobile Team Zero-Six-Zulu to V Corps D.C. Command, come in. D.C.O. Mobile Team Zero-Six-Zulu to V Corps D.C. Command, come in."

D.C.O. Mobile Team Zero-Six-Zulu this is V Corps D.C. Command, copy.

"Command, Zero-Six reporting cause of loss of electrical service to the Hersfeld/Friedewald area. Seems an AVLB crew from 3rd Armor took out about a dozen telephone poles with accompanying electrical and commo lines. Over."

Injuries Zero-Six?

"Two crew zapped but appear okay, no civilian involvement. Over."

Roger, will dispatch M.P.'s to the sight. Well good news for you Zero Six. Over.

"I'm all ears Command, Over."

You're only about 25,000 bucks away from your $100,000 cumulative damage mark then you and your driver get your 24 hours off. Command out.

"Roger Command. Zero-Six out." The Captain handed the radio mike back to the driver took a seat inside and commenced to fill in the forms on his clipboard.

"What happens at the hundred thousand mark Cap?" The driver inquired.

"They'll shut the sector down and transfer the troops elsewhere to prevent further damage."

"So they get sent somewhere else to tear up Germany and piss off more Germans?"

"Pretty much, but we get 24 hours R&R so, let's go find some more fuck ups." They pulled back out onto the road headed north.

As they drove the Captain continued to fill in forms and the driver thought back on the incident.

"That AVLB crew didn't seem too perturbed

about the seriousness of their fuck-up." The corporal noted.

"They will be when their officer receives the garnishment order which will extract the cost of repair for the wires, cables, all the telephone poles and the vehicle out of their pay until it's all paid for. On top of the fines there will probably be some reductions in rank."

Halfway to the next village the driver had another inquiry.

"Sir, that's a shitload of stuff to pay for. What happens if their enlistment time is up before the fine's paid off?"

"The Army is generous that way Corporal. They'll be given a choice."

"Which is ...?"

"Re-enlist at their reduced rank or go to jail."

"Shit!"

"Yeah."

The Captain made no comment but smirked as he noticed the corporal slow down a little on the rain soaked road.

****

Van der Valk Hotel
Shiphol International Airport
Amsterdam, Netherlands

As requested by the members of TFR-5 it was arranged by Agent John Scarlett that they would meet and spend a short time with Oleg Gordievsky, alias Josef Kuksova, as he was enroute back to KGB headquarters in Dresden, East Germany.

About a week after meeting with Scarlett in London, Gordievsky had been called back to East Germany by the head of the HVA to work out plans to set up a special joint surveillance operation in London and it was immediately following his stopover in Amsterdam that he would fly back to the East through the international traffic hub Rhein Main Airport.

Due to the restricted number of flights per day to Berlin, Gordievsky's flight plan from Heathrow was punctuated with an eight hour stopover in Shiphol Airport just south of Amsterdam.

The drive north through Germany into Holland, by Doc and Lt. Harden of the TFR, would take the better part of ten to twelve hours with another four to Amsterdam, sixteen hours in all. Much too long. As driving time wasn't an option and flight time was only about two hours one way, there was little discussion regarding travel options.

Four kilometers south of Shiphol International on motorway E19 was the Hotel Van der Valk. The meet time was set for 14:00 that afternoon. As a discretionary move it was agreed that room 405 would be pre-booked telephonically by an MI6 cutout acting as intermediary. Having never seen Gordievsky the plan was for the two members of TFR to arrive first, wait for the signal then go up to the room and initiate the meet.

Having arrived about twenty minutes early and now sitting in separate seats in different sections of the lobby, Doc and Lieutenant Harden casually glanced across the floor at the large check-in desk while pretending to read. Harden a newspaper while Doc had a pulp fiction pocket book, the latest edition in *The Destroyer* series, *The Last Drop*, featuring the fictional secret government operative Remo Williams.

Fifteen minutes later, amongst the steady stream of visitors and guests traversing the lobby, both noticed a short, middle-aged man wearing a Van Gogh and glasses. He was well-dressed and accompanied by a beautiful auburn-haired thirty-something in a full length fur coat and stylish hat holding his arm as they crossed the lobby and checked in at the desk. Following the formalities a bell boy took the couple's matching suitcases and led them over to the lifts. The eyes of the TFR men were glued to the woman as she confidently sashayed across the lobby in her black heels. Suddenly they stopped and the man scurried back to the check-in desk to retrieve a novel he'd forgotten. Doc and Harden exchanged a brief glance and returned to their reading.

Ten minutes later the pair, Harden his bulky briefcase in hand, were upstairs knocking on the door of room 405.

"Who is it?" Answered a woman's voice in slightly accented Dutch.

"Book dealers, delivery." McKeowen answered in German.

The door opened and they were greeted with the sight of the chestnut haired, brown-eyed beauty standing tall in her impeccably made up face and black high heels replete with an emerald green dress

418

and clutching a small purse.

Doc smiled and brandished his copy of the Remo Williams novel. She opened her hand bag and produced a copy of the same book Doc held. As they exchanged smiles the man she had come in with opened the door further and poked his head out.

"Kommen sie! Bitte, herein kommen!" He ushered them into the modest but eloquent main room of the apartment-like hotel suite and extended his hand.

"Josef, Josef Kuksova. Sehr nett zu kennen lernen."

"Grussen sie Herr Kuksova, Ich bin Herr McKeowen, aber mein ... my friend doesn't speak German."

"I'm sorry!" He said to Lieutenant Harden, a strong Russian accent tainting his words. "I am Colonel Josef Kuksova and may I present Major Natasha Kavolchuk, Special Agent of KGB." Doc's eyes were locked on the woman. "I thought it prudent to bring a cover agent." Kuksova explained.

"Explanations not necessary Herr Kuksova. Abject apologies to you Agent Kavolchuk, lovely to meet you." Harden smiled at her.

"Gentlemen, lovely to make your acquaintance." She said in English this time flavored with a slight Russian accent. Doc wanted to say more but he was too busy gawking at her glossy pink lips and large, doe eyes as he gingerly shook her hand.

"I think I'm in love!" He whispered to Harden as they moved to take their seats in the parlor.

"Down Simba! Put that thing away! We're on the

clock!" Harden whispered back.

Natasha moved to the bar and began to mix drinks. Gordievsky opened the proceedings.

"So Lieutenant Harden, we have only half an hour or so. To that end, when we finish, you will leave first, using the rear entrance. We will leave later this evening after dinner. Check out will be arranged by phone tomorrow at which time we will be safely to our next destination. Acceptable?"

"Agreed Herr Kuksova."

"Josef please. How may I help you?" Harden was struck by how collected Gordievsky was, impeccably dressed in his three piece, charcoal grey suit, pressed trousers, spats and a carnation in his lapel. His neatly trimmed grey hair and highly polished shoes a testament to his 'Old Worldliness' forcibly garnered respect from both Americans.

"As you have been briefed by MI6 ..." Dave ventured.

"In point of fact, it was **I** who has briefed **them**."

"Of course, apologies. I am here to locate the origin of a man or men if it turns out to be an operating cell, calling itself Ryan or some facsimile thereof."

"I have been told this."

"Truth is Colonel, I haven't got a clue where to start."

"There are several things I may be able to help you with Lieutenant."

They both took their drinks from Major Kavolchuk's tray who then crossed over to Doc as he sat on the love seat, passing him a whiskey neat. He smiled at her and mouthed, 'How did you know?'

She slipped off her high heels and tucked her stocking feet up under her bottom as she took a seat next to him on the plush couch. The Major smiled back, leaned over and whispered, "I read your file." Doc coughed on his drink. She sipped her vodka tonic. Gordievsky continued his brief.

"Firstly Lieutenant, the Russians are well aware of NATO's overall strategy to funnel them into and through the Fulda Gap in the event of hostilities." As most of the NSA had been operating on this premise for the last two years Harden showed no surprise at this revelation. "As we speak KGB with help of the East German security have approximately one hundred agents posing as long distance lorry drivers reconnoitering the roads and motorways all along the Western Front. Detailed maps of primary and secondary alternate routes across the borders and leading to major cities are being constructed on an ongoing basis and have been since late 1982."

"Maps?" Doc asked.

"Maps being drawn up to be used to rush as many troops over the borders as fast as possible before escalation to the nuclear phase?" Harden confirmed.

"Precisely. It is assumed, on both sides, that whoever is lagging behind by D-Day +14 will resort to the nukes and they are banking that NATO will not nuke its own territories."

"Presumably they are doing the same type of scouting with all the existing L.O.C.'s?" Harden asked, knowing the answer almost before he asked.

"Yes, all lines of communication as well. Is it

421

also your ambition to locate these agents?" Harden looked over at Doc who answered Gordievsky's inquiry.

"Well, it wasn't, but as long as we're in the neighborhood, what the hell?" Doc answered as he shrugged.

"Very well. Then you should know that as a means to identify each other these 'route scouts', I suppose you could call them, drive standard single or double articulated lorries, with all aspects in accordance with international European trucking regulations."

"What about cross border cargo checks?" Harden asked.

"Good question. They always carry cargo, some actual some strictly for cover. But when forced to travel empty for whatever reason, they carry multiple sets of perfectly forged shipping documents clearly indicating from where they have come and to where they are going. These papers include cargo amounts, weights, times, sale costs and complete travel tickets."

Doc finished his drink, leaned forward and interjected.

"Okay, but how do they I.D. each other and why is that important?"

"Just as in America lorries here are required to display various labels and signage at different places on their vehicles, dangerous cargo, weight and height of the vehicle etc... drivers and companies which are TIR members are allowed more free border access crossing, the inspection process is streamlined."

"TIR?" Doc asked. Kavolchuk explained.

"Transports Internationaux Routiers, an international convention formed in Geneva in 1975. Members of the TIR are required to display, on the cargo compartments of their vehicles usually on the rear right, signs with the letters T-I-R, on them. The official signs are light yellow letters on an orange field. The KGB and HVA operators have this exact arrangement with the exception that the orange fields are also rimmed around the perimeter with a thin white line. Hardly noticeable, unless you're looking for it."

"Point being we can I.D. them of we get close enough to spot the outline?"

"Precisely." Gordievsky affirmed.

"Colonel, R-Y-N? Ryan." Harden pushed.

"I have received inquiries concerning this also. We don't yet know exactly, but as best that we can venture, we believe it is code. A code name for an operation of some sort. An operational name derived from or perhaps standing for Raketno Yadernoe Napadenie."

"Which means ...?" Harden asked. Natasha answered as she rose from her seat and went to the bar to refill her glass.

"It means Nuclear Missile Attack." She explained as she poured another vodka. Harden knocked over his untouched drink as he spun around in his seat. Doc briefly stared then threw back his whiskey.

"You think the Soviets are planning a nuclear missile attack?!" Harden barked out.

"We don't know. We have no details of the operation on any level. Even that explanation is only an educated guess based on how it is sometimes written as R dash Y dash N, but also written as R-Y-A-N- in one word." She explained.

"But if you're right ..."

"Even if we are right we still don't know the significance of it." Gordievsky added.

"If you are right I'll tell you the significance of it. The problem of baby Harp seals and Artic owls going extinct just got solved!" McKeowen said as he made his way over to the bar to refill his glass.

"I have been asked to return to the GDR to consult with the HVA on an operation." The Colonel explained. "I should be back in London in a week to ten days. I hope to have more information for you then."

"We'll start checking out the movements of these TIR route scouts first thing tomorrow." Harden relayed.

As they spoke Major Kavolchuk collected all the glasses washed them and then went around removing all traces of anyone having been there. She then set out two wine glasses, opened a bottle of white wine and poured most of it down the sink. She then added a few milliliters into each of two wine glasses, imprinting her lipstick on one.

"Lucky glass!" Doc mumbled as she then went into the bedroom. Kuksova gave final instructions.

"I understand you have the contact details of John Scarlett?" Gordievsky asked as he moved to the kitchenette signally the meet was over.

"We do." Lt. Harden confirmed.

"I will be in constant touch with him. If you have anything of any importance, feel free to pass it on to him. I will get the message." Gordievsky instructed.

"Maybe I should see if she needs a hand in there? I feel bad an officer doing all the work." Doc whispered to the L.T.

"Down boy, sit! Stay! Behave or no whiskey biscuits on the plane home!" Harden ordered as through the hall they both could see Natasha mussing up the bed and then resetting the shower. Doc feigned a juvenile disappointment at Harden's remarks

"I am thinking that we will never see each other again, so may I say best of luck in your future endeavors gentlemen?"

"You have been most helpful Colonel." Harden assured him.

"Nice to have met you too Doctor."

"Herr Gordievsky, I'm not really a doctor, only a Navy corpsmen." Just then Natasha came bounding out of the back room, donned her shoes and gathered her things.

"Gentlemen, it has been a pleasure." She said as she went to McKeowen. "Doctor, I especially enjoyed making your acquaintance." She shook his hand with a smile that would melt an iceberg.

"Oh, I'm not ... ahh, thank you very much Major. Likewise. And may I say you look very healthy." As she leaned in to kiss him on both cheeks.

"If I ever need a physical perhaps I can call you." Suddenly Harden was by Doc's side firmly guiding him by the elbow to the door.

A short while later Doc and Harden were getting

onto the lift down to leave the hotel and head back to Frankfurt and on back to Neu Ulm.

"I think I'm in love!" Doc declared as they stepped off the lift. "You think that old guy is ... you know."

"She was somewhat attractive." Dave nonchalantly shrugged in agreement.

"Somewhat attractive?! She made my dick harder than Chinese arithmetic! I'm talkin' hard enough to crack walnuts!" Harden made no comment. McKeowen looked at the L.T. who, dictated by his conservative back ground, was purposely struggling to feign decorum. "What?! Tell me you wouldn't do her?!" Doc prodded while he back peddled in front of Harden as they made their way down the back hall to the rear exit. He pushed down on the cross bar and held the door open for the L.T.

"In front of the Pope!" Harden softly said as they made their way across the open field to a taxi rank across the road.

"Think I could join the KGB?" Doc speculated.

"You'd have become a communist." Harden informed.

"Think she was a communist?"

"Of course she was a communist, she's KGB!"

Doc considered for a moment before he spoke.

"I could be a communist." Doc affirmed. "Seriously, I could! What's yours is mine and what's mine is mine! How's that? Do I sound like a commie?"

"You need help!"

By the time Doc and the Lieutenant were back at

the airport terminal, getting settled into their flight back, Gordievsky and Natasha had taken a cab from in front of the hotel's main entrance and were just reaching an upscale but modest restaurant fifteen minutes on the other side of the airport.

The driver of another taxi, which had followed Gordievsky's cab to the hotel earlier, pulled into a rank across the street from the swank eatery. He watched them enter, waited a bit then manned a hand held transmitter instead of his taxi radio.

"Van der Valk One, this is Mobile Three, they've just been dropped at a restaurant about five kilometers north of the restaurant."

Roger. I will notify reception team. Van der Valk out.

"Mobile One out."

****

By 17:00 that afternoon, as the rest of TFR-5 were back together at 1187 Hunterwasser on the base at Neu Ulm making out preliminary reports of what they had found, Doc and Harden had landed back in Frankfurt and were driving south heading back to Neu Ulm on Autobahn route 5 in their government issue black Chrysler.

About twenty minutes outside the town Doc realized they hadn't eaten since just before landing that morning in Amsterdam.

"How about some chow?" Doc proposed as he pointed to a roadside sign which featured international pictures for food, petrol and accommodations at the town of Langen at the next exit.

"Got my vote!" Harden said.

After exiting east they drove a few minutes when they came on a large white van, parked off to the side of the road which had been converted into what the Americans call a 'lunch wagon'. The side had a large, top hinge mounted window cut into its side which was propped open, and there was a line of eight or ten American soldiers mixed with a smattering of civilians lined up.

"AHH! An imbiss!" Doc declared, reading the large red letters painted on the side and front of the van.

"A what?"

"An imbiss, a snack. Germans get two imbiss breaks a day." He explained as he pulled over.

"In addition to a lunch break?"

"Lunch and dinner. But so what? We get two coffee breaks a day, what's the diff?"

"The diff is we drink coffee, maybe eat a donut or croissant, not a sausage the size of a horse's dong, a liter of coke and a plate of fries! No wonder they're all so fucking huge." Dave commented.

"Lott'a people in America take their coffee breaks at McDonalds."

"Good point." He glanced down at the gas gauge. "Maybe after we eat we get some gas?" Harden suggested.

"We should be okay. It's only another 4 or 5K to the base. We can fill up in the morning. Let's chow down! You're buyin'!"

They pulled in to the road side clearing, locked

the car and walked over to take their place in line. Harden studied the guy in the van serving the food.

"That guy looks like somebody." He said.

"We all look like somebody, you're the perfect case in point." Doc quipped.

"No, no ... somebody famous."

"Again case in point." Doc pointed at Harden as the line moved forward and they were now within earshot of the driver as he made small talk with the American soldiers who were lined up as he lazily prepared their orders.

Suddenly Doc pulled Harden aside and waved the next two soldiers behind them ahead.

"Doc, c'mon! I'm hungry enough to eat Army chow! what'a we doing?"

"Take out your wallet, make believe you're counting your Deutsch Marks."

"Whiskey Tango Foxtrot?!"

"Do it and keep quiet!" Harden complied and after two or three minutes of stalling Doc got back in line and gave Harden another set of instructions. "Discreetly go back to the car, turn it around and pull it back by that grove of trees, out of sight. I'll be over in a couple of minutes with the brats." McKeowen quietly instructed.

"A brat? Fuck that noise! I want two of everything, and you're buyin'!" Harden put his money away. "Taking this espionage shit a little serious aren't we?"

Doc made deliberate eye contact.

"Remember next morning after we scammed those two chicks at LeJeune?"

"What about it?"

"You said if I was a girl you'd marry me?"

"Yeah, so?"

"Well, if you still love me get going!" Doc insisted.

Harden strolled back to the car and Doc returned to the line, moving forward as needed but occasionally, when Imbiss Man was busy prepping brats and fries for his next army customer, Doc allowed someone to go ahead of him while always paying strict attention to the casual conversation at the window of the van as the people, mostly soldiers, were being served.

Eventually, using only German slang with a local dialect, Doc made it to the window bought and paid for four bratwursts, 3 paper cups of fries and two bottles of Hermann-Kolas.

Back in the car, where they were out of the line of site of the van but could still see it, Doc handed some food off to Dave and they began to eat.

"Now what are we doin?" Dave asked, a mouth full of fries distorting his speech.

"Until Phil Collins over there ..."

"PHIL COLLINS! That's who that guy looks like!" Dave triumphantly declared.

"... decides to call it a day selling brats, closes down his wagon and heads out, we're doing nothing."

"What'a ya mean nothing?"

"The reason that fucking line was taking so long to move was that pudgy little bastard is pumping all the dumb shit young G.I.'s for intel."

"Out in the open? How?" Dave stopped chewing.

"Trolling. Casual conversation, innocent

questions. 'How long you guys here for? You drive tanks? I need to know how many of you so when I come back I can bring enough bratwursts.' Then he snows them with the story of how he wants to go to America someday." The penny dropped for Harden.

"I'll bet he does!" Dave lowered his brat and smiled. "Good pick-up Doc!"

"About time you realized I'm not just another pretty face." Doc commented as he raised the small binos to get a closer look at the vehicle. "Huh!"

"What?"

"Red mud on the rear fender and quarter panel."

"Who are you Magnum P.I.?"

"I was always partial to Philip Marlowe."

"So Phil, what's with the red mud?" Dave asked as he ate.

"Fulda Gap's caked with red mud. Could be he was doing some recon earlier."

"You reckon he's KGB?" Harden pushed as he continued to eat like a starving Somalian.

"Highly unlikely. Very strong Brandenburg dialect so probably HVA, maybe working with the KGB. But I'm new to this spy shit. In Recon we just creep in, take pictures and get the fuck out."

"You ever thought about being a detective?"

"All the time. Then I look at my old man."

"Meaning?"

"My father was a P.I. Still tinkers around, but at the end of the day he didn't make squat at it."

"Why not?"

"Let's drop it."

"Okay." Dave backed off. "So, what'a ya think Phil's up to?" Dave asked as he ripped off another

431

chunk of bratwurst and followed it with a big swig of cola which he immediately spat all over the dashboard and floor of the car. "CHRIST! What the fuck is this shit?! Pure sugar?"

"Triple caffeine drink. The kids love it. I figured we might be up a little late if we're gonna tail this guy ya know, see what he gets up to."

"Tail him. Good idea. Glad I thought of that!" As he poured the rest of his Kola out the window.

"That's why you got the bars and I got the stripes sir."

They finished their food and sat till dusk when Imbiss Man began closing down the van. Ten minutes later, with Harden on the first shift driving, they maintained a discreet distance behind him on the two and four lane black tops winding their way east through the country.

A little over 80K later they passed a sign, 'Sweinfurt 10 Kilometers'.

"Maybe he wants to do some late night shopping?" Harden joked.

"Probably needs gas. How we doing?" Doc asked.

"About a quarter of a tank. We should be okay, depending."

Doc continued to peruse the map he had spread out on his lap. "On second thought, he's probably headed for the border."

"We're only about 60K or so from the GDR and he's not likely to cross the border in that thing." As if Imbiss Man were eavesdropping, he signaled he was exiting, did so then drove another five minutes to a rest area with a dozen trucks, some passenger vehicles and a full sized restaurant with a small camping area behind it.

At the entrance to the large parking area there was a sign with two arrows pointing left and right and labeled 'PKV' and LKV'. Doc took the one marked PKV, for passenger vehicles, and drove to a vantage point across from where the imbiss wagon parked in the area designated LKV.

They deduced that Imbiss Man must have felt pretty secure in his choice of location because without hesitation he dismounted his van and strolled over to a double articulated lorry, knocked on the driver's side door and waited. Doc scrambled for the binos and zeroed in on him.

"I got the truck and the mark. Keep an eye on the perimeter." He said to Harden.

"Got it." McKeowen watched as, under the dim light of the parking lot's tall lamp posts, Imbiss Man consulted with the tall, heavy set lorry driver.

"TIR sign on the rear of the truck." Doc announced.

"Bingo!" Harden declared. "Can you make out an outline in the TIR plate?"

"I think so but light's not that good."

"We'll find out." Harden said as he reached over the seat and retrieved his bulky, black briefcase.

"Watch'ya got?" Doc asked.

"Toys!" He opened the case and produced a gadget about the size of the lid of a can of beans.

The 'toy' was a round piece of light weight metal, an aluminum alloy, half an inch thick and nearly three inches in diameter. In the dim shadows of the car he passed it to Doc.

"Is this what I think it is?"

"Yep! A tracker bug!"

"I was gonna guess an aspirin for R2D2."

"Maximum effective range of 175 miles with a constant pulse of 24 hours or intermittent pulse for 36 hours. State-of-the-Art!"

"Looks like it could double as a fridge magnet." Doc said as he rolled it around with his fingers.

"Peel the label off." Harden instructed. Doc looked puzzled as the L.T. took it back from him and peeled away the thin white label stuck to the non-magnetized side. It revealed the polished enamel label of a popular brand of German chocolate bar, Ritter Sport. "It doubles as a fridge magnet."

"I'm semi-impressed. What'a ya gonna do with it?"

"At nearly 20 grand each they only let me sign for one." He smiled producing a second device from the case and brandished it in front of Doc.

"Need I ask?"

"They only gave me one, but I borrowed the other! You know, just in case." Harden explained.

"Yeah, just in case. So you're out twenty grand if you lose one of those babies?"

"Nope! Only ten grand."

"How do figure that?"

"You're an accessory." Dave smiled as replaced one tracker than re-stowed the case. Doc put on a phony pleading voice.

"But General, I tried to warn the Lieutenant not to be so careless with government property!" He whined.

"You with me or not?" Harden demanded.

"Yeah! What's the plan Mr. Bond?" Doc inquired.

"Bug the lorry! All we gotta do is ..." They both jumped as there was a knock on the window. Both reached under their sports jackets for their shoulder holsters but didn't draw as they spotted a woman's hips wrapped in a dark purple, leather micro-mini just outside the car. Doc rolled down the window and a six foot plus, thirty something, well-worn hooker leaned both arms in on the door.

"Guten Abend Kleine! Ich bin Helki!" She announced in her best sexy-tainted-with-just-enough-slut voice as she perused the inside of the car and the two not so covert operatives. Dave slowly closed over the case. "Zwei fur eine heute abend!" She announced.

"She is Helki, and it's two for one night." Doc explained.

"Tell her, thanks but no thanks." Harden directed. Doc spoke something back to her and she gave an exaggerated grin.

"Darf ich zugucken?" Helki asked.

"Tut mir leid, aber nein." Doc replied.

"What's she want?" Harden asked.

"She wants to know if she can watch."

"Watch what?!"

"Tell ya later." McKeowen turned back and asked her something which Dave could hear contained the phrase "100 Deutsch Marks". This obviously impressed her because she immediately agreed. From his pocket Doc produced a small fold of bills, peeled off two and handed them to the

435

hooker. She strolled away.

"I offered her a hundred marks to distract our friend. Give you a chance to slip down there and bug the trailer."

"Nice!" Dave added. Doc gave a broad smile.

Ten minutes later Harden was casually strolling past the passenger side, rear of the lorry where he could hear the hooker joking with the driver through the window. He quickly and quietly planted the device and strolled away.

About ten minutes later Harden was climbing back in the car while Doc kept watch on the big truck as the imbiss van drove away.

"Just out of curiosity, what did that hooker wanna watch?"

"Told her you were a hooker too." Doc continued to watch through the binos. "A homo hooker I picked you up in Bamberg."

"That's bullshit Doc! Shouldn't go sayin' shit like that! I'm an officer for fuck's sake!"

They drove off following the TIR truck back towards the Autobahn.

"Besides, I've never even been to Bamberg!" Dave Insisted.

*** * ***

CHAPTER EIGHTEEN

Rhein-Main Flughafen
Frankfurt am Main
23:20, Tuesday, 20th September

O f all of the L.O.C.'s, Lines of Communication, air travel was the most controlled and monitored by both sides. As a result the only direct flights in Europe to Berlin were through Frankfurt and those only twice per day.

Colonel Gordievsky and Major Kavolchuk finished dinner at the restaurant in Amsterdam just before nine that evening and hailed a cab back to the hotel. Once there, they took a reasonable amount of time in the room to appear as though they were packing and again left the hotel for the airport and their 22:15 flight to Frankfurt.

While Doc and the L.T. were taking the scenic route towards the famed seven hills of Bamberg, back at Rhein-Main Oleg and Natasha had deplaned at Frankfurt and were making their way out to the lounge to stretch their legs and get some coffee.

They had been forewarned of a baggage handlers' strike in the German airports when they left Amsterdam so they were now heading to the luggage carousels which were just inside the main entrance to the terminal to retrieve their bags and carry them to their connecting flight.

The bags had not yet been unloaded from the plane so Natasha excused herself to go to the toilet

437

and Oleg announced he was going outside to have a smoke.

As he stepped into the night air to enjoy a last Western cigarette before flying into East Berlin later that night, Oleg's thoughts drifted to his wife and kids who were currently enjoying a holiday in Finland. He needed to smoke the last Marlboro in his pack because despite a thriving black market behind the Iron Curtain featuring Western goods, it wouldn't do for a high ranking official of the KGB to be seen indulging in such overtly Capitalistic behavior.

*

"TIR truck's on the move!" Doc announced, keeping watch through the Starlight binos from the passenger's seat of their Chrysler. They had found a strategically located side road to park on which rose above the sprawling parking lot and so afforded a good observation point to monitor events.

As the tractor trailer pulled out of the parking lot and onto the motorway they tailed it as it headed further east through the night for about 50 klicks past Bamberg nearly to the town of Bayreuth.

"Well, he's definitely headed for the border." Harden confirmed as he watched the tracking monitor in the black case while Doc drove.

They were about fifteen minutes outside the route 9 intersection when they decided to pull over onto the shoulder and take advantage of the dark.

"We'd better drop off here. We're too close to the

border." Harden suggested. From that point on they had to rely on the homing device as the lorry cruised across into the GDR.

Tracking the vehicle on the map they compared the route to their list of TIR sanctioned roads.

"That road he's now on is not a TIR." Doc commented.

"Get on the secure portable phone and radio Danno. Get him both tag numbers and pass on that Imbiss Man is passing troop movement and strengths to the commies!"

"Correction, selling troop movement and strengths to the commies!" Doc added.

"What about our chat with the Russians?"

"Better not mention anything about RYAN just yet. I want more info before we get into that."

"Got it."

Doc went around to the trunk of the car and broke out a second black case about half the size of a milk crate, set it on the roof and opened it. After raising a short aerial he then removed the oversized telephone transceiver, which was attached to the bulky phone system via a thick, rubber coated spring cord and dialed a number on the luminescent rotary dial.

It was the latest in communication technology, a long distance, over the horizon portable phone.

He gave an abbreviated report with the pertinent details to Danno so he could relay them to the NSA bosses with his next transmission.

After checking in with the team they did a U-turn and started to head back west.

"Well you have to admit ..." Harden spoke as he

drove. "...that was a good day's work!"

"No argument there L.T." About a minute later the car started to sputter a little. Then some more. Then it happened.

About 30 minutes from the Frankfurt city limits the car sputtered more violently and chocked to a halt with just enough momentum to coast onto the shoulder of the roadway.

"'It's only another few klicks to the city!'" Harden mocked Doc's earlier comment as he opened the door and got out. "I'll take a walk towards those lights at the next exit see if there's anything open." Harden informed.

"Sounds good. I'll stand-by and monitor the radio."

It could be a long cold night on the side of the road in the cramped car. Or so they thought.

*

440

CHAPTER NINETEEN

Route 3, Keisterbach Road
Frankfurt Flughafen

It was just after half past ten when two young Polizei in their standard green and white patrol vehicle were returning from their dinner break when they decided to swing by the Flughafen and scout for stewardesses on layovers. As they slowly cruised towards the airport the radio crackled to life with the voice of a female dispatcher.

All patrols, all patrols we have received a phone call of a disturbance, possible fight, in front of the main terminal of the flughafen. No details. Be alert.

"Central, this is Frankfurt Patrol #107, we are driving north on Autobahn Three. ETA one minute. Will investigate, out."

It was late and there were few travelers when Patrol Unit 107 turned and headed in the direction of the terminal where they spotted an old woman with a walker and a small, wheeled suitcase frantically waving at them. They pulled over and rolled down the window as the diminutive woman in the heavy wool coat hobbled over to them struggling to pull the suitcase behind her.

The Polizei in the driver's seat smacked his younger partner.

"Get out and go to her for God's sake! She's at least a hundred! Probably went to school with the Kaiser!" The younger cop complied but as he approached her she began frantically yelling.

441

"IT WAS A TAXI! IT WAS A TAXI!" She called to him.

"Calm down Mutti, come down! What was a taxi?"

"It was a taxi! It was a taxi, took the nice man! It was a taxi and three big men! In the taxi!"

"What man? What are you on about old woman?!"

"It was a taxi, took the nice man! They threw him in and ... and they sped away with him!" He signaled over to the patrol car for his colleague to join him.

"Someone was taken and it was a taxi they used?" The cop clarified.

"Yes!"

"You're certain?" He asked her. She stomped her foot as she answered.

"I'm old, not stupid! Yes! It was a taxi and it looked exactly like that one!" She pointed to the third taxi in the rank outside the terminal, its driver stood outside next to it lighting a cigarette.

"That one?!" He pointed to the same vehicle.

"Was your mother a parrot young man?! That one, only black!" She was pointing at a 1982 Ford Taunus, TC3.

"Is there anything else you can remember?"

"Yes. It had a dent in the back, like somebody kicked it."

"Dent in rear fender." He wrote in his small note book as they talked. "Anything else?"

"Yes, the driver was a Turk!"

It was at that exact moment the driver of the vehicle the old woman was describing was handing

442

a parking pass into the parking attendant in the exit booth.

In the back seat Oleg Gordievsky was sandwiched in-between two pugnacious looking thugs both with 7.62mm Marakov pistols pressed into his ribs. Professional enough to fully realize his situation, Oleg sat perfectly still. The driver paid the fee and exited the main gate of the car park.

A photo from the CCTV cam above the gate recorded the transaction.

Meanwhile Natasha had returned to the luggage carousel where she and Gordievsky were supposed to have met, but there was no sign of her boss. After a cursory look around the terminal she still couldn't locate him and immediately suspected something. She stepped outside, saw the old woman, the police and their car and quietly moved to within earshot as the old woman was speaking.

"It was a taxi, took the nice man! I was waiting for my son to come and collect me and I saw them! They threw him in and –"

Seconds later Natasha was frantically feeding several coins into the phone box back near the main entrance and dialing a direct long distance number. Her party picked up on the third ring.

Hello, Agent –

"Agent Scarlett, they've taken Oleg!" She spoke into the receiver with a calm but clear sense of urgency. He recognized her voice.

Bastards! Never thought they'd do anything so drastic!

"John, if they get him to the East they'll torture him then kill him!"

Let's don't get ahead of ourselves Natasha! We have some chips to play too! It's probable they'll take him through East Berlin first just to get him over on their side of the fence. Where are you?

"At the flughaven in Rhein-Main."

Listen to me carefully, this is important! You have a decision to make. It may be the most important decision you will ever make!

Not wanting to voice it out loud agent Kavolchuk knew what was coming.

You must decide to stay on this side or go back!

Natasha's mind slowly numbed as she looked over to the two policemen jumping back into their patrol car.

When she left her home in Moscow two days ago it was for a short 48 hour trip to the West with an immediate return. Now she had mere seconds to decide the rest of her life.

You know full well what they will do to you if they ...

"Kill us both?! Yes, I know!"

"I don't know what Oleg has told you about me, but if you stay, I give you my word we will protect you and give you a complete new life!"

Despite the suddenness of the situation thrust upon her, Kavolchuk's training kicked in and she pulled herself together.

"What must I do?" She firmly asked.

Get into town and head straight for the British embassy, they'll be expecting you. Tell them you're name is Ludmilla Kuksova and you're there about your brother. When you're there ring me from a secure line. I'll take care of the rest. Understand?

"Yes. Please do all you can Agent Scarlett! He's a good man that's why he came to you in the first place!"

By now the Polizei in unit FP-107 were exiting the airport in search of the mysterious taxi.

The green and white Polizei cars, Audi 5000's, were never meant to be race cars but, being no strangers to chasing criminals in high speed pursuits and with ready access to the finest engineered cars in the world, there were other vehicles German criminals would have preferred to have been chased by.

"Central Control, this is 107, in search of a black 1982 Ford Taurus, dent in left, rear fender. Possibly posing as a taxi, driver described as being Turkish. Vehicle suspected of involvement in forced abduction approximately ten to fifteen minutes ago. Over."

Central to 107. Can you advise direction and present estimated location?

"Roger Central. Rhein-Main parking security sets time of exit of vehicle at thirteen minutes ago. Over."

107 Central, be alerted we are activating and monitoring all cameras in the Rhein-Main and Frankfurt Kreuzung areas, will notify as soon as we locate. Out.

"Roger Central. FP-107 out."

The Frankfurt Kreuz intersection is a clover leaf where the Autobahn 3 and the Autobahn 5, the two busiest motorways in Europe, meet. An estimated 300,000 vehicles per day pass through the area and having virtually invented the CCTV the Germans were the first in the world to arm all major traffic intersections with cameras. So, not widely known to the general public, were the thirty-seven cameras, where the Polizei were able to scan 270 degree arches of the entire Frankfurt Kreuz intersection.

It was only a matter of minutes before the black 1982 Ford Taunus was spotted by Central Traffic Control driving through the Kreuzung.

Until they could get some kind of confirmation as to their suspect car's whereabouts, Frankfurt Polizei patrol unit #107 had taken a chance that the Ford Taurus taxi had travelled along the main road, route A3, once leaving the airport parking lot. Their gamble paid off.

FP-107 and all units, be alerted, suspect vehicle has been located and is heading north at regulation speed towards the F.K. Over.

"Central, 107 in pursuit. We are five minutes from the Autobahn. Can you give a location marker for suspect vehicle please?"

107, one moment please. Ten seconds later Central came back on. *107 be alerted suspect vehicle is at km marker #12 from airport exit. Over.*

"He's only one kilometer in front of us!"

"Maybe we have an early Christmas Karl?" The junior cop driving commented to his partner.

"Could be Dietrich. Could be."

Ten minutes after starting their search, thanks to the luminous mercury vapor street lamps lining the moderately busy Autobahn, the black Taurus was sighted about half a dozen car lengths ahead.

"Keep your distance. We don't want to spook him." Karl ordered.

"Ya klar."

"Central,107. We have suspect vehicle in sight at kilometer marker sixteen driving east/north east at 70 kilometres per hour. Will follow."

Roger 107. Do you require back-up?

"Negative central. No danger is imminent. Out."

****

It had been less than ten minutes from the time Harden set out on foot down the autobahn when a patrol car pulled up beside Doc as he lay reclined in the driver's seat trying to catch a catnap. A loud tapping on the window with a large flashlight snapped him out of it.

"Offnen!" The cop ordered as he signaled to open the window. Although fluent in the language Doc also knew when not to use it.

"Evening officers. How may I be of assistance?"

"What are you doing so late on the road with your car parked in this way?"

"Ran out'a gas. My friend and I are engineers contracted to the U.S. Army for this big exercise they're doing here." Doc fished his false D.O.D. I.D. out of his pocket, but the cop ignored it.

"Ha, das ist gut! American engineers who can't read za gas gauge!"

"Actually officer, that's because the gas gauges in America go the other way." He demonstrated with his finger as if it were a gauge needle.

"Oh! I did not know zat. Now I must apologize for being rude. I'm sorry!"

"No problem officer." *Asshole. Should have told you Chinese women's vaginal openings are horizontal. Probably would have bought that too!*

"Come. Ve give you a lift."

"Thanks! My lieutenant is up ahead looking for a petrol station. If we drive we should see him." McKeowen spoke as he gathered up the commo case and Harden's big briefcase. Doc locked up and climbed into the back of the patrol car and they were off in search of Harden.

*

"You're too close! I told you to stay back!" Karl commanded. Now thirteen klicks from the airport traveling east on route A3 the tension for patrol car #107 started to mount.

"I am back far enough! He won't notice us! There are three cars between ..." Then it happened. The taxi suddenly hit the gas, pulled around a van and sped away.

"SHEISSE! GIBT GAS MAN!" Karl fastened his seat belt, switched on the siren and manned the radio as they took off.

"Central, FP-107, be alerted we are now in high speed pursuit of suspect Black Ford Taurus, travelling east on Autobahn 3."

Roger 107. All camera's being positioned, will notify all units. Keep us advised. Central out.

"Don't get too close. If he crashes we want room to avoid getting involved."

"Dietrich, someday you will make someone a

wonderful wife. But until this time, please let me drive!" Karl calmly answered as they swerved around a slow moving farm vehicle.

"Karl?"

"Ya Dietrich?"

"Go and fuck yourself, ya?"

*

"Sounds like there's a chase on!" Overhearing the radio Doc commented form the rear seat of the squad car as they cruised west along the A3 towards the A661. The cop in the passenger's seat manned the radio.

Central, FP#109. We are just east of the A3/661 intersect. How do you wish us to proceed? A second unit radioed in.

The passenger cop in 109 turned in his seat and spoke to Doc.

"Just some local gangsters. They are watching too many American gangster films."

"They all want to be Edward G. Cagney or Jimmy Robinson or sumsing, starring in *Scarface*!" The other cop mocked. Doc smiled and suppressed a laugh as he interrupted.

"Guys ... ah ..."

"Ya?"

"Not important, never mind."

Just then, up in the distance, they spotted Harden walking in the dark along the shoulder of the road. They pulled over, picked him up and continued on. Cursory introductions were interrupted by the radio.

109 this is Central.

"Central, 109, go ahead."

109, be prepared to intercept should suspect vehicle cross the 661 intersect.

"Roger Central. Moving into position. 109 out."

In the back seat Dave leaned over and whispered to Doc.

"Catch me up."

"Trouble at the Airport. They think it's locals, possibly small time drug dealers. They're also up ahead on Route 3 about three or four klicks east, heading this way. Apparently a kidnapping." Harden's face turned to stone.

"Who's' been kidnapped?!"

"Don't know."

"Ask them."

'What?"

"Ask them!"

From the look on Harden's face Doc put two and two together.

"You're not serious!" Doc sat up straight and looked at the L.T.

"Ask them!"

McKeowen spoke to the cops who said they did not yet know who was involved, but that it was almost certainly local Turkish gang members. In as broken German as he could muster, so as not to let on he was fluent, Doc pushed for details and the cops radioed in. Central came straight back with an answer.

109 be alerted. Patrol 107 states four men in vehicle, a driver and three men in back. Other than description of the vehicle, that's all that's available at the moment. Central out.

"Thank you Central, 109 out."

Doc relayed the news to Harden who seemed a bit more agitated.

"I'm not getting a warm fuzzy feeling about this Doc. Think we can convince them to join in and follow those guys?" He suggested.

"Might be a case of going to the well once too often L.T. I mean they are being cool about –"

All units, all units. Be alerted shots fired from suspect vehicle, vicinity of A3 and A661 intersect.

"Now what?" Harden asked as the siren was turned on and they shot from 60 kph to 120 in a matter of seconds.

"Be careful what you wish for." Doc quipped. The car pulled into the far lane and headed for the A661 intersection.

Less than two minutes later FP#109 had joined in the chase.

"Central, FP#109 in pursuit of the black Taurus." Doc and Harden strained to make out the people in the black taxi but it was too far ahead, swerving far too much and the occasional crack of gunfire discouraged the Polizei from getting too close.

"Now I will get too close!" Karl in #107 stated with angry determination. "Dietrich get out your gun!"

"What?!"

"Take out your gun! I will get close and you can take out one of the tires!" His partner complied and the cop car, now racing at near 160 kph suddenly pulled ahead and in front and sped up to and nearly alongside the black Ford.

As the passenger, Dietrich was able to roll down his window and take aim steadying his hand between the window frame and the side mirror. Just as he squeezed off one round which just missed the taxi's rear left tire. The cop car suddenly lurched to the left and swiftly dropped back.

"What the hell are you doing Karl?! I almost –"

Karl pointed ahead to the taxi as the distance between the two vehicles grew. The muzzle of an MP40 Schmeisser machine gun peered out the rear window of the taxi and let loose a short burst.

Both cop cars swerved but 107 took a few rounds across the grill which didn't seem to affect the vehicle.

"107 this is 109. All okay up there?"

"Ya109. He appears to be shooting low. Warning shots I'd guess." By this time they were fast approaching the north south major artery of 661.

At the A661 intersect, which was also a clover leaf affair, the kidnap vehicle tried to lose the chase cars by feigning an exit by getting off at the next ramp only to remount the autobahn again on the other side. This put the KGB car on the east side of 661 now further ahead of #107.

However knowing the territory the two Polizei vehicles split up and one stayed with the Ford as the other took the next on ramp, only 300 meters ahead, and had now rejoined the pursuit.

"Central, 107. Be alerted, suspects now heading north on the A661."

107, Central, understood.

"109 this is 107."

"Go 107."

"Before we started this Steve McQueen scene they seem to have been set on following Route 3. Stay with them. I'm going to take the Babenhäuser Landstrasse exit back over to state route A3. You follow him. If I am right they are likely to turn west again on 43 along the river once they hit the city. The Gerbermühlstrasse is closed for construction that means there is only the Alte Brücke at Sachsenhausen to cross over the river. We'll get there first and intercept them. If they stay on the river road we can intercept them by the next bridge."

"Copy that 107. Will do."

"Good plan Karl." Dietrich commended. "Glad I thought of it!"

"Dietrich, go and fuck yourself ya?"

"109, 107 out. Break. Central, this is 107, did you copy?"

Roger 107. All units, suspects appear to be heading towards Sachsenhausen district in the city. Units 105 and 103 stand by to incept. 111 standby on the north side of the river. Break. Units 109 and 107, status please?

From the back seat of 109 Dave and Doc both listened intently as one of the cops radioed in a request.

"What's a 'hubschrauber'?" Dave asked having picked the word from the radio transmission.

"The party just heated up. We're heading into the city. Cop've requested a helicopter." Doc relayed to Harden as two more shots rang out from up ahead.

"Good thing we're undercover, huh?" Doc quietly joked. Harden didn't laugh.

"That doesn't make any sense! I don't get why they'd do that? The city traffic will kill them, even at this late hour!"

"These are not amateurs L.T. There's got to be a good reason, and I got a bad feeling we're about to find out what it is."

Doc switched to speaking in low tones as they remained hunched down in the rear seat of the Audi.

"You think the bad guys raided the house and snatched Mr. Cassini?" Doc ventured. Dave copped on to the code McKeowen used to avoid the two Polizei understanding his meaning, Oleg Cassini for Oleg Gordievsky.

"That driving, the machine gun, three men stuffed in the back seat. Smells like Reds to me." Harden confirmed.

"But if they got him and she's not in the car ..." Doc suddenly reasoned.

"Relax! She was along with him for cover, strictly window dressing. They wouldn't want the extra burden and they're not sloppy enough to just go pluggin' people for no reason." Doc didn't appear convinced. Dave gave further reassurance. "As soon as we get a breather we'll commo Danno and the guys. If she's around she'd have the sense to contact somebody on this side of the fence. We'll call around. We'll have to anyway."

"How do you mean?"

"If those are the bad guys up there and they have him, our mission is in the process of being redefined as we speak."

The officers of FP#107 guessed right and the KGB did head north until they hit route 43 when, disregarding all traffic lights and signs they turned back west and raced along the south side of Main River towards the city.

Simultaneously FP#107, siren blaring, sped up into the Sachsenhausen district on the south side of Frankfurt a full five minutes ahead of 109 but seconds behind the KGB car which had just sighted the Alte Brücke, the first passable bridge into the city.

Without warning the taxi cut right across two lanes of traffic of the river road and fishtailed onto the six lane bridge, but not without consequences.

Three passenger cars, another taxi and a fully loaded beer truck were some of the several vehicles the KGB men cut off with their latest death defying maneuver causing the beer truck to lose control. Skidding to the left, up on only his right side wheels and across the on-coming lanes the truck eventually tripped over the divider and fell onto its side.

Something in the neighborhood of 1500 plus beer bottles shattered across the intersection coating most of the road with foamy, golden Hofbräu. Several passers-by scrambled to retrieve some of the unbroken bottles but the reverie was short lived.

FP#107, less than a minute behind the Ford Taurus attempted the same maneuver to get onto the bridge. Unfortunately for them, this meant speeding over the beer coated road bed.

Karl fought the wheel with all he had but there was no controlling the squad car at that point and it was hard on the driver's side that FP107 crashed into and through the bridge rails on the west side of the span taking one of the metal lamp posts with it over the edge.

From inside the vehicle the surface of the river came up at them in seconds to slam into the car's windscreen, while up on the bridge the car seemed to fall the thirty meters in slow motion, narrowly missing the base of one of the bridge's support caissons.

Water flooded into the car from all sides as the river quickly engulfed the entire vehicle and the green of the trunk and tail lights were the last of what the few spectators looking over the rail of the bridge saw of FP#107.

Squad car #109 skidded to a halt just at the entrance to the bridge and the two officers scrambled out of the car and ran over to the railing to scan the river for their colleagues.

"Well, that's the end of that fucking chase scene! God damn it!" Doc said as he climbed out onto the road and slammed the door, the carnage of several wrecked cars and the beer truck behind him.

A car screeching to a halt across on the North bound lanes caught their attention. It was a cream Mercedes SLC with beige interior. A well-dressed elderly gentleman carrying a small black bag sprang from the car not bothering to close the door and jogged over to the shattered rail to speak to the Polizei.

Doc nudged Harden.

"What?!" Harden snapped as Doc pointed towards a big black "A" in the left lower corner of the back windshield. "So? He did good in school so he got an 'A'. So what?" The L.T. quipped.

"You're a cantankerous bastard sometimes, ya

know that?! 'A' is for Artz , it's German for doctor."
He explained as he spied the keys dangling from the
ignition.

"You suggesting we commit a heinous felony
just to avert an international intelligence disaster,
further the cause of freedom and strike a blow
against communism?"

"That, plus I always wanted to ride in a
Mercedes!" Doc added.

Seconds later, with Harden at the wheel, along
with their commo gear in the back seat they were
speeding north across the bridge and into the city.
As they pulled away Doc glanced up and into the
rear view mirror in time to see two more patrol cars
pull into the crash scene. Harden was trying to spot
the taxi.

"Shit we lost them! They could have gone
anywhere!" Harden declared.

"Relax! Go straight for about a klick, the road
will dog leg right, they either followed it or turned
west at the intersection."

"How could you ..." Dave was interrupted as
they nearly kissed the ass end of stopped bus at 80
kph but swerved around it. "How could you
possibly know which way –"

"I was stationed up on Bremerhaven for a year.
We used to come down here to party all the time.
Stay in the left lane." Doc instructed as the dog leg
in the six lane road lay up ahead. "Slow down!"
Doc ordered as he perused the road around the
intersection. "THERE!" He pointed across the
intersect at a mangled post box which had been
knocked over, letters strewn across the path and into

the street. "LEFT, LEFT, LEFT!!"

They were nearly across the large Konrad-Adenauer-Strasse intersection and into the oncoming street as Dave slammed the wheel hard to the left. They fishtailed across the intersection, up onto the oncoming median and took out a row of decorative bushes before regaining forward momentum, cutting across the north west sidewalk and narrowly missing a small group of late night revelers who had no sense of humor about nearly being taken out by a reckless driver.

"Shit these things handle pretty good!" Dave commented as he glanced over at Doc who nearly had hand prints imbedded in the leather covered dash board.

"We're coming up on a city landmark, the Eschenheimer Türm ..." Doc informed.

"The what?!"

"It's a ten story tall, peaked medieval watch tower. The road will split. Go left at the fork you should come out ahead of them!"

The beautiful decorative tower quickly came into sight and the taxi could just be seen in the distance as it slowed to take the right fork and drive around the structure. Dave quickly cut left onto the shorter route.

As the intersection was the meet point of no less than eight inner city roads, four of which were avenues, even just after midnight the road traffic as well as the pedestrian traffic was considerable. The fact that the area was heavily peppered with cinemas, bars and restaurants, most of which served alcohol, contributed to the late night congestion.

Dave fought the wheel hard as the Merc swerved left ripping across the small open plaza of a café and behind the imposing tower throwing two seater tables and fold-up chairs in several directions.

When they came out on the other side of the Türm they were heading into the oncoming traffic.

As Dave leaned on the horn while dodging the oncoming cars Doc was able to spin around in his seat in time to see the black taxi, now behind them about 50 meters as it skidded 90 degrees and shot north up one of the adjoining road.

"YOU DIDN'T TELL ME IT WAS THE WRONG WAY!!" Harden yelled as he shot between a bus and a van before finally regaining control. He brought the car back over into the proper lane.

"Sorry, they must have switched traffic patterns in the last couple of years. Besides, we caught up to them didn't we?!"

"Where the fuck are they?!"

"Hang a 180! They took a north bound road."

Less than a minute later Doc and Harden had caught back up to the black Ford just under a kilometer away. They were now on the Eschenheimer Landstrasse winding their way north leading out of the city.

Suddenly the rear windshield exploded spraying glass across the passenger compartment.

"What the fuck?!" Doc ducked down in the seat several more single shots whizzed by.

"Fuck this noise!" Doc produced his 9mm Colt from his shoulder holster.

"Doc remember, we got a friendly in that

459

vehicle!"

"I know." Doc peered through the hole of the spider-webbed rear window and spotted a silver BMW gaining on them.

"What'a ya see?" Harden asked.

"They got back-up!"

"Sneaky bastards! They had an over watch for security!" Harden declared as he swerved the car through the narrow lanes barely avoiding another head-on collision.

"Now we know why they wanted into the city so bad!" Doc observed.

Several more low caliber, single shots rang out but hit nothing.

"Friends in low places! Hold on Doc!"

"Wha-?" The interrogative was mute as Dave slammed on the brakes, whipped the wheel to the left and pulled up hard on the parking brake. The Merc slid across the two adjoining lanes, spun 180 degrees and was now driving backwards down the boulevard.

McKeowen was right on top of it. With his Colt in his right hand sticking out of the passenger's side window, he steadied his arm and shoulder on the window frame and let loose six shots in rapid succession.

The first two careened off the windshield but had their intended purpose, they distracted the driver the few seconds required for him to partially lose control and briefly expose his right front tire broadside to the other four bullets one of which hit home. The deflated tire caused the chrome steel wheel to act as a wedge digging into the asphalt and shifting the momentum of the two ton vehicle.

There was barley time for the rapid sequence of events to register in the driver's mind as one minute he was focused on the two unknown men in the cream Merc up ahead the next he was looking straight down at the asphalt street and his BMW was ten feet in the air going end over end at 80 kph.

It didn't end well for the two KGB agents in the BMW.

After slamming roof first into the street, the passenger compartment was smashed flat, the car skidded forward upside down for another 30 meters while spinning like a giant Hanukkah dreidel before crashing through the showroom window of a ladies clothing store.

"Still got the taxi?" During the action Dave was doing a good job of keeping the taxi in sight through the rear view and side mirrors and as he pulled the stop and turn maneuver again so they faced forward, and they were able to pick up speed.

"Yeah, I see the Ford!" Dave declared. "He's slowed down a bit! Looks like he anticipated his comrades taking us out of the equation!"

"Don't ja just hate it when things don't go as planned?"

By now they had transitioned into the suburbs of the Eshenheimer district north of the city, a good fifteen klicks from where the chase had begun. The last of the main road was coming up fast and was about to narrow down to four lanes.

The taxi suddenly sped up to over 120 kilometers per hour.

"I think we spooked him L.T." Dave hit the gas.

"Probably hadn't expected any company this far out."

"Hey Doc, back when we were over the river on the Autobahn heading north didn't you translate the radio traffic about the backup units?"

"Yeah, what's your point?" Doc asked as he topped off his clip.

"Wasn't there supposed to be two cop cars in on this side of the river with us?"

"Three actually. One up here someplace to head them off at the pass."

Just as he posed the question Harden was forced to swerve sharply left to avoid a piece of wreckage which looked a lot like a Polizei car fender. Immediately afterwards they came upon multiple remnants of what definitely used to be a cop car strewn across two to three hundred meters of the four lane suburban roadway.

"Not anymore!" Cursed Doc.

"They're turning off!" Harden announced. Both focused hard as they raced behind the KGB and into the small village of Riedberg where the roads closed in to two lanes and buildings suddenly began to encroach on the roads.

Doc noticed a peculiar sensation taking hold. The faster they went the more harrowing the event became and the outside noise seemed to fade away until only the shifting of the gears and the rev of the engine buzzed in his ears. Glancing over at Harden he sensed the L.T. was in a separate yet similar bubble.

Fortunately it was approaching one in the morning and foot traffic in the small town was all but non-existent.

Through the north end of the brief village and out into an open field area the black Taurus left the road and careened across a recently harvested field bouncing for about 200 meters, slowed, stopped and the doors flung open.

Two KGB darted for the tree line lining the drainage ditch off to the left while the other one, crouched against the car provided cover fire.

"What the fuck?! They have their high beams on!"

The two runners stopped, turned and fired while the last one ran to and between them.

"Banana peel pull back!" Doc commented as he watched the well-executed maneuver. "Very nice!"

"And they're heading straight for that drainage ditch!"

"Guess that definitely settles the question of who they are." As the Russians made a very well disciplined retreat across the field Doc and Harden stood beside the Mercedes and with good fire discipline were pooping off rounds like a three dimensional range exercise with live targets.

"They're not shooting back anymore!" Doc observed.

"I only see three bodies!" Harden declared.

"Counting Gordievsky there was four reported! You think the bastards shot him and dumped him off somewhere?!" Doc wondered out loud.

"Or he's still in the car!"

"SHIT!" At that they both halted fire and double timed to the Ford Taurus about a hundred meters away, out in the field.

463

Just as they reached the taxi the last of the Russians vanished into the dark of the large drainage ditch on the other side of the tree line. Doc reached the Ford first and maintaining a stiff armed bead in front of him slowly visually cleared the back seat of the vehicle. Dave ran up and repeated the move on the front seat from the other side.

They lowered their 9mm's and looked at each other with blank faces. Ideas, conjectures and theories raced through their minds.

But the show wasn't over.

From behind the tree line the unmistakable whirl of helicopter blades slicing through the air was heard as a small Sikorsky passenger helicopter rose out from behind the trees like a large mechanical firefly. They could make out the pilot and passenger's silhouettes as the chopper rose to about 200 feet facing their direction. Both Task Force Romeo men open fire and where instantly answered with a fusillade of 7.62 ripping down both sides of the Taurus.

When Doc and Harden recovered from trying to become one with the Mother Earth, the bird was quickly fading to a palm sized ink spot in the night sky.

They stood and brushed themselves off.

"Theories my dear Watson?" Dave asked as McKeowen after they rummaged through the car.

"Clean as Liberace's fingernails."

"Or his pecker." Doc slowly circled the vehicle but stopped and stared at the back.

"Got'a give these Reds credit."

"What?!" Dave made his way over to Doc.

"The plates called in were 82 FRK 7652." The tags they currently on the taxi in front of them didn't match up.

"Bastards switched cars on us! We fell for a fucking decoy!" Harden cursed.

"Must've been back at the Türm!" Doc guessed.

"When we lost them for that minute."

"Pros!" Doc mumbled as they reloaded and holstered their weapons and started the long slog across the ploughed field back to the stolen Mercedes Benz.

"So how do you like Special Operations so far L.T?"

"I think I'll like it a lot more when I get about 24 hours sleep and a steak the size of Rhode Island into my belly!"

Two minutes later they were back in the Merc and driving down the narrow village road.

As if the night hadn't given them enough shit to cope with about a hundred meters out of the village the car's engine started to sputter and choke then gradually died. There was just enough momentum to coast it onto the gravel shoulder.

Harden, at first composed as he slowly and deliberately climbed out of the car, once outside lost it.

"God damn cheap bastard! YOU'RE A FUCKING DOCTOR! FILL YOUR FUCKING GAS TANK!!" He yelled to no one as he continually kicked the bumper.

Across the gravel and dirt road a light flicked on upstairs in a farm house and an old woman stuck her head out the window. Spying the two unlucky spies and their empty Mercedes under the yellowish lamp post she yelled.

"WAS IST DENN LOS? MACHT RUHE ARSCHLÖCHER!" She yelled then slammed the window.

"She said –"

"Yeah Doc, thanks! I think I know what she said"

****

As the chase ended at around 03:00 that morning Doc and the L.T. had missed the 18:00 commo window the evening before when Danno sent his daily sit rep and, as they were stranded about 15 klicks outside Frankfurt, which was about 4 hours by car outside their base of operations, they certainly were going to miss the 06:30 commo window that morning.

Forty-five minutes after being stranded a good Samaritan who happened to have a Geri can of petrol in his truck came along, gave Doc and Harden a few liters of petrol which allowed them to get back into the city where they grabbed their commo gear, abandoned the Mercedes and walked into the city center to find a room for the night.

They checked into a low budget hostel not far from the Hauptbahnhof, or main train station, on the other side of the river but not before finding a pay phone outside an all-night kebab restaurant, which was situated inside the massive station.

Once the call was through to Neu Ulm Harden

got the barracks orderly at 1187 Hunterwasser to run upstairs and wake Danno.

L.T.! Everybody in one piece? Danno asked as soon as he came on the line.

"Yeah, we're good here Danno."

Where are you guys? What's the plan, sir?

"Coordinates and orders to follow, so listen up. There's a chopper run up from Neu Ulm to V Corps headquarters twice daily. Get Mac to contact our liaison, Major Hopkins at G2 and finagle all three of you guys a lift into Frankfurt. The next run should be just after the evening rush hour and should leave the small airfield there at around 19:00. Pack everything up, bring your commo gear, Doc's medical gear and the weapons up with you. Bring the rest to the base supply officer and have him sign for it and secure it."

Rendezvous location sir?

"Once you're in the city go to ..."

Just outside the call box Doc had activated a new gadget they brought along. A pocket sized GPS they had packed in with their other various commo gear items. Doc held the device to the glass of the phone booth for Harden to read.

"... 50.10° N, 8.66° E, got it?"

Got it L.T.

"In your a.m. commo set an intermediate transmit time for 20:00 ahh ... tomorrow –"

"You mean today sir?"

"Yeah, twenty hundred local, nineteen hundred Zulu. I'll fill you in once you're here. Questions?"

Just one sir.

"Yeah, what!?"

467

When's the last time you slept?! You sound like shit!

"You're wheels up at 19:00 sharp, 18:00 Zulu. Don't be late! Out."

By half five that morning, Doc and the Lieutenant were finally, after nearly forty-eight hours, able to get a shower and let their heads hit the pillow.

****

Doc and Harden, with the commo gear tucked safely away under their beds, were up and about late that afternoon in their two bed room suite at the hostel they had checked into the night before. They showered again and had the desk call out for a couple pizzas to be delivered.

As soon as the food was finished they decided to stay in the small, stark room and went to work on the new plan of action. First priority was to check in state side as soon as Danno showed up with the gear and give their NSA mission handler an update on events.

"You think they'll alter our mission brief L.T.?" Doc asked moving to sit on the bed facing the L.T. who was leaning on the small desk at the foot of the two beds.

"Hard to say. From what I understand he's the most valuable asset the West has right now. The down side is NSA and CIA haven't exactly seen eye-to-eye with MI6 since the Sixties. Short of doing something illegal I don't see how we can help this guy."

"Ya know sir back in the day, all the most successful gangsters, Rothstein, Luciano, Lansky, made it to the top by playing both sides of the fence." Before this Dave's thoughts were in and out of the conversation, this got Harden's attention.

"What'a ya getting at?"

"You still got Scarlett's secure phone number?"

"Yeah, why?"

"He might be interested, maybe even grateful that we're keeping in touch after his most generous favor."

"What makes you think so?"

"Another important tenant of the Underworld code was reciprocity when someone did you a solid, you returned the favor."

"How is it you know so much about gangsters?"

"Cultural history I guess. I'm from New York. Besides, my grandfather was a made man."

"I see."

"His people use to have a saying. 'Due face della stessa medaliglia!'"

"Sorry Doc, forgot my high school Italian. What exactly the fuck does that mean?"

"It's not Italian, its Sicilian. Crime and politics, two faces of the same coin."

"And?"

"If you really need or want something bad enough, you play both sides the same way. Against each other."

"Remind me never to cross you."

✱

Danno Byrd, Ray MacDonald and Ricky Matson made it into Rhein-Main Military Airbase without incident that evening and were able to hop one of the van-cabs common in Europe with their packs and a small crate containing the weapons they might need. They arrived at the Hauptbahnhof hostel just before half past seven and split up to wait at different entrances to the shopping mall-sized train station.

With Harden babysitting the other gear in the hostel room, McKeowen walked the few short blocks to the train station, met the guys and brought them back to the hostel.

The L.T. had pre-booked a six bed dormitory room for the team and paid a week in advance, so by nineteen thirty they were all gathered together in the dorm for the initial pow wow.

"L.T., what'a we here for? Exactly I mean." Ricky queried.

"A plan."

"What kind of plan sir?"

"An iffy plan, but a plan all the same. First, Danno, you set up a 20:00 transmission tie with the handler?"

"That's a roger sir."

"Good, take this down for your transmission." Danno broke out a pencil and piece of note paper and wrote as Harden dictated the details of the message to be sent. He would encode the actual message later just before transmission. The L.T.

dictated.

"Met with asset Juliet Kilo. Strong lead on RYAN. TFR handler to contact MI6 re: update on same. Request orders. TFR standing by. Got that?"

"Talk to you as soon as I get confirm of message received. Where can I transmit from?" Danno asked as the L.T. tossed him a key.

"Here, go down the hall to 207. Doc and I spent the night there last night, but –"

"How was it for you Doc?" It was MacDonald again.

"A gentleman never tells!" Doc answered.

"Will you two Bozos get serious for once?" The L.T. was more annoyed at being interrupted than about the juvenile jocularity. Behind the L.T.'s back Doc mouthed over to Ray, "I'll tell you later." Harden continued.

With Scarlett's card in hand Harden ordered everyone to stand by and as Danno shifted and to room 207 to set up and send his evening commo, Harden went off to find a private phone.

He was back in twenty minutes with news.

"I'm just off the secure line with Agent Scarlett. They got word of Gordievsky's kidnap from another agent who was with him. They're pretty sure the Reds hopped the fence with him to a safe house they use up in East Berlin." Doc's eyes shot over to the Harden who quickly turned to face Doc. "She's okay. They have her under diplomatic immunity at the British Embassy here." Doc breathed a sigh of relief. "Doc, don't get any ideas!" Doc feigned indignation and pointed to himself. "After Danno gets back from updating the NSA handler I need us

471

to come to a consensus regarding a plan of action. Doc and I cooked something up while you bunch were on holiday down in Neu Ulm."

"L.T.?"

"Yeah Mac?"

"Please tell me we didn't leave our martinis, margaritas and saunas to come up here and actually execute an actual real world mission of some sort?"

"Actually, you did Mac but, I was gonna call you off to the side later however, since you brought it up ..." Mac's face got serious as the smile quickly melted away. "SINPAC sent a twixt through the handler at NSA. You've been detached from the TFR. Effective midnight tonight. They need you back at The Teams." Silence pervaded.

Just then Danno came back into the room to report the commo situation and picked up on the negative vibe right away.

"SHIT L.T.! Ya told him?!" Danno declared. Harden shook his head yes. "Ya promised we'd all be here when you told him."

"Tell me what exactly shithead?!" MacDonald demanded.

"That I'm fuckin' with you sergeant! That's what!" Harden chuckled.

"Hey Ray?" Doc calmly called over.

"What?!"

"If you need it, I got some burn cream in my kit."

"Okay, one to the Officer in Charge. Good one, good one L.T." Mac conceded with much relief but no trace of sincerity.

"Danno, what'a we got from the handler?"

Harden asked.

"They want us to stand-by sir."

"Anything else?"

"Negative sir. That's all. Stand-by. They probably wanna run t through channels."

"Kind'a what I suspected." Dave said. The room got a little more serious. Harden reached in his pocket and produced a piece of note paper. "This is the address where MI6 is pretty sure the KGB took Oleg Gordievsky. It's over the fence, in East Berlin. If they're right and he's there now, there's no doubt in my mind he's wishin' he was somewhere else."

"You thinkin' what we all think you're thinkin' L.T.?" Matson asked.

"We are likely the only operational team within striking distance on deployment, equipped and trained for such a mission."

"What about the SAS? They got some fellas who are okay at this sort of thing?" MacDonald threw out.

"Scarlett says even before he asked the ministry they said no."

"A hostage rescue!" Ray squealed with the delight of a little girl on Christmas morning.

"MacDonald, when's the last time you had a psych eval?" Ricky asked.

"Right after my third divorce. But the docs reckoned I ain't got no dane bramage."

"You're forgetting one thing we ain't got L.T." Matson pointed out.

"I'm not forgetting that Ricky. My assessment is if we don't hear back by the next commo window at zero six-thirty, I say we go." Harden tossed out to the group.

"That's ten hours from now sir! There's no telling where they could have him by then!"

"It's only been about twenty-four hours since they grabbed him. There's only a couple of places they could have taken him in that amount of time. There's no chance they'll have gotten him back to Lubyanka in Moscow besides they'll want to start working on him as soon as possible and not waste time bouncing him all over the globe. The KGB have multiple safe houses in the West as well as an entrenched HQ in East Berlin. After the chase we gave them I don't see them staying on this side of the fence."

"So what then?" Matson asked.

"If we hear back from NSA and they don't mention a rescue or if they specifically nix it L.T.?" MacDonald asked. Harden quietly perused the team.

"There's not a prayer in hell I'm gonna order anybody to disobey orders or-"

"Sir," Ricky Matson interrupted. "I just want you to know, and I think I speak for us all when I say this, that even though you're an officer, and a Navy one at that, most of us ...okay all of us ... will follow whatever FUBAR'd scheme you two squids have dreamt up."

For the first time since they launched nearly a week ago Harden appreciated one of team's wise-assed remarks. Harden pushed on.

"Okay, that settled here's the details ... getting no news from the handlers, Doc and Mac using your false papers, will cross over and go into East Berlin through Checkpoint Charlie-"

"Sir?! Doc I can see going but why Mac?! Why not me and Doc?!" Ricky protested.

"Doc for linguistics and Mac because if everything goes to shit."

"How do you mean sir?" Matson pushed.

"If it all goes to shit we have to have someone to sacrifice to the commies so Doc can escape."

"You're not gonna let up, are you L.T.?" Mac asked.

"Someday. Maybe. When the mission's over." Harden added. "The others and myself will stand-by to act as emergency back-up and as a stand-by exfil team. Along with their phony credentials, they'll take a portable transponder and signal us when the target, designated for the purposes of this mission as Juliet Kilo, is located." Doc held up one of the pocket-sized transponders as Harden spoke.

"At that time, depending on what kind of condition he's in, we'll move to exfil him by the most expeditious means." McKeowen explained.

MacDonald glanced over at Doc and they both smiled as everyone else stewed in their seriousness. One by one Lieutenant Harden made eye contact with each man.

"Last chance gentlemen, you too MacDonald. Are we in agreement? If we don't receive orders by ..." He glanced at his watch. "... next commo, we launch a rescue op of our own volition over the fence. Questions, comments, snide remarks?"

"Yeah sir, just one. What's volition?"

"Fuck you MacDonald!" He answered.

"Thank you sir."

475

CHAPTER TWENTY

Intercept & Decipher Room
Lubyanka Building
KGB Headquarters, Moscow
13:20, Sunday, 25th September

As opposed to the multiple, massive CIA, NSA and FBI receiving and transmission centers, the primary KGB Intercept & Decipher Room only occupied the basement of the Lubyanka Building. The work area was divided down the long axis of the space into two sections of continuous consoles.

The message receiving stations, six consoles in all, were subdivided by point of origin of the messages, that is from which side of the 'Iron Curtain' they originated, East or West. All six consoles and operators would first authenticate the operator, receive the message and then confirm it. Messages were then decoded and routed accordingly.

The four message traffic personnel who handled the messages coming in from KGB and HVA operators in the West had to tag the messages with a special in-house code which allowed the decipher team to tell from where and from whom it came. The recent increase in the sheer volume of message traffic from the West along with several new directives from Director Chebrikov, clearly indicated to the veteran staff that something was afoot.

That afternoon the basement buzzed with activity and things were noticeably more tense than whenever the Americans had launched some form of military activity in the past.

As a precaution not only had Chebrikov, since the launch of *Operation REFORGER*, ordered that a decoding team be moved into the basement to allow deciphering to commence as soon as the traffic was received, but in the last ten days six additional stations had been squeezed into the cramped, 19th Century dungeon-like work space, and it was these which occupied the right hand wall.

Just that morning Chebrikov, who seemed now to be ever present at Lubyanka, had ordered that four new decoding personnel be added to the cipher staff. As there simply was no more room in the basement they were given an office area up on the ground floor.

Now, in addition to the pounding of keyboards, the whir of reel to reel recording tape and the cacophony of voices of operators the din of workers removing furniture and consoles to be relocated upstairs added to the chaos.

"Are these figures correct Major? Have they been double checked?" Chebrikov asked as he perused the hand written entries in the 'received' log book on the desk next to the code room supervisor.

"Yes Director. Once from the log when they first came in and secondly by me as they were distributed after deciphering."

Chebrikov moved across the basement past the workers at the consoles who seemed to be working at a steady pace. Reaching into a basket he retrieved a stack of messages which had not yet been passed to the decoders upstairs. There were over a dozen.

"How long since these came in?" He questioned one of the operators responsible for Western European intercepts. The operator scrolled down on his screen and checked his message list.

"They are from a few minutes after 12:30 Director. 12:34 to be exact Director."

"Are any of these repeat transmissions?"

"No Comrade Director."

"One dozen messages in the last hour?! Is that possible?"

"Yes Sir. It would appear so." Chebrikov flipped through them a second time.

"Carry on." Viktor ordered as he passed back by the Supervisor's desk to make his way upstairs. He didn't stop, he merely barked another order as he passed by.

"Major get me a full tally of the amount and types of messages intercepted by HVA in the last 48 hours! And cross reference them by code level." He vanished up the stairs and out of sight by the time he finished issuing the order to the major. "I need that within the hour and I need you to forward the information to The Presidium, to the attention of myself!" He called down the stair well.

"Yes Comrade Director."

Thirty minutes later Chebrikov was being escorted into the General Secretary's office in The Presidium.

"Viktor are you well?"

"I should be asking you that question Comrade General Secretary!" Viktor brandished a broad smile as he shook Andropov's hand. Whether from fatigue due to his physical condition or status the General Secretary didn't bother to stand. Andrei Gromyko sat off to the side of Andropov's desk.

"What? Is there something the matter Viktor?" Andropov asked.

"Comrade Secretary, what makes you think something is wrong?"

"He forgets who had his desk before him!" Andropov quipped to Gromyko as he tossed a message across his desk to Chebrikov. Viktor picked it up and read it. It was the report he requested less than thirty-five minutes ago from the Major supervising the code room at Lubyanka.

"Regular, somewhat dramatic increases in NATO message traffic in the last six to eight days, wouldn't you agree?" Andropov questioned.

"We expected as much, they are after all engaging in a sizeable military exercise." Gromyko commented. "Do we think something is actually happening or is it just an exercise as the yanks claim?" Gromyko added.

Andropov begrudgingly sipped a cup of medicine through a straw in front of him as he spoke.

"Andrei, the fact that you have not been allowed into the U.S. and therefore not able to give us firsthand accounts of the situation, causes us to work without a major piece of the puzzle. More difficult to predict what they intend." Viktor relayed.

"The attack will be disguised as an exercise, it will come on or around a holiday and they will be fully prepared to use nuclear weapons!" Andropov forcefully asserted.

"Yuri, with the internal resistance Reagan is encountering against his mad Star Wars scheme and the massive world-wide protests blanketing the West how can you be so certain they will attack or if they will use their nuclear armaments even if they do?!" Gromyko, with a clearer understanding of the American political scene than anyone in the room, challenged.

"We have been battling the Capitalists for more than three decades. Never believe what you think you know about them, never believe what they say and never believe you know what they are doing!" Andropov argued.

Viktor then directed his comments to Gromyko.

"It has no doubt started out as an exercise and we have no definitive proof to the contrary but, as the Secretary General has repeatedly pointed out, if they attack they will unquestionably design their attack to look like an exercise."

Viktor took a seat across from the lethargic Andropov.

"Comrade Chairman, as we all know it is of the highest importance to keep a close eye on the functioning of communications networks and systems of the enemy since through them information is passed about the adversary's intentions and above all, about his plans to use nuclear weapons and practical implementation of these. It only remains for us to do all we can to accurately detect their second stage preparations for all-out war." Chebrikov made his way over to

Andropov's Dooms Day board and lifted the black cloth as he spoke. "I believe that changes in the method of operating communications systems and the level of manning them, which we have recently detected may in themselves indicate the state of preparation for RYAN."

"What have you seen so far, specifically Viktor?" Yuri enquired.

"They are using completely new message trafficking procedures as well as a completely revamped code. Also our operatives are reporting new, much more sophisticated field procedures than used before in previous exercises we've observed."

"Interesting development, wouldn't you say Comrade Gromyko?" Andropov added in a challenging tone.

"Can we decipher the traffic?" Gromyko asked.

"I've assembled a team. They're working as we speak."

"Viktor, from now until Friday the 7th of October I want updates three times each day, through the weekend. Sooner if you think there is something significant."

"Yes Secretary Andropov!"

"I'll be sure to keep you apprised of my whereabouts." Yuri finished his medicine and chased it with the remnants of a small glass of scotch. He appeared to be slightly more slumped in his chair and stared into the distance. Gromyko and Chebrikov quietly excused themselves.

Outside in the vestibule the two stepped to one side, out of ear shot of the guards.

"Viktor." Gromyko took Chebrikov by the arm.

"Yes Minister?"

"What is your honest opinion ... let me rephrase that. What is your gut feeling about this situation?"

Chebrikov's instinct was to answer honestly, from the gut as it were, he was after all now not only in the upper echelon of the inner sanctum of the kingdom, but an integral part of it.

However, his instincts had also been tempered in the furnace of oppression hallmarked by the secrecy which inundated the Soviet system. Chebrikov had himself played an active role in the purges of the old Brezhnev regime immediately following Andropov's ascent to the throne. The very purge which followed the purge of the Khrushchev survivors with Brezhnev's ascent to power.

Here, no less than in the West, politics was politics.

Before answering Viktor briefly glanced down, blanked his face and then made eye contact with Gromyko.

"Comrade Gromyko, with the exception of Anatoly you are the only one of us who has actually been to the West. We can only imply what the capitalist leaders are thinking and planning by what they infer through their actions. And right now, they may have the bulk of their forces in our back garden, on a high state of readiness."

"But do you actually believe they would launch an unprovoked attack on us? All that stuff about 'no competition for industry, security for their largest exposed boarder, reduction of oil, steel and raw materials to rock bottom market prices, record prices for their oil like on his Dooms Day Board?!"

Gromyko asked in an increasingly pained voice.

"I can't pretend to know the future but, the General Secretary makes a very convincing argument. The indicators which he predicted two years ago are materializing. Excessive intelligence collection, scheduling a major military exercise on our doorstep."

"But that's just-"

"Shuffling the cabinet to weigh it down with military minded hawks. Aggressive expansion of their missile program."

"Reagan hasn't done that yet."

"Yet." Viktor clearly stated in a tone signaling he fully expected such to happen.

"Well Comrade Director **do you** accept all these other premises?"

"Comrade Gromyko, the only thing I will say with any certainty at this time is, that most likely they will attack on a holiday, deep during maneuvers, when they have a substantial force in place and between midnight and dawn. For now we will work twenty-four hours a day, seven days a week until October 5th giving us just enough time to launch a defensive. We will use the time from now until then to prepare for their attack. At that time a decision will be made as to what needs to be done based on where the Americans chose to fulminate their aggression."

Viktor politely shook hands with the minister and took his leave. Gromyko called after him.

"You are serious about this?"

Chebrikov stopped, turned and took a few steps back. "A friend of mine was travelling in America.

He hitched a ride in a car from a local when his rental car broke down on the road. He saw a baseball bat tucked in between the seats. My friend asked what it was for. The Texan answered; 'For self-defense.'

'What do you mean? Why?"' My friend asked.

"Because it is better to have a baseball bat in your car and not need it then to **not** have one and need it."

Despite the fact that the HVA and KGB working in tandem had revolutionized 20th Century military intelligence data collection methods and amassed the largest collection of Intel data to date, unlike the NATO Pact powers, the Soviets were mysteriously unable to analyze the data and apply the information to strategic thinking.

Like American police investigators working for a state prosecutor it was as if they were collecting data to be taken at face value to prove an established point rather than gathering evidence to reveal the truth.

Outside The Presidium Chebrikov's car pulled up and as soon as he got in, the driver turned and handed him a sealed message. The Director opened it.

PACKAGE RETRIEVED.
ENROUTE TO SAFE HOUSE.

"Lubyanka." He ordered.

"Yes sir!" He glanced at the message again and nodded in approval as the car pulled away.

Back up in his office, when he was alone,

Andropov slowly crossed to his Doomsday Board and looked at the box labeled, 'Massive increase in general communications traffic'. He took up the white grease pencil and lined out another of the half dozen boxes still not crossed out.

*

It had just gone nine-thirty when the guys of TFR were considering their next move. It would be at least another two and a half hours before they might hear back from their handler so the logical conclusion was to wait it out over a few drinks.

"FUCK, FUCK, FUCK! FUCK ME!!" Harden pounded on the bar, apologized and slid a twenty Mark note across to the barmaid.

As there had been no immediate response from their NSA handler, the men of Task Force Romeo had decided to do a little recon, at a local watering hole down the street from the hostel.

"Your friend is upset. Hopefully he will become more upset." The heavily ringed and tattooed barmaid commented to Doc as she brandished the twenty Mark note before floating it into the tip jar by the till behind the bar. She poured another round for the guys who sat lined up on the other side.

"We lost a big contract today." Doc defended Harden's outburst. "He takes his work very seriously." Mac explained while sizing her up. She started to pour Dave another drink as well but Doc stopped her. "Make his a Goldschläger."

"Must have been very big contract!" She

declared.

MacDonald tapped the L.T. and nodded to the two mannequins dressed in black leather hoods in the corner above the bar holding the big Grundig TV. The news program being broadcast was obviously covering the chase scene from the morning before.

"What kind'a shit are they talking about us?" Harden asked as he leaned over to Doc sitting next to him.

"Actually none at all. They're just describing the vehicles and interviewing eye witnesses."

"Hey Doc?"

"Yeah Mac?"

"After Danno and I left V Corps the other day we stopped off in the city center, you know, to do a bit of recon."

"That wouldn't be the Red Light District kind'a recon would it?" Doc discreetly inquired.

"We asked the taxi driver where the hot places are. He told us about this place over in the Red Light District, *Mackie Messer's*."

"Mackie Messer's, I know it. It isn't in the Red Light District, the Red Light District is here in the city center."

"You sure? Because I distinctly remember he said, 'the area they call Sex-in-Houses!'"

"Sex-in-Houses? Guess there's a reason SEALS don't exactly have a reputation for languages. Sachs-en-hausen blockhead! It's Sachsenhausen, the Medieval District. It's mostly for tourists. That's where we first chased the bad guys too, where we intercepted the Polizei?"

"Intercepted?! Crashed into more like!" Dave grumbled from a bar stool on the other side of MacDonald. Mac carried on with his anecdote.

"This driver told us all the Turkish drivers hang out there because it's the only place in the district where the German taxi drivers don't give them shit."

"What's your point?"

"Well, it's a bit of a long shot, but you said the guy driving those KGB mugs was a Turk. If this Mackie Messer's is a stomping ground for them ..."

"What'a think L.T., worth a shot?" Doc asked Dave who, judging by the L.T.'s horribly contorted face had just downed his Goldschläger.

"Might as well! Can't dance!" Dave coughed back.

Fifteen minutes later the five of them were over the river in Sachsenhausen and huddled up catty cornered across from the entrance to the club which was situated about halfway down a wide alley in the middle of the block. The line to get in was backed out onto the street.

"Popular place!" Ricky Matson observed.

"Yeah, interesting clientele too!" Ray added.

Nearly the entire crowd sported some item of leather to include a few characters with masks and leather hoods. Others were dressed in turn of the century shirts, vests and suspenders.

"Betty Page meets The Wizard of Oz!"

Upon spotting one well-dressed young lady, except for the blouse she was wearing which left both her breasts fully exposed, Ray MacDonald was seized with a shock of patriotism and a sudden urge to volunteer for hazardous duty.

"Lieutenant, maybe we should split up? You guys could spread out and secure the perimeter while I go and do some recon in and around the club area?"

"Good idea Ray!" Harden agreed.

"Really?! Great!" He turned to launch himself in the direction of the alley when he felt Harden's hand on his shoulder.

"Yeah, you're right Ray, we should split up. Doc, get yourself into that freak show and take a meander through the place. See if you can spot any Turk types and if you do, get a bead on him. Danno you and Ricky get back to the room. At ten minutes after midnight establish commo with NSA and get a sit rep. Ray, as per your suggestion, we're gonna split up. You get down to that corner where you can still keep an eye on that taxi rank. Remember, black Ford Taurus. I'll take the other side of the street."

"Meet up L.T.?" Danno asked. The L.T. checked his watch.

"It's nearly twenty-two thirty. Everybody meet back at that pizza joint on the corner at twelve-thirty. Questions?" Harden asked. Ray raised his hand. "None? Good, let's go." Harden ordered.

Everyone moved out and left Ray standing in front of a sex shop with his hand in the air. He was quickly approached by a tall tranny in a blond wig and high heels.

"You are perhaps looking for some action, big boy?"

****

It was just after half past midnight when they later rendezvoused at the pizza place on the corner and had been just about twenty-four hours since Oleg Gordievsky had been snatched by the KGB.

Danno's report when they all met up after establishing commo with the NSA wasn't what they hoped for. Not only were no orders with regard to the missing agent forthcoming but the men of TFR were ordered to keep standing by for more orders. Doc found nothing in the club of any help and as they reached the far corner where Ray MacDonald had been posted for the last two hours Doc spied a taxi in the taxi rank outside a kebab shop.

"What's got your interest Doc?" Harden asked.

"Keep walking. A taxi in the rank across the street. All the others are Mercs or BMW's."

"And?"

"The fourth one in's a Ford Taurus." Doc pointed out.

"So it is! But it's red."

"So it is!" He glanced up and down the street where he saw a pair of hookers on the corner, one of which had her compact out checking her top layer of make-up.

"L.T. gimme some cash outta the Op fund will ya. DM's." Doc spoke in a low tone.

"How much?" Harden asked as Doc looked over to Danno.

"Hey Danno, how much the hooker's cost when you two were here the other day?"

"How the fuck should I –" Danno weakly protested.

"How much?!" Doc insisted.

"50 Deutsch Marks for half an hour!"

"Guess that means you'd get about 42DM change, huh?" Danno didn't laugh. Harden handed over a fifty DM note and Doc took the lead. "You guys hang out here like you're trying to decide what to do next. I'll meet you around the corner in five."

He took the note and meandered up to the hookers who suddenly became all smiles as they watched him approach.

A few minutes later there was one happy hooker fifty Deutsch Marks richer and Doc who was bent over next to the blind side of the taxi pretending to tie his shoe lace while he scanned the interior of the rear wheel well with the hooker's compact mirror.

Five minutes later he was around the corner with the guys.

"Well Sherlock, what'a think?" Mac asked.

"It was the butler in the kitchen with a hammer." Doc retorted.

"Thought so."

"Interior of the wheel well's black. That car's recently been painted and it was a quickie job too."

"Gentlemen, I think we need to take a taxi ride!" Harden suggested.

"Good idea, L.T. I was just thinking the same thing meself!" Ricky added.

"What if it's not the same driver?" Danno asked. Just as he did Doc produced a folded up piece of paper from his back pocket.

"Maybe this will help." He handed the paper to Harden.

The others stared at the 81/2" X 11" sheet of

thinner-than-normal, off-white paper as the Lieutenant held it open. There was an image of a man from the shoulders up, taken at an angle through an open car window, printed in tiny black dots across the page, below which was a short paragraph of information.

"What the hell is it?" Mac asked.

"It's an LDX. A long distance xerography. All the Polizei stations are equipped with them most of the cars too. Some people call them fax's." Doc explained.

"This our man Doc?" Harden inquired.

"It's the Turk who was driving the Taurus sir. It's a copy of a pic taken from the security cameras at the toll booth of the airport parking lot."

"Feels almost like rice paper!" Mac said as he grabbed at it from the Lieutenant's hands. It tore in half.

"Tears like rice paper too, don't it, dumbshit?!" Doc jibed.

"This info underneath of any use to us Doc?" Harden asked as he held the two pieces together.

"Not really L.T. Nothing we don't already know."

"Where the hell'd you get this?" Ricky asked.

"Got it from a squad car sitting outside the club. I asked them nice and they gave me a copy. Also I promised to call them straight away if we come across the guy."

"These cops got printing machines in their fucking squad cars?" A shocked MacDonald asked.

"You're not in Kansas anymore, Dorothy! This is Germany. The newer squad cars have 'em, yeah."

Harden had already formulated a plan in his head and started to issue orders.

"Alright, everyone beepers on, switch to channel three. We take one hour shifts. As soon as he's spotted –"

"L.T.?" Ricky nudged the Lieutenant and nodded across the street. The front two taxis in the rank quickly picked up passengers, all drunk, and the rest were creeping forward as their drivers moved their cars up in the line.

The Taurus was now second in line. The driver was the man whose image was on the LDX printout.

"Sir given the number of drunks out here tonight he might balk at taking a ride with five Amis –" Doc proposed.

"What the fuck's an Ami?" Danno asked.

"Derogatory term for Americans."

"Way ahead of you Doc!" Not wanting to lose their only lead Harden quickly issued orders. "As soon as he's first in line you, Mac and Ricky grab the cab. When you get him just outside the city, somewhere not too busy, you can have a heart-to-heart with our little brown KGB chauffer."

"Can I say bad things about his sister L.T.?" Asked MacDonald.

"Maybe not go that far Mac."

"Darn!" Mac cursed.

"Maybe just beat the living shit out of him until we get where he took the monkeys and Gordievsky. Rendezvous with Doc back here."

Doc how we gonna talk to this rag head if he doesn't speak English?"

"Because of the mass U.S. military presence here

and the large amount of money they rake in from us, they all have some level of English. You should be able to what you need out of him." Doc informed. "Here." Doc passed a folded over note he had just quickly scribbled out to MacDonald.

"What the hell's this?"

"Leave it in the glove box after you lose the Turk. It's a note for the cops. I'll be in the all night café on the corner." Mac and Ricky nodded and took off across the four lane street.

"Danno, you and I are heading back to the hostel and establish commo with MI6 and get Scarlett to give us an update on our missing Russian agent. Doc, call us by land line at the hostel as soon as Mac and Danno get back here. See you back at the room."

Danno and Harden walked away as the other two, feigning to be drunk, crossed the road and climbed into the taxi and drove off down a side street.

Doc scurried up to the lieutenant and Danno halfway down the street as the taxi pulled out and drove off. He pulled Harden aside.

"Sir, you still have those fake passports you showed me before we left the States?"

Harden hesitated but then answered with a smile and a nod.

"And are you thinking about doing something that is so against regulations that we could all wind up in the brig for a very long time?"

"Get back to the café and enjoy a tall coffee. I'll see you later back at the club house." Harden with a hand on McKeowen's shoulder responded before walking away.

"Son-of-a-bitch!" Doc quietly declared as he suddenly realized something.

By virtue of the fact he was the officer in charge Harden had to maintain a certain air of leadership and so couldn't reveal how far he was actually willing to go to complete this mission. But as far as McKeowen was concerned, he just did.

What Harden also knew very well was that had any of the others realized the actual significance of Operation Ryan, they would take any and all risks necessary as well.

****

An hour and a half later Mac and Ricky were enroute back to town in the Turk's cab, minus the Turk.

The taxi was ditched behind some buildings in a rundown Turkish neighborhood just outside the city where it was likely to be stripped clean by sun up.

After ditching the Turk and taking his cab, Mac and Ricky made their way back into Frankfurt on the U-Bahn met up with Doc as planned and explained what they had found out.

It didn't take much persuasion but the Turk, who had passable English, was convincing in his story of how he drove the four men to a border crossing during which time the KGB men made several references to what they would need to do when they reached Berlin.

The three TFR team members made their way

back to the hostel to share their info and prep for their mission over the fence.

"What'd ya write in that note you left inside the glove box?" Ricky asked Doc on their way back to the hostel.

"It was to the Polizei, I told them this was the cab used in the airport kidnapping the other day. Driver was reportedly mugged by some Neo Nazis."

"Another unfortunate racial incident!" Ricky shook his head in mock sympathy.

"Poor bastard."

*

West Wing
The White House

Reagan had been working overtime since the shoot down of KAL 007 to depolarize his critics, solidify his domestic and foreign programs and forge a bigger, stronger world-wide alliance against the Soviets. But when the Russians had blown it by initially denying responsibility, then being outted by the evidence, the Administration truly felt they had the Reds on the ropes. They smelled blood.

The next box for Reagan to check was to get all the NATO leaders to sign off on the last part of the REFORGER exercise which was participation in the ten to fourteen day *Able Archer* portion which would simulate the anticipated nuclear exchange between the Soviet Bloc and the NATO forces.

The scenario envisioned that the world leaders,

along with their cabinets and staff, would actually take the better part of a day and be "evacuated" to safe areas where the ability to govern in the immediate aftermath of annihilation of their respective countries would be assessed.

Naturally it was imperative that Reagan's entire staff were behind him as well.

The National Security Advisor, although not an official Cabinet post, is no minor position in the administration and to that effect the office of the APNSA, Assistant to the President for National Security Affairs, has their office located in the West Wing of the White House.

Coming out of a National Security Council meeting over in the West Wing that morning was exactly where Casper Weinberger cornered Robert "Bud" McFarlane, the current APNSA.

"Bud, can I have a quick word?"

"Sure Cap, what's up?"

"We just got word from London. Thatcher's on board with the *Able Archer* exercise. We heard from Prime Minister Kohl's people yesterday and it's looking good for the French and possibly even the Danish."

"It's going well, I know. All the leaders are backing it. So?" McFarlane knew full well what was coming as Weinberger assumed a defensive posture.

"Word has it that you're not going to get behind us on this full participation drive?" The Secretary of Defense tried but failed to assume a non-confrontational air. Having just heard about McFarlane's objections to involving world leaders in *Able Archer* through the grape vine that morning, he was still not fully convinced that one of the team was willing to stay on the bench. McFarlane had been expecting feedback and so had been mentally prepared.

"Look Cap, NATO and ourselves have dumped a shitload of time, effort and capital into this exercise. And it's important. We need it, I think we're all gonna learn a lot. But I think we need to be careful about just how realistic we make this thing."

"What'a you talking about?"

"The Soviets aren't like normal people. They're worse than Hoover and his crowd ever were with respect to paranoia. They're suspicious of everybody and everything all the time. When I worked exchanging intel with the Chinese, they weren't always up front, but at least I knew where they stood. When I was posted in the Middle East they didn't pull any punches but, even at the worst of times, we had good feedback on where they stood. These are the **Russians** we're dealing with now. They change leaders like we change socks. Ya never know what way the wind is blowing with those people!"

"I get your point Bob, but ... Look, you did a bang up job getting Thatcher on board the SDI program so ..."

"So you're applying the same tactic in the hopes it'll work?" As McFarlane checked Weinberger he became a little more irritated.

"You think as the sole hold out that you're going to affect anyone's decision on this?" Weinberger argued.

"I'm behind the SDI program and have been

since day one. I took the heat for the Beirut bombing and am behind the Chief 100%, in most things. But if this thing goes south and backfires, there's only one person I have to face. And that's the guy who looks back at me in the morning when I look in the mirror."

"What the hell you talking about?!"

MacFarland took a breath and stared at the floor.

"Cap, with all your planning, strategizing and striving to make this as realistic as possible, has anyone considered the possibility that there are some people who might not understand that it's just an exercise?"

"Like whom fer instance?"

"The Russkies." McFarlane smiled, patted Weinberger on the arm, turned and walked away.

Twenty years McFarlane's senior, and technically outranking him Weinberger went into the confrontation that morning fully confident that he was going to convince McFarlane to reverse his opinion. As Weinberger knew, confrontations don't always unfold as predicted and now 'Cap' stood and stared in disbelief as 'Bud' disappeared down the marble hall enroute to the Oval Office.

*

A single strand of smoke flowed at 90 degrees from the lone iron pipe serving as a chimney poking from the roof of the century old cabin which sat out on the featureless tundra. A cold wind blew across the wet, rocky land as a light but constant rain tapped at the windows.

Inside cabin a wrinkled arthritic hand set the glass syringe back on the stainless steel tray next to the half dozen medication vials, three of which were empty. The old man, owner of the hand, resumed reading a sports magazine. Within the small, shadowy room a thin haze of smoke emanated from the potbellied stove in the corner.

Fifteen minutes passed in silence until one of the three men in the room walked over to the semiconscious man seated against the back wall.

"Comrade? Comrade, can you hear me?" There was no response. The middle-aged officer turned away from the man tied to the steel chair which in turn was bolted to the heavy wooden floor boards. There was no accurate way to tell how long the prisoner had been there, but two things were certain. He had been beaten and he had not been allowed to use the toilet for some time.

The officer looked over at the elderly doctor seated across the dimly lit space.

"How long?" He asked. The doctor, obviously annoyed at the imposition on his reading time, didn't look up from the magazine as he answered.

"Theoretically we should wait at least four to six hours before we ..."

"Again."

"But -"

"Again!" The officer demanded.

"As you wish Colonel." The elderly doctor lifted himself from his seat by way of the table next to him. "But if he suffers a seizure I won't –" The doctor was cut off as the Colonel raised a hand.

"Herr Doctor!"

"Colonel?" The doctor casually answered as he walked back to the small table against the wall by the prisoner.

"You needn't be concerned for your patient's welfare on two counts." The Colonel made his way back over to the bound man. "Firstly he doesn't exist." He pulled the prisoner's head back by his matted hair and studied his contorted face. His glassed over eyes peered through his drooping eyelids. "Secondly, they are already digging his unmarked grave."

The doctor shuffled to the table, prepared another syringe of sodium thiopental and crossed over to his victim.

As he slowly injected the drug he wondered what heinous crime this man could have committed to be slowly tortured to death. When finished he didn't see to the injection site, he just walked away.

"Will there be anything else Colonel?" The doctor asked.

"No, you may leave Otto. Give my love to your wife and children." The man tied to the chair gurgled and spat a mouthful of blood onto the floor. The Colonel smiled and squatted down in front of him, lifting him by the chin.

"Now, Oleg! What shall we talk about?"

****

CHAPTER TWENTY-ONE

Control Room, PBS Studios
Arlington, Virginia

The camera slowly pulled back holding steady on a middle-aged man in a baseball cap who looked old beyond his years. His roadmap of a face was carved into a leathery brown skin and he wore a light jacket over a plaid, red, wool shirt, Farmer John jeans and a pair of worn work boots.

He sat on a low stool in front of a yellow, domed arctic tent flanked by large protest signs hanging from poles on either side in what was obviously a makeshift campsite. Behind him the White House gradually came into view and it became obvious he sat just outside the black, wrought iron fence.

It was early morning and the odd car drove through frame as a female reporter's voice broke in above the subdued sounds of the street.

This is William Thomas Hallenbeck, Jr. Mr. Hallenbeck has been arrested a total of 13 times. For sitting in front of the White House.

The camera pullback stopped when the reporter came into frame left.

He is an anti-nuclear activist and has been engaged in what is now become known as the White House Peace Vigil. He has been sitting at this same

501

spot in Lafayette square since the morning of June 3rd, 1981 and has sworn to continue the seemingly growing protest against nuclear proliferation until complete disarmament is a reality.

The picture cut to a head and shoulders shot of a middle-aged man sitting behind a desk, well-groomed and wearing a dark blue suit jacket and dark maroon tie. A light blue sign with black letters mounted on the wall behind him read: 'The McNeil/Lehrer News Hour'. He looked straight into the camera and although he held a sheaf of papers with both hands he never referred to them as he spouted his report from the studio.

Just one month ago today one million people took to the streets and met in New York City's Central Park. Their motivation? To halt nuclear arms proliferation and put an end to the Cold War.

Officially the largest demonstration of any kind in America's history, there are still no signs of a slowdown to nuclear proliferation or of a negotiated settlement of the now near forty year old Cold War.

Large black and white stills of the Central Park demonstration as well as others flashed on a screen to his left as he spoke.

A month before the Central park demonstration 70,000 people linked arms to form a human chain between three nuclear weapons centers in Berkshire, England. The anti-nuclear demonstration stretched for 14 miles along the Kennet Valley.

Nor are there any apparent slowdowns in the momentum of what has come to be called the 'Peace Movement'.

The Central Park protest was the culmination of what organizers are calling the 'International Day of Nuclear Disarmament' which saw demonstrations in more than fifty locations across the country and included a march from Los Angeles across the United States to Washington, D.C. in conjunction with nearly 3 million people across Western Europe engaged in protests against nuclear missile deployments all demanding an end to the arms race.

The President's Press Secretary Jim Brady was seated on his living room couch at home with his wife that evening following the major network news coverage.

"Do they see this in Europe too?" His wife asked as she moved to the small bar next to the telly to mix him a martini.

"Only in England but they won't see it until tomorrow."

"You think this will affect the President's domestic image?"

"I'm not overly concerned about what these two have to say. Couple of Left Wingers who got lucky covering Watergate so they got their own show."

She brought him the martini and took a seat on the couch next to him.

"If there's no strong central support for them then how is it they just got their news program extended to one hour, have no commercials and everybody's tripping over themselves to be interviewed on air?" She challenged.

Brady shrugged and sipped his drink. The report continued.

"Today half in Italy a million people took to the streets in several cities and more than 250,000 people protested in Bonn, Germany while 250,000 demonstrated in London, and 100,000 marched in Brussels with nearly one million assembled in the Hague in the Netherlands."

The camera shifted to a second, well-groomed female studio reporter as newsreel footage played on a screen to her right.

"In Britain some 400,000 people participated in what was probably the largest demonstration in British history while an estimated 100,000 Australians also participated in anti-nuclear war rallies across the nation's largest cities.

Austrian anti-nuclear protesters demonstrated and at one stage all twenty-six border crossings into the Czech republic were blocked by protestors and police."

Once again the man picked up the report.

"In what clearly signals a new tactic of the Peace Movement a coalition of lawyers in Israel has filed a P.I.L. against the government's nuclear program at the Israeli Apex Supreme Court in Tel Aviv.

In a throwback to the Sixties anti-Viet Nam peace movement, professionally manufactured 'Ban the Bomb' as well as peace sign tee shirts and placards have begun to appear world-wide in every known language to include Swahili!"

There has been no word concerning any protests inside the Soviet Union."

****

"Alright, last time. 'Yes I am'." Doc coached.

"Ya, Ich bin." MacDonald parroted.

"Good. 'No I am not'."

"What about my accent?"

"Forget about it. We're not tryin' to pass you off as German, just some schmuck trying to learn a few words so he can go home and get laid by impressing the Newfies."

The next day Doc and Mac, dressed in their newly purchased European leisure wear and carrying a cheap, tourist type camera went through their rehearsed routine one last time before they turned the corner of the back street south of the Brandenburg Gate when Checkpoint Charlie came into sight. To reinforce their image as daytime tourists they carried no luggage.

"Okay, let's hear it. 'No I am not'." Doc directed.

"Nein, Ich bin nicht."

"Good. Just glance at me for your cues, let me take the lead. The first thing I'll ask is if they speak French Canadian. Highly unlikely any of them will. They want to question you, I'll translate."

505

"You speak French Canadian?"

"Fuck no but they don't know that! I'll tell them you're only here for a day or so and want to see the ... unique architecture of the East."

"Especially the Karl Marx Alley!" MacDonald answered as he proudly beamed.

"Very good! You're not a stupid as you look!" Doc complimented.

"Nope, that's just a disguise."

"Just show 'em your Canadian passport and they'll have to speak English or German. The guys on guard duty are usually Black Shoes anyway. They don't waste their elite units on permanent guard duty."

A minute later, still on the American side, they showed their Canadian passports and driver's licenses to the Army M.P.'s which were checked as the two were signed in and lead to separate rooms where they were questioned as to the purpose of their visit to the East, cautioned about contraband and reminded of the 19:00 curfew and the fact that they were expressly forbidden from contacting any known communists, officials or members of the Russian or East German military.

"Thank Christ that M.P.'s English was minimal!" McKeowen commented.

MacDonald breathed a sigh of relief once outside again.

"It probably wasn't language proficiency. Probably his educational level." Mac quipped.

"Actually, that wasn't so bad." Mac commented once back outside.

"That was the easy part!" Doc replied as they

slowly walked the 200 meters of open no-man's-land, passports held up in full view of the CCTV cameras and in open sight of the waiting Russian and East German guards.

The guys caught a break in that there was an unusual pile up of workers and West Germans with relatives trapped in the East who were anxious to get through the Wall and back before curfew otherwise they would be subject to arrest by the communists. Also, the guards tended to be reluctant to get too tough with passports from declared neutral countries such as Canada, one of the few countries in the West which recognized the DDR.

With Doc dong all the talking and Mac standing there assuming a particularly stupid look on his face they were through the communist side in a couple of minutes.

"That wasn't so hard!" MacDonald commented, the guard shack behind them.

"Said the big red lobster to his mate as they crawled into the cozy little wooden crate on the bottom of the ocean!"

They left the communist checkpoint behind and headed for the east side of town consulting the tourist map they brought with.

"What'a ya worried about Doc? We got the address on Mollstrasse from this guy Scarlett and it's only a klick from the Spree! We'll be there and get the signal out by 14:00. After that it's the CIA's headache. We're home by supper time." MacDonald assured.

"This is the part where you're supposed to say, 'what could go wrong?' You know, just to be sure and induce really bad karma!" Doc added.

"You nervous Doc?"

"No more than usual when I'm illegally behind the Iron Curtain in direct contravention of orders from the Chief of Naval Operations, the Joint Chiefs of Staff and pretty much every muther fucker in the Pentagon who out ranks me there including the janitor."

"What are you worried about?"

"The part where we're supposed to sit on him until the Agency guys show up. I didn't sign onto this gig to be a baby sitter!"

"The L.T. said their response time is 15 to 20 minutes. They're already on this side of the fence waiting the signal."

Twenty-five minutes later they crossed over the not-so-busy Mollstrasse where they were clear of the business district and deeper into the charcoal grey of the residential neighborhoods.

A virtual forest of half completed, abandoned concrete high rise apartment buildings sprawled across over-grown lots defined the next five or six blocks they descended into. The nearly deserted streets combined with the light grey dust and colorless buildings to impose a Sci-Fi, dystopian-like ambience to the entire scene.

"Jesus! I thought Arkansas was a mess!" Doc declared as he looked around at the government induced devastation.

"Where's all the workers? The tools, machines? It's like somebody snuck in the middle of the night and stole everything! Even the fucking people!" Mac wondered out loud.

An old woman pulling an empty grocery basket on wobbly wheels averted her eyes and walked a little faster as she passed the two strangers.

"It's like a giant construction site that got half started then ran out of steam!"

"Or money!" Doc observed.

Three Russian armored patrol vehicles, BRDM's, suddenly sped by as they approached the Schönhauser Strasse.

"We're in a fucking George Orwell novel!" Mac blurted out.

Down a small laneway off a side street of Schönhauser they found their first landmark, a boarded up butcher shop.

"Number 24." Doc said aloud as they stopped, looked to the ground and began to search the area. "Here!" Doc pulled a small drainage grate from a storm drain against a building, fell to his knees and fished around in the drain. He came up with a heavy, black plastic bag. He quickly replaced the drain grate and ripped into the package.

"Mac, remind me not to talk shit anymore about the CIA." He finished unwrapping two Colt 9mm's with shoulder holsters, six clips of ammo and four stun grenades.

They divvied up the caché, did a quick functions check and moved out continuing down the cramped alley perusing for addresses.

"We need number 127. It's supposed to be fronted by a pub."

"I like the sound of that! Ya suppose there'll be women?"

"If there are, they'll probably be able to bench

509

press both of us." Doc responded as he moved ahead down the alley stopping about fifty meters up where he took up a defensive position. Mac carefully leap frogged ahead.

"Doc, 122!" He called in a loud whisper pointing to a doorway. Doc scurried forward and they both ducked into a doorway about twenty meters down from the store front they guessed was #127.

"You find it strange we been down this alley the better part of twenty minutes and haven't seen a soul?" Doc theorized.

"Now that you mention it. And what about security? You think they would'a had someone on a rooftop or something as a reception committee!"

"Maybe they pulled in their over watch, trying to suck us in. Three prisoners beats one!"

"You mean **two** prisoners Doc! I don't eat borscht."

"Fair enough. How ya wanna do this?" Mac took a moment to consider.

"Play it as stealthy as possible until we make contact."

"Then what?"

"Kill anything that moves!"

"Subtle! I like it!" Doc said. "Look, we get this guy, fuck waitin' around for the cavalry! I say we grab him and go! We can ring the Agency boys from a remote, safer location. You agree?!"

"As long as he can still walk, sounds like a plan."

"And if not we stay here, establish a defensive stance and pray for the guys in the white hats to show up first. Agreed?"

"Agreed."

They slipped along the alley and took up positions on opposite sides of the bar door. Doc tried the handle and as expected it was locked. He signaled Mac to back across the alley and look up for a window. Mac spotted a potential means of entry and pointed up.

Mac being the bigger of the two holster his Colt and placed his palms on the wall to the left of the entrance. Doc followed suit with his weapon and climbed up onto Mac's shoulders. The sign post served as a good foothold and with the window sill as a handhold he could see the dirty window had less than an inch of space between it and the sill but it was adequate to get a finger hold into and lift the window enough to see into the room.

In more financially profitable times it had apparently been used for a party/function room and just as with the abandoned apartment blocks a few streets away the eerie sensation of a sudden, rapid evacuation permeated the space.

Doc climbed in through the window, signaled down to Mac to stand fast then disappeared into the building.

The minutes dragged as Mac mentally ran through his options if the shit suddenly hit the fan. Potential to break through the door and get Doc, best mean of egress ...

Without warning the front the door slowly opened, Mac's heart skipped a beat and found himself drawing a bead on a guy in front of him. The haze cleared and it was Doc, weapon at his side.

"What the fuck?!" Mac declared more than

asked.

"You're gonna love this!"

They were careful to close the door over and rig it with a beer glass balanced on the door knob after they entered as they still held their weapons at the ready as they moved through the first floor.

They scanned the burnt, abandoned wreckage of the interior searching for any clue that someone might have been there in there in the last few days. They found the basement completely flooded and the mold on the water ruled out any recent mishap. Everything that survived the fire, which had obviously occurred some time ago. Virtually every stick of furniture was heavily charred and useless.

"Well, they didn't bring him here. It's an empty hole for sure!"

"This fucking place hasn't seen anyone since Reagan made *Bedtime for Bonzo* fer fuck's sake!" Mac declared as his adrenaline level crept back to normal.

"Fuck me Alice!" Doc blurted out

"Who the fuck is Alice?! Why do you always say that?"

"Something we used to say back in high school when bad shit was about to happen." Doc sighed.

"Well, at least we ain't got no extra holes in us!" Mac sighed.

"Curfew kicks in in a few hours and the light's fading, we'd better head back to civilization."

They left the dead end pub and exited to the left and went further up the alley to avoid leaving the same way they came in. Just as they reached the end of the street what appeared to be a company of East

German Infantry was marching by in formation.

"That's one big guard contingent! They always post their guards like that?" Mac asked as they stood to the side of the road trying to blend in with the small crowd of civilians that had gathered to watch.

"No, it's not normal. Let's go!" As soon as the Soviet company had passed they picked up the pace as they turned off Mollstrasse and headed back west towards the river.

When they reached a point about three blocks away from Checkpoint Charlie they could see something wasn't right. From a distance they saw that the checkpoint was in the process of being closed off despite it only being 17:30. Not only were barricades being erected but the entire area was being cordoned off and reinforced with extra troops and vehicles. Additionally civilians, probably looking to get home to the West, were being herded off to the side and held under guard.

"At least we know where those BRDM's were going." Doc observed.

"Ya suppose they're onto us?" Mac proposed.

"Nah, they wouldn't go so far as to activate an entire company to guard the gate and wait for two guys. Would they?"

"In The Teams we're told the Russian Spec ops guys at Spetnaz work with entire specially trained HK battalions dedicated to intercept Seals and Army SF units."

"What's 'HK'?"

"Hunter-Killer." Mac shrugged.

"Whole battalions?! You just made my day. Join

the Navy and see the world my ass!" Doc took one last look at the commotion around the gate, turned and started walking back the way they had come. Mac followed suit.

"Where we headed?" Mac asked not really expecting a definitive answer.

"Somewhere else. No point hanging around here."

They headed back towards the Mollstrasse to formulate a plan.

****

"Charlene?!" George Schultz called out to his secretary through the intercom on his desk. "CHARLENE?!" Now ignoring the intercom he yelled through the door.

Schultz's office in D. C. had been non-stop chaos for the last three days dealing with what was now being called the 'escalating Russian situation'.

"Mr. Secretary, you called?!" Her response dripped with sarcasm as she pushed through the door.

"Sorry Charlene, things are ..."

"Hectic Sir?"

"In a different frame of mind I would employ a slightly stronger adjective. I need a status report on the TFR project. What's the last commo the NSA has from Lieutenant Harden?"

"I don't know sir but I'll telephone their handler's office right away. Meanwhile here's the list you asked for." She handed him a sealed envelope and with a puzzled look he tore it open. "The President's intended new appointees to vacated positions." She explained. He carefully but quickly perused the list. "More bad news Mr. Secretary?"

"Things just went from hectic to ..."

"FUBAR'ed Sir?"

"That's the word Charlene. Let me talk to the TFR handler when you get him on the line please."

"Right away Sir. Will you be meeting General Vessey for lunch?"

"No. Send out to the commissary for a corned beef on rye, a Tab and get yourself something as well, if you have no plans that is."

"Thank you Sir. I'll get NSA on the line straight away."

Less than a minute later Schultz was on the secure line with the TFR's assigned handler.

Sir on the last scheduled link they indicated they had a strong lead on the item we're interested in and then we had an extra rotational commo link at 20:00.

"What was that for?"

Apparently their lead ran into a problem. No details available.

"When's your next commo link with them?"

18:00 tonight Sir.

"Encrypt and send this." Schultz ordered.

Ready Mr. Secretary.

"'Temp heating up here. Possibility of increased HUMINT traffic your sector. Be alert.' You got it?"

Yes Sir.

"Run that by Admiral Butts get his okay before you send it."

Will do sir. Anything else?

"Yeah, find me as soon as you have a decode of their 18:00 transmit."

Will do Mr. Secretary!

**

From the second floor of one of the partially constructed but now abandoned apartment buildings where they had spent the night Doc and Mac huddled out of sight of the street behind a large pile of neatly stacked cinder blocks and some tarps.

From the window opening the ranks of marching Russian troops seemed endless. The two dozen T-32 tanks at three a breast which led the column had long passed and 150 to 200 meters behind the battalion sized, fully armed, battle ready troops, supply and service vehicles could be seen slowly keeping pace. With various vehicles and on foot military units had been passing through the deserted streets past the windowless, half constructed, concrete apartment blocks of the Prenzlauer District since first light that morning.

"So much for being home by supper!" Doc quipped.

"Look on the bright side Doc!"

"What fuckin' bright side?!"

"At least we get to see a parade!" Mac smiled. Doc stared at him.

"You need a lobotomy!"

It was just after eight that chilly morning. Doc and Ray MacDonald had passed the night in a rundown park about a klick from where they now were and had, since discovering the safe house they were told Gordievsky was to be found in had been burnt out, had been trying to piece together what was happening around them. One conclusion they immediately reached was that if the Communists were too busy yesterday to notice they were at large, they damn sure were out beating the bushes to find the two by today.

"That ain't no May Day parade! Those bastards are moving out with full issue." Mac observed.

"Beans, bullets, and bandages!" Doc added as he fell back on his ass, sat there and stared out and through the rows of the many unfinished, multi-story apartment blocks.

"You alright?" Mac enquired.

"They're Russians!"

"Yeah." Ray answered as calmly as he could, given their situation.

"They're not East Germans."

"Nope."

"They're Russians with Russian tanks, AK-47's and they probably got some Russian SS20's, SCUDS and some more BRDM's around here too!"

"Yep, probably." Ray reaffirmed. "What are getting' at?"

"We're FUBAR'ed!" Doc declared.

"NAHHHH! SNAFU'ed, maybe even TARFU'ed, but not FUBAR'ed."

"Ray, as flattering as it might be all those leg commies and their hardware are not out there looking for a couple of dumbshit operators! The fucking balloon has obviously gone up! We're trapped deep in East Berlin and by way of weapons all we have are two Colts, a few grenades, some bricks and a few lengths of rusty steel pipe!" He pointed to the construction rubble around them. "How do you figure we're not fucked?"

"When we see the first of the mushroom clouds go up, then we're FUBAR'ed!" Ray argued.

"Point taken." Doc did a third functions check on his Colt. "Maybe Berlin's not on the list?"

"Berlin's on the list." Ray affirmed still watching the parade through the small window opening in the wall.

"How do you know? Maybe they want to keep Central Europe nuclear free. Save the culture, all that stuff?"

"Berlin's on the list."

"How do you know?"

"I worked with the CIA last year. I saw the list. Berlin's on the list." Doc, flooded with indignation, drew back from his team mate.

"You couldn't have just said, 'the check is in the mail? The doctor will be with you in a minute!' I mean if you're gonna lie! 'I promise I won't cum in your mouth?' Ya know, something not so obvious!"

"Doc?"

"What?!"

"I'm from the government I'm here to help you."

"Thank you! That's much better!" Doc conceded.

"We need a plan, you're the Recon guy!"

"So?"

"So what's the plan?" Mac pushed.

Having gotten his frustrations out, Doc gathered his thoughts, grabbed a chip of concrete and cleared the dust from a small section of floor to draw a make shift map and assess the situation.

"We're two and a half, three klicks from The Spree River. We've only a couple hundred in dollars and seventy-five in East German Marks."

"Well, the up side is the entire Eastern Black-market runs on dollars and with 75 East Deutsch Marks we could probably live in a penthouse suite with room service for a month."

"True, if only they had penthouse suites and room service."

"Details, details. Don't bother me with details!" Mac nervously joked.

"The way I see it we have three choices. Make it to the river and find a place to swim to the West, try and find a way to jump the train between the Friedrich Strasse station and Checkpoint Charlie or find a crossing by foot."

"The Strasse station is locked down better than Fort Knox and Checkpoint Charlie is the closest foot crossing for about five or six klicks and is likely to be closed by now and just as heavily fortified." Mac pointed out. Doc stared at his crude map.

"Any chance we can get a hold of the Agency guys to get us out?"

"No chance. The L.T. gave them a thirty minute window for the pick-up. That was yesterday."

"Shit!" Doc swore. "How long'd the L.T. say that homing device was good for?"

"I think he said about six hours. Depends on the distance. Why?"

"I just came up with a plan. Crack open your

camera and get that thing out and activate it." Doc instructed.

"We activate the beacon won't they take that as we found the Russian?"

"I'm hoping that they'll realize something's wrong if the signal keeps moving. Besides, there's a back-up plan."

Mac got busy carefully removing the homing device concealed in his Nikon F-1.

"What's the back-up plan?"

"By now the Reds have to know we're here. No idea who we are, but they know we're here. I'm banking they're gonn'a bet we're gonn'a try and get out as soon as possible through the shortest route available. If we're lucky they'll fuck around for a couple of hours with the tunnels they know exist. If we're really lucky they'll piss around for another half a day looking for a tunnel they don't know about."

"I agree so far." Mac declared as he adjusted the homing device before activating it.

"The last thing they'll expect is for us to try and cross over and get out up north."

"North?! Shit Doc how far is that?"

"That depends on exactly where we can arrange an exfil. Maybe around 300 klicks."

"Five to six hours by car. But I can't help but notice the flaw in your plan." Mac argued.

"What, no car? Not an issue. In the words of my dear old cantankerous father, we'll cross that bridge when we come to it."

Mac held up the device and shrugged at Doc as he gave it a half twist to the left. There were three short beeps and a tiny red light flashed on. "Houston we have lift off!" Mac declared. Dc checked his watch.

"Okay, zero-eight-twenty. We have until fourteen hundred, fourteen-thirty to make exfil. Come on, we gotta find a pay phone."

As soon as the coast looked clear they made for the bare concrete stair case, left the building and headed east deeper into communist controlled territory in what they hoped was the direction of the north-south Autobahn.

*

**Boris Solomatin's Office
Lubyanka Building
KGB Headquarters, Moscow
11:15 Local, 27th September**

In the two and a half weeks since he accepted Chebrikov's offer of forming a new department of the KGB dedicated to monitoring U.S. activities in the European Theatre, Boris Aleksandrovich Solomatin had hardly spent a night sleeping in his own, well-appointed Moscow flat. Instead he was semi-permanently camped out in his new office at Lubyanka.

Already having a detailed knowledge of the NATO and Western nations' political hierarchy, particularly Britain and America, Boris was in a good position to launch into his intel gathering phase straight away. Coincidentally, not one week after Solomatin set up shop in Lubyanka, KGB field agents in the U.S. reported an interesting item which was not paid much attention to by the U.S. Press, but appeared buried on page six or seven of one of the major dailies, always a lucrative source of intel for the KGB.

There were to be about a half dozen key position replacements in the Reagan Administration. Upon learning this Solomatin immediately went to work putting together a report then scheduled a meeting with KGB Chairman Chebrikov.

It was agreed when they set the meet, the first official report Solomatin was to submit as head of the new department, that as a sign of mutual respect, Chebrikov would come to Boris' office.

Chebrikov showed up right on time and was pleased but not at all surprised to see Boris at his desk, head down, sleeves rolled up and an ashtray filled with cigarette butts. Taking his cue from this scenario, they got right down to business.

"I have something I think is of interest." Boris opened with.

"Tell me." Chebrikov instructed as he leaned forward to light Solomatin's fifth cigarette in the last half hour.

"There are some significant shifts in lower and upper hierarchy in the administration coming up. Are you in a hurry or do we have time to go over this?"

"May I?" Chebrikov indicated the intercom box on Solomatin's desk.

"Of course!"

"Major Kirkof, cancel my appointments for the

afternoon." Chebrikov ordered into the machine.

Yes Comrade Colonel! The voice on the other end answered. Chebrikov took a seat next to the desk.

"Where do we start?" Chebrikov queried.

"One of the major elements of which we are virtually certain is that the initial attack will occur on a holiday weekend." Boris began.

"If we assume the next holiday we're talking about November 7th only weeks away!"

"If not in October then yes, certainly the fourth or seventh of November." Solomatin conceded as he took the thick folder offered him by Boris.

"Agreed, essentially the same time frame." Chebrikov added. Chebrikov perused the substantial folder and smirked at the title.

"The Seven Dwarfs, I like that!"

"They are listed more or less by rank, but it doesn't follow that the higher ranking individuals are the most important changes. First up we have Reagan himself. Though not due to leave office any time soon he is included for the sake of thoroughness. A notable change in his strategy however is worth mention." He took a long drag on his cigarette and gulped a half cup of cold coffee. "As things have escalated, so too have his opponents, particularly concerning his nuclear arms strategy. His somewhat skewed philosophy of mutual assured destruction is coming under increasing fire by some of his own people and we believe this is partly the reason, these changes are being instituted."

"Is there anything significant in his speeches

these last two weeks?"

"Not that we've noticed. Just the usual Soviet bashing, exaggerated statistics and a somewhat stronger push for Star Wars support. But nothing new."

"Next is Bush." Chebrikov read from an identical folder he held.

"Though not seen as a hard core hawk or a hard line conservative he does submit to Reagan on all military issues, strange as he's a war veteran, one would have thought him more independently minded, particularly on military issues. However, back in 1980 he was quoted in the press as being optimistic about coming out on top of the Soviet Union following a nuclear exchange."

"He said that?!" Chebrikov asked. Solomatin rifled through a second folder and produced a single page from which he read.

"'You have a survivability of command and control, survivability of industrial potential, protection of a percentage of your citizens, and you have a capability that inflicts more damage on the opposition than it inflicts on you. That's the way you can have a winner.'" The article quoted Bush. "Amazing! The fact that they think there can be a winner is only usurped by the fact that they think **they** can win!" Solomatin snuffed out his sixth cigarette. "We don't yet have a complete picture of the administration as a whole in terms of opposition, but yes it does appear the majority of Reagan's people see America as being able to fight and win a nuclear confrontation."

"Remarkable!" Chebrikov sighed.

"But we think Bush may have an ulterior motive in his public views." Chebrikov sat up at this and was interested in what was to come next. Solomatin added.

"Such as?"

"He regularly meets with industrialists, but not just random industrialists. Primarily those who have a strong history of political involvement."

"It's common knowledge that it is the industrialists who select the presidents in America, how is this different?"

"He apparently favors those with a history of backing presidents. Backing them with substantial financial support."

"Do we think he has his eye on the White House?"

"He's made no outward overtures but I think it's worth following." Solomatin suggested.

"If Bush gets in it will affect the overall picture. Interesting. Well done."

"Now, the Defence Secretary ..." Solomatin continued.

"Weinberger, the hawk!"

"Yes. Considers the standoff between the U.S. and the Soviet Union akin to the situation between Britain and Nazi Germany in 1938, with himself playing the part of Winston Churchill. Worse yet he has clearly stated on several occasions that any attempt at arms control is nothing but appeasement."

"And regularly attends mass on Sundays!" Chebrikov sarcastically added. Boris continued.

"The newest member of our Hit Parade is the

most outspoken opponent of arms control. Richard Perle has recently been appointed as Assistant Secretary of Defence. He will now work hand-in-hand with a man he strongly agrees with, Ikle, who is an ardent anti-arms control man and who is responsible for peeling back the original SALT agreement we struck with the U.S."

"Yes I remember he also wrote a speech last year advocating a 'five year plan' of escalation leading to a situation whereby the U.S. would win a nuclear confrontation with us."

"Yes. Also worth noting is that Perle cut his teeth as the security advisor for Senator Henry Jackson, Reagan's chief arms control officer."

"Ah yes! 'Scoop' Jackson, a chief arms control officer who has made a career out of being an obstructionist!"

"Also dubbed 'the Prince of Darkness'." Solomatin added as he produced a *New York Times* article and read it aloud. "'The sense that we and the Russians could compose our differences, reduce them to treaty constraints, and then rely on compliance to produce a safer world. I don't agree with any of that.'"

Chebrikov sat in silence as he scanned the documents. Solomatin offered an analysis.

"In conjunction with the fact that National Security Adviser Clark categorically opposes all U.S.-Soviet contacts of any kind clearly signals to me that the hardliners have gained the upper hand."

Chebrikov flipped through the remaining few pages of the report.

"Reagan appointed Eugene Rostow to head the

Arms Control and Disarmament Agency who flatly opposes any sort of arms control or disarmament agreement with the Soviet Union, and also led the CPD fight against the SALT II agreement. 'Arms control thinking drives out sound thinking.', he stated." Boris explained.

Chebrikov gradually began to experience a sinking feeling as he absorbed the data and realized he would have to present these findings to The Premier and soon. Solomatin continued.

"He also told the Senate that the U.S. could certainly survive a nuclear war citing Japan as an example saying, 'They not only survived but flourished after a nuclear attack.'"

"The man's insane! And an attack of hundreds of nuclear warheads instead of two? Who will survive that?!"

"He told them that he estimated that between ten million and one hundred million might be lost but argued the human race is 'very resilient'. Victory is possible if the Americans are prepared to fight."

"An obvious reference to supporting nuclear proliferation!" Chebrikov shifted in his seat as he spoke.

"This one was confirmed day before yesterday. At the end of last week Reagan personally appointed a Mr. Richard Burt to head the State Department's Bureau of Politico-Military Affairs, the State Department's primary liaison with the Defence Department."

"Okay."

"Burt is a former *New York Times* reporter and one of the few journalists sympathetic to the CPD.

527

He called the SALT agreement 'a favor to the Russians.'"

"I see! So he is a strong proponent of peace and nuclear arms controls." To quell his rising fear of the picture being presented him Chebrikov continued to employ sarcasm. He stood and moved to the window.

"Last up is a quote from Pentagon official Thomas Jones who last month told a reporter from *Time Magazine* ..." Solomatin brandished a clipping of the original article as he spoke. "... that the U.S. could easily survive a nuclear exchange and fully recover within two to four years, if the populace digs plenty of holes, covers them with wooden doors, and buries the structures under three feet of dirt.' And my favourite quote, he passed another article, 'If there are enough shovels to go around, everybody's going to make it.'"

Viktor Chebrikov now, reinforced by Solomatin's Intel report, was convinced more than ever he was on the right track, closed over the folder, leaned back and stared blankly out the window.

"Apparently Reagan's 'Peace through power' argument is more dependent on power than peace."

Boris, observing Viktor's 1000 yard stare, suddenly realized this job wasn't just a favor to keep him around or give him something to fill his time as he may have initially suspected. The overall situation was far more serious then he thought.

"Comrade Director, are you alright?" Boris hesitated then answered in a mechanical voice without moving a muscle.

"Interesting picture we have here Boris. Excellent work, by the way." He snapped back to reality. "What are you working on at the moment?"

"I was thinking to prepare a presentation for the Politburo."

"Let me give the information to Secretary Andropov first and I will enquire whether or not he wants a full scale briefing after. If he does, I will let you do it."

"Thank you." Boris turned to leave. "Comrade Director?" Solomatin followed him to the door.

"Yes Boris?"

"If this thing happens ... if a hostile exchange appears imminent ... give me your word I will be returned to active service!"

Chebrikov, the reports tucked under his arm, smiled and patted Solomatin's shoulder.

****

CHAPTER TWENTY-TWO

Harden, Danno and Ricky were where they had been since yesterday when Doc and Mac took off for East Berlin, in the hostel room anxiously awaiting word on the situation. The in-house wall phone buzzed at a little after zero-nine hundred and all three fell over themselves diving to pick it up. Ricky got there first.

Hello is this room 217? A young female receptionist asked.

"Yes!"

I have a trunk call for anyone in room 217?

"We'll take it!" Ricky handed the phone off to the L.T. and signaled the thumbs up to Danno.

"Hello?!"

"Is this Mr. Hawkeye?" It was Doc who had to assume the payphone he was speaking from was being monitored.

"This is Mr. Gere, can I help you?" Harden responded.

"Mr. Gere, can't talk long. Things crazy here. Lots of business activity but the C.E.O. wasn't in."

"We thought as much. What are your plans Mr. Zhivago?"

"My colleagues and I have decided to try our luck at your northern facility. I'm told the meeting there is scheduled for about two to four hours before your next scheduled conference call. Perhaps you could phone ahead and arrange for a vehicle to meet us?"

"There's nothing available out of our Maryland

office at the moment but we might be able to arrange something through our London affiliate."

Both of them heard the coin drop into the phone signaling there were 30 seconds left on the call.

"Okay then, I'll contact you at a later time. Thank you for your help." Doc signed off.

Yesterday afternoon an hour after contact time had passed and there was no beacon signal coming in from Doc & Mac, the monitor was shut down as a precaution. Harden took a seat on a bed to brief the other two.

As soon as they hung up Harden ordered Ricky to lock the door, stand by and Danno to set up the commo gear and switch the homing beacon monitor back on.

"They made the meet but apparently Gordievsky wasn't there. I don't know for sure but there must be trouble at Checkpoint Charlie because they're heading north to seek an alternate egress. Ricky, when we're done here see what you can find out on the TV news stations about the border crossings. We can't wait until 18:30 to ask the handler besides I don't want to tip the agency off that anybody's over the fence."

"Will do sir."

"Ya know how nobody wants to be the guy that starts World War Three?" Harden speculated to Danno who just nodded. "Well we got two armed, rogue operators lost in Communist territory and that is not only not going to go over well with Moscow but Washington..."

"... is gonna shit a brick!" Danno added.

"Two bricks!"

Just then there was a loud knock on the door. Harden and Danno quickly threw a blanket over the beacon monitoring gear and Danno slid his 9mm off safe and under the blanket, maintaining a firm hold on it. A nod from the L.T. signaled Ricky to answer the door.

"Who?" He asked with one hand on his side arm behind his back.

"U.S. Marine Embassy Guard here for Lieutenant David Harden. Open up!" Ricky looked at Dave who hung his head and mumbled.

"Shit again?! How the fuck ...?" He waved for Matson to unlock the door. One Marine stepped into the room while the other waited just outside.

"Lieutenant Harden?"

"Yeah."

"Sir we have a car downstairs waiting for you."

"Sorry lads, I know you guys are not real big on chit chat but I'm not going anywhere this time without an explanation."

Ricky and Danno simultaneously tensed up.

"I don't know what you mean by 'this time' sir but we have orders to take you to the Ambassador's Liaison sir. He's waiting in the Frankfurt Annex. That's all we know."

Harden solemnly perused the room.

"How did you guys where ...? Never mind. Alright, fair enough." He turned and handed Danno Scarlett's business card with his secure number on it. "Call this guy, explain the situation and I'll be back as soon as I'm done. If I'm not back in an hour, make that two, pack up and head back to base."

"Roger that sir."

532

It was a mere fifteen minute car ride to the Fifth Corps Annex building in the central city where the Ambassador's office maintained an annex office. Harden was escorted up through the sub-level car park and up to the fifth floor and shown into a small, windowless room where a well-dressed, official looking guy about Dave's age waited sitting half on half off the desk.

"Thank you Sergeant." The stranger dismissed the Marine guard who took up their positions outside the sound proof office and once on their own the well-dressed man, who remained expressionless, didn't move to the back of the desk but instead crossed his arms and stared at Harden. Dave thought it prudent to remain standing.

"Lieutenant Harden, do you know Mr. Brandon Croke?"

"Can't say as I do. And I don't know you either."

"Franks, William Franks, Ambassador Burns' Liaison." Franks suddenly decided to take a seat behind the small desk of some previously ousted occupant.

"As you know, due to the political situation, we don't have an embassy just now in the DDR. But we do have Mr. Croke. Mr. Croke is not permitted to have his family behind the Iron Curtain, so he lives alone. In a big house with two servants, a 67 year old maid and a 70 year old butler both ardent communists who naturally make regular reports to the HVA who make regular reports to the KGB who make regular reports to Moscow about Mr. Croke's every movement.

He requires armed guards from both sides of the

fence anywhere he goes because, among other groups, Mr. Croke has been issued death threats by The Asian Dawn, The Red Faction Army, The P.L.O. and the Students for a Democratic Society."

"Very educational. Presumably that's why he gets the big bucks." Dave quipped.

"He is the United States Charge d'Affaires for what used to be the American Embassy in the German Democratic Republic. It is his job to maintain some semblance of diplomatic relations with a political party whose leader openly declared, in the United Nations, that he will bury us." Dave looked down to check his shoe shine as he started to sense where this was going. "I guess some might consider that fair in that our leader, your leader and my leader that is, most recently labeled their leaders 'The Evil Empire'."

"Mr. Franks –"

"I know, 'get to the point'! Okay. Mr. Croke's job is difficult. No, a pain in the ass. Wait. I can do better. IT SUCKS!! Do you wanna know how bad it sucks? It sucks so bad that I wouldn't take it for twice the pay grade, six days a week off, and the official employee uniforms were string bikinis with Brigitte Bardot, Raquel Welch and Farrah Fawsette as my personal secretarial staff."

"I suppose what you're trying to say, in your own subtle way, is Mr. Brandon Croke doesn't need anyone to make his job any more difficult?"

"Perceptive Lieutenant!" He pointed a finger at Harden. "Very perceptive." He rose and came around from behind the desk. "We received an official complaint from the DDR, through Mr.

Croke to the Embassy in Bonn to the effect that there are suspicions that two, maybe more, individuals possibly Americans, are unaccounted for and possibly lose in East Berlin. I'm on a very short schedule, down here just for the day so if you could –"

Realizing that his mission's classification was well above whatever classification this guy had, and so resolved not to reveal any details, Dave saw his chance to get something out of this little power party.

"Any idea how that might have happened Mr. Franks?"   Franks picked up on Harden's attempted end run.

"You come off as the kind'a guy who keeps up on current events Lieutenant, so I assume you've heard things aren't going so well between us and them? Today as of zero seven hundred hours the DDR Politburo decided to close all checkpoints pending a review of all political relations between the East and West."

"Any idea if it's a blanket order across the Iron Curtain?"

"No, not yet. But it's being looked into." It dawned on Franks he was being milked and he didn't like it. Milking people for information was his job. "I have no idea, nor do I want to know, who you are, why you're here or who you know in The Diplomatic Corps, however unless you want to be the guy who starts World War III, you need to clean this up. Whatever this is!"

"Funny you should say that. Mr. Franks, you know I'm not at liberty to give you details but you've got to trust me when I tell you that we are literally this close to what we need. And that will in turn help us avoid WWIII."

Franks stared intently at Harden then placed his briefcase on the desk, opened it and handed Harden a standard, white sealed envelope.

"I suspected as much. This came through in the Diplomatic Pouch less than an hour ago. It was stamped 'EYES ONLY!'

Dave opened it. It was a message from Agent Scarlett at MI6 through the British Embassy in Bonn.

Have locale on JFK.
CONFIRMED!

"Thank you Mr. Franks." Harden moved to leave. Ah, just one more thing."

"What?!"

"Can I trouble your drivers for a lift back to the hostel?"

****** ***

Century House
Central London
MI6 Offices

John Scarlett was livid. Everyone had seen him pace before, nothing out of the ordinary but this morning was different. His long legs strode across his office on Westminster Bridge Road as he travelled nearly wall-to-wall in unrestrained anger.

Saxon, his assistant, sat off in a corner staring out the wall-length, plate glass window into the misty haze of the central city.

For the second time there was a knock at the office door which again went unanswered as Scarlett continued to rant and rave.

"BASTARDS, BASTARDS! FUCKING BASTARDS! If it was one of their fucking over paid, Nancy agents there'd be a fucking general mobile-fucking-ization!" Scarlet spewed as he continued his twenty minute long tirade initiated by a phone call he had just received from the U.S. Intelligence Liaison informing him no American agency was in a position to attempt to help rescue his #1 asset, Oleg Gordievsky.

Finally the third series of knocks was responded to as Saxon rose and scurried over to the door carefully dancing around Scarlett's return journey across the room as he continued to pace.

It was a messenger who stood at the door who leaned his head partially in and whispered.

"Is he upset?"

"Docs a pope shit in the woods?" Saxon whispered back.

"Well, I'd best not disturb him then! Give him this! Just off the wire." He thrust the single sheet of teletype at Saxon and disappeared.

Saxon gave the message a quick peruse and then mustered up the courage to approach the ranting Scarlett.

"Bloody one hundred million fucking dollar annual budget and they sit in their fucking holes like a fucking bunch of ball-less, bastard rabbits! Home of the fucking bloody Brave my fucking arse!"

"Sir, I sense you're a tad upset, but -"

"NOT FUCKING NOW!!" Scarlett screamed at Saxon.

The habitually compliant Saxon suddenly stepped in front of Scarlett purposely blocking his path and held the message up at face height.

"JOHN! READ THE FUCKING MESSAGE!!" Saxon yelled.

Temporarily shocked out of his vexation, Scarlett at first hesitated then, in order to save face, feigned increased anger as he snatched the paper from Saxon's hand.

Saxon stepped back out of striking distance as he watched Scarlett's face melt into a gradual broad smile.

"FUCK ME YOUR ROYAL HIGHNESS!" Scarlett shouted compelling Saxon to step back again as his boss started to do a jig around the room. Saxon grabbed the message from Scarlett's hand and re-read it. It was from Lieutenant Harden.

TFR has located item.
Will follow JFK to Dallas.
Can you support?

Through a covert network in Scandinavia and satellite imagery surveillance the U.S. Intel services had located what they believed to be a known KGB safe house in the south of Finland.

Deducing that Gordievsky was far too valuable to kill straight away, which they would probably do

538

eventually, the Reds would take the better part of a week to extract information from him but first they would move him closer to home territory for safety.

Knowing that the Americans had a well-developed HUMNIT web in and around Lubyanka likely to spot the KGB, the next logical location was Finland where the Allied HUMINT availability was weakest.

"Are we going to Texas?!" A shocked Saxon fearfully inquired.

"Get me commo with TFR, last I heard they were in Frankfurt. Then get me Commander Shillings at Two Squadron, RAF Hereford! Tell him to prepare for an emergency, long distance covert, night exfil. Forget Hereford, I'll place the call myself! Get me commo with TFR! NOW!" Scarlett commanded as he dialed the phone.

"HOW?!" Saxon yelled back.

"I don't give a shit! Carrier pigeon! Go through the NSA if you have to. Tell them we have information regarding *Operation Ryan* for them, it's classified 'Eyes Only'!"

Saxon, not having access to the code the message was sent in could only sense it concerned Gordievsky. A minute later it dawned on the junior agent that the initials of Gordievsky's cover name, Josef Kuksova, were 'JK', as in JFK and that Dallas was not a good place for JFK to be.

Saxon got to another phone in the office as Scarlett was already on the line with the SAS Commander.

"Commander, how soon can you have a four to

six man cell prepped and ready to deploy for an emergency exfil?"

"I'll need details ASAP, but about four to six hours. What do we need for transport? Air, sea, land?" The commander inquired.

"Most likely air. We're pulling three or four men out of Finland. It is more of a hostile rescue mission actually."

"Hostiles in Finland, hmmm. Ivan's backyard." Scarlett didn't like the sound of that. "Where, exactly are we talking about?" The Commander pushed.

"Night exfil, somewhere in the south east. I'll get you coordinates as soon as we have them." There was an inordinately long pause. "Well commander, can you do it?"

"Sir I understand your dilemma but to prep, brief and deploy a cell in a matter of hours behind enemy lines or hostile territory, you're asking something that is simply not in our brief! I'm not sure."

"Commander, we need to be sure! We're running out of time, we can't risk another miscalculation and these are resources we simply can't squander! Sorry I can't tell you more but ..."

"Mr. Scarlett, would that I could accommodate you but it will take some planning and that will take time, neither of which is possible without emergency approval from headquarters at MoD."

Reverting to his former state Scarlett slammed the phone down and resumed a profanity punctuated pace across the room.

Saxon, one ear on his phone conversation with the other on Scarlett's, finished up his call and decided to take a chance on an idea which occurred to him.

"Sir what about the TFR people still behind The Curtain? Do we intend to help them?"

"I've been working on that. Set up a burst transmission with our commo people for ... noon."

Saxon's plan of distraction was working. He turned to leave then turned back.

"Sir about the rescue mission, we don't need Number Two Squadron! There are already British units deployed in the BRD and all over the North Sea! If the Yanks know for sure where he might be and its logical the KGB snatch team will avoid all the known routes back into the U.S.S.R., then they'll likely take him to a peripheral territory." Scarlett gave him a questionable look.

"What do you mean 'assets already in the area'?"

"For REFORGER!" Saxon clarified. Scarlett turned and stared at his assistant.

"Saxon I take back almost everything I've ever said about you! You apparently can be useful!"

"Sir, is that all the bad things you've said about me or –"

"Let's don't push it!"

"I'll just find out the nearest unit and set you up an   appointment with Communications. Sir."

****

Although clearly more muscular and in much better condition than the average executive traversing Canary Wharf in Central London, this thirty-something, well dressed executive seemed to take an inordinate interest in his surroundings.

For the better part of an hour he had been walking around the bustling business district, weaving in and out of the buildings and studying the traffic patterns for a good part of the time before he took a seat on a bench on the wharf. He just seemed to sit and observe the pedestrian and vehicular traffic more closely occasionally scribbling a note in a small note book he took from his brown leather brief case.

Meanwhile, across town on the West side of the city, a similarly dressed and well-built gentleman stood tucked away in a doorway taking a few snap shots of hospitals and various medical facilities in and around Central London.

The Royal Marsden, the Chelsea and Westminster Hospitals, with their cluster of nearly one dozen buildings, and The Chelsea Outpatient Centre were all located within a kilometer of each other. Thinking it was strange that all the hall lights in the buildings appeared to be on at this late hour he watched closely as the linen delivery trucks pulled into the delivery ramps of the main building and began unloading what seemed massive amounts of fresh, clean duvets, sheets and pillow cases.

Had he been there early that morning he would have seen the same trucks collecting the dirty linen. But he wasn't.

It was just after six p.m. when the moon began to rise and both men were again on the move, this time towards the nearest respective underground stations.

Arriving at the Aldgate East Station in East

London about twenty minutes after he boarded the train, the man from Canary Wharf headed up Old Castle Street to a boarding house nestled in between a small office building and a modern tower block still under construction.

He used a key to enter the premises, a well maintained 150 year old, Victorian residential structure and made his way directly upstairs. However the man didn't stop on the first floor he climbed the second set of stairs to the two bedroom second floor level and entered the smaller of the two bedrooms.

On the other side of the door, in the bedroom, a small office was set up. In lieu of a bed a three man bench sat against the wall and a forty-something female secretary sat at a small desk. Next to the bench was another painted wooden door leading into the adjoining bedroom.

The man signed into a small log and took a seat on the bench next to the man who had been in the hospital district earlier. Neither spoke.

The woman rose from the desk and went to the other door, opened it and peeked her head into the adjoining room.

"Colonel, #167 is here." She announced.

"Thank you, send him in." She stepped back and held the door open.

"The Colonel is ready. You may report." She instructed.

Without speaking he entered the room and she pulled the door closed behind him.

The man behind the desk switched on a tape recorder sitting to his left and spoke into the small mike next to it.

"This is cell 17 field report of 27 September, 19:45. Agent #167 reporting." He nodded to 167 who removed a note book from his breast pocket and spoke.

"A total of seven major medical facilities were observed over the last three days. Hospitals, administration buildings associated with them and clinics."

"Continue."

"Several things stood out to me, Comrade Colonel. I found it unusual that non-essential lights such those in hallways etcetera were on all night, personnel were seen going in and out of all the buildings throughout the night and it was clearly apparent all the facilities were stocking up on extra linen, sheets, blankets and so forth."

"Are you certain you saw this 167?"

"Yes Colonel, it particularly caught my attention because all deliveries were under cover of the night. In Moscow all deliveries to medical facilities are during the day. What is there to hide?" The Colonel switched off the recorder.

"Major!" He called out Seconds later the woman came through the door.

"Yes Colonel?"

"Who is next?"

"We are awaiting 171 to arrive but 365 is here Comrade Colonel."

"Send him please."

"Yes Colonel!" The next agent entered and took a seat next to the colleague he knew only as 167.

"365, did you see anything that would lead you

to believe they are preparing for shortages, emergencies, problems of any kind?" 365 opened his standard issue note book and flipped through a few pages. The recorder was again turned on.

"Colonel, it has become clear to me, during the last seventy-two hours of careful observation that workers in the financial district were working increased hours. These are the financial elite of The West yet they stayed in their offices well into the evening, well past the English tea time of six p.m. Some of them much later than that." The Colonel sat back in his chair and motioned for 365 to continue. "Petrol delivery vehicles were lined up at London docks most of the day for the third day in a row as were various other delivery vehicles.

"Sir may I?" 167 interjected. The Colonel nodded.

"Colonel, enroute to a hospital complex yesterday I happened on a food storage warehouse taking deliveries."

"And?"

"I've never seen that much food in one place, and I am from the Ukraine. The trucks were lined up back into traffic all day."

"Yes, we've similar reports from New York, and Chicago in The States and Bonn as well." The Colonel confirmed

"Sir, I am only a low level operative but, if Lubyanka is looking for signs of preparation for war ... it looks to me as if the Westerners are preparing for the worst."

"I fear I have to agree with you 167."

"What are we to do Comrade Colonel?"

"I'll get this to Moscow right away. Resume your observations tomorrow and continue to report."

The inexperienced agents had no way to know that, despite their experiences in their Soviet Union home towns, work schedules, delivery times and in-house hospital routines varied greatly from what they had come to know as 'normal'. Delivery schedules in the Soviet Union were restricted because supplies under a communist system were always restricted.

In short they were reading into their observations and allowing their imaginations to run away with them.

****

The weather was chilly but clear and dry as Doc and Ray came over a small ridge and in the distance, the Autobahn came into sight. They had covered about six klicks so far that morning and as they constantly scanned their perimeter for foot or vehicular traffic they spotted a dark red, corrugated metal barn about 300 meters ahead but still about 200 meters short of the Autobahn. The same thought struck them both at the same time and they headed for the suitable recon spot.

Once there they crouched behind a stack of oaken casks up against the side of the corrugated structure and assessed the situation.

"What'a ya think Doc?" Ray quietly asked as he peered over a couple of the wooden barrels next to some machinery parts.

"There's no chance we'll make exfil before dark without a vehicle. I could hotwire any Soviet vehicle but there's nothing around here. I don't see any movement either but it's cold enough they could be inside."

"There's only one way to find out I guess!" Ray got up to creep around the side of the building and as he did there were some more barrels in his path.

Back around the corner Doc pressed his nose right up against one of the barrels and sniffed.

"Son-of-a-bitch, booze!" Doc declared. Then the bottom of his stomach fell out as he heard the unmistakable click of a gun hammer being cocked directly in back of his skull.

"Turn! Slowly!" A husky voice commanded in German. Doc did as told and had to look up as he was face to face with the chest of a six foot six and a half foot farmer type with two Lion sized paws wrapped around a Kalashnikov looking back down at him. In lieu of hair the farmer's bald head was covered with a continuous tattoo which appeared to be a map of something. His fully buttoned up collar strained to contain the over flowing, half tattooed neck and Doc quickly estimated that a yard stick would be hard pressed to measure his shoulder width.

Doc smiled a nervous smile as Gargantua wrapped both hands more tightly around the weapon which appeared as a toy in his hands.

Without warning the giant's smile melted from his face and he lowered his rifle. Doc grabbed it and Ray peeked out from around the side of the human edifice, smiled and waved as he held his 9mm at the framer's back.

Doc thanked the War Gods that Ray had the presence of mind not to give them away by speaking English. The farmer raised his hands and Doc turned the Kalashnikov on him.

"Kommen!" Doc commanded and led the two around to the front door. With the weapon he motioned and the big man pulled open the large sliding door. Both Doc and Ray fought back a smile as they perused the spacious interior.

The entire inside of the barn was fitted out as a distilling operation. Three full sized boilers, distillation pipes, tons of potatoes piled against the exterior walls and a half dozen workers all stopped dead in their tracks and became engaged in a stare-off with Doc, Ray and one embarrassed big guy.

Maintaining a bead on the farmer Doc stepped closer to Ray who was behind the farmer, and whispered.

"I need you to focus! You're a deaf mute. Got it?"

"A what?"

"Deaf mute." Ray nodded. Doc ejected the magazine from the Kalashnikov, ejected the round in the chamber and walked over to hand the weapon back to the farmer.

"We are not the police. We are not interested in what you are doing here." The stunned farmer looked back and cautiously took his rifle as an older man in coveralls, wiping his hands with a heavy cloth approached. Ray pulled the barn door closed.

The old man sized them up before speaking to the farmer.

"Co ty myślisz?"

"Ja myśle możemy im zaufać." The farmer responded slowly.

"Mów po niemiecku!" At the command the old man turned to Doc and reverted to German. "Who are you?" Doc realized the risk of the story he had been mulling around in his head since they left Berlin but saw no alternative.

"We are fishermen from the North. We were arrested by the Stasi last week because our captain was running contraband from Denmark. My friend can't speak, he is mute, so they thought he was playing games. They threatened to kill us. We escaped."

The old man made no attempt to hide his skepticism.

"Just like that, you escaped from the Stasi?! What happened they leave the door open for you?" The other few workers had by now gathered around and garnered a good laugh at the old man's joke.

Doc pulled aside the open flap of his coat to reveal his 9mm. "No. We opened it for them."

"You trying to tell me you killed a Stasi?!"

"No father." Doc stepped closer to the grey haired man. "I'm telling you we killed two Stasi. And we are happy to kill more if we have to."

The old man mumbled something, again in Polish to the youngest boy there, a teen, who ran to a table aside the nearest boiling vat and returned with a half empty bottle of crystal clear liquid.

"To dead Stasi!" The old man swigged then passed the bottle to Doc.

"Na zdrowie!" Doc offered and drank before

passing the bottle to McDonald.

"What do you want here?" The old man asked.

"We need to make it back to the north, there our relatives can help us." The old man nodded with understanding.

"Janusz!" The man called over his shoulder and one of the men stepped forward. "This is Janusz. His German is shit but he can drive like the wind. His truck is next to be filled." He indicated a dark blue box van near the back of the barn. "When it is full he will leave for Kiel. You can ride with him."

"We are grateful." Doc nodded to Ray as he slid out of his coat and headed back towards the truck as he rolled up his sleeves.

"Where are you going?" The old man asked.

"In football there are no free tickets to the World Cup!" Doc proposed as he took a second swig from the near empty bottle then began to help with the loading. The old man smiled.

Forty minutes later, with Doc and Ray riding up front, their new best buddy Janusz, was heading up Autobahn Route 24 North.

It would be a three and a half to four hour ride and so Doc made one or two half-hearted attempts at conversation but discovered the old man wasn't exaggerating about Junusz's German. Doc spoke, Janusz grunted with an occasional nod.

It was coming up on noon so Doc motioned to Janusz to turn on the radio. Janusz grunted and Doc switched on the radio purposely a bit louder than normal.

Ray leaned over from the passenger's side and whispered to Doc. "These papers we're carrying are essentially useless. The only option if this guy gets nosy is to pop him."

"Pop him? What'a you Don Corleone?" Doc jibed.

"Then we got the problem of a body. I'll talk, you grunt and shrug. You're good at that anyway."

"Fuck you!"

"You'll never go back to dogs." Doc retorted as he leaned in and fiddled with the radio. It was set to DDR-1 but he quickly found the West German station RIAS where ZDF news was underway.

As the only one of the three that understood the broadcast, Doc had to keep his presence of mind as he listened. He stared straight ahead and fought to remain expressionless at what he heard.

Finally, an hour after they turned onto the Route 20 cut off, they saw a sign indicating 10 klicks to their intended destination, Lübecker just outside Kiel.

Janusz dropped them off in the middle of the fair sized town, they thanked hi then waited until he was heading back out of town and out of sight that they spoke.

"Well that was a lucky bre-"

"Shut the fuck up and come here!" Doc said as he dragged McDonald into the wide doorway of a closed up bank building.

"What the fuck's wrong with you!? We're outta the woods!"

"Ray Sweetheart, we ain't even **in** the woods yet!"

"What the fuck are you on about?" The penny dropped and Ray's face turned serious as he stared at Doc. "What did you hear on that radio?!"

"I heard why Checkpoint Charlie was closed."

"Why fer Christ's sake?!"

"Russia has officially severed all diplomatic ties with the West!" Ray fell back against the doorway. "Effective zero nine hundred this morning." Doc added.

"Jesus Christ Doc! Talk about outta the fucking frying pan!"

*

At nearly the same time as Doc and Ray had been speeding north on the East German Autobahn, the remaining members of Task force Romeo were huddled around the bar staring up at the television in the hostel's lounge listening to the English version of Andropov's shocking announcement being read out over the local news.

Byrdo came into the lounge, looked around and saw the L.T. and Ricky alone over at the small bar in the corner of the hostel's bar/TV room.

"Hey guys, got some news! We just got a Flash message from the handler. There has been a complete –"

"– termination of all diplomatic relations. We know. It's on the news." Ricky interjected and threw back his vodka.

"Yeah, but that ain't all." He handed the message to Lieutenant Harden who read it then crumpled it and leaned on the bar.

"It's good news. I can tell." Quipped Ricky.

552

Without turning to them the L.T. spoke.

"We've been directed to abandon the mission and return to D.C." The voice of the news commentator came back into focus.

In what is widely seen as an attempt to quell international speculation concerning his declining health, while at the same time facing down what is seen as the aggressive advances of the Reagan Administration, Soviet Prime Minister, Yuri Andropov, today held a rare in-person press conference in Moscow.

Foregoing the standard protocol of using lower ranking Politburo members to make the announcement, the Communist Chief had to have help to mount the podium to announce what amounts to a declaration concerning the current state of U.S.-Soviet relations.

A photograph of Prime Minister Andropov appeared behind the news commentator as a recording of his speech began to play. He spoke in slow deliberate terms:

The Soviet leadership deems it necessary to inform the Soviet people as well as other peoples and all who are responsible for determining the policy of nations, of its assessment of the course pursued in international affairs by the current U.S. administration. In brief, it is a militarist course that represents a serious threat to world peace.

If anyone had any illusions about the possibility of evolution for the better in the policy of the present American administration, recent events have dispelled them completely.

The recording stopped and the photo in the background faded out. The commentator resumed.

Political analysts say this statement only serves to bring the current war scare into sharper public focus. For Washington, the incident seems to express all that is wrong with the Soviet system and to vindicate the administration's critique of the Soviets while for Moscow, this development encapsulates and reinforces the Soviets' worst case assumptions concerning U.S. policy.

"What's this mean L.T.?" Danno, standing at the bar dumbfounded, asked. Before Harden could answer Ricky took up the question.

"I'll tell you what it means. It means this might be a good time to buy stock in one of those idiotic bomb shelter companies you always see on TV." Harden was quick to interrupt.

"Let's not get ahead of ourselves! Unless we hear differently, our primary mission is still to find out exactly what the hell RYAN is and right now Gordievsky is our best bet to do that!" Harden clarified.

"Sir, what about these new orders?" Ricky asked.

"What orders?" Harden answered.

****

Once in area of Lübecker Doc and Ray had about two klicks to walk into the town. The plan was to find a phone box, chance another call, this time to Scarlett's classified number and then pray to the war gods that MI6 could get them out.

"Well, the homing beacon is dead." Ray announced as he reassembled the camera lens while they still walked along the road.

"Guess everything comes down to one phone call!" Doc pointed across the four lane blacktop road to a wall mounted phone box in a gas station. They made their way over to it.

"One phone call." Doc announced as he held up their only East German two Deutsch mark coin.

"Just like jail." Ray cracked.

"Let's hope the lawyers are in!"

Dialing the number from memory Doc fed the box and placed the call. It was picked up on the third ring.

"Hello, is this Mr. Red?" Doc asked.

"No I'm sorry. There's no Mr. Red here."

"I was advised by your reprehensive that –"

"I'm afraid you have the wrong number. I'm late for a meeting so I'll have to go. Sorry." The line went dead.

"What the fuck ...?!" Doc cursed.

"What happened?!"

"He fuckin' hung up!!" He stared into the phone's transceiver. "Fuckin' Limey bastard!"

"So much for the lawyers being in!"

"Fuck me Alice! We risk our ass for his asset and he fuckin' hangs up!"

"You know what they say in training Doc, we're

all fuckin' disposal."

"Yeah, like fucking Kotex!" They plopped down on the ground, their backs against the building.

"Now what?! Fuckin' swim to Denmark?" Ray proposed. There they sat under the phone box to let the event sink in. Suddenly the phone rang. They both scrambled to reach it but Doc was closest.

"Yes?" Doc desperately asked. It was Scarlett's voice which came on the line.

"Had to ring back on a secure line. If Ivan picks this up you're bloody well fucked! We have 10 to 15 seconds so pay attention! Presumably you're in or around Kiel, so make your way to the fish processing plant and cannery on Steinbecker Strasse. Find Johan Jorgen, he works in Personnel. Code word is FUBAR'ed. Questions? Good. Best of luck." Again the line went dead. Doc stared at the phone.

"Well?!" Ray begged as Doc slowly replaced the receiver.

"Not sure. I think we were just given a contact."

"Tell me the contact's not back in fuckin' Berlin?!"

****

556

CHAPTER TWENTY-THREE

16:10, Tuesday, 27th September
Opposite the East Wing
The White House

Concerned about a Soviet commander in the field not bothering to go through Moscow before he pushed "The Button" during a tense situation, particularly following The Cuban Missile Crisis, President Kennedy ordered the development of a contingency where-by the U.S. Commander-in-Chief would have the capability to retaliate regardless of where he was. Ergo the design and development of OPLAN 8010 and "The Nuclear Football".

Inside a metallic briefcase, which is carried in a black leather satchel, there are a few things contained in the package euphemistically referred to as "The Football".

A book with classified launch site locations, a list of retaliatory options, an instruction booklet on activating the Emergency Broadcast system and of course the all-important launch codes. Also there is a list of emergency evacuation sites where the president can be taken in the event of forced evacuation due to an attack.

In line with the op plan, extensive consultation is undertaken with the President and a decision is jointly agreed upon, at which time a launch option is chosen. When there's uncertainty as to what to do in a tight situation the saying goes, "Drop back and punt." This was the situation during and immediately after the Cuban Missile Crisis which contributed to the evolution of the attack plan codenamed "Dropkick". The institution of that plan lead to the invention of "The Football"

While not an actual launch capable mechanism, The Football acts as a secure communications device to pass on the order to launch with the required authentication codes to the National Military Command Center.

Amongst his perpetual entourage of aides the President has one or more military with him at all times whose duty it is to carry The Football with him, usually chained by steel cable to his wrist. The 0-4 pay grade or above officer, previously cleared to security level Yankee-White, meaning they all but dug up your deceased relatives to finger print them, is rotated by military branch to make the responsibility equitable.

"Do you have the biscuit sir?" Reagan's aide asked as they scurried down the hallway.

"Yes, yes, right here." Reagan tapped his left breast pocket as they left the White House halls and headed for the rear exit leading out to the South Lawn.

As they did a pair of binocular optics gradually focused in as the large Sikorsky Sea King, known as Marine One, gently touched down on the plush lawn.

"A Tokarev SVT-40 with a good scope and this 'crisis' would be over right now." The slender Russian agent lying on the roof remarked as he refocused the binos.

"Always ready to shoot first and ask questions later eh Sergei?" His colleague lying beside him shot back. "What if everybody thought that way?!"

"The reason we are in the middle of a world-wide political crisis is precisely because more people don't think that way! There is no problem too large that cannot be solved with a well-placed bullet!" He watched through the powerful binos as Reagan and his entourage crossed the lawn and boarded the chopper. "Either we are at fucking war or we are not!" Sergei cursed.

Logically divided into sectors as any military operation is, the various operatives of the KGB and the HVA were assigned to central locations according to known concentrations of Allied military and political activity throughout Britain, the BRD, the northern European countries, France, Spain, Portugal, Italy and The United States.

All of the sectors were further subdivided into watch areas which were in turn divided into cells of varying numbers of operatives. Watch areas were labelled by their geographic location, BRD North etc. Cells were referred to by species of dog and individual cell members were tagged a letter-number combination. Although not many, there were a considerable number of operatives, largely veteran KGB, assigned to areas in the United States. Unknown to U.S. intelligence, the KGB currently had a team right in Reagan's back yard, literally.

Team D composed of Operatives #17 and #18, assigned to cell Hound Dog had been camped out on the roof of a hotel two blocks from The White House since an hour before dawn.

It was around 15:37 when KGB operative D-17 nudged his partner as they alternated surveillance duty on the roof of the hotel. They watched as the President's entourage boarded Marine One on the White House lawn.

Having been alerted by the NBC Six O'clock News the night before that Reagan would leave on a ten day trip abroad that morning they were ready and manned from the roof terrace of The Intercontinental Hotel on 14th Street, less than 1,000 meters from the East Wing.

"Shit!" Sergei again cursed

"What?"

"He has the football!"

"He what?"

"He is taking the fucking Nuclear Football with him!"

"But he's only supposed to be going to –"

"Exactly!"

"Let's go! We have to call this in!" They crawled backwards until they reached the roof's interior stairway and headed down to scramble out of the hotel and back to their safe house to alert their cell commander.

Not ever having risked such close observation of the U.S.'s Head Man before, the Soviet agents had no way of knowing the Nuclear Football was like Reagan's blood pressure medicine and his seemingly endless political scandals.

Always with him.

*

Just after their phone call with Scarlett Doc and Ray made their way two klicks into the small city of Lübecker proper and found the cannery. As Ray milled around outside while pretending to be a worker Doc ventured inside and upstairs to the main office where he sought out their contact Herr Jorgen.

The moment Doc entered the sprawling office Jorgen knew who he was. The code word was redundant as Jorgen rose to meet him and, knowing his office wasn't safe, steered him off to a small supply room.

"The schedule will be tight, but your movement has been arranged. Tonight at 21:30, be at loading pier number 3. It is used only in the daytime and so will be abandoned. There you will meet my son, Mikhail. He will take you up the Trave River by small motor launch about 12K to the mouth of the Baltic.

Once on the Baltic you will meet the fishing boat *Nina Marie*, posing as seasonal fishermen and go out with the morning tide." Jurgen suggested they pass the time in a local dockside kneipe which had a back room they could eat and rest in until launch time.

The next leg went as planned and once they were aboard the *Nina Marie* that evening, Doc and Ray were given basic tasks such as Flemishing down the lines and cutting bait to lend a hand during the 50 nautical mile journey back to western waters.

MacDonald lost the coin toss on that one and would spend the next 10 to 12 hours stinking of squid and whitefish guts.

They caught a good tide and just under five hours after shoving off the *Nina Marie* made her rendezvous point where the guys were transferred aboard the British submarine *H.M.S. Swordfish*.

As they disembarked the trawler Doc thought to give the remainder of the operational cash to the captain to buy the fishermen drinks when they got back. In his gratitude he forgot to take into account just how much cheaper drink was in the communist east.

That crew would drink and remember him for a very long time. Of course, due to the swollen heads the next day, the wives would remember him too. But not in the same light.

Doc and Ray were grateful for the ensuing four hour journey aboard the sub, which afforded them time to get a hot shower and some chow. They were able to cobble together a full-of-shit but believable after action report as they ate, which didn't take long as it was after all, English military food they were eating.

At around eight in the morning they met with a U.S. Navy CH-53 off the coast of Denmark, were hoisted aboard and flown to the carrier *U.S.S. Lexington* which was in the North Atlantic on maneuvers in support of the REFORGER exercise.

To their surprise Agent Scarlett was there to meet them on the flight deck as the helo touched down. They had to shout above the din of the deck.

"How was your sub ride?"

"Ahh, you know, it was a sub. 120 men go down, 60 happy couples come up." Doc answered. "Does the L.T. know where we are?"

"Yes. He and your team are enroute here as we speak."

"Did D.C. okay this?" McKeowen asked.

"Okay what?" Scarlett mocked as they ducked into the base of the island structure on their way up to the briefing room.

"I see!" Replied Doc.

"Said the blind man to his deaf wife!" MacDonald added.

"And she picked up the hammer and they saw!" Doc finished off. Scarlett shook his head.

"You lads have been in the sun too long."

"So Mr. Crimson, what's the plan?"

"Follow me." Scarlett led them up the port side ladder and into a door marked 'RESTRICTED'. The small compartment they entered housed a table, eight chairs and had been set up as an impromptu meeting space as indicated by the maps of Northern Europe hanging on two of the bulkheads.

"The Commanding Officer was nice enough to have his chaps set this space up as a briefing room for us." He motioned for them to sit. "This will be short as I imagine you'll want a bit of rest before your team comes in." Scarlett took a seat himself.

"And when exactly is that sir?" Doc asked.

"ETA zero eight hundred tomorrow. Best we could do what with the war games on and all. Most resources are allocated to REFORGER."

"By the way, thanks for all the help." Doc offered.

"I'll not give any details until we're all assembled, however while you two were on holiday gallivanting all over Eastern Germany your lieutenant was nice enough to offer to give MI6 a dig out with another attempt at recovering our missing friend." Doc and Ray exchanged shocked expressions. "I know what you're thinking. All I ask is that you listen to my complete briefing and I promise all questions will be entertained."

Ray was clearly reluctant as he slid down in his chair. Doc wasn't exactly turning cartwheels either. Scarlett clearly saw their reluctance. "Gentlemen, listen to my brief, if you're not satisfied with what I have, simply decline the mission." Fully suspecting these two were a major force on the team Scarlett considered pushing further but decided against it.

"One last thing and I'll let you go. While aboard use the code word 'Llama' if you are approached by anyone and I do mean **anyone** save the Commanding Officer, Captain Bartholomew. Everyone knows there are spooks aboard, difficult to keep that kind of thing quiet, however, that being the case they have been ordered not to communicate with you."

"NICE!" I'm finally immune to Legs!" Ray gleefully quipped.

"Very well, thank you for your time. There's hot food and a pair of bunks for you in a the ahh ... brig."

"What?!"

"It's the only place we could arrange you to be away from everyone else. It was either that or the chain locker. After you've eaten, report to the Captain-of-the-Guard, use the code word and he'll sort you out. I'll send a runner when Lieutenant

Harden and the others arrive."

Doc and Ray rose to leave and Doc ducked out through the hatchway first as Ray hung back just enough to lean over and whisper to Scarlett.

"Agent Scarlett?"

"Yes Petty Officer?"

"Did you ever actually meet James Bond?" Without moving but making direct eye contact Scarlett answered.

"Petty Officer MacDonald, I am James Bond and now that you know that, should you tell anyone, I'm afraid I'll have to cut off your head and put it in a safe!" Once outside with Doc Ray laughed.

"I'm getting; to like that Limey!" Ray commented.

Doc responded in his worst-best mock British accent.

"Well Gov, I still thinks 'e's a bit of a pompous fuck. Dja'know what I mean mate?"

❋

Back in his Lubyanka office Chebrikov had spent the better part of the morning studying Solomatin's 'Seven Dwarfs' report on the new appointments in the Reagan Administration as well as other developments such as his two page recommendation of increased permanent KGB surveillance of the NATO pact countries.

Chebrikov had ordered a copy of the report sent to Horst Vogel of the East German HVA the day Solomatin presented it to him and requested Horst's feedback before he proceeded to his meeting with the General Secretary. Late that morning Chebrikov and Horst were on the line together.

"The fact that he has shifted a significant number of people in his upper echelon is relevant. But the fact that he installed such hardliners is clearly indicative they are preparing for the worst." Vogel espoused.

"But what if they are merely 'tightening the screws' so to speak?" Chebrikov challenged.

"Then they are no less posturing for a war footing, but they are aiming to force us into the first move. It's an old trick. Hitler did it with Poland, the Japanese used it against us in their war. There is even a precedent with the Americans against the Spanish when they concocted that ludicrous story about the *U.S.S. Maine* to launch the war with Spain over possession of Cuba."

"Ludicrous story or not, it worked." Chebrikov affirmed.

"My point exactly." Vogel said nonchalantly.

"What strategy do you suggest?"

"Have you observed any other significant developments?"

"We have received a report that Reagan is on a ten day journey."

"And?" Vogel prodded.

"He has taken the nuclear football with him."

There was a longer than expected pause.

"Are you certain of this information?" Vogel queried.

"It's come from our best team in the States."

"Do you agree with Comrade Solomatin's

analysis, Director Chebrikov?" Chebrikov had no illusions about the significance of their current conversation and therefore the weight of his next answer to Horst's question.

"I'm afraid I do."

"My analysis and your opinion of a report by your most trusted, experienced and informed field agents speaks for itself. Taken in conjunction with this latest information ..."

"Certainly they couldn't be so stupid?! That blind to the final consequences of an overt attack?!"

"Herr Chebrikov, there is a reason we supply you with over forty percent of all the scientific and technological materials and information obtained from the west."

"And why exactly is that Herr Horst?"

"Attention to detail my dear comrade. Attention to detail! In all matters."

Again thee was a short silence.

"I have a meeting with the Secretary General in one hour. Thank you Horst. I suppose the path is clear."

"I'll contact our field agent leaders for updates and get them to you as soon as we get them. Meanwhile, please keep me informed of developments as they happen. And Boris..."

"Yes Horst?"

"Remember, every major war which has been fought in the last two centuries has usually been won by those who struck first. *Fortuna Eruditis Favet*!"

"Fortune favors the prepared. Thank you Horst. You are a good ally." Chebrikov hung up and sat in his office for a long time staring down on Red Square before he summoned his car to take him to The Presidium.

*

Early that afternoon as scheduled, Boris Chebrikov arrived at Yuri Andropov's plush Presidium office to present the report he had not yet told the Politburo he had commissioned.

It was an anxious twenty minutes while Boris sat, in front of Yuri's desk, as quietly as possible while Yuri read through the report.

When finished Andropov didn't speak, he just sat staring straight ahead, report still in hand.

"General Secretary?" Chebrikov leaned over and repeated his inquiry. "What do you think?" Andropov spoke slowly and methodically.

"I know Solomatin. Therefore I know this is not panic talk. He's not the kind of individual to pander to that sort of thing." For one of the few times in his long career Chebrikov was unsure of what to say.

"I agree Comrade." He sat forward on his chair. "So you feel there's some credence in this political reshuffling in the West?"

Andropov carefully laid the folder on his desk and sat back. "What we decide next will inevitably affect the course of not only Russia but possibly the course of world events."

"There can be no doubt General Secretary. Perhaps that is why we should convene the Politburo?"

"To what end? Discuss, argue then finally, after hours of debate in the Politburo, like the American Congress vote as if we were a Western power?" Andropov sighed, leaned on the edge of the desk and with some effort, eased himself up and shuffled across to his Doomsday Board. There was one unmarked square remaining. "To what end?" He reached for the grease pencil.

Chebrikov turned in his seat and watched Andropov as he crossed the room.

"General Secretary, if we are in agreement concerning the intentions of the West, we must form some census of opinion about what course to follow." Andropov didn't reply he just stood staring at the board. "General Secretary?! Are you alright?!"

Andropov tried but was unable to answer as he suddenly began to fight for breath. Chebrikov quickly rose and crossed over to him.

Yuri's face was ashen and appeared to be turning blue. Chebrikov quickly moved to ease Andropov over on to the couch, laid him down, loosened his tie and ran to the door.

"GUARD! GUARD! CALL FOR HELP! GET THE DOCTOR! QUICKLY!" Chebrikov dashed back into the office and loosened Yuri's belt and raised his feet with a cushion.

"Yuri, help is coming! Hold on!" Within minutes a medical team arrived and were administering to the struggling General Secretary.

He was given an injection and an oxygen mask was fitted around his face and turned on full as he was carefully lifted onto a gurney to be wheeled down to a waiting ambulance.

As they reached the door, Chebrikov by his side, Andropov struggled to lift his arm and signal to them to halt in the doorway of the lift. He managed to grasp Chebrikov's jacket and pull him into earshot. He spoke through his oxygen mask.

"Do whatever ... needs to ... be done ... to stop them!" He ordered. They rushed him into the elevator, through the lobby and out into the ambulance.

Minutes later the leader of the entire Communist world was unconscious on a forced oxygen feed, had an I.V. drip in both arms and was being rushed to hospital by his dedicated medical staff.

*

Seventy-five miles off the coast of northern Germany the U.S.S. Lexington sat at anchor in the North Sea to allow her fighter squadron to practice touch and go's, a standard airborne exercise whereby the assigned aircraft were launched, circled around and came in at recovery speed, only to touch off the deck with the arrester cables on the flight deck retracted. The aircraft would then continue out over the bow to circle back around and repeat the maneuver.

About a mile off the starboard bow a Navy Blackhawk hovered at 5,000 feet.

"Sorry Lieutenant, with that tail wind we arrived on station a little early. Looks like it's gonna be another fifteen to twenty minutes before we'll get clearance to go in." The chopper pilot spoke through to Lieutenant Harden's headset as the L.T. squatted between the pilot and co-pilot's seat in the cockpit of the Blackhawk. They had a bird's eye view of the touch and goes as the jets circled around off the port side of the flat top. Back in the passenger's compartment Danno and Ricky were reclined amongst all the commo, demo and other operational gear Task Force Romeo had carried with them.

"You guys just relax. It's gonna be a little while." Harden yelled back at them. Ricky signaled a thumbs up,

Danno with a bed roll for a pillow and his feet up on the demo locker just kept snoring.

Finally the carrier recovered the last of her aircraft and the Blackhawk was given clearance to come in.

Doc, Ray and Scarlett were on deck near the island structure to greet the L.T. and the guys as they touched down and a small work party of the ship's crew scrambled out to the bird to help offload the gear.

"So you two assholes had a little excursion in Ivan's backyard?" Ricky asked as they made their way down to the improvised briefing room below the flight deck.

"Place is like a fuckin' zombie movie!" Ray answered.

As the others filed in to the room and took their seats Scarlett pulled Harden aside.

"Are you sure you want to get involved in this? I must tell you that we have new information and we

571

strongly suspect that the Soviets have been being helped by Poul Schlüter himself."

"Who the hell is Poul Schlüter?"

"the prime Minister of Denmark."

"Jesus! You serious?"

"We've had an MI6 man on him for the last three months. The higher ups are debating on a course of action."

"Interesting." Harden answered, his hesitation obvious as he digested this latest development.

Doc, peering through the hatchway out to where the two stood, quickly picked up on Harden's situation and made a decision. Stepping back outside the compartment he came up alongside the lieutenant.

"Agent Scarlett, could we have a moment?" McKeowen requested.

"Of course." Suspicious but with no choice Scarlett agreed and stepped to the side.

"Doc –" Harden started but was cut off as Doc held up a hand.

"Sir, a good part of my job is counseling people after they get bad news. Now I'm not gonna pretend I know what it's like to be an officer-" Harden pulled back and stared at Doc.

"Funny you should bring that up Doc! How is it you got a Bachelor's of Science, 20 creds toward your Master's and you're not an officer?"

"Couldn't qualify sir."

"On what grounds?!"

"My parents are married."

"Walked into that one, didn't I?"

"Sir, I know what you're wrestling with. Given

572

your brief history in field ops and the fact that you've already pissed off most of the honchos of most of the major intel services ..."

"And not to mention I've been arrested for illegal possession of classified data!"

"And the fact that you almost triggered an international incident by losing two of your tea m behind enemy lines…"

"Get to the fucking point Doc!"

"Just want to remind you of the question you asked me a couple of weeks ago about how you're doin' with the team when we started down this Yellow Brick Road."

"Consider myself reminded. Let's get this meet underway."

"Aye aye sir." They went into the room pulled the hatch over and dogged it down.

"Agent the floor is yours." Lt. Harden took a seat.

"Thank you Lieutenant Harden. Very simply gentlemen I'm here to formally ask for your help. In turn we will get you what you first came here for. All your answers concerning Operation Ryan." Everyone exchanged glances. "All I'm asking is the opportunity to present my plan. Our plan." He had their attention. "I've had the best strategists in MI6 on this for the last 72 hours. If at the end of my little dog and pony show you're not happy, I'll forward you a full report of everything MI6 has on Ryan, you can go home and that'll be that."

"Scarlett?" It was Ray MacDonald. "Exactly how important is this little Russki?"

"Agent Gordievsky has 30 years in active service

with the KGB. He is the highest ranking individual of any Soviet agency ever to cross the fence. He is as valuable to the Allies, the U.S. as well as the U.K., as Fred Ilke would be if he defected to the Russians."

"If that cantankerous old fuck defected the whole fucking Communist Bloc would implode in a matter of weeks!" MacDonald quipped. Harden turned to Danno.

"Danno, what's the last word you got from the stateside handler?" The L.T. asked.

"The last message we have from them was the midnight commo." He reached into his pocket and came up with a folded up radio transmit. Harden, as was the rest of the team losing patience with the NSA handler and the agency's constant   delays.

"What'd they say, exactly?" Harden pushed. Byrdo exchanged glances with Doc then, as Doc was closet to Harden, handed him the decoded message to pass to the L.T. But Doc opened it and read it aloud.

"They said to go for it." Ray, instinctively realizing Doc was lying, waited to see what Harden would do. Doc handed him the message to afford Harden the chance to read the actual message. He didn't. Instead the lieutenant stared at it for a second and crumpled it up.

Just then there was a loud bang on the hatch.

"WHO?!" Scarlett yelled.

"Message for the officer in charge, sir!"

Grumbling, Scarlett undogged the hatch and opened it halfway. A ship's runner stood outside. He looked at Harden.

"Sir, the C.O. requests the O.I.C. of your group to report to the C&C on the double." Harden turned and looked at the Seaman. "I'll be there just as soon as we finish this briefing."

"Sir, you're requested to report to the bridge on the double. The Captain is waiting."

There was a brief stare-off.

"It's important sir."

"SHIT!" Dave exclaimed. "Scarlett, set up your brief ASAP. Rest of you stand-by till I see what the hell this is about." With that Harden followed the runner topside.

"Have a good time sir!" Ray called after him.

"Don't forget to write!" Ricky added.

"We'll keep a light on in the window L.T."

Top side in the C&C the C.O. was in a conference with several of his officers huddled around. He stopped talking and signaled Harden over to the small group as soon as he entered the space.

"Lieutenant Harden I have no idea what you're doing aboard my vessel, and it was made clear to me that I don't need to know. But this Twix just came in from NORATL Fleet Command. I strongly suspect it may affect your mission." The C. O. handed Dave the message.

"To: All Stations: BE ADVISED,

EFFORTS TO REVIVE POLITICAL RELATIONS W SOVIETS UNSUCCESSFUL.

EFFECTIVE AS OF 00:01HOURS, DEFCON 3

IN EFFECT. THIS IS NOT A DRILL."

**

CHAPTER TWENTY-FOUR

The Keller Residence
Smithfield, Ohio
Illinois, U.S.A.

Mrs. Keller removed the roast from the oven while her husband was glued to the television.

"They say there's people sleeping outside some of the banks in Lincoln and Madison." She called in to him as she prepared the **dinner**. "Does that mean there's gonna be a run on the banks ya think?"

"Nah! Don't worry about it. Just some old loons getting panicky." He called back.

She brought the roast in and set it on the table.

"Jim! Do we have to watch the television while we eat?!"

"I just wanna see the rest of the Six O'clock News."

"Alright but remember *Arthur* is on at seven! I wanna see it, they say it's really funny!"

He leaned in and turned up the volume on the floor model Motorola but the news broke for a commercial.

A well-groomed man in working clothes came on screen and stood in front of something covered with a large curtain

As we all know, no one can escape an atomic bomb, but there is something practical and patriotic you can do to prepare for an atomic attack! Even a

577

millionaire could not construct a completely A-bomb-proof shelter, but the average home owner can make a worthwhile refuge room right in the average basement of his own home!

He pulled a large rope and the curtain fell away to reveal a 24x10x8 foot tall, flimsy looking modular structure reminiscent of an over-sized plastic shower.

What is it you ask? Why it's the cutting edge of technology! "The Family Foxhole!" The high-tech, nuclear-bomb shelter manufactured by Ajax Survival Equipment & Shelter Systems – exclusive inventors of The Family Foxhole!

Made of solid, 100% fiberglass it folds flat for shipping, can be installed below ground in three days, and costs a third less than the equivalent in reinforced concrete! By building your Family Foxhole, you will also be building the state of mind that can resist the pressures of Communist aggression as well as the shocks of an actual atomic war!

The Family Foxhole is designed to house four or five people, but the modular units can be used individually or linked together for larger groups.

"Fucking Band-aid on a severed limb!" Mr. Keller mumbled as he sipped his bottled Budweiser. His wife quickly produced a glass and poured the remainder of his Budweiser into it, removing the bottle and taking it out to the kitchen.

Remember, no one can escape an atomic bomb, but there is something practical and patriotic that you can do! The Family Foxhole, from Ajax Survival Equipment & Shelter Systems! Call and order one today!

Out in the kitchen Mrs. Keller, overhearing the commercial, stopped spooning the hot vegetables into the serving dish and stared down into the sliced carrots. The steam rising from the veg appeared to form into a mushroom cloud. The hair on her forearms stood on end and all wet silent. She was momentarily mesmerized.

Pulling herself together she had to clear her throat before calling out.

"CHIL ... CHILDREN! SUPPER'S READY!"

*

After returning to the below decks compartment Harden was informed by the team that Scarlett's people would have a complete briefing as well as a crude sand table model ready in the C&C in one hour. Meanwhile Scarlett requested that Harden meet him in the radar tracking room. Dave had, as of late, come to trust Doc McKeowen's opinions and so asked him along as well to see what Scarlett was up to.

As the two entered the closet-sized, darkened space there was a radio operator at a small console to their left and to their front another console operator. The out-of-control Jewish-Afro, faded blue jeans and red and white Converse sneakers signaled he was a civilian. He sat at the larger of the two consoles which sported three screens, only one of which was on. The guy next to him was a petty officer radio operator. Scarlett commenced the introductions.

"Lieutenant Harden, Petty Officer McKeowen this is Mr. Bernard Horowitz. He's on loan to us from NASA." Both Doc and Harden immediately noticed the fact that Horowitz suffered from what Drill Instructors called Dunlap's Disease. Despite only being in his late twenties his belly had dun lapped over his belt.

"Actually, I'm not stationed on this boat. I'm hitching a ride while I test out some new protocols for our airborne surveillance. They figured REFORGER would be a good opportunity to play with our toys in a lot of different situations. Bill Casey said if I came across you guys I was to lend a hand if I could."

"FUCK!" Harden yelled without warning.

"What?!" Doc asked.

"When this is over, I'm gonna havt'a find a girl, fall in love, marry her, get her pregnant and hope it's a boy!"

"L.T. you been drinking?" Doc asked. "What are you babbling about a baby boy?"

"I'm gonna need a baby boy because before this thing is over I'm gonna owe that old bastard Casey my first born son!"

Horowitz leaned back in his chair and smirked as if he had just realized something.

"So, you two are part of the crazy bastards squad

huh?!"

"Excuse me?" Harden queried.

"TFR! The Fucking Renegades! The Dirty Not Quite Half Dozen!" Horowitz smirked. "There's a pool back at the agency on you guys!"

"What the fuck you talking about?" Doc prodded.

"Shit, I got a hundred bucks with a guy in Photo Analysis says you're all gonna die!"

"Thanks for the vote of confidence, asshole!" Harden protested.

"Oh don't take it personal L.T.! I got 500 bucks and a bottle of 25 year old Jameson's with some clown at the NSA says you're gonna make it."

"That's relief." Harden said. "So what's all this about Agent Scarlett?"

"Put me down for a hundred." McKeowen quickly threw out.

"Show them Bernard."

"John, please, what am I, your fucking son-in-law?! It's Bernie."

He flipped a few toggle switches, adjusted the large dial to his right and started typing on the keyboard. Screen number two sprung to life but appeared blank. "Gentlemen! If I may call your attentions to screen number three!" Bernie took a dramatic pause while the pixilated screen sorted itself out and focused. "Eyes on the ground are good. Problem is multiple real time perspectives. That's why God made Red Wagon!"

The last of the screens came into focus to reveal a shot of the flight deck amidships with the camera focused on what looked like a model airplane. They were looking at one of the first drones.

"Where in the hell you gonna find a pilot small enough to fly that thing!" Doc jibbed.

"Not that small really. It measures five foot five nose to tail!" Bernie said as he casually set into operate the console.

It's a surveillance drone.

"Why can't we rely on the reports from the Danish Intelligence Service?"

Not being known to the general population of the armed forces, much less to the general public, drones were still a mythological creature to most. Harden, being an Intel officer knew full well what they were looking at.

The ship's radio operator sitting next to them, never having seen one, slid his head set down around his neck and gradually took notice. Bernie continued the crash lesson in aerial surveillance.

"Red Wagon will tell us what's happening in real time as well as what nastiness might be on the ground in a five to six mile radius."

"Red Wagon! Like from *Citizen Shane*!" The radio guy proudly boasted.

"Yeah, ah ... no Scorsese. It's *Citizen Kane* and the secret word is 'Rosebud'! Red Wagon' is our code word for 'The Drone'."

They watched via the deck camera as the drone taxied down the flight deck, picked up speed and lifted off the foc'sal to vanish beneath the bow only to glide back up again a few seconds later. Scarlett continued to fill them in.

"The target area is Valkeakoski, Denmark. We have independently confirmed information that he's being held just outside there." Scarlett explained.

"That drone crashes within 100 miles of Valkeakoski they'll know we know and move his ass out faster than an apartment full of Gypsies in Hoboken on rent day!" Doc pointed out.

"Have you ever considered a career in literature Petty Officer McKeowen?" Scarlett casually inquired.

"Nobody reads anymore and writing doesn't pay for shit! So Bernie, give us the scoop on these drones!" Doc requested.

Bernie gleefully kicked into documentary mode.

"During the Yom Kippur War back in '73 the Soviets were supplying the Arabs with entire surface to air batteries."

"Entire S.A. batteries?" Doc questioned.

"Yeah! They really put the hurtin' on the Israeli fighter jets. Egypt and Syria were loaded with them. The U.S. had drones they were using over in Viet Nam but they were only good for surveillance and the optics were shit."

"So the Jews upped the game? Who'd a thunk it?" Doc sarcastically remarked.

"You know all those little Jewish kids you hear about always getting beat up for their lunch money in school? Well they all headed back to the Homeland during the war to lend a hand. In addition they developed and implemented real time recon and later actual target relay capability for the drones."

"Impressive!" The L.T. noted.

"They not only took out the majority of the Soviet batteries but with constant upgrading were able to completely neutralize the Syrian air defenses during the last year in the war against Lebanon." Bernie adjusted some switches and a dial on the console and the drone's on board camera kicked in to reveal a crystal clear P.O.V. facing down deck from the drone. "Result? zero pilots lost!" Bernie triumphantly announced.

"Looks like we picked the right man for the job!" Scarlett boasted as if he were personally responsible for Horowitz being there.

"You seem to know quite a bit about Jewish war history." Harden queried.

"Duh! My name is Horowitz! I have dual citizenship and Israel has been at war since it was founded. Any wonder why we know about that stuff?"

"Point taken. How'd you wind up working for us?"

"Simple, my family has developed three very important traditions over the years. Never let anybody see you eat a ham sandwich, never let your mother know you slept with a non-Jewish girl, or at least buy her a Star of David necklace to wear when she comes over for the High Holidays."

"And third?" Doc asked.

"Always fight on the winning side."

They watched the screen which now showed the drone's view as it made landfall over some coastal farms and quickly shifted altitude to what appeared to be only a few meters off the ground. A red light blinked on the console and the letters, "N.O.E. Mode" flashed in the lower left hand corner.

"I'll take her in at Nap of the Earth until we get to

the built up areas then up to about 25, 30,000 feet when she's closer to target to avoid detection."

"What's her ceiling?" Harden asked.

"Theoretically forty thou plus, but that can get a bit shaky especially if there's weather. Twenty to twenty-five though will give us what we want once over the target area but if it looks clear I'll bring her in a little closer to snoop around. Speakin'a which, this is gonna take a few hours. If you gents have other business I'll send for you when we're in the neighborhood if you want a live feed, but we'll be videotaping the area for immediate transmission and replay to NSA anyway."

"Cheers Bernie!" Scarlett nodded for them to leave.

"It's been an education Bernie!" Doc said as he patted the tech on the back then leaned into whisper in Bernie's ear.

"When you win, half that bottle's mine!"

"Deal! Just bring me back a souvenir!" They shook hands and Bernie leaned into the console to resume work.

*

The Russian Colonel was seated across the room near the doctor's table, the doctor long since gone.

A second officer, a major, came into the cabin from the outside shaking the cold off himself as he stomped his wet boots on the threshold. He didn't speak he just made for the warmth of the potbellied stove. There was a ten minute pause before either spoke.

"What do you think?" The Colonel asked nodding to Gordievsky. No longer tied to the chair Gordievsky's apparently lifeless body now lay on the cabin floor next to the steel frame of a bed. The second officer took his time lighting a cigarette on the surface of the hot stove.

"I think we are already here too long. Three days is too long. We should move him."

"Move him to where?" Puffing his cigarette the major crossed over to the prisoner, squatted down and lifted his head from the floor by his hair. Gordievsky's face was expressionless, his eyes glassed over.

"To Lubyanka, let them work on him. They will uncover if he has turned or not."

"It's possible. Still, it would be nice to crack this one of our own accord. Perhaps earn a station in some location a couple of hundred miles closer to the equator."

"He looks like shit." The major remarked as he crossed back across the room and poured himself a vodka. "So what now?"

"I suppose we can do as we like. Now that the so called 'relations' have been broken, no one will ask questions if he disappears."

"Interesting idea."

"Have them tie him up and put him on the bed then have one of the men drive into the village for some food."

"Any preferences?"

"Anything, just no more fucking whitefish! And have them bring more vodka."

CHAPTER TWENTY-FIVE

I t was nearing 13:00 when, escorted by a Marine guard, a ship's runner appeared down in the brig to rouse the men of Task Force Romeo and bring them to the Captain's private briefing compartment.

Together again as a unit for the first time in nearly a week they were pleasantly surprised at what greeted them in the briefing room.

The Commander of the U.S.S. Lexington stood at the front of the compartment, the X.O. seated next to him. Scarlett and his #2 man Saxon were seated at the conference table which had been decked out with soft drinks, plates of man-sized sandwiches and donuts.

"Jesus! Better than McDonalds!" Danno remarked as they entered the space and moved towards the chairs at the front of the table obviously reserved for them.

"Better than my mother's house!" Ricky mumbled.

"You still live with your mother?!" Danno challenged.

"Yeah! What about it?!"

"Nothin', nothin'." They took their seats up near Scarlett and Saxon. "Just think it's kind'a sweet, that's all." Danno whispered as they sat.

"Go fuck yourself!" Ricky whispered back.

Once everyone was settled in, the C.O. nodded to the Marine guard in the back who stepped out and secured the hatch behind him. The Captain opened the proceedings.

"You gentlemen can dig in, just keep the noise to a minimum we need to get this briefing underway and wrapped up so you can get all your high-speed low-drag toys together so you can go and do whatever it is the Navy pays you for."

"A humph!" Danno sat up straight and cleared his throat.

"Problem Petty Officer Byrd?" The Captain asked.

"I'm actually Army. Sir."

"As long as you're on my vessel son you're in the Navy. Consider it a promotion as well as a step up in your quality of life and status."

"Yes sir." Danno meekly replied.

"Gentlemen, in less than an hour and a half the Lex will be on station and ready for you to launch to your objective. Mr. Scarlett, all yours."

"Thank you Captain."

Bartholomew took a seat off to the side and Scarlett stepped up. With a remote control he lowered a small projector from the overhead as someone switched off the lights. A screen automatically lowered to cover the front bulk head and the overhead projector lit up.

"Jesus! We're on the starship Enterprise!" Danno commented.

"No son, you're on the U.S.S. Lex! Never forget that!" The Captain barked in the dark.

"No sir. Won't forget that."

Ricky leaned over and whispered to Danno "You're just scoring all kinds of points today, aren't you Danno!" Danno flipped him off.

The first image to come up on the screen was a slide of the European operational area.

"We are situated here in the North Atlantic currently steaming east, north east towards a point approximately here. We know we are being monitored by the Russians so we need to get you as close as possible to infill range without arousing suspicion." He switched slides to a chart which overlaid the map.

"Your infil is broken into basically three legs. Leg one is by chopper to Uppsala, Sweden here where, because of the distance, you will transferee to a fixed wing aircraft for your night drop onto the objective here in Valkeakoski on the Finnish side.

Following infill and following the effect of the recue you will move by foot to the exfil point which will be achieved by CH-53." A hand went up. "Please hold your questions." Scarlett requested.

"No sir, no question. I was just wonderin' if we could get some more cold Cokes?" Ricky asked.

Harden reached over and slapped Ricky in back of the head.

"Please continue agent Scarlett." Dave offered.

"Thank you lieutenant." The MI6 agent continued. "No idea how many Ivans you may face or what support they may have but D.I.S. have a sniper-observer team on station and report there are at least half a dozen or more on the target area. There's only one road in so remember lads, like a duck mating - in and out." Ignoring the request to hold questions, Harden broke in.

"The Danish or Swedish governments gonna get their panties in a bunch about this? I mean stomping around in their operational areas, stirring up Russkies and all?" Harden asked for the sole reason of knowing how much deeper they were heading down the rabbit hole.

"Only if they find out about it!" Scarlett smugly answered. Harden was not amused as Scarlett reached over and patted him on the back. "Don't be too concerned old Boy. That's why they call it 'plausible' deniability."

"How the hell is the Danish Intelligence Service in on the game and their higher ups aren't? I mean snipers on station with regular reports?" Harden persisted. Scarlett let out an exaggerated sigh before responding.

"In the case of the Swedes we have over flight. As for the Danes I have an old friend, works in the D.I.S., know him from the early Falkland days. One of his chaps got himself in a nasty bind over there with an Argentine woman just as hostilities broke out. We happen to have had a forward unit of SAS lads over there so ... I 'borrowed' a few to ..."

"To take care of business. I remember that incident! While we were feeding you intel about the Argentines NSA spent two weeks trying to find out who that guy was!" Harden finished. "Agent Scarlett, do you have any idea how much headache and paperwork people like you cause people like me?" Harden protested. Scarlett responded in a deliberate manner.

"With all due respect Lieutenant, you're no longer behind a desk, behind closed doors or behind friendly lines. You are, as you Americans say, 'off da porch and a runnin' wit da big dogs', as it were.

Isn't that why you lads sign up for these types of assignments in the first place? And let's don't forget that without people like me we wouldn't need people like you." An awkward quiet permeated the compartment.

Scarlett resumed the briefing indicating relevant landmarks as he spoke.

"Still don't like that pompous fuck!" Doc whispered to MacDonald as Scarlett carried on.

"We know he is being held in a small house in the south of Valkeakoski, Finland which is about 40K south of Tampere about 180K north of Helsinki. This is a 950 kilometer trip from the Borre peninsula in Denmark, which is where you will launch from for your leg two of the infill just ... here." He pointed to a spot on the map. "This is required due to the operational limitations of the aircraft available. Finally, following what I'm sure will be a textbook mission, you'll exfil here by and be returned to the *HMS Illustrious* via a second, British CH-53E Super Stallion which will have made a stopover in route to you to be fitted with fuel bladders."

"Why not back here to the Lex?" Doc asked.

"We have other priorities than to act as your personal big, grey taxi Petty Officer." The Captain jumped in. "We'll be departing station as soon as you launch off so we can support the rest of the REFORGER exercise." The Captain clarified.

"Yes sir, I only meant that we've become accustomed to the unusually high level of professionalism you have shown us that we ..."

"Stow it wise guy." The Captain cut in.

"Stowing it sir. We sincerely appreciate your accommodating us as much as you have sir."

"*Illustrious* will be in a better position by the time of your exfil and return."

"Thank you agent Scarlett." Harden interjected.

Scarlett changed slides and showed a 1 to 100 overhead of the objective area near the village of Valkeakoski, Finland.

"There's a disused football stadium here, about a klick away near the lake. The exfil Stallion will launch from *HMS Illustrious* with conventional NATO markings, covertly land just outside Uppsala on the tip of Sweden and change her markings to Soviet insignia for the ride to her staging area."

"The Russians have nothing like a Sea Stallion. They'll recognize it right away!" Danno pointed out.

"Which is why you chaps receive Hazardous Duty Pay each month."

"I wondered what that $55 a month was for. Good to know." Danno remarked. The captain shook his head.

"The CH-53 will be standing by three or four kilometers off station to the west. Due to fuel considerations this makes response time by the chopper about one and a half to two minutes to the stadium, depending on weather and visibility. I couldn't arrange a face-to-face with the CH-53 crew so let me know your preferred plan to signal the chopper to rendezvous for your exfil and I'll see that it gets to the RAF chaps."

"And the exfil point is where exactly?" Harden asked. Scarlett indicated a spot on the map near a school.

"A primary school yard, about 350 meters the other side of your objective. It's the closest spot clear enough to act as an LZ." Scarlett informed. "You'll have a secondary more detailed briefing at the second launch point with more updated information regarding weather, the aircraft and any significant developments which have transpired before you mount up for the drop. Questions, comments snide remarks anyone?"

"Yeah, I got one." Doc raised his hand.

"Yes Petty Officer McKeowen?"

"The KGB aren't exactly known for their warm-hearted compassion."

"And your point is?"

"If you got it right this time and your asset is there –"

"He's there!"

"... and things didn't exactly go his way, you want us to bring back the body?" Scarlett made no attempt to mask his anger as he ignored the question and changed subjects by going directly to the next topic.

"Captain Bartholomew has kindly had an area cordoned off on the port side of the hanger deck for your exclusive use to prep for the mission. Mr. Scarlett will have a sand table set up for you by that time. That'll be all." Scarlett had a p.s. as the team stood to leave. "And gentlemen, Her Majesty thanks you for what you are about to do."

As everyone filed out through the hatch the C.O. called over to the L.T.

"Lieutenant Harden." Bartholomew called over.

"Sir?"

"A minute." He motioned Harden aside out of earshot.

"Keep an eye on those clowns of yours. They come off as a bunch of immature assholes but I suspect they're good men."

"There's a reason they're rated as the top one tenth of the top one percent of the military sir."

"No doubt. At any rate, I just want to say, bring them back in one piece. The Navy is always short of those kinds of individuals."

"Thank you sir. I will."

"And Lieutenant Harden?"

"Sir?"

"Kick some Russki ass!"

"Aye aye sir." As they shook hands Harden distinctly felt a twinge of envy in Bartholomew's voice at not being able to go along.

Less than fifteen minutes later, with Marine guards posted in a wide semi-circle to act as a perimeter, Task Force Romeo were in a forward corner of the hanger deck, preparing for their second rescue attempt.

As he packed his ruck sack Lt. Harden noticed Scarlett approaching from the side.

"Lieutenant Harden, I want you to know-"

"How much you appreciate us doing this and we're all invited to tea and cakes with the Queen when we get back?"

"Not quite. I just want you to know that if there's ever anything-" With a hand on his shoulder Dave cut him off.

"Rest assured Agent Scarlett, as soon as we're all back with Comrade Gordievsky, one way or the other, you'll be running interference for us with the NSA, the CIA, Naval Intelligence and the White House. That will be appreciation enough."

"I get the picture Lieutenant. The key to success in this business is always having a trump card up your sleeve. Not to worry. I'll grease the skids before you're even back."

"I'm gonna have to hold you to that John."

"You do that David. Now just to show my undying support ..." He signaled across the deck to Saxon and a British soldier standing by who then came over to the two. "In England when one gives a dinner party it is customary to bring a little something. Usually the wine, but in this case ..." Saxon entered the Marine perimeter carrying a small chest with an SAS man in a kilt directly behind him dragging a large, footlocker styled container.

"I brought you some toys. The small black crate is assorted demo and ammo while a full array of electronics is in the big black case. This is Sgt. Campbell of Two Para, he'll see to any questions or help you need with the equipment."

Campbell smiled and nodded to Harden.

"Additionally, I've arranged with the ship's armorer to provide anything you might need in the way of ordnance and ammo."

"Appreciate that Scarlett."

"Petty Officer McKeowen, is there anything you need?"

"Negative Mr. Scarlett. Haven't really dug into my med kit yet so I'm pretty well stocked but, anything I need I can commandeer from the ship's sick bay."

Saxon and the SAS man opened and started to unpack the crates as Harden turned and leaned into the four foot square table in the corner supporting the rough scale model Saxon had thrown together while the team were in the briefing.

"Scarlett, I need to know that we're sure this time. I need to know he's there."

"Red Wagon has had eyes on target on and off since yesterday. Before that Danish Intel Service infilled a two man sniper team into the area who have been camped out there in the woods for three days."

"Yes, you mentioned them earlier. Impressive!"

"It's they who first got us word he was there." Packing their gear in the back ground Danno and Ricky overheard the conversation.

"This guy Scarlett's got his shit together!" Ricky commented to Danno.

"He apparently has connections with every security service in Europe. Wouldn't surprise me if he was honcho of MI6 this time next year next." Danno shot back.

"Handy friend to have when you need him."

"Will the two Dane's be available after we infil?" Harden continued with Scarlett.

"That's up to them. They're completely autonomous but your man has their freqs so you can establish commo when you land. Their call sign is 'Sam and Dave'. Yours is 'the Beatles'."

"Hey guys, bring it in, let's have a look at the sand table." Harden instructed. Ray called over as he made his way over.

"Sir what's our call sign?" MacDonald asked.

"Apparently we are the Beatles. You get to be Ringo."

"But there's five of us! Can't we be the Rolling Stones? Ya know, we keep movin', keep rollin'? That sort'a thing?"

"Rockin'! I like that!" Ricky added.

"What about Agent Scarlett?" Danno asked. "What's his call sign, sir?"

"Tom Jones."

"Very sexy!" Ricky remarked.

"Oh please Lieutenant Harden, can't we be the Rolling Stones?! Please, please, pretty please with sugar on top?!" Ray MacDonald pleaded like a child.

"Danno as soon as we're done here get on the radio checks and coordinate with Sgt Campbell for compatibility with his long range gear. And I suppose the new call signs." Ray, Danno and Ricky cheered and did a happy dance. The Marine guards stared and shook their heads.

"I'm about to go on my first real world mission behind the lines with a bunch of freakin' five year olds!" Harden whined in mocked frustration.

Suddenly he felt part of the team.

They turned their attention to the model, a match box represented the single story cabin structure and sat center table. It was surrounded by fields with a tree break off to the west and a school house to the east. There was a crudely labeled river, some hedges and a low fence surrounding the cabin on all four sides. A sheet of paper marked 'football stadium' was taped a distance on the other side of the school house.

"Danno you and Ricky will set security here and here. Doc and I will go in through the front door as soon as Ray is in position here acting as over watch then back-up."

"Got it."

"Ray don't move till you hear the all clear. If you don't hear it 10-15 seconds after we're in, you're Doc Holliday at that's the O.K. Corral! Get the picture?"

"In Technicolor L.T.!"

"At that point Danno you and Ricky will approach from the left flank, Doc you and I are going in through the front door from the south at an angle as close as we can get before we're detected."

"Knock, knock!" Doc muttered as he packed a third I.V. kit into his M-1 med bag.

"What about a possible roving patrol?"

"Agent Scarlett's provided us with two silences. Ray and Danno, one each. You see a guard and we haven't gone in yet take him out."

"Doc you'll open the door by whatever means required, but if we get that close I suspect it won't be locked. If it is rig yourself a C4 charge in the bird on the way over to use on the lock and knob mechanism before we touch down. As soon as it blows Doc and I will initiate with two stun grenades. Everybody moves on the first grenade. Doc you go high, I'll go low as soon as the second grenade fires. No one but Doc and I will fire inside the house. Doc shoot low unless you can visualize a confirmed enemy target. We fuck up and hit Gordievsky at least we won't kill him."

"That mean everything outside the structure is fair game sir?" Danno asked.

"Free fire zone Danno!" Danno grabbed three more magazines from the ammo case.

"One day's beans and 3 days bullets only!" Harden ordered.

"A.G.S. route sir?" Doc asked. Scarlett looked puzzled. Ricky leaned over and whispered a clarification to Scarlett.

"All Goes to Shit route. A plan if the chopper doesn't show."

"All Goes to Shit! How quaintly American." Scarlett replied.

"A.G.S. is to maintain radio silence for twenty-four hours, E&E to rally point Zebra, here at this factory about eight klicks to the west." He indicated on the sat photo Scarlett had provided.

"Sir."

'Doc?"

"He might not be able to walk. In that event we're gonna have to be prepared to carry him the eight klicks. Just putting that out there."

"Good call Doc! In that event we'll shift gear around and take turns at one klick intervals. Clear?" Harden issued.

Everyone nodded.

"Agent Scarlett, our alternate exfil will be twenty-four hours later at a point in the vicinity of the factory TBD pending a sit rep from us. In the event we haven't established commo with you in that period tell the exfil aircraft to look for IR strobe, Morse signal by red Maglite or as a last resort red smoke.

"Questions, comments snide remarks? MacDonald?"

"As the only SEAL here I'd just like to tell you guys ... I've worked with better operators."

They waited for it as McDonald smirked. "But not many!" He added.

****

Special Operations life is traditionally marked by long periods of boredom highlighted by moments of sheer terror. The CH-53 ride that evening was long, uneventful and full of boredom. They eventually touched down just before 22:30 in a remote field just outside Guldborg on the Berre peninsula in Denmark.

After the team disembarked the chopper lifted off again into the dark and turned back west. From the tree line a young Danish man in civilian clothes appeared from the dimly lit field and greeted them in a heavy accent.

"Which one of you is ranking officer please?"

"I'm Lieutenant Harden."

"I am Oversergent Poul Hagen, Jæger Korpset Regiment, Danish Special Forces temporarily attached to the Intelligence Service."

"Good to meet you Oversergent." Following behind the two as they headed off the LZ Doc leaned over to Ray.

"Shit Mac, looks like we're in the wrong navy!"

"How's that?"

"He looks like he's just out of high school and

already outranks us!"

"Yeah, maybe. But I bet he can't do this!" Mac formed an oval shape with his mouth and flicked his cheek with a finger making a dripping sound.

The Danish SEAL led them through a wind break of trees and up to a single story farm house adjoining a barn where they entered through the rear door. Inside they grounded their gear to the side and took seats around the kitchen table.

"Our sniper team is still in place and will cover your landing and entry into the target house. I have a good description of the operational area for you to include some recent infrared photos." An old woman in a house coat and slippers came into the room and he spoke Russian to her.

"She's Russian?" Doc asked.

"Ukrainian. This is her house." Hagen informed.

"How many languages do you speak?" Danno asked.

"Only five. Not counting Danish of course."

"Of course!" Mac echoed. "Wrong fucking navy!" He mumbled.

"Thank her for us." Harden suggested.

"No need. She is being paid, paid well. Besides, she hates the Soviets."

The old woman, who looked as though she had been around since the 1917 Revolution, nodded and shuffled to the stove to tend whatever was cooking. Hagen continued his brief.

"You will have approximately one hour here to prepare your gear or make any last minute checks you require before the aircraft arrives. Your chutes, oxygen tanks and masks are in route with the aircraft. Launch time is zero two forty-five." The old woman spoke to Hagen. "She says there is hot fish soup and some bread if you would like it." The large plate of bread the old woman placed on the table didn't stand a chance once the plate hit the table. A steaming tureen of fish stew followed and twenty minutes later the team members had forgotten that in less than a few hours they might all be casualty statistics.

With all the last minute gear checks already completed there was nothing left to do but wait.

They had only briefly enjoyed the imposed serenity when MacDonald suddenly became attentive to a dull roar outside.

"How far's the airfield?" Harden asked.

"About four or five meters." Hagen answered which drew a puzzled look from the Lieutenant.

"I think I hear the airplane approaching." Ray said as he looked up from where he was sitting by the window. "Hey boys ..." Mac parted the curtains and peered out onto the road as the dull rumble grew louder. "... taxi's here!"

"Sounds like a truck engine to me!" Dave countered as he came across the parlor and peered out the window. "It's a fucking tractor trailer!"

"That's what a Bronco sounds like." Mac reassured him as he too looked outside and spied the dark blue trailer truck with removable side rails lettered in large white letters.

'Christianson Long Distance Furniture Haulage'.

"Before you put it together!" Ray the quintessential adrenaline junkie, smiled in anticipation of the upcoming operation as he rose and went outside. He was quickly followed by the rest of the team.

"Fucking impressive!" Doc grinned as he perused the truck pulling up on the side of the two lane, macadam road being led by a black Land Rover.

Ignoring any pretext at formalities a burley, middle-aged man climbed down out of the passenger's seat of the Rover, signaled his five man team with some orders and started directing them as they got out of the tractor trailer.

"No sense wasting time on introductions I guess!" Harden said.

"They must be on the clock!" Doc suggested.

"One question. Where's the runway?" Harden queried.

"You're standing on it son." The burly man retorted as he approached the guys standing in front of the house. "Who's the honcho here?"

"I am."

"Bring your men inside and I'll give you the skinny." He directed in the slightest of Scandinavian accents as he grabbed a parachute from the bed of the trailer and headed in the door.

Mesmerized by a sight none of them had actually seen before, they stood as the man's crew opened the trailer truck and got to work.

The huge, canvas side flaps of the trailer were the first to be peeled back revealing the O.D. green fuselage of an OV-10 Bronco with the twin stabilizer strapped to the top. The single overhead wing was flat on the deck of the trailer underneath and beside the fuselage. One of the crew stopped work and yelled over to the spectators in front of the house.

"It's gow'n take us better part of coupl'a hours ta get this puppy ta'gether. Best if you all go inside and listen up on the Chief!" Unsure if they were fluent in Hillbilly or not he stared at them awaiting their reaction. They didn't move. "Gown now! Scat, scat!"

Harden shook his head as they piled back through the front door and into the parlor where the chief was waiting for them.

"This just keeps getting better and better!" He swore. "Now I'm about to go on my first real world mission behind the lines with a bunch of five year olds in a model airplane assembled by the cast of *Deliverance*!"

Inside they formed a semi-circle around the big burley guy in jeans, red flannel shirt and brown leather flight jacket.

"My name is Chief Warrant Officer Stokes, U.S.N., Retired. I'll be your briefing officer on this little cross border excursion as well as your pilot. And no, there will not be an in-flight movie!"

"I love this guy! Saw him at the Sands in Vegas last year." Ray whispered to Doc. Stokes continued.

"First things first. Your limo for tonight is a little number I helped design back during Nam and have been pushing for the Navy to use ever since. We borrowed this particular one from the U.S.S. Nassau out in the North Sea. It's an OV-10 Bronco. She

604

takes a crew of two, has an air speed of 460 klicks per hour with a maximum effective range of 2,224 klicks at a ceiling of about 9000 meters. She's got a twenty foot wing span and can be airborne with a fifty foot clearance at 500 feet. So L.T. soon as we're done here I'm gonna need two'a yaw men ta grab that tape measure over there, start out by that big oak up the road on the left and mark me off four hundred fifty, four hundred seventy-five and five hundred feet with the white stakes them boys outsides got fer ya."

"Danno, Ricky?" Harden called.

"Got it sir." Danno nodded back.

"Additionally, you'll be jumping captured Soviet chutes for your HALO in ..." He opened the carrier bag of the chute. "You'll know from your basic jump course what this is, affectionately known as a dial-a-death release."

He held up the body harness of a chute where all the canvas straps converged on the center chest strap and were connected by a four inch silver disc with a similar spring loaded cover plate all held in place by a flimsy 'C' clip.

"Your little excursion is just short of 900 klicks so that means your ride time will be about two hours. It ain't gonna be all that comfortable but we'll get you there on time and on station." Harden leaned over to Doc and asked a question.

"What's a HALO?"

"High Altitude Low Opening." Doc pulled back but tried not to attract attention as he shot back in a low whisper. "L.T., you never HALO'ed?"

"I'm assuming you've all jumped Broncos

before?" Stokes threw out to the team.

"I haven't but I'm familiar with the required protocol." Doc volunteered.

"Same here." MacDonald added. Danno and Ricky also nodded.

Harden meekly raised his hand.

"You've never jumped a Bronco Lieutenant?" Stokes asked.

"No sir. Not exactly."

"What have you jumped besides 130's or 141's sir? I mean what small aircraft?" Stokes pushed.

"Ahh ... not too many aircraft, that is not too many different kinds of aircraft, Chief."

"Well, 123's, choppers? Which ones **have** you jumped?"

"Ahh ..."

"Lieutenant, exactly how many jumps you got altogether, I mean counting HAHO, HALO and static?"

"Including this one?" Hardin stalled.

"Well, yeah if it makes a difference." The Chief pushed.

"Ahhh ... one."

Everyone turned and stared at Harden.

"Ballsy move!" Danno whispered to Mac who nodded in agreement.

"You mean you've only done one HALO?"

"No Chief I mean this is my first jump. Ever." The Chief cocked his ball cap back and stared at Harden.

"Well fuck me Alice!" Stokes blurted out.

"Hey Chief, you from Jersey?!" Doc asked.

"Don't sweat it Chief! We'll sort him out."

MacDonald interjected with a hand on Harden's shoulder.

"If you say so. Getting back to the subject at hand. As you know due to its limited airspeed when fully loaded, combined with the fact you can't stand up in the cargo bay, the OV-10 has a unique delivery technique ..."

"Chief, we'll sort him out on the details! Trust us." Doc insisted. Suddenly, the more they spoke, the more Harden felt trust evaporating from his mind.

Both Doc and Ray along with Ricky and Danno knew about the Bronco's method of jumper delivery. Only Dave was in the dark. But only for the next couple of hours.

"Okay. Questions? None? Then let's get this road on the show! Chute up, rig ya gear and let's take us an airplane ride!"

Doc took advantage of the break when Stokes ducked outside to check on the assembly process and pulled Harden aside out of earshot. Danno and Ricky took the tape measure and went out to the road to pace-off the stakes.

"L.T., what the fuck?! You must be this tall to ride this ride!" Doc declared with no attempt to hide his shock. "I mean I get the balls angle, wantin' ta get on the teams and all that, but we're dealing with a somewhat technical skill here!"

"Doc, what the fuck am I gonna do cancel the mission because I never jumped before? Hell even you jumped for the first time once!"

"Yeah, after four weeks of training, gear rigging classes, about a hundred parachute landing falls, tower training and five practice jumps ..."

"Stow it! I'm not only on this mission I'm, the honcho!"

"So what'a ya gonna do, order me to keep your ass alive?!"

Despite his macho attempt Harden was embarrassed by his current situation.

"SHIT! Sorry Doc. Just that ..."

"Fuck that! May I respectfully suggest a new stick order, sir?"

The Lieutenant nodded and Doc continued.

"Mac goes out last, you're in front of him and I'm in front of you. Danno and Ricky lead out. Danno's a good navigator, he can guide us in on his compass. At least you'll have some kind'a chance with two of us babysitting you on the way down."

"What else?" He asked.

"We'll double check your gear after you chute up and I'll show you how to release your pack once you hit 100 feet off the deck."

"Okay."

"Maintain a hard arch on exit no matter what. You'll tumble forward on the exit but don't surrender your arch, you'll stabilize quickly. Keep centered on me, that is keep aimed at me buy steering with your body like a kite. When you're ready to deploy, maintain position, left arm over your head like this ..." He demonstrated. " ... grab the drogue chute firmly, which will be in your right cargo pocket, yank it out quickly and forcefully throw it out and well clear, then resume your arch. Then check your canopy and man your toggles. After that watch me."

"What about steering?"

"Don't worry about it. If Danno gets us where we need to be, he'll signal when to deploy so hang time should be less than thirty seconds. If you're facing away from the pack yank down on one off your toggles and you'll turn a 180. Then hold fast."

Doc finished just as MacDonald, who was already chuted up, with his pack strapped to his front drifted over and addressed Doc.

"Did you go over the OV-10 exit tech –" Mac was cut off as Doc interrupted him.

"The bird about ready?" He blurted out. Ray picked up on the fact that Doc still hadn't explained the unique exit technique of that particular aircraft.

"You got anything you wanna add MacDonald?!" Harden challenged.

"No sir. Don't believe in taking cheap shots." Mac extended his hand and they shook as he spoke. "I just wanted to say that I have a new found respect for your courage, dedication and loyalty to the mission. I know how important this little Russian guy is and if you're willing to do a HALO into Ivan's backyard never having jumped before, well, good on ya sir!"

"That's it?"

"That's it L.T."

"Well thank you Petty Officer MacDonald that means a lot to   me."

"You're entirely welcome Lieutenant Harden. And I hope to see you on the Teams one day."

"Thank you!"

"Just one question sir."

"Yeah what?"

"If you burn in on infil, can I have that watch? I mean that's a really cool watch. Looks expensive too! I bet I'd get a lotta pussy with that watch."

"Go fuck yourself MacDonald!"

Outside the aircraft had been assembled and the Chief along with his co-pilot were strapped into the cockpit and firing up the engines.

Harden thanked Oversergent Hagen and the old woman and joined the team out by the aircraft as the vehicles were pulled off the road and parked around back.

They passed under the twin stabilizers and boarded the short ramp, with Mac the first in followed by Harden then Doc with Ricky and Danno in last. They took their seats on the deck facing the ramp with one of the assembly crew acting as a guide to get them seated in a tight row, their legs straddling each other with their rucksacks pressed into the lower back of the man in front.

When they were settled in Doc produced a small, black plastic film container from his cargo pocket, popped the top and started passing out small white pills to the team. The L.T., sitting with his back to MacDonald who was against the cockpit firewall, saw him passing a two to MacDonald before Doc offered two to him.

"What's this?" Harden asked gazing at the little white tablets in his palm.

"White crosses, bennies."

"White what?"

"Speed, keeps ya awake without giving you the shakes."

"I'm not sleepy." Harden protested handing them

back. Doc ignored him.

"Pop one just after take-off. It's a long flight and you're gonna get stiff and sleepy. They'll kick in just before jump time. More importantly, keep ya alert after we hit the ground."

One of the crew did a last minute walk through checking positions and gear as he passed down the narrow space on the side of the stick of jumpers, stepped out off the ramp, waved bye-bye and secured the hatch. The team heard him pound twice on the fuselage, and the engines revved to full. They felt the aptly named Bronco buck at the power surge and suddenly blast down the country road turned combat runway.

It seemed only seconds before they tilted 30+ degrees nose up and lifted off into the night.

"Hey Ricky, guess you get your wish." Doc called forward as they leveled off ten minutes later.

"How's that Doc? You got Raquel Welch on the DZ waitin' for me?"

"Better than that. You finally get to infill with me."

"I got a chubby Doc!" Ricky yelled back.

"Hey L.T., you okay? Lookin' a little pale." MacDonald asked.

Harden just sat back against Mac's pack and closed his eyes, trying not to be sick to his stomach. The co-pilot leaned back through the hatch and tapped Mac on the shoulder.

"Everybody doing okay?"

"Hey, lieutenant, pilot wants to know if you're okay?"

"Ask him if we're gonna make it in this toy or is

611

the rubber band gonna break halfway there?" Harden answered.

"Better off in a small aircraft, flying N.O.E. Impossible to spot on radar." Ray explained.

"What the fuck is N.O.E.?" Harden yelled back to MacDonald.

"Nap of the Earth. We fly low level, along the contours of the earth. Keeps us under their radar screen."

Just then the plane took a three to five second nose dive before leveling off again.

"Like that." Ray said.

"That why I ... already wanna ... puke?" From a pocket on the side hatch Doc handed back an air sickness bag.

"We're in good shape as long as we don't have to ditch." Ray continued as he tapped the L.T. on the back.

"Why? Can't these things ditch?" Harden asked as he held the bag tight to his mouth and upchucked some of his fish soup into it.

"Oh yeah, they can ditch alright. Dozens of them have ditched over the years."

"Then what's the ... YAAAK ... hang up?" He asked wiping his mouth.

"No one's ever survived a ditch." Ray said.

"YAAAK! Good to know." Danno turned and leaned back to Ricky from in front of Doc.

"What'd he just say?" Ricky shrugged as he answered.

"Said it should be okay."

"SHOULD BE?! WHAT THE FUCK YOU MEAN, 'SHOULD BE'?"

"Go back to sleep Danno, I'll wake ya at the next rest stop."

For the next hour and a half the flight was uneventful.

Finally, up forward in the cockpit Chief Stokes checked his altimeter and his radar then began to drop altitude. Shouting over the dull roar if the engines Doc continued Harden's crash tutorial.

"Once in the air keep your eyes on my right foot, maintain your distance but don't let me get any smaller than about two palms width. I'll signal before I pull, as soon as I do you pull. Green?"

"Green! Hey Doc, how we gonna jump if we can't stand up?" Dave asked as he wiped his mouth again and sealed the air sickness bag.

"Take too long to explain. If you're done puking get your O2 on."

"Well what about ..."

All eyes turned to the starboard side of the plane over the ramp as the red light came on. Danno, first near the ramp, yelled over his shoulder and gave the hand signal.

"THIRTY SECONDS!" The command was repeated as it was passed back along the stick.

The lights in the cargo hold went out and the rear hatch slowly opened to reveal a sprinkling of white specks along the distant horizon which interrupted an otherwise inky black canvas. Simultaneously as the ramp lowered to just below deck level the aircraft picked up speed.

"Hey Doc!"

"Yeah L.T.?!"

"I burn in you can have the watch. Just don't give

it to MacDonald!"

"Fuck him! If he wants it let him dig through the goo!"

The red light started to flash.

"Get ready L.T." Doc instructed as he tapped Hardin on the leg.

"But –"

Suddenly the red light went off, the green light came on and the aircraft pulled into a straight up, 90 degree climb at full throttle.

Like the last five cookies in a cylindrical can the TFR team slid silently out of the Bronco and into the black of night.

Silently, except for Lieutenant Harden's blood curdling scream which Doc and Mac thought drowned out the twin engines of the aircraft for a full ten seconds.

As if on cue the men gradually drifted from each other, assumed their hard arches, and floated into a loose diamond formation with Danno on point as he scanned the ground and spotted the tiny, pea-sized stadium off to their right.

****

CHAPTER TWENTY-SIX

Vicinity of Hotel Saint-Gilles
Brussels, Belgium
Vicinity of NATO Headquarters

Sitting out on the tenth floor balcony of a city center apartment pretending to read a newspaper, operative #5 watched as a two door limo approached the hotel entrance across the boulevard and pulled up to the door. With a pair of opera glasses he quickly and covertly scanned the rear licence plates.

"He's on the move!" He said in Russian to #3 who had just sat down to eat inside. #3 reached across the table and manned a large hand held walkie-talkie and spoke in English.

"You're up."

"I am under it!" Responded the other voice. #3 looked out to #5 who smirked and shook his head.

"It's 'on it! I am on it! You Ukrainian farmer!" #3 yelled back into the radio.

Seconds later as the limo pulled out into traffic so did a Belgian taxi from the underground parking facility in the block of flats across the boulevard.

Team A composed of Operatives #3 and #5, assigned to cell Bloodhound, were not run-of-the-mill operatives. Both had been pulled from the ranks of the highly skilled SPETNAZ only three weeks earlier. Their assignment was considered among the most critical of *Operation Ryan*.

As setting up direct surveillance on NATO

Headquarters itself was far too risky as well as impractical, they had been posing for the last ten days as Alaskan fur traders and were camped out in an upscale flat across the boulevard from the Hotel Saint-Gilles. Aside from being the pleasant duty afforded them by virtue of their seniority and rank, they were considered a lynch pin in Andropov's overall plan. What they observed and reported would directly affect his course of action.

Maintaining the tail was no problem in late evening traffic and once out of the city on a rural stretch of the A10 the taxi could drop back and keep his distance but when, about twenty minutes outside the capital, the limo took a sudden right turn off the motorway the fake taxi driver was caught off guard and overtook the exiting limo. Nearly causing a pile up, he crossed over the grass median and raced back to the adjoining exit.

Crossing back under the motorway he was shocked to see the limo, now minus any passengers, coming the other way heading back into the city.

Following his instincts he kept to the spur road rather than follow the empty limo. He got lucky.

200 metres ahead just off the dirt road, he spotted an O.D. green military station wagon with what appeared to be two or three officers in the back. His curiosity piqued, he dropped back and followed them through the hilly terrain northwest along the A10 spur road to what appeared to be a bunker facility just outside the village of Opwijk.

From a safe distance, through a pair of binos he watched as the three U.S. officers were let out of the vehicle and now joined by four others two German and two Belgians, were escorted across a short field to an underground bunker complex the Soviets had not known about despite their small stable of their double agents.

Twenty minutes later the taxi driver was at a roadside restaurant and on the phone back to his handlers in the city flat.

After having been compelled to confirm what he had seen three times, #'s 3 and 5 entered into a ten minute argument about how to word the flash message to their Cell Chief who in turn passed it on to his HVA handlers out in the border region.

Back in Moscow contingency plans for this exact scenario had been drawn up a year prior. Following Andropov's urgent plea to the Politburo when he told them that the Allies would attack and that it was only a matter of time, several steps were taken. Amongst them was a plan to deploy up to 2,500 extra operatives into Western Europe to insure that the Soviets had adequate warning of exactly when and where the Allies had planned to launch their first attack.

In the event of an actual, verified emergency, the HVA were prepared to launch reinforcements of additional operatives of up to two thousand personnel into the field to pre-assigned areas across the continent with orders to get to their respective sites, hunker down and wait to report movements.

Within an hour of Bloodhound's reported observation those HVA agents were being mobilized.

The day after Chebrikov visited Andropov in the hospital the first of the reports of increased activity started to flow into HVA headquarters then on to Lubyanka. Now with senior officers heading for underground bunkers there could be little doubt of NATO's game plan.

Somehow, despite the overwhelming number of Soviet operatives blanketing Western Europe, the extra agents being deployed and the fact that the Communists had more than one senior infiltrator actually employed inside NATO Headquarters, they had missed the fact that it was the first day of the *Operation Able Archer* phase of the REFORGER '83 war games, the names and dates of which were not classified, frequently used in the open and so should have been known to the Soviets.

***

Colonel Chebrikov didn't wait for the elevator but took the stairs two at a time to get to the second floor. Walking at a brisk pace he was shocked to see Yuri's wife out in the corridor beside Andropov's hospital room.

"Tatyana is he alright?!" The distressed, slender woman was on the verge of tears as she looked back at the colonel.

"I don't know, they won't let me in." He crumpled the piece of paper he held and put a hand on her shoulder.

"I'll talk to them." He assured her. She smiled through teary eyes. He restrained himself as he entered the large room, glanced at the two nurses and then at the doctor making an entry into his friend's chart.

"You'll have to excuse us." Chebrikov demanded more than announced. They three acknowledged, stopped their activities and filed out of the room. He moved to Yuri's bedside and sat.

"Yuri?" He quietly spoke.

"Viktor!" They embraced.

"Are they treating you well?"

"No drinking, no red meat. What do you think?"

"You'll be out of here in no time, back at your desk and then we'll have a drink and a steak together."

"Don't bullshit a bullshitter! I'll be dead by the end of the month, if not the end of the week!"

"Comrade General Secretary, you mustn't ..."

"Give it to me."

"What?"

"The bad news you came over here with." Chebrikov smoothed out the paper as best he could then offered it to Yuri.

"This was sent out three hours ago." Chebrikov reported.

After nearly two decades at Lubyanka Andropov recognized the KGB flash message as Chebrikov held it out to him and it was with fear, anger, contempt and a guarded sense of gratification that he spoke his next words to Chebrikov.

"I don't have my glasses, read it, please."

Viktor took it and read aloud.

"To all operatives; we believe the predicted 7-10 day window has commenced. Any and all information regarding enemy movement should be reported immediately. Bypassing of all intermediary channels is authorized. We believe the enemy have made the decision to attack. NATO forces should now be considered to be at DEFCON 2."

There was a long silence before Andropov spoke.

"Increase alert status to High, move the forward deployed units to within ten kilometers of the predetermined battle line markers and have all navy and air units on full alert within the next 48 hours."

Chebrikov slowly folded the message and pocketed it. He took Yuri's hand and kissed him on the cheek and left without speaking. Out in the hallway, out of sight of Tatyana, he flagged down a passing doctor.

"Do you know who I am?"

"Yes Comrade Chebrikov! Of course!"

"Did you know that the Spring thaw doesn't reach Upper Siberia until mid-June. Sometimes early July?"

"I... I didn't realize ... I never knew that, Comrade Chairman." The puzzled doctor stammered back.

"The General Secretary's wife will be admitted to his room at any and all times she wishes. She will be allowed to bring him anything he wishes. Do you understand me?"

"Yes Comrade Chebrikov! Of course comrade Chebrikov!"

"I would like to ring my wife. Where's the nearest private phone?"

"Please, you may use my office, Comrade Colonel! I'll see that you're not disturbed. If you need –" Chebrikov walked away in mid-sentence.

CHAPTER TWENTY-SEVEN

With a full moon over their left shoulders Task Force Romeo were grateful for the partially cloudy sky as Danno steered them through the dark, navigating with the only useable landmark, a flashing red aircraft warning light atop a radio tower about seven klicks northeast of the objective. As they approached their target at nearly 120 miles per hour from the southwest, they were confident that Danno would get them in close enough to do a low pull and minimize their hang time. With this in mind each man focused intently on their point man as they mentally rehearsed how the plan was to unfold once back on earth.

Finally, at about 5000 feet Danno signaled, veered slightly south and carefully scanned the landscape below through the minimal ambient light as ground rush increased significantly.

Suddenly all the plans based on the improvised sand table Saxon had so painstakingly assembled for them back on the U.S.S. Lex went to shit.

At about two thousand feet, just as he let go his drogue to deploy his main canopy Danno looked down and spotted the target building a thousand meters out. Scanning the perimeter he spotted one of the SPETNAZ guards looking directly up through the sights of his Kalashnikov drawing a bead on the falling cluster of jumpers.

Danno scrambled to unstrap his CAR 15 from his side just as his canopy deployed above him but there wasn't enough time before the opening shock pulled him back, jerked the weapon from his hand and left it dangling from its pack strap.

Danno's life passed before his eyes.

He thought he saw a brief flash of light in the distance out of the corner of his right eye but then, nothing. Nothing happened, no report of a shot, no apparent damage to his body and a quick glance around showed four other dark canopies in a tight cluster, fully deployed. The Russian sentry had simply vanished.

Less than a minute later the team was on the ground, the chutes had been hastily piled up, covered by a thin layer of brush and the team were assembled in patrol position carefully and swiftly moving towards the cabin which lay just over 600 meters away on the other side of a lightly wooded area.

As they swiftly and quietly swept forward through a small clump of trees Harden, now on point, halted and pointed down to a dark lump in a small clearing. The others carefully approached and looked down at a crumpled corpse, a Kalashnikov lovingly cradled in its arms. Danno glanced down at what was left of the former soldier. The head appeared to have been ripped violently ninety degrees to the right but the eyes were wide open on what used to be the side of the head, peering straight up at the sky and closer together than normal as they floated in a dark pile of bone splinters and mushy brain matter. They still appeared to register shock.

"I swear it looked like that evil fuck smiled when he looked up at me!" Danno whispered.

"Well, now he just looks like a dead flounder." Ricky said over Danno's shoulder.

"His head exploded from the inside out!" Doc informed.

"Looks like our Danish snipers got the word." Harden threw in realizing full well, as did the others, this meant that it was now public information that there was a sniper acting as over watch in the neighborhood.

They resumed patrol formation and moved on.

"Hey L.T., what do Danes drink?" Danno whispered.

"Who the fuck knows, why?"

"Cause whatever it is I'm gonna buy them a fucking case of it!"

As they came within one hundred meters of the cabin reality again struck. Two man patrols in the immediate vicinity could be seen on either side and through the windows of the cabin movement of more than one body inside could be discerned. The number of occupants of the building was impossible to determine as the small windows had been partially blocked with translucent curtains.

At least three separate two man patrols were spotted at various distances around the perimeter and suddenly something occurred to Doc. If this particular dance was for couples only, where was the dead sentry's dance partner?

With the objective more heavily guarded than expected, the decision to abort never crossed anyone's mind as Ray made eye contact with each in turn, smiled and whispered.

"Time to make the donuts!" He silently lit off

into the darkness across the right flank of the objective.

As per plan Ray made a wide arch to the right to come up behind the back of the structure while Danno and Ricky took the left flank and moved out about 150 meters through the trees before turning 90 degrees and creeping forward.

Doc and the L.T. crouched behind a cluster of small trees to allow time for the flanking attackers to assume position before giving the signal which would be the two of them selecting targets and initiating fire.

Just then they spotted another patrol of three Soviets coming out of the woods on the far side of the cabin.

"That makes it close to a dozen I figure." Harden whispered as they crouched behind a tall pile of split logs.

"Nice!" Doc whispered back. Harden gave him a puzzled look. "A target rich environment!" Doc clarified.

Harden made a last minute adjustment to his gear, signalled and they moved out until they were fifty to sixty meters apart. Due to the uneven terrain the L.T. was soon slightly forward of Doc.

Without warning the missing SPETZNAZ sentry made himself known as, knife in teeth, he dropped from a tree onto Doc knocking the wind out of him and both of them to the ground. Banking on Doc not wanting to break silence, he managed not to arouse Harden's attention in the process as the L.T. was now eighty to ninety meters away. Maintaining a choke hold on Doc the Soviet quickly rolled over on top of him to pin him to the ground.

Out of breath McKeowen's mind raced to decide which of his weapons was the most accessible. The decision became mute as a large blade flashed across the corner of his eye and he reflexively struggled to bring both arms up to counter the attack. Using a lop-sided, partial push-up he was able to block the knife hand and counter the Russian's grip around his throat which bought some time, but not much.

All this way from the fucking slums of Jersey City to get knifed, again! I don't think so!

It took a bit of struggle but with two hundred plus pounds of Russian pinning him face down to the ground Doc still managed to unclip his holster and draw his 9mm from his right hip. However, with only one arm partially free the best he could do was get the muzzle twisted around behind himself and into the Russian's ass. It was enough. The shot fired and the Russian screamed as the projectile ripped through his right ass cheek, entered his left one and came out his left lower abdomen.

As the Russian writhed in pain clutching his lower stomach with both hands Doc rolled free, holstered his 9mm and retrieved his M16.

As the report of the round resonated across the valley several things happened at once.

Lieutenant Harden spun around and realized he'd lost sight of Doc. Cursing to himself he was forced to hit the deck as a burst of AK fire raked the foliage just above his head. He scrambled to safety behind a tree and again scanned for Doc. No luck.

The Russian patrols all split up in a rehearsed

manoeuvre and while one pair converged on the cabin several headed in the direction of the shot. Harden pulled it together just in time to stave off their movement with a double burst in their general direction. Peering around a tree he saw all but two had disappeared, one helping the other limp to the cabin. Back behind the tree the L.T. nodded his head and smiled in self-satisfaction.

Meanwhile Doc's eyes stared blankly as he squatted and peered down at the bubbling, sliced open neck of the SPETNAZ, while he wiped the blood from the Russian's knife on the dead man's trouser leg.

"Yankees two Bears zero!" Doc mumbled while he tucked the knife into his web belt as a souvenir.

Assessing the situation he saw there was no noise or movement in any direction which sent a red flag to his brain. He hit the deck and crawled to cover.

Meanwhile, well out of sight of McKeowen and Harden, Danno and Ricky, lying fifty meters out from the north east corner of the cabin, had to make a decision. With the plan now gone to shit they had to attack, but in which direction?

Without speaking they had simultaneously decided to fight to the rear of the cabin and get inside. They shrugged at each other, stood in a crouched position and slowly crept to the right to move around and center their attack through the back door about one hundred meters away.

They didn't get very far.

No sooner had they taken a step when in the distance they watched as first one then two more Russians, weapons in hand, burst out through the door and made for the thick underbrush behind the cabin.

They didn't get very far either.

"You take left I'll take right!" Ricky instructed and in unison he and Danno raised their weapons and drew a bead to fire. It was an unnecessary gesture.

The first Russian through the door looked down as he continued running and it appeared he thought he stepped on something. There was a flash of light and the two behind him were twenty feet in the air with a leg tumbling in one direction and an arm in another before anyone realized what was happening. A short burst of automatic weapons fire from the bushes raked the third man across the face and chest and all fell silent again.

Ricky and Danno quickly adjusted their bead on some rustling bushes but quickly lowered their weapons as Ray slowly rose from the underbrush, smiled and waved hello.

The three jogged towards each other and met about twenty-five meters behind the cabin.

"You two get inside and get the Ruski I'll stand over watch!" Ray directed. Danno gave a thumbs up and with Ricky on his right flank they moved towards the door at 45 degree angles.

Meanwhile Doc had caught up with Harden.

"You all right?" The L.T. asked.

"Yeah. What's the plan?"

"Well it would appear MacDonald is around back ..."

Just then several bursts of fire ripped through both front windows from inside and the cabin again fell silent. Doc and the L.T. took up positions at 45 degrees to the front door about 50 meters out behind some small trees and waited to see what happened. Suddenly the door flew open and they heard Danno yell out into the darkness as he stepped into the doorway and waved the other two forward.

"CLEAR!"

On entering the small wooden building Doc and the L.T. glanced at the three bullet ridden bodies on either side of the room as they scanned the sparsely furnished space. MacDonald was occupied rummaging through the contents of the table to the left then turned his attention to the roaring fire in the potbellied stove. Doc made for the bed to the right while Ricky acted as sentry at the rear door.

"No sign of the Russki L.T." Danno announced.

"Fucking Scarlett!" Harden cursed as he kicked a chair across the floor.

Then, as they continued to scour the room, amongst the partially eaten, tinned mackerel, half bottle of vodka and still smouldering cigarettes Doc found a civilian tie and a shoe under the bed.

"He was here!" McKeowen announced.

"SHIT! Ya think they moved him?" Danno asked.

"No time. Whatever condition he's in he's in the immediate A.O.!" Doc answered as he looked at the back door threshold then over to the bed "The only blood I see is less than a day old and doesn't look arterial."

"That mean anything to you Doc?" Mac asked as Doc crouched by the blood stain.

"Yeah. If it's his it's not likely to be from a

628

serious wound, means they were smacking him around a bit. Probably looking to break him."

"This is un- fucking-acceptable!" Harden declared. "Ray, you got any more toys out back?"

"Negative sir. Recovered my two Claymores and used the 5 kilo AP to erase those other two assholes."

"Okay, we're gonna do a perimeter search. Danno Ricky fan out across the back, Doc with me out front. He damn sure didn't come out through the front and there's obviously no basement and no rafters, then look for tracks out back. We got twenty to twenty-five minutes max to hit the trail if we're gonna make our taxi before he heads home without us!"

"Roger that L.T."

"Move out."

"Be careful! He's not expecting us and if he's out there he' sure to be a little jumpy!" Doc warned.

A few minutes later outside Ray came across the other shoe then, at about 100 meters out to the west of the cabin he came across fresh traces of tracks on the wet ground. As soon as he saw the first distinct track he realized they were not only fresh but made by someone in socks or bare feet.

As he rounded a small rise of land there, ten meters ahead, was Gordievsky, tee shirt, trousers and bare foot, laying back against a thick wooden fence post shivering violently.

"I'm a Navy Seal! I'm here to -" Ray didn't get to finish as Oleg raised a Makarov pistol and fired three shots in rapid succession. Ray dove to the right and hugged the ground while yelling.

"AMERIKANSKI GOD DAMN IT! FUCKING AMERIKANSKI!!

Hearing no more rounds fired he peeked up over his arm to see the Russian staring glassy-eyed into the distance, pistol still raised to shoulder height. As Ray was debating whether or not to talk him down or shoot him Doc appeared off to the left.

"OLEG!" Danno and Harden caught up as well. "OLEG! IT'S DOC!" Gordievsky slowly turned towards McKeowen and, after what seemed to MacDonald to be an eternity, blinked, lowered the pistol and keeled over.

"Well, at least we found the little fucker!" Danno declared as Doc jogged up to the Russian and did a quick evaluation.

Without being ordered to, the others formed a hasty perimeter and did an ammo check and redistributed rounds as needed.

"Sit Rep Doc?!" Harden called over as he faced outboard scanning the terrain.

"Hypothermia, malnutrition, shock, and his vitals are shit! He could go downhill at any minute!" Doc reported as he worked.

"In other words he's good to go?!" Ray said as he cleared a lump of mud from his gun muzzle.

"Yeah." Doc said. "I'm gonna havt'a get a couple of I. V.'s in him before we move out."

"Danno, the bird should be at his staging area by now, contact them. Send, 'we have package. Stand by for yellow smoke'. Instead of the school are we'll bring them in over in that field. Activate your homing beacon and let's get the fuck outta Dodge! Ray give Doc a hand, get Gordievsky on the other side of this fence, then off to the other side of the road, near the field so Doc can plug him in. We'll bring the chopper in over there." Ray retrieved the Makarov pistol as he relocated to Doc's position and Danno manned the radio as they spread out and moved back towards the small dirt road south of the cabin.

The road next to the field was less than 150 meters away and the team was in position five minutes later. Hunkered down in the drainage ditch to minimize their profiles, they took up defensive positions and scanned the night sky as Doc worked at full speed to get a pair of I.V.'s in Gordievsky, get them taped tightly down and begin a more thorough physical exam as they waited.

"I hear the bird!" Danno declared as he pointed off to the south east.

"SHIT!" Ricky made his own declaration.

"What?" Harden spun around and looked at Ricky who was pointing down the road.

"We got company!" Just as the chopper came into sight approaching from the west through the darkness, 500 meters off to the east a combat reconnaissance patrol vehicle known as a BRDM lead by a BTR command jeep came around the turn on the dirt road at full speed and slid to a halt, the SPETNAZ Colonel clinging to the side door of the BTR. In the moon light they observed the Colonel as he climbed up onto the back of the jeep and with binos scanned for any signs of the team.

"They'll see the bird but can't see us. Sit tight until they move." Ray whispered from his vantage point.

"Matson. Stand by with your two-O-three to pop some yellow smoke on the other side of the road out by that clearing." Ricky was already loading his 203. "Doc, think you can get him across the road and out to the LZ?"

"Does Belinda Carlisle need me to go down on her?" Doc answered as, down in the ditch, he threaded Gordievsky's two I.V. bags with a 12 inch piece of parachute cord, slung his pack on and draped the I.V.'s around his neck.

As Doc prepped to go the Russian patrol appeared to make a decision and moved out in the direction of the TFR.

At one hundred meters Harden gave the order and they opened up on the Russians. Harden immediately began directing traffic as Ricky popped the smoke over on the intended exfil point.

"Concentrate fire on the lead vehicle! DOC GO! Suppressive fire only until they start to maneuver. Once Doc's got him over the road banana peel on my order!"

"Fuck L.T.! You sounded like John Wayne just then!" Ray quipped as he fired off several suppressor rounds.

"Fuck you! Pilgrim!" Harden responded with a bad imitation of The Duke.

No sooner had the words left Harden's mouth when the first fusillade of small arms fire with tracer rounds emanated from the small convoy and ripped over their heads.

From the cover of the drainage ditch t was impossible for the Soviets to bring effective fire to bear.

"They'll move to out flank us as soon as they're deployed. Concentrate fire on the BRDM as the troops get out." Ray yelled out loud in between bursts as the first two Russians collapsed to the ground. "Scratch two!" Ray said as he adjusted his fire position.

"Beginner's luck!" Ricky commented.

"Tall guy, left of the BTR." Ray yelled over to Ricky, squeezed the trigger and fired. The left side of the tall guy's face disappeared and his torso collapsed.

"Fuck you MacDonald. Nobody likes a show off."

"Matson, give us a couple of smokes at our eleven o'clock then you and Danno get across the road and set up a cross fire position near the LZ!" Harden yelled.

As the yellow smoke round burst on the north side of the fence about 150 meters from where Doc had Gordievsky, the CH-53 veered in to the intended LZ.

Dumping his pack but keeping his weapon, and with Oleg's left arm around his neck, Doc limped his patient to within 25 meters of the smoke, laid him down and dashed back to his gear to join the fire fight.

Smoke is an effective screen for movement but it works both ways. As the breeze shifted into the TFR's position the Russians, who had been stopped cold by MacDonald's marksmanship, took full advantage and the SPETNAZ Colonel lost no time in directing the NCO squad leader of the BRDM unit to arch to the left while he would lead the occupants of the second vehicle in a wide arch right to set up a pincher against TFR.

Staring out the side window and down to his mutilated colleague the young Soviet driver of the BTR decided to stay in his vehicle.

As the chopper approached the LZ the guys out on the road began to prep for a banana peel pull back when tracer rounds from the Russian's 7.62's found the chopper's range.

The TFR members watched in dismay as the bird banked hard right exposing its lightly armoured underbelly and climbed back out of sight.

"Gonna be a long fuckin' walk!" Harden said to MacDonald who had stopped returning fire and seemed distracted before he shot a thumbs up back across the road to the L.T. In the interim Ricky had reloaded his 203 with an HE round.

So as not to lag too far behind the advancing troops the BTR started to come up the middle along the dirt road which is exactly what Ricky was hoping for. The driver may have been long on balls but he was short on brains as he slammed on the brakes and skidded to a near halt, swerving to the right in a vain attempt to avoid the high explosive 203 round whizzing at him five feet off the deck.

The well trained, Russian troops around the BRDM saw it as well, scattered and hit the deck as the 203 round hit the windshield of the BTR.

Inside the driver screamed, sucked in his breath and simultaneously grabbed his helmet with both hands as he hit the floor under the dash. He slowly became aware that the fire fight outside had ceased altogether as there was a low 'tink' against the windshield and then silence.

Through the urine soaked wet crotch of his trousers he felt for his balls, smiled that they were intact, and slowly sat up and stared through the spider webbed windshield. He spotted the short, fat 203 round lying sideways on the other side of his windshield where the glass met the hood. The driver, on the verge of laughing hysterically, slowly climbed out of the vehicle and decided he wanted a souvenir form his first real combat mission.

Combatants on either side were nowhere to be seen as the surreal scene played out.

The Russian troops slowly stood and reformed as they heard Harden loudly curse in the distance. The BRDM along with the troop escorts began to move again and the fire fight resumed.

As rounds whizzed on either side the young driver quickly pocketed the half pound cartridge and scurried back into the jeep.

Less than a minute later the lower half of his body, from the balls down, were spattered across the dash board and inner windshield. Harden looked shocked at what he had seen then glanced over to Ricky.

"I had my Gunner's Mate in the armory replace the fuse. Kind of an experiment." Ricky shrugged. "Guess it worked."

With a half dozen Russians now less than 300 meters from their left flank, Ray yelled over to the L.T.

"AHHH, SIR! NOW MIGHT BE GOOD TIME." MacDonald prompted and Harden gave the order.

"MATSON, MORE SMOKE. BANANA PEEL LEFT! ON MACDONALD!" As they moved the Russian fire quickly increased but withered as the team scored more hits and the Russians fought to regroup.

With TFR's exact location now public knowledge the Soviet NCO on the other side of the road had redirected his troops who were now making straight for the road in an attempt to cross it and rush TFR's right flank.

Once all four TFR guys were across the road, through the small wire fence and within fifty meters of the dwindling yellow smoke they were able to locate the semi-conscious Gordievsky.

In the reduced fire the chopper was heading back in to the intended LZ so Harden did a quick head count and came up short.

"WHERE THE FUCK IS DOC?!" With the approaching chopper's rotor wash suppressing the knee high grass it was clear Doc was nowhere in the immediate area.

"Don't know." Somebody yelled.

"Keep moving! Head for the bird!" Harden ordered.

"FUCK THAT NOISE! IF THOSE OTHERS CROSS THE ROAD WITH THAT BRDM WE'LL NEVER GET AIRBORNE!" MacDonald yelled as he dropped his pack, pulled one of the Claymores and headed back towards the road to confront the half dozen advancing Russians and look for Doc.

Meanwhile the rest of the team, running low on ammo fought to suppress the sporadic enemy fire while loading Gordievsky and the remainder of their gear onto the bird.

With Danno and Ricky holding off the last four Russians who had mistakenly advanced well ahead of the BRDM, Harden was hoisting Oleg up into the arms of the Crew Chief. Gordievsky grabbed Harden's lapel, looked into his eyes and mumbled, "RYAN! PHASE TWO!" Just as he went unconscious.

Harden refocused on the fire fight with the Russians who were alternately firing and trying to direct the BRDM through the plowed up field to within range of the chopper. He considered waving the bird off now that the asset was aboard but then reconsidered that they had at least another minute to wrap things up. Or get their asses blown off.

Running hunched over, further out from the bird, Ray scanned for Doc but was greeted with heavy fire from the Russians now less than 200 meters away over on the edge of the road. He felt like he hit his leg on a stone or a branch as he knelt to return fire. He scored one KIA but only wounded the second, both of which were enough to buy him enough time to set and arm the Claymore and get back.

Suddenly, as he again took aim, two of the Russians on the left flank fell in rapid succession before he could fire. The other four hesitated and scanned the area around them.

Holding his CAR-15 Doc popped up from behind a fallen tree and fired at the remaining few but fell back behind the log as his weapon failed to fire. Two of the SPETZNAZ rushed his position.

Across the road Mac took aim and fired two

shots, each hitting its mark.

With only one troop left the NCO decided to live to fight another day and headed for the far tree line.

Mac covered Doc as he watched him cross the road at a point that was now two to three hundred meters behind what remained of the Colonel's men and the now crawling BRDM.

Doc had broken a cardinal medical rule and abandoned his patient, but with good reason. He had out flanked the NCO on the left and come up from behind. Now, apparently, he intended to push his luck.

As he crossed the road in a low hunch he signalled for Mac to double back through the drainage ditch and link up with him.

Meanwhile, back at the LZ, everybody had been loaded onto the bird along with Doc's gear. Just inside the door the Crew Chief shouted into his head set in answer to something the pilot had just said. He then turned to Danno.

"Sorry Petty Officer, the Skipper says we're outta here with or without your guys!" Danno looked him in the eye and shouted back.

"I'm not a petty officer! I'm in the fucking Army!" Then grabbed him by the jaw and forcibly turned his head outboard of the chopper.

They both watched as the two tiny figures of Mac and McKeowen came up from behind the BRDM and disappeared from sight.

"GET YOUR C.O. TO LEAPFROG THAT TREELINE AND SET HER DOWN ON THE OTHER SIDE SO WE'RE OUTTA SIGHT!"

"BUT THAT FUCKING TANK -"

638

"ITS NOT A TANK! AND NEVER MIND IT, WE GOT IT HANDLED! DO IT!"

The Crew Chief radioed the instructions and the bird lifted off over the tree line to its left. As the Stallion climbed the small cannon on the front of the BRDM elevated along with it.

With Ray now climbing up and hunched down behind the open top hatch of the BRDM popping rounds at anything in the area that moved, Doc climbed up over the left track fender and was able to pull the pin then lob a frag grenade to Ray who threw it forcibly down into the compartment so it bounced around. Inside the three man crew had no chance as they scurried for the hatch opening just as Ray slammed it shut.

Doc and Ray rolled off the slow moving vehicle but didn't clear the concussion blast soon enough and were partially stunned and temporarily deafened.

By now the Colonel, a hundred plus meters ahead of the armoured vehicle, was down to himself and one combat capable man but had no intention of calling it a day.

Looking back at the smouldering wreck of the BRDM he cursed, pulled several magazines from his ammo belt, stuffed them in his cargo pockets, tucked his pistol into the rear of his belt and stripped off his web gear, hat and overcoat. In his shirt and trousers he dashed across the field toward the tree line and the low hovering Super Stallion, his lone troop following suit.

Back on the ground Ray started to come around first and, not seeing anyone nearby rolled over. He

639

heard a groan and crawled towards it.

"Doc?!" Following the groan he found McKeowen twenty meters off to his right lying sprawled across a muddy furrow of the plowed field. Ray moved to Doc did a quick visual survey for injuries then slapped him in the face twice.

"What the fuck you doin'?!" Doc yelled as he shoved Ray away.

"Checkin' your reflexes. Saw it in a movie! You hurt anywhere?"

"Yeah my face! Ass hole!"

"Com'on!" Ray instructed as he got to his feet.

"WHAT?!"

"COME ON!" Ray shouted. CHOPPER'S WAITING!" Doc was slow to get up but made it.

Just as they began to move out the chopper slowly raised its hover. Doc and Ray assumed the team were returning to recover them and moved to where the smoke was. They weren't the only ones.

The Russian Colonel had intended to attack the bird single-handedly but smiled as he realized the same thing they did. He crouched about 50 meters on his side of the tree line, watched and waited.

Now with no more small arms fire being received there was a renewed sense of security in the helo as it rose and drifted to leapfrog over the trees, the Crew Chief hanging out the door. He spotted the yellow stained area of the original DZ and directed the bird in. Doc and Ray made a dash for it but didn't get far as the remaining Russian troop opened up on them as they hit the deck.

With the shots 200 meters or so away from the bird, the orientation of the chopper coupled with the noise of the rotor, the TFR members and crew inside were unable to see or hear that there was still a fire fight in the vicinity and so the bird continued gliding in sideways over to the intended LZ.

As the chopper hovered then came in to touch down the doors on the pilot's side opened just as the skids lightly touched down.

On the other side of the bird, with the wood line now at his back, the SPETNAZ Colonel appeared and walked stiff armed, pistol in hand, straight at the blind side of the CH-53. At about fifty meters out he opened fire through the skin of the opposite door and into the bird.

Inside everyone hit the deck and scrambled for a weapon.

With no return fire coming from the chopper the Colonel's confidence was bolstered. Remaining stiff armed and maintaining fire, he continued straight at them.

Out in the field Doc shouted over to Ray as the Russian troop had them pinned down.

"RAY! STAND BY TO FIRE!"

"GO!" Ray yelled back and like a pop up range target Doc jumped up and dashed two or three meters straight in the direction of the Russian then dove for cover. The tactic worked as the Russkie drew a quick bead on Doc giving Ray enough time to get off three quick rounds. One body shot followed by a head shot settled the matter.

A hundred meters away in the chopper Danno was able to get to his CAR-15, roll out the open door and off the deck out into the field. He hit the ground hard on his left side but was unseen by the now fanatical Colonel and quickly flicked his selector switch to full auto and emptied the magazine in the colonel's general direction.

The first few rounds hit low and to the right but he quickly corrected and the next three penetrated the abdomen, chest and face of Gordievsky's former torturer in rapid succession. He kept firing until the mag was empty and from the knees down the Colonel no longer had any legs

Inside the chopper Gordievsky propped himself up on one arm, smiling as he spotted Doc and Ray running for the bird.

Five minutes later they were airborne at altitude and on track to fly N.O.E. until they hit open water.

"Hey MacDonald?" Danno called over above the din of the aircraft. "You feeling okay?" Mac sat with his back against the half empty fuel bladder.

"Feelin' a little weak, but that's probably due to the adrenaline level going back down. Why?"

"No reason." He quietly but quickly leaned over and tapped Doc on the shoulder as he worked on Oleg. Doc looked over at Mac.

"Cut his trouser leg open." Doc instructed. "Look for an exit wound. If there is none, clean it, dress it and wrap it tight." Danno went to work and two minutes later he was done.

"Anything else Doc?"

"Ricky, you good?!" Doc shouted over.

"All's green Doc! Good show eh!?" He grinned back with an enthusiastic thumbs up. Ricky was obviously still riding his adrenaline high.

Doc glanced over at the L.T. who had apparently cleared a space for himself on the deck and was taking a break from all the excitement by catching a nap. Doc nodded over in Hardin's direction to Danno.

"I think he might have pulled a muscle getting aboard or something. I saw him holding his shoulder. Check him out will ya?" Doc said.

"Ya think I should wake him? He looks pretty worn out from all the excitement." Danno asked.

"Wake him, get his camo top open and do a quick check for any marks or bruises, then let him get back to sleep."

Meanwhile the fly boys were wrestling with their own set of problems. The back-up Russian troops had been well trained and had not only the why-with-for to open fire as they dismounted the vehicles but were good enough to get more than one hit on the bird as they advanced. Oil lights were flashing, the fuselage slowly yawed and the collective started to get sluggish.

As they wrestled the controls the co-pilot/navigator spoke through his head set to the pilot.

"What about dumpin' the extra fuel bladder?"

"Won't leave us enough juice to make it to the carrier." The pilot answered.

"SHIT!"

Harden wasn't responding to Danno's rousing so he decided to gently unbutton the L.T.'s shirt and do a quick check. He reached the last button and peeled back the camo top then pulled back white faced.

"Doc! DOC!" Harden had taken three rounds, one in the right shoulder, one in the neck and one in the upper right chest.

"JESUS CHRIST! Are we ever gonna get a fuckin' break here!?" Doc cursed. He shifted across the deck to where Harden lay and went to work. "Danno, collect everybody's compresses, rip open my M-1 kit and get my last two I.V.'s out and prep them!" Enlisting Ray's help Doc immediately applied pressure to the chest wound as Danno got to work with Ray on the I.V.'s.

Rolling Dave onto his side he checked for an exit wound but found none.

"Danno get the cuff outta my kit and get me a BP." Doc spoke as he cut away Harden's shirt sleeve. Danno moved quickly.

"Ricky, get his boots off! Check his legs!" McKeowen further instructed.

They worked frantically but methodically for the few minutes.

"Doc B.P., ninety over seventy-six!" Danno reported.

"SHIT!"

As he worked on the unconscious L.T. Doc picked up on the overwrought activity up on the cockpit and deduced the crew was not in a good place either. He could see they worked in an agitated state as well.

Just then Harden's eyes slowly opened but only halfway. He smiled up at Doc and, struggling, took off his watch and held it up to him. Doc took it and maintaining focus on the job at hand as he quietly passed it to Mac. Ray took it and fell back against the bulkhead of the aircraft.

Danno slid the stethoscope from his ears and looked over at Doc.

"Doc, BP is ninety over sixty and his pulse is one ten and climbing!"

Dave's eyes closed back over.

"FUCK!" He looked around the compartment then out the window into the inky black. "Danno, get him in the Trendelenberg, tourniquet his thighs then gimme a minute!"

He repacked Dave's chest wound and crawled up front to the cockpit where he tapped the co-pilot on the leg.

"What's the ceiling on this thing?" Doc asked.

"What?"

"The ceiling! How high can you get this thing? Our L.T. is hit, Gordievsky's fighting dehydration, broken ribs and disorientation but he's stabilized and we can manage the leg wound but L.T.'s B.P. is fucked. If I don't get it back up, he's yesterday's news!"

"In case you haven't noticed Doc we got our own problems right now! Not the least of which is a fuel problem! We took a good few hits!"

"By flying higher you'll use less fuel and maybe not solve all our problems but maybe alleviate them some. Besides, if it comes to it and we have to auto rotate in the extra altitude might make a difference!"

The co-pilot stared over at the impertinent corpsman. "Take it up and hold it as long as you can! That's all I ask!" The pilot and co-pilot exchanged glances then slowly pulled back on the stick. The chopper began to climb. Doc scrambled back to the rear and went back to work on the L.T. whose BP rose slightly as they climbed. It wasn't much but, with the tourniquet trick and two I.V.'s he temporarily stabilized.

Thirty-five minutes later as the last of the second IV was draining into Harden and Gordievsky had regained consciousness, slivers of light broke over the ocean horizon and the Crew Chief announced to the team that they had spotted *HMS Illustrious* off the port side.

The co-pilot manned the radio.

"HMS Illustrious, HMS Illustrious, this is SF-312 Sea Stallion, we are heavily damaged and low on fuel. Requesting immediate clearance to set down on your flight deck."

CH-53, this is Illustrious, we have you on radar. Please enter into hover at our three o'clock position and maintain holding pattern until notified of clearance to approach. Thank you so much.

"That's a negative *Illustrious*. I repeat we are heavily damaged, have only partial control, flying on fumes and have multiple wounded aboard. We will attempt to reach your mid deck and auto rotate in as we are losing power."

Sea Stallion, I say again we are in the middle of launch and recovery operations! This is not a bloody sea borne taxi –

"Please scramble your Alert-5 aircraft and Damage Control crews! We're coming in! Hold your launch traffic! I say again, hold your launch traffic! Stallion out!" Initially the TFR guys were relieved to see the British flattop approaching through the front wind screen, but when they saw a Harrier on deck prepped for take-off and realized their situation, eyes widened and hearts raced.

646

As the carrier deck grew bigger and faster than it should have, the conscious envied the unconscious, everyone grabbed onto something, squeezed until their hands turned blue and unconsciously stopped breathing.

The hardware and fixtures of the carrier's flight deck very rapidly came into focus and the blurred, gray streak of a jet whipped past the front of the chopper and shot off the jump ramp.

The near collision caused the bird to shutter hard and twist to starboard and both Stallion pilots had to strain at the controls.

"FUCK ME ALICE!" Doc yelled.

"WHAT IS IT DOC?!" Ray yelled.

"THAT HARRIER PILOT HAD BLUE EYES!"

****

CHAPTER TWENTY-EIGHT

The North Sea
Off the Coast of West Germany
Sick Bay, *HMS Illustrious*

Less than ten minutes after slamming onto the deck of the British carrier Lieutenant Harden was prepped and in surgery. Oleg Gordievsky, thanks to Doc's efforts, was conscious and had been stabilized.

On the other side of the low overhead but spacious sick bay, while changing out Oleg's I.V., Doc surreptitiously eavesdropped on MacDonald's version of events as he chatted up the young nurse changing his leg bandage while he sat on the end of an examining table.

"Well, there were only four of them but I realized I had to take them out one by one and my knife was the best bet, you know, to maintain silence and all." MacDonald explained leaving no embellishment unturned.

"Petty Officer, might I venture to ask you a question?" The attractive dark haired nurse queried.

"Why yes ma'am. As an officer you're perfectly entitled. Ask me anything you like!"

"Does this sort of malarkey go over well with the American girls?"

Just then the ship's C.O. complete with entourage, entered the sick bay.

"ATTENTION!"

"Carry on, carry on! As you were gentlemen."

648

Paddy Kelly

The C.O. directed as he approached an orderly over by the sink and extended his hand.

"Good mission gentlemen! Agent Scarlett has informed me of the -." The bewildered orderly dried the bedpan he had just removed from the autoclave and gave the Captain a quizzical look before employing his thick Mancunian dialect.

"Beggin' yer pardon sir, I ain't been on no mission!" The orderly half mumbled. Despite there being a dozen people scattered around the compartment, you could've heard a mouse fart.

Across the space MacDonald gently waved his hand causing the Captain's adjutant to lean in and whisper into the C.O.'s ear.

Dusting off their embarrassment, the entourage shuffled over to MacDonald's treatment table. The nurse respectfully took a step back.

"Agent Scarlett has informed me of the bang up job you chaps did for us!" The C.O. re-informed.

"Thank you sir. It's an honor and a privilege to have served Her Majesty and the umpire!" Ray hopped to his feet and saluted smartly.

"Well ... that's awfully good of you. I'd like to read you a priority flash message."

"Please do sir!" Ray invited. Doc shook his head.

"To Commander *HMS Illustrious*, Director MOD has informed me of outstanding job by Agent Scarlett and MI6. Please extend kindest regards to all involved. M. Thatcher, Prime Minister."

"All involved!" Ray mouthed across the room to Doc as he pointed back and forth between himself and McKeowen who slowly scratched his right eye with his middle finger.

649

"Well done chaps, I say some serious congratulations are in order! As soon as you're up to it, please feel free to join me in my cabin for a bit of the hard stuff!" Doc cleared his throat and, without shouting, spoke loud enough for the whole space to hear.

"If by the hard stuff' you mean Irish whiskey, I most graciously accept your kind offer Captain, however, need I remind everyone we still have a little problem hanging over our heads?" He nodded over to Gordievesky.

Oleg grabbed Doc's sleeve and leaned up to him and whispered.

"Doctor McKeowen, get me Agent Scarlett!"

✱

Century House
Westminster Bridge Road
Lambeth, Central London
MI6 Headquarters
16:21, Local, 29ᵗʰ September

Since the days of WWII, in spite of 'The Special Relationship', there has been no love lost between the American and British Intel agencies. In the intervening years not much had changed. Having assisted in the rescue, the NSA were giving no quarter in their fight to have first dibs on the debrief of the defected Russian agent.

The short National Security Agency rep with his

British diplomatic 'envoy' waited outside yet another office in Century House, their third of the morning. While the NSA rep paced the hall the British envoy sat on a bench outside casually reading *The Daily Mail*.

The office door finally opened and the same lanky fellow who disappeared behind it twenty-five minutes ago reappeared. The NSA rep scurried over.

"Terribly sorry sir. But I'm told there's no Mr. Oleg here. Hasn't been all morning I'm afraid."

"HEY, ICABOD! It's Gordievsky! HIS NAME IS GOR-DI-EVSKY! You people invented the god damned language! How come I'm the only one talkin' it?!" The rep scolded in his best American.

The fellow pretended to ponder deeply for just the right amount of time and then came to a revelation.

"Perhaps Mr. Speers might be of some assistance! I'll just ring down to his office." He headed back to the door then suddenly stopped. "Drat! I just remembered! He's on holiday." The British envoy smiled behind his morning edition.

Meanwhile, as the Ministry played Three Card Monty with the NSA, Oleg Gordievsky, sitting in an office just a few floors above, had been back in the safety of MI6 for nearly a full twenty-four hours when he finally got to speak with the man he had been demanding to see since his rescue, his British handler John Scarlett who now, as was his habit, slowly paced the room.

Still weak from his ordeal and the effects of the drugs used on him by the KGB and thus unable to retain heat, Oleg sat at a table wrapped in a blanket in Scarlett's 19th floor office, with the heat blasting away. Ricky and Danno stood off to the side. Doc and Ray leaned against the back wall as Oleg spoke.

"The Soviet Union not just Yuri Andropov, not just the KGB, but as a system, is geared to expect an attack and to retaliate very quickly to it. As we speak the entire system is on hair-trigger alert. They are very, very nervous and this makes them prone to mistakes and accidents."

"What are you trying to tell us Oleg?" Scarlett pushed.

"John you fail to grasp the magnitude of the situation!" Gordievsky emphasized. "This NATO REFORGER 'exercise' could not have come at a more dangerous, intense phase in relations." Mounting frustration laced his voice. "Not only don't they believe but they cannot grasp the fact that it is only an exercise! They actually believe your people are preparing a full scale attack against them!" Silence permeated the room.

"Scary shit!" Doc whispered to MacDonald who continued to be mesmerized by what they were witnessing as they leaned against the wall opposite the office entrance. Oleg continued.

"You must understand that no more than a child can accept the fact that you do not cease to exist when you are not in his presence, can Andropov and the cronies of the Politburo accept you do not intend to wage war! They are paranoid by nature it is ingrained in the Soviet history. Do you understand what I am trying to tell you?! They think it is real!"

Scarlett stopped in front the Russian.

"Oleg, the Americans have put months and millions into this exercise to say nothing of what the rest of NATO has put into it! Virtually every message sent in the clear has been marked 'Exercise Only!'" Agent Scarlett mistakenly still clung to reason as the basis for his arguments.

"John, Reagan himself, the so called 'Leader of the Free World', has declared the Soviets 'The Axis of Evil'! And not only does he think there is a god, he thinks that his god's sole purpose is to crush all evil in the universe. Worse he believes he is an instrument of this god whose purpose it is to do away with this evil!"

"Oleg, I'm not minimizing your argument but-"

"We had his ranch under surveillance last July ..." Doc and Ray were impressed and nodded. "... the man owns a fucking white horse!"

To everyone in the office-turned-debriefing-room the reality that this was not something out of an Ian Fleming novel, but hard core reality was slowly sinking in. As the reality of Gordievsky's arguments sank in Scarlett sat and fell back into his seat. Oleg pushed harder.

"If you cannot convince the Americans to pull back on these "games" immediately and give Andropov some assurances they do not intend to attack Russia, there is the very real possibility that we will wake up tomorrow to a world which is in the process of being incinerated!"

"But-"

"Agent Scarlett, if I may?" Doc interrupted.

"Petty Officer McKeowen?" Scarlett acknowledged without turning to face him.

"Sir, if all this comes down to is a matter of saving face by the British and Americans, I'm sure, before you approach them if you have a reasonable explanation the administrations can sell to the public, they'll be compelled to consider it. I mean considering we're talking about avoiding an all-out nuclear war with the Soviets and all!" Scarlett spun in his chair and now faced Doc.

"Well, Petty Officer, now that you've promoted yourself from a humble Medic –"

"Hospital Corpsman, Mr. Scarlett. Marine Force RECON Hospital Corpsman. Medics are in the Army."

"... to International Peacekeeper, just what do you propose we try and sell to your bosses to get them to put an end to the largest military exercise the planet has ever seen?"

"Sir I – " MacDonald started.

"DAMAGE! Money and damage." Doc declared as he pushed himself away from the wall, stood upright and approached the table.

"What?" Scarlett questioned.

"The language administrators and politicians understand best is money. Damage costs money. Collateral damage." A smile crept across Mac's face as Doc continued. "Every war, as does every exercise, yields collateral damage."

"YES!" Gordievsky understood where McKeowen was heading. "So if this is the largest military exercise the planet has ever seen, logically so too would be the collateral damage by the troops!" Oleg added.

"That might work Doc." Ray chimed in. "I saw a

copy of the collateral damage estimates about a month before we launched. They allowed $1 Million but that was probably exceeded in the first two to three weeks!" MacDonald proposed.

"I don't mean this the wrong way John, you don't mind if I call you John do you? John." Doc continued. Scarlett scowled but said nothing. "Regular military aren't exactly the sharpest knives in the drawer sometimes, and last year when I was assigned to the Medical Liaison's during an exercise, I saw an incredible amount of damage to civilian properties, houses, businesses, civilians themselves. Two civilian fatalities along with over 250 military personnel injured. That shit runs up a tab, and let's face it, it can get expensive and money talks." Doc smiled at Scarlett. "Know-what-I-mean, John?"

Less than a minute later Scarlett was dialing the phone.

"Operator? Put me through to Sir Charles Powell's office immediately! Tell him it's Scarlett of MI6 and that I have a Priority Red One message for him. I'll wait."

Not sure I can reach him at the moment sir. May I ask what it's regarding and perhaps I can pass the message on at his earliest convenience? Came the tentative reply.

Scarlett briefly held the phone away from his face and cleared his throat as he threw a sarcastic smile towards Doc and the others then resumed the conversation.

"What's your name please?"
Percival, Percival Smyth. Why?

"Percival, listen to me my dear man, listen to me carefully please. YOU HAVE NOTHING ELSE TO DO! DO YOU UNDERSTAND ME YOU PETTY FUNCTIONARY SOON-TO-BE-REPLACD BY A FUCKING CIRCUIT BOARD GLORIFIED ANSWERING MACHINE?! IF THAT'S NOT CLEAR ENOUGH, KNOW YOU THAT I WILL BE SPEAKING WITH SIR POWELL IN THE NEXT THIRTY TO SIXTY SECONDS OR THE ONLY FUCKING WAY THEY WILL BE ABLE TO IDENTIFY YOUR FUCKING REMAINS IS THROUGH YOUR DENTAL RECORDS! THAT IS IF I BOTHER TO SHIT YOUR TEETH OUT AT ALL!"

"That's what I like about the Brits! They got a way with words, ya know?" Ray whispered to Doc.

"Yeah, that and the diplomacy thing." Doc whispered back.

Scarlett slammed the phone down and shrugged as he turned to Doc. "What the hell. If it all goes pear shaped I understand that in America there are hundreds of minimum wage jobs in mall security."

"You can have a one week truck driving course for about a hundred dollars." MacDonald added.

"Either that or you could become an officer." Doc piped up. "They'll pretty much take anybody these days." Doc added.

Ray reckoned that deserved a high five.

✱

The Private Residence

British Prime Minister
18:17 Local, 30th September

Attired in a Saville Row tuxedo an aide made his way through the large rooms of similarly dressed dignitaries until he found the Prime Minister. Once located he discreetly whispered into her ear from behind.

"Madame Prime Minister, sorry to bother you but, it's the Foreign Secretary's office. Urgent."

"Thank you Cyril." Thatcher excused herself from the small clutch of politicians she had been standing with in the ball room and followed the aide to an upstairs office to access a phone. "This is the Prime Minister, to whom am I speaking?"

"Sir Charles Powell, Madam Prime Minister. I have some urgent news. How soon can we meet?"

"Sir Charles, what could be so urgent that we –"

"Operation Ryan Prime Minister."

Twenty minutes later a black Bentley escorted by a pair of motorcycle cops and a squad car, blue lights flashing and sirens blaring, screamed to a halt in front of Number 10. The chauffer jumped out and held open the door as Sir Powell, briefcase in hand, scurried up the steps and disappeared behind the famous black enameled door.

He was met by the same aide who had earlier relayed the message to the P.M. and was then escorted to Thatcher's office. The doors closed behind him.

"Sir Charles, just how serious is this thing?"

"Not to put too fine a point on it Madam but ... it makes the Falklands look like a primary school yard tiff."

✱

The Oval Office
White House
15:23 EST, 30th September

"Mr. President, I'm assured by the highest authority that our intelligence reports are 100% accurate." Margret Thatcher concluded her plea to Reagan.

Reagan switched the intercom phone on his desk to hold and looked over at Secretary of Defense Casper Weinberger who, along with Adm. Butts of Naval Intelligence, Bill Casey of the CIA and Secretary of State George Schultz, was seated on the Executive couch adjacent to the President's desk.

"Mr. President, the Brits are right! We've detected their missiles are on full alert. They've scrambled their bombers and fighters in Poland, Czechoslovakia and East Germany and the NSA reports that the KGB has tripled their number of field operatives in the last two weeks!" Schultz informed Reagan.

"To top it all off we can't locate half their submarines!" Admiral Butts informed the President.

Reagan reclined in his tall backed, black leather chair and put both hands on his desk.

"What's Thatcher doing?" He quietly asked.

"She's waiting to see how we're going to

658

respond, but strongly advises we take it down a notch." Casey responded.

"Ron you must understand the mentality of those people! They still live in the 1940's and ever since Hitler attacked them ... !" Weinberger felt compelled to add.

"What if they're preparing a first strike? They certainly have the capability, we know that much." Reagan argued.

There were no takers. Reagan switched the phone back to intercom.

"Margret?"

"Yes Ronald?"

"I'm sustaining the JCS's recommendation to prep and upgrade to DEFCON 2."

Given the weight of the higher ups currently huddled in the Oval Office, the stunned silence was that much more stunning.

****

JCS Ready Room
The Pentagon
17:17

Reliable Intel, based largely on satellite observation of the Russian's military posture, had it that the Soviets had upgraded to their equivalent of the U.S. defence forces' DEF CON 2, the final warning of an imminent attack and the last stage before pressing the button for an all too real massive retaliation.

On Soviet controlled airfields Russian nuclear bomber pilots sat in their cockpits, engines running, waiting for orders to fly. Three hundred ICBMs were prepared for firing and 75 mobile SS-20s were being hurriedly moved to hidden locations all along the western border of Russia.

Satellite Intel further revealed that Soviet surface ships had dashed for cover, anchoring beneath cliffs in the Baltic, while her submarines, with their arsenals of nuclear missiles, slipped beneath the Arctic ice and had cleared for action.

Given the magnitude of the crisis Joint Chiefs Chairman General Vessey was the man for the job. However, even he, despite the multitude of critical situations he had faced, had never been in it this deep.

The frenzied activity of the JCS Ready Room was only the center of the bedlam which now permeated the Pentagon as messages flowed in and out of virtually every office of the nerve center controlling the entire U.S. military juggernaut as air wings across the country were fired up, naval resources were issued emergency orders and troops in the field were put on full alert.

Now Reagan wanted the JCS to upgrade to DEF CON 2.

Despite the late hour the Ready Room looked like Grand Central Station in Manhattan at Rush Hour.

"Line one, it's an MI6 guy!" An adjutant said to Vessey as he poked his head through the door.

"MI6?! What the fuck...? Trace this!" Vessey ordered.

"We got it running." The messenger replied. Vessey flicked the phone to intercom.

"This is General Vessey of the Joint Chiefs. Who am I speaking to?"

"General Vessey, this is Agent John Scarlett of MI6. Please hold." Oleg, with his distinct Russian accent, came on the line.

"General Vessey, we have never met but all you need to know is that I am a Soviet spy who has defected to the British."

"Yeah? How do I know that?" The adjutant reappeared.

"Sir, CIA confirms the call is coming from inside central London." The Adjutant whispered. Vessey nodded. The voice on the other end continued.

"On August the 17th a field report made its way up the command structure in V Corps, Frankfurt. It was delivered via classified courier to the Pentagon where it made its way to your desk by the morning of the 19th. The report detailed problems with the transfer cranes you employ to hoist the Minute Man missiles you have deployed along the Eastern European border. This otherwise minor problem could potentially delay launch time by thirty to forty minutes."

Vessey sat upright as he listened to the guy on the other end of the line spouting his own Top Secret information to him. A guy with a Russian accent no less.

"How do I know –" Vessey pushed.

"Have whoever is listening in on the other line check my facts." Vessey stared up at his adjutant. "I will hold."

After verifying who Scarlett and Oleg were and confirming their information Oleg explained the atmosphere in the Kremlin at that exact moment to include that as the Americans were preparing for an attack by the Soviets the Russians were preparing for a first strike on the Americans.

Finally convinced, Vessey went into action. He put Oleg on hold again and dialed out on another line.

"This is General Vessey. Who am I talking to?"

"Sir this is Colonel James, Lieutenant General Williams' adjutant. How may I help?"

"Colonel, this is a Code Purple order. Effective immediately, REFORGER 83 to include *Operation Able Archer* is to be put on hold! I say again, put on hold! All units are to cease all activity, stand down and hold in place until further notice! I say again Code Purple order! Is that clear?"

"Yes General, Code Purple. I'll notify the Lieutenant General immediately sir!"

"And James?"

"Sir?"

"Make it clear to the General that we've simply incurred too much collateral civilian damage and relations have become strained. Too strained to risk continuing. Is that understood?"

"Yes General Vessey. Perfectly clear sir. And perfectly understandable sir. Our D.C.O.'s are being run ragged! Is there anything else sir?"

"No, that's all. I'll expect an all sector preliminary report by zero-nine-hundred. Out." Vessey plopped down into his chair and breathed a deep sigh of relief then relayed the message to MI6 still on hold.

Vessey scanned the faces of the leaders assembled around the long table.

"Not every day you get to avoid an all-out nuclear war!" He mumbled. After a few minutes reprieve, he realized he had one more important call to make.

In the White House Master Bedroom a servant knocked on the door and woke the President.

"Mr. President, it's General Vessey from the Joint Chief's on the line."

"Thank you Malcolm, I'll take it in the library." Vessey laid out the situation for the half asleep President ending with what Oleg had passed on, including the fact that their satellites had detected that the missile bay doors around Moscow were opened indicating they were in 'deploy' mode.

White faced and silent Reagan stared into the distance for a full minute before regaining composure.

"Mr. President, are you still there?"

"How could they have actually believed that we'd really attack them?" Reagan asked. Flabbergasted at Reagan's naivety, Vessey fought the impulse to retort.

"I don't know sir but I'll keep you informed." He pushed the disconnect button on the phone,

A full ninety minutes later Vessey sat alone in his private Pentagon office down the hall from the JCOS meeting room staring at a large wall map. He pushed away from the table and moved to his small liquor cabinet in the corner and poured a large scotch. Next he used the desk intercom.

"Doris, ring my wife please. Tell her I'll be home later then you'd better get home yourself."

Yes General, thank you. Shall I say how late you'll be?

"Not as late as I could've been."

Sorry General?

"Just say 'late'."

Yes sir. Goodnight.

It would be well past noon the next day before Vessey left his Pentagon office.

*** * ***

664

CHAPTER TWENTY-NINE

BMEW Radar Tracking Facility #7
16 Kilometers East of Moscow
23:59 Local

At the same time General Vessey was instructing his secretary, believing a nuclear catastrophe had been averted, the SON ZN radar tracking facility on the far eastern Russian border had, for the last twenty-four hours, been receiving hourly updates on the status of the skies over the Soviet Union.

These relays originated from the Soviet early warning satellite system known as SPRN, which was code named 'OKO' and within seconds that information was relayed to the all the BMEW tracker stations across the world's largest land mass to form single country.

BMEW Bunker Facility #7 was one of more than two dozen spread across the expanse of the Soviet Union but, due to its proximity to the capital was deemed one of the most critical.

Down in the bunker the young officer strolling along the bank of 16 radar screens noticed one of the operators a few chairs up quickly reach for his teletype printout and tear off a page. The operator hurriedly approached the officer.

"Yes Sergeant?"

"Sir, I have something. It looks to be a flash warning from OKO."

"Show me." The officer perused he paper.

665

The bilateral strategy of Mutually Assured Destruction, MAD for short, dictated that any detection of inbound missiles would immediately activate the other side's 'Launch on Warning' systems. In the event of this happening both the U.S.A. and the U.S.S.R. had a simple straight forward, standing policy – immediate nuclear counter attack.

Meanwhile, at the Serpukov-15 Launch Control Command Bunker, 10 Kilometers East of Moscow City Center, the tall, forty-four year old Lieutenant Colonel Stanislaw Yevgrafovich Petrov, Assistant Commander of the early warning and launch command facility, had just settled in for another tedious night of routine paper work.

However, no sooner had Petrov lifted his first mug of strong Turkish tea to his lips when one of his junior officers burst through the office door and thrust a piece of paper at him.

"Shit!" Was his only response as the quiet night Petrov had envisioned quickly evaporated.

"Who sent it?"

"Tracking Facility Number 7 Colonel!"

"Are you sure Captain?!"

"Sir I took it from the teletype myself less than a minute ago! They have transferred tracking and we are now scanning." The Captain stood frozen awaiting Petrov's response.

"Take me to the primary relay console operator who is tracking this sector! Then get me BMEW Command on the line!" The Captain led the way back down the metal stairs of the office to the spacious monitoring room. Seconds later they were at the console.

"Are you still on it Sergeant?" Petrov questioned the operator.

"Yes Comrade Colonel, I have it here." The operator indicated a point at about ten o'clock high up on the screen.

"Reset your tracking ratio twelve to one and confirm point of origin!" The Colonel ordered and the operator quickly obeyed.

"Sir it appears OKO has intercepted an ICBM launch from ...**within** the Continental U.S.!"

"Sukin syn!" Petrov swore. The Captain who had been on the phone handed the head set from the console to Petrov.

"BMEW Comrade Colonel!" The Captain informed.

"This is Lieutenant Colonel Petrov, Serpukov-15 Launch Control. Do you read incoming?" There was a brief pause as Petrov rolled his eyes. "FROM ANYWHERE YOU IDIOT!"

Suddenly a shrill, intermittent, screeching alarm filled the spacious room. An angry Petrov slammed down the phone and stared at the green radar screen.

"Sir, OKO reports possible further incoming ballistics!" The sergeant at the desk blurted out.

"Do you see more blips?!" Petrov could feel his pulse begin to rise.

"Negative sir! Not yet!"

"Where in the hell is Krasnaya?!" The Colonel demanded.

"He went out for a cigarette, Colonel." The captain said.

"Shit! Turn off those fucking flashing lights!

Come!" Petrov barked over his shoulder to the captain and hurried back to the staircase.

As he exited the tracking room Major Vasily Krasnaya entered across the room from the outside chamber. The sergeant switched off the flashing red lights and alarm.

"What's happening?!" The bespectacled, middle-aged Krasnaya demanded.

In a different time and place he would have been an SS officer bullying defenseless civilians.

"We are receiving reports of incoming ICBM's from the U.S.!" The console operator sergeant reported.

"I knew it would happen sooner or later! Capitalist bastards! Are they confirmed from OKO?!"

"Yes Major!" Krasnaya turned white and stepped back.

Meanwhile Petrov and the Captain had made it back up to the command office.

"Check if BMEW handed off to SON ZN for acquisition and intercept!"

"Yes sir!" The Captain grabbed a wall phone and dialed.

The warning lights began to flash again, more missiles were apparently in the air.

Now an electronic voice filled the bunker:

ATTENTION! ATTENTION!
MISSILE ATTACK IMMENENT!
ATTENTION! ATTENTION!
MISSILE ATTACK IMMENENT!

"This makes no sense!" Petrov fell back into his seat to focus himself, fully cognizant that the captain, as was everyone else in the bunker by now, frozen in place.

His facility was clearly detecting incoming hostiles however he was yet to receive verification from the BMEW acquisition an tracking and acquisition installations. Although such verification was not required Petrov, realized he had seconds to make a decision before retaliation would be pointless. He tried to focus as he broke into a cold sweat.

Just then the large glass wall map down stairs above the bank of radar screens lit up like an evil Christmas decoration as further warnings began to flash.

LAUNCH! LAUNCH! LAUNCH!
LAUNCH! LAUNCH! LAUNCH!

Petrov and his men were apparently the first to discover that the U.S. had just gone to war.

The deafening sirens continued to wail.

LAUNCH! LAUNCH! LAUNCH!

"Switch all screens to live feeds!" He ordered the captain.

Before him, on half a dozen monitor screens in the office, there appeared still images of the tops of missile silos in the Midwest prairies of America being relayed from the OKO spy satellites.

"The silos are still closed!" The captain observed.

"There's a two to three minute delay in reception and image transmission from the OKO satellites system!"

Comrade Colonel, incoming readings are endo-atmospheric sir! The desk intercom squawked as the sergeant called up on the intercom from the floor below.

"ARE YOU POSITIVE?!" Petrov demanded.

YES SIR, CERTAIN OF IT!

"The command screens show the same!" The Captain confirmed from across the office. Petrov's eyes were glued to the satellite imagery.

"WHY THE HELL HAVEN'T WE HEARD ANYTHING MORE FROM SON ZN, GOD DAMN IT?!"

"Sir, by the time they detect anything more our launch window will have been reduced to one minute!" The Captain urged.

"THIS DOES NOT MAKE FUCKING SENSE!" Petrov slammed his fist on his console. Across the room the Captain readjusted his screen to get a closer reading.

Multiple blips confirmed at 2,257 kilometers and closing. The intercom croaked from below.

"Confirmed inbound Comrade Colonel." The Captain chimed in. "What are your orders sir?!"

"Maybe it's a secret test by Central Command to test our readiness!" Petrov quietly mumbled. "FUCK! Alert the Novators!" He finally blurted out.

The Novator 53T6's were distributed around four

sites surrounding Moscow with an additional site dedicated to protecting the SON-ZN radar facility which was used for guidance and tracking.

With 17 ICBM's at each primary site and 16 for the radar facility, there were a total of 84 ballistic missiles at 10 kilotons each. Enough to level every major city in the United States with residual fallout to render 80-90% of the rest of the country uninhabitable for a very long time.

He fought back the panic as images of his wife and family being swept away in a fiery windstorm flashed across his mind.

At that moment it hit Petrov like a dart between the eyes: He was the man fate had chosen to have his finger on the button.

"Is it possible the Americans are only launching one or two missiles to test our response?" The Captain queried.

"It makes no sense!" He mumbled again as his brain raced at warp speed to find a solution. "NO! A U.S. first strike would be all-out! So five missiles is an illogical start!" He ripped off his hat and jacket and loosened his tie as he spoke down to his desk. "Protocol clearly dictates that any strike, especially a pre-emptive strike, is to be launched at **exo-atmospheric** altitudes! Check again these readings are endo-thermic!"

The Captain manned his control board.

"Confirmed endo-thermic readings Colonel!" The captain reported. "Perhaps they are chancing one missile to be undetected to provoke us to launch so it will look like a first strike from our side?"

"They know our protocol as well as we know

671

theirs!"

Wavering between duty and denial he focused all he could. "This detection system is new and likely not yet wholly trustworthy, they never are!"

With SON Radar Tracking Facility less than 16 kilometers West of Moscow this meant by the time they detected the reported missiles there would be less than two minutes to impact. Every second burned making a decision brought them closer to annihilation.

"Captain, go back down, confirm trajectory, tell me if you see actual missile trails on radar while I monitor the status of the Novators."

"Yes Comrade Colonel!" The Captain ran for the stairway.

Down on the floor all operators' eyes remained riveted to their screens, Major Krasnaya's eyes were glued to the screen just behind the sergeant who first picked up the alert.

"Sergeant, confirm missiles' trajectory status!"

"Major sir, I have. But the ground radars fail to report corroborative evidence so I can't track trajectories." The sergeant reported.

"That's because those detection systems can't see beyond the horizon!" Major Krasnaya countered.

The Major approached the two. "SERGEANT, DO YOU READ MISSLES IN THE AIR?" Krasnaya demanded.

"Sergeant, do we see missile trails?" The captain intervened.

"The computer verifies incoming, but negative reading on radar sir!"

"Major, Colonel Petrov has ordered the Novator

silos opened and readied but not launched!" The Captain informed.

"And we have not yet heard word back from the ground radar installation at Sakhalin!?"

"No Major, but-"

"Yet the computer confirms there has been a launch and that multiple American ICBM's are inbound?!" Krasnaya pushed.

"Yes sir, but Colonel Petrov thinks –"

"I don't give a damn what the Lieutenant Colonel thinks! DO YOU CAPTAIN WANT TO BE THE MAN WHO ALLOWED THE AMERICANS TO DESTROY THE SOVIET UNION WHILE WE STOOD BY AND DID NOTHING?!"

"No sir, but –"

"Then use your key, open the case and give me the codes and I will enter them myself!" The young Captain hesitated. "That's an order!"

"Yes ... yes Major!" The sergeant, along with the rest if the room, froze and stared opened mouthed at the two officers.

The Captain opened the wall mounted case, removed the large red envelope and handed it to the enraged Major who tore it open and removed the two yellow plastic cards containing the codes.

The horrified captain stood by as Krasnaya sat between the two side-by-side consoles and quickly began to enter the first set of codes.

The young captain ran from the control room to alert Petrov who was still trying to determine the Novotar's status.

Unlike the U.S. fail safe systems which required two separate keys, two separate operators working in tandem and had two separate launch buttons located ten feet apart, the Soviet fail safes were much more basic. Everything was on a pair of consoles both in easy reach of one operator.

As the Major finished entering the second set of codes the Captain came back through the door with Petrov.

Both officers watched in horror as Krasnaya slammed his hands down on both buttons at the same time

"NOOOO!!" Petrov screamed from the top of the stairs. "YOU FUCKING FOOL!! IT'S A MALFUNCTION!" Petrov yelled racing across the floor to the console. "YOU WAR MONGERING BASTARD!" Petrov screamed again as he hit the bottom of the staircase ad raced to where Krasnaya sat, roughly yanking the Major from the console hard enough to fling him and his chair across the room.

Wide-eyed and panting heavily Petrov immediately reached for the scramble phone to alert Air Defense Command Headquarters.

"This is Colonel Petrov of the Serpukhov-15 Facility! I am reporting an accidental launch from my sector! Scramble the intercept aircraft from Kamchatka immediately!"

Colonel Petrov, sir, that's not possible! The duty NOC on the other end responded.

Petrov yelled into the phone.

"I AM ORDERING YOU TO SCRAMBLE THE INTERCEPT AIRCRAFT! MAJOR KRASNAYA HAS ENTERED THE CODES AND JUST INITIATED LAUNCH OF ALL THE SILOS

TO THEIR PRIMARY TARGETS!!"

Petrov glanced over at the disheveled Major climbing up off the floor.

Comrade Colonel, sir, I am sitting right next to the vault! It is still open. I can see your sector's confirm launch code envelopes sitting here. Right in front of me!

Petrov frantically scanned the radar control panel, the wall display and the other operators sitting stiff-backed at their posts. The red warning lights continued to flash as the launch command recording continued to sound.

ATTENTION! ATTENTION! MISSILE ATTACK IMMENANT!

"BUT ...THE CONSOLE LAUNCH LIGHTS ARE LIT! THAT MEANS A LAUNCH IS UNDERWAY!" Petrov insisted.

No Comrade Colonel! The console lights merely indicate that the launch buttons have been depressed. In the new system your order is relayed to us and we clear for launch! I am double checking as we speak. There is no indication of a launch in your sector at this time! The silos appear to be open, but no ordinance has been launched. The major must have entered the wrong codes.

The command operator heard no response from the launch room.

Comrade Colonel? Comrade Colonel, are you there?!

The black head set hung from the console by its thick, rubber coated spring cord gently swinging

675

back and forth a foot above the pale green tiled floor.

Petrov pulled his side arm and strode over the major who now sat back on his roller chair, smugly adjusting his hair and uniform. Grabbing Krasnaya by the collar he pressed the pistol to his throat.

Staring right through him with more hatred than he had ever felt in his life. More than wanting to be somewhere else, more than wanting to be finished with the Army or even more than he wanted to be back home with his wife, at this exact moment he wanted the man sitting beneath him dead.

"Major Vasily Sergei Krasnaya, by the power given me by the Supreme Soviet Command I place you under military arrest for attempting to launch an attack without authorization!"

Colonel? Colonel Petrov, are you there? The command operator continued to call out through the dangling headset. Petrov pushed Krasnaya back and the roller chair slammed into the wall behind him. Moving slowly back over to the communications console with his pistol leveled at Krasnaya, Petrov lifted the set to his ear.

"Yes, I am here. Send security to my facility immediately!"

Yes Colonel!

Minutes later, as the security detail led Krasnaya away in handcuffs Petrov, now back up in his office, turned his small desk radio up and sank into his high backed chair.

The chorus of *Every Breath You Take* by Sting was fading out.

CHAPTER THIRTY

Conference Room X-Ray
CIA HQ, Langley, Virginia
Wednesday, October 5th

*I*n *a press conference held late last night by the F.B.I. in Washington it has been revealed that Arne Treholt, former Prime Minister of Denmark, has been arrested and charged with High Treason after secret dealings with the Soviets were exposed by the KGB defector Oleg Gordievsky.*

This has been ...

General Vessey aimed the remote and switched off the wall mounted color T.V. set.

Save Lieutenant Harden who wasn't officially due for hospital discharge until day after tomorrow, the four members of Task Force Romeo sat around the table awaiting Secretary Schultz's visit for a personal debriefing and to receive pat's on the back.

"Turns out that little Oleg guy was a useful son-of-a-bitch!" Ray MacDonald offered as he adjusted his leg propped up on a second chair. Vessey frowned at him and the leg drifted back down to the floor.

"You gentlemen have all received medals before so I won't go through the whole rigmarole." The General started. "I'll nod when the Secretary is ready and you'll all stand and form a line over here facing out. Rank order naturally, ranking man, I guess that's you MacDonald, here to my right."

"Yes sir."

The Marine guard outside opened the door and Secretary George Schultz strode into the room followed by a Naval Adjutant and a civilian aide. Vessey rose to greet him and they shook hands.

"Mr. Secretary, how was your debriefing with the President?"

"Let's just say there was not a word of criticism of the Soviet Union from the Cold Warrior." Schultz dropped his long coat, hat and scarf on a side chair and stepped to the table where a pile of five small, dark blue awards boxes sat then addressed the troops.

"I don't have to dwell on the fact that what you five people did for this country can never be fully repaid. Especially since it's classified and has to stay under wraps but, maybe someday, somebody'll write a book, make a movie or who knows what. At any rate, from the president, myself and a grateful nation, thank you for your service. General shall we?" General Vessey fetched the medals, opened the boxes and passed them one at a time to Schultz. The Adjutant followed behind handing over the printed, detailed citations accompanying the medals as Schultz pinned them on.

"Sorry these can't be read aloud in front of your units but each of your commanders will receive a general message informing them of your outstanding service." The Adjutant explained.

The Secretary finally came to the last man in line, Hospital Corpsman Second Class McKeowen

"A corpsman! Proud tradition you men have. More medals and awards for heroism than any other

678

unit, branch or department in the Armed Forces!"

"We appreciate the recognition Mr. Secretary." Doc acknowledged.

"Congratulations Petty Officer McKeowen."

"Thank you Mr. Secretary."

"I guess you'll be anxious to sign up for this new multi-force SOCOM commando unit Lieutenant Harden's putting together?!"

"I'd like that very much Mr. Secretary, but if it's all the same to you, I'd like to get back to RECON and log some more team time first. Got my orders right here." He brandished a large manila envelope.

"Good idea McKeowen. Maybe give Commander Harden some time to work out the kinks in this wild scheme of his first."

As the secretary passed back by MacDonald, first in line, Mac couldn't control a giggle. Schultz turned to him.

"Commentary, Petty Officer?"

"Apologies Mr. Secretary, but Lieutenant Harden could be a bit of a pain on occasion. As a Commander I'm sure he'll be intolerable."

"Well, that's something you're gonna have to learn to deal with."

"Oh not me sir! I'm on the next plane back to the San Diego and the Teams myself, back in sunny Calif –"

"Oh we get sun here in D.C. On occasion." Schultz added.

"Sir, I don't -!"

Schultz turned to Vessey who smiled back.

"I take it Petty Officer MacDonald hasn't yet been informed of his new duty assignment?" Schultz inquired.

General Vessey smiled and shook his head 'no'.

The look on MacDonald's face was later described by Doc as a 'true Kodak moment'.

"You should be proud MacDonald! You're the second troop Commander Harden requested when I gave my blessing for his hair-brained multi-force unit. You're staying here in D.C. son! At least until we can find SOCOM a home!" Vessey took a pace back and saluted MacDonald. "Well done, Petty Officer MacDonald!"

Ray returned a weak salute.

"Sir I can't stay here! My team's- Second choice?! That's not possible! How could I possibly be number two?! Mr. Secretary, sir, there must be some mistake!"

McKeowen leaned forward, looked over at Mac and smiled as he held up a single finger indicating he was Harden's first choice.

****

Capitol Building
Washington, D.C.
09:25 October 29th

The small gaggle of press were scattered over the Capitol steps forming a half circle around the portable podium on the top step. They were there to cover the presidential candidate's daily speech.

The Presidential campaign had been hot and heavy and Walter Mondale, in light of the fact that fear of nuclear war was a major sore point for the Reagan camp, had assumed the role of nuclear freeze activist.

"The so called logic of 'peace through strength' is wrong! It's tantamount to making war in the name of peace!" He declared in his current speech from the steps of the most recognized building in D.C.

"Yeah, kind'a like fucking for virginity!" The ex-Viet Nam Vet turned reporter quipped to his cameraman standing next to him. The cameraman in agreement.

In a press conference ostensibly in relation to his election campaign but widely held as a thinly veiled challenge to Reagan, Mondale charged that so far, despite all his rhetoric, President Reagan had not personally held a summit meeting with even one Soviet leader.

At that very moment Reagan sat in the Oval Office surrounded by his campaign manager and several staff members watching the challenge being strategically broadcast in his own backyard.

"Certainly has a flair for the dramatic!" An aide commented.

"You have to give him credit for the location!" Reagan quipped as his only real opponent in the upcoming election continued to address the assembled Press Corps.

"I think we'll have to admit that the peace through strength strategy did not provide the credibility we were hoping for Mr. President. It's time we started to consider the fact that the Democrats are in striking distance." The aide counselled.

Without taking his eyes from the TV screen Reagan mumbled an order.

"Get me a meeting with Schultz."

Reagan, as the incumbent, was favored to take the election but his aggressive four year campaign against the Soviets had begun to backfire. The Right Wing warmongering Americans who had helped put him into 1600 Pennsylvania Avenue four years ago had since been given a wakeup call with the unrestrained nuclear proliferation of The Cold War and the threat of all out nuclear confrontation.

Only days after Mondale's challenge, Reagan was debriefed by Schultz on the Gordievsky affair and the famous Hotline to the Kremlin, commonly known as the "Red Phone", was installed and successfully tested.

Now on what could be considered the most historical day to date in the history of diplomacy, a televised phone call to Moscow was about to take place.

"Mr. President we have a direct connection to Moscow, sir." The aide informed Reagan who was sitting at his desk. The phone rang. "It's Moscow calling sir. Just press this button to talk."

Like a nervous little kid at his first school dance, Reagan exchanged glances with the small crowd gathered in his office and to the T.V. cameras broadcasting nation-wide and being taped for later international distribution.

He gingerly took the transceiver from the aide who discreetly stepped aside.

"Mr. Gorbachov? How's the weather in Russia?"

Mr. President, a pleasure to meet you, so to speak. But this is Minister Gromyko. Just a minute, I'll put the General Secretary on the line.

Gorbachev's voice came on.

Mr. President, a pleasure to meet you.

"Mr. General Secretary, I wonder if I might invite your Secretary of State to visit my country in the near future?"

I will arrange his schedule immediately Mr. President.

A week later, in what was literally a 48 hour press marathon broadcast around the world, Reagan brought Soviet Foreign Minister Andrei Gromyko to the White House where he was greeted with great fanfare and a throng of photographers from around the world.

Taking Gromyko aside, Reagan told him, no doubt with the Petrov incident indelibly etched in his mind;

"My dream is for a world where there are no nuclear weapons."

Outside a very small circle of Intel operatives, little did anyone know how close the airplane had really come to crashing into the mountain side.

****

683

CHAPTER THIRTY-ONE

Long Beach Harbor
The Queen Mary
20:15, Thursday 10, November

With Natasha decked out in a dark green satin evening gown and heels pushing Harden in a wheelchair dressed in his dress whites, flanked by Doc and MacDonald in their dress blues, the four came off the boarding ramp and turned onto the promenade deck of the Queen Mary, anchored at Long Beach and currently hosting the Annual United States Marine Corps Ball.

As they made their way down the passageway of the Luxury Liner Doc reached down and handed something to Dave Harden.

"What's this?"

"Had that made up for you."

"What is it?"

"What's it fucking look like? It's a shoulder patch."

"I can see it's a patch! From what unit?"

"Some fuckin' Intel officer you are! Four crossed swords over a globe?" The penny dropped and Harden smiled. It was the Special Operations Command or SOCOM insignia.

"Thanks Doc, this means a lot." Dave examined the patch which represented his concept of a unified special operations force from all four services united under one command. "I never thanked you for what you did on that chopper. I-"

"Stowe it! The Navy pays me a hundred and ten dollars a month hazardous duty pay. Besides, I've never lost a patient on a medi-vac and you were certainly not gonna be the first!"

They made it up the ramp to the door and into the ornate, grand ball room just as the Marine Corps Hymn finished and were then allowed in.

A six foot tall, ornately decorated, four tiered cake stood on a long table at the foot of the stage and forty or more tables, arranged in a herring bone pattern, filled the room.

Hundreds of Marines and sailors, all decked out in their respective Class A's, festooned the expansive ball room with a full orchestra on stage.

Doc and company found space at one of the large round tables by the bar, ordered drinks and settled in. Danno who had arrived earlier, spotted them and came over.

The orchestra were on break and as being back in a safe environment slowly sank in, they avoided conversation and let the mood permeate. The silence didn't last long.

Minutes later, carrying an embossed silver serving tray, a young ship's steward approached them and addressed Doc.

"Excuse me sir –"

"You don't have to call me sir, I'm not an officer. My parents are married."

"Never gets old Doc." Harden quipped.

"Ahh ... are you Petty Officer McKeowen? The guy they call Doc?" Doc sized up the steward, the tray and the bottle of 25 year old Jameson's sitting on the tray.

"Why yes I am son! How can I help you?" He asked as he took the bottle from the tray. The steward handed over a note as well.

"This is for you sir ... Petty Officer ... Doc." The steward explained.

Doc opened the note.

'Good job on not getting killed!'
- Bernie Horowitz.

"Well thank you my boy! We appreciate your attention to duty! Rest assured your commanding officer will receive a letter detailing how important your services were to this country!"

Not sure of how to react the steward left.

Doc passed the bottle to Dave then emptied his untouched champagne on the deck under the table. As he opened the whiskey Dave chastised Doc.

"Ain't you had no upbringing?!" He jibbed as he spilled his glass across the linen table cloth. That's how you dump cheap champagne."

Dave poured them each a good measure and all mouths dropped open as Natasha threw hers back like a dockworker.

"So Lieutenant, where's this hot nurse you met in therapy?" Danno asked.

Just then Dave pointed across the floor to a short but attractive, dusky blond in the dress whites of a naval nurse.

"Well, what'a ya think?" Dave solicited from the group.

Doc looked across the table to Danno. They both shrugged.

"She's okay. For a mouth breather." Danno commented.

"The hell with both you enlisted pukes!" Dave answered. When she arrived at the table Dave suggested the two meander over to the bar so, with her pushing his wheel chair, they headed out.

Wandering over to the table where Doc and Natasha were now engaged in a serious lip lock, Ray leaned into Doc and whispered.

"Never trust anything that bleeds for five days and doesn't die."

"Didn't you see the sign as you came over here?"

"What sign?"

"Men at work! Now fuck off!" Doc instructed.

Just then MacDonald spotted a well-built, tall dark-haired female Marine standing over by the bar, on her own. Natasha glanced over, saw MacDonald ogling the woman and nudged Doc who leaned over to Ray as he gawked and killed his drink.

"Careful Ray. They still teach hand-to-hand in The Corps!"

"Just call me Julius fucking Caesar! "Veni, vidi, veni!" Ray mumbled as he set his empty glass on the table, downed Doc's drink and headed in her direction.

Doc smiled and returned to Natasha's lips. He looked into her eyes then sat back. She sensed he was about to get serious and also sat back maintaining eye contact.

"So, now that you've worked both sides of the fence, how do you compare American men to Russian men?" Doc asked her.

She shrugged reached for the bottle and poured them another round as she mulled over her answer.

"Men are men. They are not so complicated. It is easy to keep them happy. They are basically having two emotions: Hungry and Horny. If you are not seeing him with erection, make him sandwich." Again she downed hers.

"Well, my little Russian pastila, I just had dinner so I don't need no sandwich!"

"OH!" She suddenly gasped.

"What?!"

"I just noticed. Everyone is in best military dress! Maybe I just dash back to hotel and change into my uniform!" Doc stared at her. "What do you think? Should I wear **all** of my medals as well?"

"You look just fine, Sweetheart. Besides, don't you have a Red Star, do you?"

"Yes! Given to army and navy personnel for exceptional service against enemy!" She slowly perused the room full of buff sailors and Marines. "Looks like I am surrounded!"

"You have got to be the first communist ever to attend a Marine Corps Ball!" They kissed again. "Why don't I go back to the hotel with you and help you change out of that dress?"

She shifted from her chair next to him to sit on his lap. She wiggled her bum a couple of times.

"I see you don't need sandwich!" She smiled.

No sooner were they back into it when Dave and his date showed up back at the table.

"HI! Sorry to interrupt..." A partially lit Harden spouted.

"Bullshit! WHAT?!" Doc didn't bother to hide his annoyance. "Lieutenant we're tryin' to improve East-West relations here, seriously." Harden wrapped his arm around his date's waist.

"Well, Petty officer McKeowen, you will be interested to know that Lieutenant Chambers, R.N., U.S.N. here just happens to have a time share beach house not a half an hour from here down in Huntington Beach. And did you further know that said house has two bedrooms neither of which is currently occupied?"

"Are you suggesting we relocate our area of operations, Lieutenant?" Doc asked. Natasha smacked Doc's shoulder.

In less than five minutes the four were heading for the nearest exit. On the way across the parking lot Doc walked up next to Harden's wheelchair.

"It's a burro."

"A what?"

"It's a burro." Doc said to Dave. "Back at C.U.N.Y. our school mascot was a burro. You know, as in one of the five boroughs, Manhattan, Brooklyn, Bronx, Staten Island and Queens. Queensboro. A burro a donkey."

"A jackass?!"

"A donkey!"

"Seriously, a fucking Jackass?!" Harden loudly repeated.

"We were at the Queens campus so we were referred to as Queensboro, ergo burro."

"The Fucking Donkeys! The Jackasses! That's fucking great!" They stopped in the middle of the partially lit parking lot. "Fuck me Doc! That almost makes it worth gettin' my ass shot off for! I mean we're talkin' about jokes for months! Hell possibly years! They'll be jokes about this well into the next century! Seriously!" Doc stood stark still allowing Harden to have his moment. Then tucked the half empty bottle into Harden's lap, grabbed the Russian beauty and headed off.

"We'll follow you. Don't let that asshole drive!" Doc yelled after them.

With Dave's nurse pushing his wheel chair, whiskey bottle in hand, they made their way to their cars.

"It's the BUROS!"

"Doc, I got an idea!" Harden suddenly yelled out.

"Good! Write me about it. Promise I'll write back." Doc yelled back over his shoulder as he and Natasha headed for their car.

"Oh, no need to write back! There'll be plenty of time together!" Harden said as he climbed into the car, just before Doc stopped dead in his tracks as the penny dropped.

"Fuck me Alice!" He quietly declared. "DID YOU FUCK WITH MY ORDERS, YOU LOW LIFE, FUCK OF AN OFFICER?!"

"Tell ya about it over breakfast!" Harden called back.

Back up in the ball room someone let out a war hoop and the first Marine, held by his arms and legs by two other burley Marines, was flung across one

690

of the lengthy dinner tables crashing through the dishes, crystal glasses and on into the remnants of the birthday cake.

An age-old, closing tradition of the Marine Corps Ball had begun.

Carrier landings.

***

CHAPTER THIRTY-TWO

24 November, 1983
The Rural Settlement of Sazeni
Moskovaya Oblast,
107 Kilometres East of Moscow

All across the U.S. folks were sitting down to Thanksgiving dinner but out on the frozen tundra of central Russia, far from the parades, cameras and hero worship engulfing Washington and Moscow, a worn, middle aged 25 year old woman was chopping wood to fortify the already significant stacks surrounding the modest one bedroom cabin randomly planted on the Russian plains.

It was late morning and the air was still, crisp and cold with the sun struggling to climb above the horizon when she lowered the axe and lifted her head to hear better.

Pulling back the fur lined hood of her parker she stared out across the ice and snow to spot a dark, military jeep bouncing down the single lane, dirt road towards the cabin.

Smiling more broadly then she had in the six months since her husband had been stationed outside of Moscow, she dashed to great him.

Minutes later they appeared to be glued at the hip as they walked, holding each other, down the drive to the small three room house they had occupied since their marriage nine years ago.

Stanislav Petrov was home.

692

General Yury Votintsev, Commander of the Soviet Missile Defence force had been the first to get debriefed by Petrov as he underwent intensive, prolonged questioning for the better part of two weeks. This despite the fact that Petrov was not only initially praised for his quick thinking and bravery of actions, but even promised a reward. A reward which would never come.

It was nearly a week and a half after she was notified he had been released from custody before Petrov's wife heard from him again. Although he was being held in detention he was, with a little inside help, able to get a short message to his wife that he was alright and would soon be home.

The last part was based on sheer hope, not on any concrete indications that he would be released by the authorities in the near future. Unlike most of the Soviet operatives involved in RYAN, Colonel Stanislav Petrov was, after many 'debriefings', allowed to return home but was informed he would be kept from any military duties pending a full inquiry.

Knowing better than to ask for details before they were offered, as Stanislav settled back in, his wife wisely decided to keep thc conversation superficial as she fixed dinner in the shadows of the encroaching evening.

"So, how are you? Are you okay? Did they feed you well?"

"Well enough, I suppose." He responded as he casually sat re-reading one of his favourite novels, Steinbeck's *Cannery Row*.

"What did you do at work?"

693

Children of the Nuclear Gods

"It was a routine couple of weeks. We had a little trouble with one of the computers, but we fixed it. Nothing serious."

She served the fish and potatoes and they ate.

THE END

EPILOGUE

"Just listen with attention to the ideological nuances on Radio 4, BBC Television and the BBC World Service and you will realize that communism is not a dying creed."

Oleg Gordievsky,
3 August, 2005

We are here only by virtue of the fact that Colonel Stanislav Petrov refused to press the launch button reputedly stating, "I will not be the man to start WWIII!".

For his astuteness in a high pressure situation that Dave Harden later described as, "Fucked up like a soup sandwich in the rain!", Colonel Petrov was decorated by both The White House and later the Politburo.

The lengthy investigation which followed the false missile reading incident determined that the computer system had indeed malfunctioned, misreading intense sun light on high altitude clouds and misinterpreting these as nuclear missiles.

The incident became known publicly in the 1990s following the publication of the memoirs of Gen. Votintsev, the former Commander of the Soviet Missile Defense Forces at the time of the incident.

Oleg Kalugin, a former KGB chief of foreign counter-intelligence officer who knew Soviet chairman Andropov well, said: "Andropov's distrust of American leaders was profound. It is completely conceivable that if Petrov had declared the satellite warnings valid, such an erroneous report would have likely provoked the Soviet leadership into becoming bellicose and firing on the Americans".

Later research has shown that up to 50% of most people, regardless of nationality, would have hesitated or refused to "push the button" when ordered to do so. However 50% was considered far too little by both sides. To that end automated launch systems have now been installed.

Out with the cold, in with the new.

Now we can all sleep better a night?

In 1992, nine years later, the first Soviet President Boris Yeltsin turned over the Flight Data Recorders from KAL 007 and went so far as to share the Russian military tracking data from the incident with the N.T.S.B.

Subsequent investigation has revealed that, for whatever reason, the INS tracking on flight KAL 007 was not engaged and so the pilots could not have known they were so far off course.

The FBI reported at the time that they determined the Flight Data Recording box, the 'Black Box', had not been tampered with as the seals were still wholly intact.

The ensuing debacle by the American military leadership and the resulting disaster of Eagle Claw in Iran did give rise to the present day Combined Special Forces Command.

The Cold War remained rooted not only in ideology but deep distrust and carefully cultivated fear, on both sides from the end of World War Two in 1945 until Gorbachev's Perestroika initiative in 1989.

Most people credit the fall of the Berlin Wall as the result of the end of the Cold War but I credit the end of the Cold War with scaring the bejesus out of both sides as a significant factor.

*

As a late note; Now since February 24th, 2022 with Russia's unprovoked invasion of Ukraine by President Putin, (the little man mentioned on page 259), and NATO's escalating involvement, it seems the Cold War virus again rears its ugly head and some people didn't agree with Perestroika. . .

Also by Paddy Kelly

Ghost Story (A play)

Operation Underworld

The Wolves of Calabria

The Broad in the Kimono

The American Way

Politically Erect

Kelly's Full House

American Rhetoric

Children of the Nuclear Gods

The Galileo Project

When Two Tribes Go to War

The Hermes Project

Synopsis or option information available on line at:
paddy.incanto@gmail.com
or Paddy Kelly Amazon or from
Fiction4All